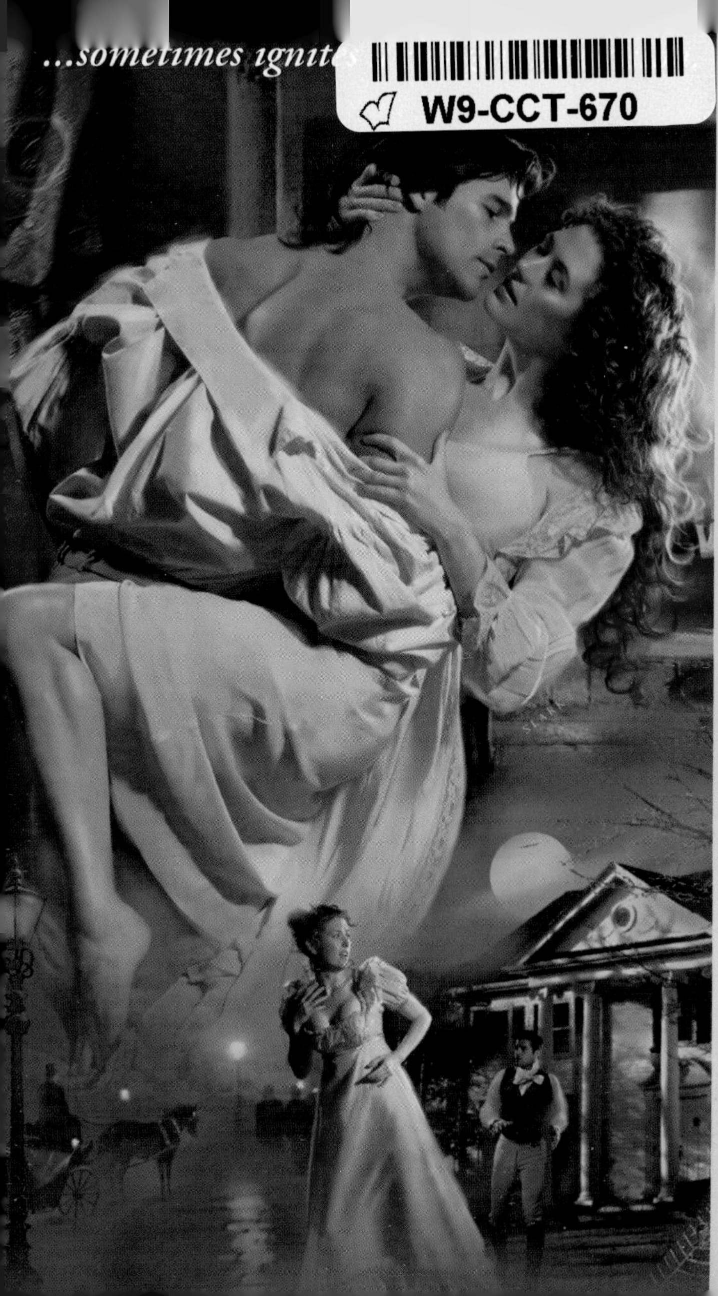
...sometimes ignit

"There is one last thing," she said as he reached the door.

"Which is . . . ?"

"I need to know if you truly believe I am innocent of killing the earl."

He gave her a hard-edged smile. "For the present, let's just say my mind remains open. If you're innocent, there'll be a way to prove it. If you're not—" His eyes held a promise of retribution so dark she had to work to suppress a shiver. "But then, since you're telling me the truth, there is no need for concern."

So saying, he opened the door and strode off down the hall, leaving her alone.

Jillian sank down on the brocade sofa, Blackwood's handsome image still etched into her mind. Her heart beat faster the instant he appeared, and even with the ruthlessness stamped onto his features, he was the most attractive man she had ever met.

It occurred to her that in accepting the earl's assistance in proving her innocence, she might be in more danger than if she had been captured and carted off to prison.

Praise for bestselling author
KAT MARTIN

"Pure entertainment from page one!"
—Jill Marie Landis

"Shimmers like a bright diamond in the genre."
—*Romantic Times*

"Can always be depended upon to produce a story that is a 'can't-put-down.' "
—*Rendezvous*

More acclaim for
Kat Martin

"[She] keeps getting better and better. . . . A premier historical writer."

—Affaire de Coeur

"Displays an unusual sensitivity . . . tackles the more complex wonder of enduring love."

—Publishers Weekly

"A master of the genre."

—Reader to Reader

Books by Kat Martin

The Fire Inside
Fanning the Flame

Available from Pocket Books

KAT MARTIN

FANNING THE Flame

POCKET STAR BOOKS

New York London Toronto Sydney Singapore

An *Original* Publication of POCKET BOOKS

A Pocket Star Book published by
POCKET BOOKS, a division of Simon & Schuster, Inc.
1230 Avenue of the Americas, New York, NY 10020

ISBN: 0-7434-1916-2

First Pocket Books printing August 2002

10 9 8 7 6 5 4 3 2 1

POCKET STAR BOOKS and colophon are
registered trademarks of Simon & Schuster, Inc.

For information regarding special discounts for bulk purchases,
please contact Simon & Schuster Special Sales at 1-800-456-6798
or business@simonandschuster.com

Front cover illustration by Tom Hallman;
tip-in illustration by Gregg Gulbronson

Printed in the U.S.A.

1

~∽~

London, England
April 1806

The battle raged inside his head, the crack of musket fire, the thunder of cannonade, hot lead tearing into flesh and bone, men weeping in fear and despair.

It's a dream, he cried inside his mind, trying to convince himself, to awaken from another of the nightmares that plagued his sleep. Inch by inch, clawing his way back to consciousness, Adam Hawthorne, fourth Earl of Blackwood, sat upright in his huge four-poster bed. His heart was pounding. Sweat ran in rivulets down his naked chest and dampened his hair, urging it into heavy black waves that stuck to the cords at the back of his neck.

Though a chill pervaded the room, Adam shoved the feather comforter down past his waist and a shiver swept over him, pebbling his skin above the crisp linen sheet. He was used to nights like this one. He had suffered the terrible images for more than six years. Penance, he believed, for the part he had played in the war.

Running a hand over his face to erase the last vestiges of slumber, he swung his long legs to the side of the bed and stood up. Through a slit in the gold velvet draperies, the first gray light of dawn filtered into the room. Adam poured water into the porcelain basin on his dresser and performed the necessary ablutions, then pulled on buckskin breeches and a full-sleeved white shirt and shoved his feet into a pair of high-topped Spanish riding boots.

Making his way downstairs, he headed for the stable at the rear of the town house for his daily morning ride.

His groom, Angus McFarland, a big ruddy Scotsman, formerly a sergeant in the Gordon Highlanders, stood waiting, a beefy hand gripping the reins of Adam's prize black stallion, Ramses.

" 'Ave a care, Major. The lad's a bit full o' himself this mornin'."

Adam nodded. "We'll give him a run, then." He patted the stallion's sleek neck. "You'd like a good run, wouldn't you, boy?" The horse was as black and shiny as polished jet, with perfect conformation and a surprisingly gentle disposition. Once Adam had spotted him at Tattersall's, he had spared no expense to have him. It was his single real indulgence since he had unexpectedly come into the Blackwood title and fortune.

Adam patted the soft dark muzzle, then reached into his pocket and held his hand out, palm up, offering the animal a lump of sugar. "A little fresh air always makes the world seem better."

"Aye, and so it does," the Scotsman agreed. Adam swung up onto the saddle and settled himself on the flat leather seat. After eight years in the cavalry, he felt more at home on a horse than he did with his feet on the ground. He bid farewell to Angus, more friend than employee, and headed for his daily outing in the park, Ram in high spirits, dancing and snorting with untapped energy as they rode through the London streets.

At this early hour, the park was empty. Adam set the horse into a gallop, nudged him into a flat-out run, and they pounded around the carriageway. The sun had crested the horizon by the time horse and rider drew to a halt beneath a plane tree on a rise near the duck pond. Adam let the big horse blow, the stallion's sides heaving in and out with spent effort, both of them feeling the benefits of wind and early morning sun.

Giving Ram an absent pat, he turned his attention in another, more interesting direction, scanning the grassy field below in search of his quarry, spotting her on the same wrought-iron bench she had been perched on each morning since he had come upon her three days ago.

The expensive clothes she wore, today a pale green muslin sprinkled with small embroidered rosebuds, marked her as a member of the upper classes. She was shorter than average, with a slender frame and fair, unblemished skin. Beneath the rim of her lace-trimmed bonnet, he could just make out her face, the refined lines and straight nose, the nicely shaped dark copper eyebrows. He imagined her eyes were blue, but at this distance, he couldn't be sure.

What amazed him was how badly he wanted to find out.

On the bench below, the woman smiled at the

growing cluster of ducks that swam or waddled toward her, fanning out to surround her feet. To each in turn, she passed out bits of bread, watching with delight as several of them plucked a morsel from her hand. She laughed as a mother duck clumsily waded ashore, six tiny ducklings lined up in a row behind her.

He thought she might have glanced his way, spotting him on the knoll, but perhaps he only imagined it. He wondered who she was and why she came to the pond by herself, so early in the morning. He wondered if, as he did, she sought solace from turbulent thoughts.

He wondered if she would be there again when he came to the pond on the morrow.

Departing the carriage from her morning journey to the park, Jillian Alistair Whitney whisked through the big double doors of the Earl of Fenwick's town mansion, a brisk spring breeze having driven her early from her daily morning outing. She grabbed the rim of her bonnet to keep the wind from blowing it off as the butler, Nigel Atwater, closed the heavy portal behind her.

"A bit chilly, isn't it, to be out gallivanting about?" He glared down his long beak of a nose with disapproval, mirroring the sentiment of a number of the servants, though Atwater was the only one secure enough in his position to let it show.

"The wind came up rather suddenly," she said matter-of-factly, refusing to let him know how much his censure hurt. "Perhaps we're in for a bit of a storm." It wasn't important what the servants thought, she told herself, and even if it were, there was little she could do to change things.

From the start, Lord Fenwick had scoffed at the gossip her presence in a bachelor household caused. He was, he had said, old enough to be her grandfather, was, in fact, a close friend of her father's, a man who had seen more than forty years by the time he sired a child.

Jillian thought of the proud man who had died sixteen months past, a man who had doted on her, loved her to distraction, but left her without a farthing to see to her needs. If it hadn't been for Lord Fenwick ... ah, but the earl *had* come to her rescue, and gossip was a small price to pay for all he had done.

Jillian tugged off her kidskin gloves and started up the stairs to her bedchamber, a cheery room done in pale blue, ivory, and gold, her mind on her situation and the solitude she found each morning in the park. She always went early, before the fashionable set arrived. She hated their knowing glances and speculative smiles and at that early hour, she had the park all to herself.

At least she had until three days ago, when she discovered she wasn't alone.

"Beg pardon, Miss Whitney."

She had almost reached the top of the stairs when she heard the butler returning to the entry. "If you please, Miss, his lordship would like a word with you in his study."

Jillian paused in the process of untying her bonnet. "Certainly. Thank you, Atwater."

Making her way back downstairs, bonnet in hand, she walked along the hall to the suite of rooms in the west wing of the mansion that included the earl's private study, her mind still on the tall, dark-haired rider and magnificent black horse she had spotted on the knoll. There was something frightening about him. Something dark and forbidding. Something mysterious and intriguing.

In truth, he was attractive, in a hard, ruthless sort of way, sitting there astride his horse. At first she had been frightened, then it occurred to her that he would scarcely need to press himself on an unwilling woman. Handsome as he was, likely he could have whatever lady he chose.

A noise in the study drew her attention. Jillian knocked on the gilt-trimmed ivory door, then, at the sound of Lord Fenwick's gruff voice, turned the gold knob and went in.

"Ah, here you are, my dear. I thought I heard you in the entry. You are certainly one for getting an early start."

She walked to where he sat behind his rosewood desk, his stained meerschaum pipe gripped casually in an age-spotted hand. She bent toward him, kissed his wrinkled cheek.

"I'm always up early, my lord, as you well know. Morning is the best time of day. Everything is bright and cheerful, and it is quiet enough to hear the birds."

He chuckled, carefully set his unlit pipe down on its stand, and rose from behind his desk.

Oswald Telford, Earl of Fenwick, was a man well into his sixties, with patchy gray hair and a paunch beneath his white piqué waistcoat. He had never been a handsome man, with his sugar-bowl ears and slightly bulbous nose, but he was dear to her and she to him.

"Tonight is the Marquess of Landen's soiree," he said. "I thought you might like to attend."

She shook her head a little too quickly, steadied herself enough to smile. "Your gout is still acting up, and in truth I should rather remain at home. I thought perhaps we might spend the evening playing chess."

For an instant, a twinkle appeared in eyes a cloudy shade of blue much paler than her own bright hue. With a look of regret he shook his head. "I should like nothing more than to stay here and trounce you soundly, my girl, but I am not getting any younger, and I need to see you settled. It is beyond time I found you a husband, and the only way I can accomplish the feat is——"

"You are not that old! And at any rate, I am already on the shelf."

"At one and twenty? I hardly think so."

"We've had this conversation before. I thought you understood my feelings on the subject." Those being that she didn't want a husband. At least not the sort the earl would have to buy for her. She wanted a man she could love, one who would love her in return. She wanted the kind of happiness her father had found with her mother.

Jillian had never known Maryann Whitney. Her mother had died giving birth to her only child, but her father had never remarried. He had loved his wife that much. And Jillian refused to settle for anything less than that same sort of devotion.

"Every woman needs a husband," Lord Fenwick grumbled, but he didn't press her further and Jillian was grateful.

"There are endless soirees," she said, "as evidenced by the stack of invitations on your desk." But the stack continued to dwindle as the gossip about them mounted.

As usual the earl ignored it. He was set in his ways and taking her in was as far as he was willing to go in her regard. "I refuse to have that old battle-ax of a cousin of mine in the house just to still the wagging tongues," he had said.

But sooner or later, without a proper chaperon, they would be ostracized completely.

Jillian summoned a smile she suddenly didn't feel. "Perhaps by the end of the week you'll feel better."

The earl fought not to show his relief. "Yes, I'm certain I shall."

But Jillian was worried about him. He'd been looking a little more peaked every day. She would have to make certain he got plenty of rest and brew him some rose hip tea.

He had come to her aid when she had no one else to turn to. He had lost his only son the year before and perhaps he was lonely. Whatever the reason, he had taken her into his home, become the father she had lost, and she meant to take care of him.

And she didn't give a damn what the gossipmongers said.

Adam sat astride his black stallion at the top of the knoll. The day was fair, the breeze no more than a whisper. Ramses pawed the ground and snorted, lifting his magnificent head to study the lean bay gelding standing placidly beside him. Today Adam wasn't alone.

"Nice view." Clayton Harcourt Barclay, Duke of

Rathmore, stared down at the woman seated on the wrought-iron bench near the duck pond.

"So I discovered several days past." Adam had known Clay since Oxford, where they had been close friends. Since Adam's exit from the cavalry and subsequent return to London, they had become good friends again. "Do you have any idea who she is?"

Clay flashed a roguish grin. He was a handsome man, tall and broad-shouldered with thick, dark brown hair, the sort who could charm the garters off a lady with little more than a smile, which he had done with considerable regularity before he had wed.

"Actually, I do know who she is." Clay had recently married the Viscount Stockton's rebellious little red-haired daughter. Though the two had their problems in the beginning, they had worked them out, and Adam had rarely seen a happier man.

"The lady's name is Jillian Whitney. We met several months back at one of Stockton's dinner parties. Lately there've been rumors about her. They say she's the Earl of Fenwick's mistress."

Adam felt as if he had just been hit in the stomach. "Fenwick? I can scarcely credit that. The man is thrice her age and more."

"True, but he's still a man, and Miss Whitney is a very attractive young woman."

Adam silently agreed, wishing he could get a closer look at her.

"As the story goes, her father was a longtime friend of the earl's. When he died, Miss Whitney was left near penniless. She lived with an elderly aunt until the woman died, then Fenwick took her in. He claims she is merely his ward, but there is speculation she is far more than that."

Adam swallowed the bitter taste in his mouth. Little surprised him anymore, jaded as he was, yet it was difficult to imagine the smiling young woman who sat placidly feeding the ducks had been spreading her thighs for the ancient Lord Fenwick.

"Fenwick has never been known for his charity," Adam said. "I'd say he got a nice bit of muslin in return for his generosity."

"I suppose so . . . if the gossip is true."

Adam's attention swung away from the woman and fixed on his friend. "You're saying it isn't?"

Clay shrugged his powerful shoulders. "It wouldn't be the first time the gossipmongers have been wrong."

Adam pondered that. He had felt the vicious bite of slander himself, on more than one occasion.

And yet in his experience—which, where women were concerned, was quite extensive—most of those he had known would sell their souls for a few expensive baubles.

Clay lifted a knowing, dark brown eyebrow. "Since it is highly unlikely that mere coincidence brought us here this morning, I assume you would like an introduction."

Adam's mouth only faintly curved. It wasn't exactly the reason he had led Clay in this direction. Or maybe it was.

"Why not?" he said, and nudged his boot heels into the sides of his horse.

Jillian straightened as she saw the two men riding off the knoll in her direction. It took her a moment to recognize the Duke of Rathmore as the man on the right, but she had met him and his wife a couple of months ago, and he wasn't a man a woman would forget.

She stood up as they slowed their horses and both men swung down from their saddles. Rathmore went through the formalities, making polite morning greetings, then introduced her to the tall, raven-haired man beside him, Adam Hawthorne, Earl of Blackwood, the man who had watched her from the knoll.

"I've seen you here before," Blackwood said to her, more candidly than she would have expected.

"Yes, I'm quite an early riser. I prefer to enjoy the park before the crush arrives."

"That is my preference as well." He was lean, his skin darkly tanned, as if he often spent time in the sun. His features were strong, even harsh: black slashing brows and lean cheekbones, a mouth that looked hard, but was perfectly curved, except for a faintly cynical lift at one corner. A thin scar ran from his temple along his jaw, giving him a danger-ous air, and yet it was a face of uncommon beauty, the sort a woman would notice the moment he walked into a room. His looks combined with the powerful presence he exuded to make the earl a potent force.

"Morning is the very best time of day," Jillian went on, groping for something to say that wouldn't sound inane, forcing herself not to look away from the midnight blue eyes that assessed her with such bold regard.

Blackwood barely nodded. "Yes . . . the sunlight has a way of sweeping the demons away."

It was an odd thing to say. She studied him with

renewed curiosity and thought she saw something shift behind his eyes, as if the door he had accidentally opened had once again slammed closed.

"Lord Blackwood was in the cavalry for a number of years," the duke said mildly. "I don't think he'll ever get used to spending much time indoors."

"I can understand that. I prefer the country myself." Jillian smiled a bit wistfully, thinking of the small, ivy-covered cottage where she and her father had lived in Buckland Vale, a little village near Aylesbury.

"Is that where you got your interest in birds?" the earl asked.

"The ducks, you mean?" She glanced down at the creatures once again wobbling toward her from the pond. "I've grown quite attached to them, I'm afraid. That's Harold, there; and this little brown hen with the spots on her face, that's Esmerelda. If I don't bring them a bit of bread in the mornings, I worry they won't get enough to eat. Silly, isn't it?"

The duke cast her a glance. "You sound like my wife, Kassandra. She adopts every stray animal that comes her way. Just yesterday she ran across a litter of abandoned kittens in the mews. She was up half the night feeding them with a rag dipped in milk."

But he didn't look disturbed about it. In fact, he looked rather proud of her efforts.

The earl—Blackwood—however, continued to watch her as if he played a game of cat and mouse. There was no doubt which one of them was the prey. Jillian shivered beneath that intense regard and returned her attention to the duke.

"I hope your wife is well."

"Quite well, thank you. I'll be certain to give her your regards."

She nodded, hoping they would leave, but Blackwood seemed in no hurry. Since that was the case, she made ready to depart. "It has been a pleasure to see you again, Your Grace, but I'm afraid you'll have to excuse me. It's past time I returned to the house."

"Yes . . ." Blackwood cut in, assessing her in that unsettling way of his. "Should you be overly late, I'm certain Lord Fenwick would become quite concerned."

Was that mockery she heard in his voice? Had he heard the gossip about her? It always seemed ridiculous to her, considering the earl's age and health. She couldn't imagine how it had ever got started. The duke didn't seem the sort to be amused by such things, but Blackwood . . . he was difficult—no, impossible to read. Her stomach clenched to imagine what the men might be thinking about her.

"Farewell, Your Grace," she said to the duke.

"Have a pleasant day, Miss Whitney."

She tipped her head to the earl. "It was a pleasure to meet you, my lord."

Dark blue eyes swept over her. "The pleasure was mine, Miss Whitney, I assure you."

Still uncertain what she heard in his voice, Jillian turned and started walking away. She expected the shuffle of boots as the men remounted their horses and rode off the way they had come. Instead, only one of them departed. Without looking back, Jillian knew which one remained. She could feel the dark earl's gaze on her back until she disappeared out of sight on the path leading off into the trees.

                    *   *   *

In the early mornings, he rode. At night he walked the streets. His years in the army, days and nights of living out of doors, made it nearly impossible for him to fall asleep without at least a little fresh air. More than a year ago, after the death of his older brother, Carter, Adam had sold his commission in the Eleventh Light Dragoons and returned to London to assume his duties as earl. His nightly outings had quickly become a habit, and Adam knew every lane and alley in the West End.

He knew the exact house, a huge Georgian mansion in Brook Street, where the Earl of Fenwick lived.

What he didn't understand was what had drawn him there this evening.

Adam swore an oath into the darkness. *For God's sake, the girl is the old man's mistress!* She had bartered herself like a piece of meat for the expensive clothes she wore, for the fancy black coach and flashy matched grays that carried her each morning to the park.

He knew about women like Jillian Whitney. He had nearly married Caroline Harding, would have, if he hadn't found her in bed with his cousin, Robert.

And there was Maria. His face bore a constant reminder of her betrayal. The duel he had fought with her husband left a far deeper scar on the inside than the one he carried along his jaw.

And yet when he imagined the young woman beside the pond, when he remembered the sound of her laughter as she fed the ducks, he didn't feel the anger and hostility he felt when he thought of Caroline or Maria. Instead, he felt an odd sort of calm, a peacefulness he hadn't known since before the war.

The huge house loomed ahead, lamplight gleaming from a dozen different windows on the first and second floors. He wondered which room was Jillian Whitney's, wondered if the old man was brazen enough to install her in the countess's bedchamber next to his own. He imagined how the servants must feel about the old earl's mistress being kept right there in the house, and suddenly felt sorry for Jillian Whitney.

He paused in the shadows across the street, leaning back against the trunk of a tree. Had she really been so desperate? Had her father left her with no other choice?

Other speculations rose into his mind, but the echo of a gunshot brought them to a sudden end. There was no mistaking the sound, not after eight long years in the army. And the shot had come from inside the Earl of Fenwick's house.

Adam moved in that direction, careful to stay in the shadows. A scream came from somewhere inside and a few seconds later, the front door burst open.

"Help! Someone call a watchman! The Earl of Fenwick has been shot!"

From the corner of his eye, Adam caught a flicker of movement between the mansion and the house next door. A small, cloaked figure ran from the rear of the house toward the alley behind the mews. Moving silently, ignoring the shouts of the servants who streamed out into the street, he rounded the house next door and headed toward the mouth of the alley to stop the fleeing figure he had seen.

Waiting in the darkness at the entrance, he could

hear the pounding of light, frantic footfalls. Hidden beneath the hood of a billowing cloak was the barely discernible shape of a woman. Adam stepped out of the shadows directly in front of her and she careened hard into his chest.

His arms clamped around her as she struggled to break free. "Let me go!" She tried to twist away, but he merely tightened his hold. "Please. Dear God, please let me go!"

Adam stared down at her, a grim smile etched into the corners of his mouth. "Why, Miss Whitney. I hadn't expected we would meet again so soon."

She looked up at him and the breath seemed to stall in her lungs. "Blackwood," was all she said.

2

Jillian started to tremble. Behind her she could hear the servants shouting. Any minute the night watch would arrive. She glanced frantically around, started struggling again, tried to wrench herself free. Blackwood's hold was implacable.

He shook her, not gently. "Calm down or you'll hurt yourself. Tell me what happened."

Jillian's eyes filled with tears she couldn't hold back any longer.

"It's L-lord Fenwick. I heard a loud clap of noise and when I ran ... ran into the study, I found him lying on the floor. He was covered in b-blood, staring up at the ceiling, and I-I knew he was dead." She swallowed, tried to force the words past the lump in her throat.

"Go on," Blackwood commanded.

"One of the servants rushed in and started ... started shouting. He said that I had killed him. He said that I-I had murdered the earl. I tried to tell him I wasn't the one who shot him, that I would never do anything to hurt him, but the man wouldn't listen." She looked up into those fathomless dark eyes. "They'll put me in prison. Oh, God, please . . . please just let me go."

His hard mouth tightened. His features looked cold and forbidding. "I can't just let you go and even if I could, what would you do? Do you have friends in the city, someone to take you in?"

Jillian bit down on her trembling lip. "I'll find someplace to hide until they find the person who k-killed him. Please, I didn't do it. You must believe me."

Several seconds passed and the beating of her heart grew more fierce. Something flickered in those dark brooding eyes and his hold grew tighter on her arm. "Come with me."

Perhaps she should have run. If her mind hadn't been so muddled, perhaps she would have. Instead, she obeyed the command in his voice and his unrelenting grip on her arm and let him haul her down the alley.

The first passage seemed endless, winding through the darkness behind a row of houses. It led into another that was darker yet and stank of rotten leaves and horse manure. They headed into another corridor, took several more turns, weaving in and out between buildings, ran down more darkened paths, then he dragged her into a stable constructed of fine red brick.

For a moment they paused and she fought to catch her breath. As they hurried from the rear of the building to the opposite side, the magnificent black stallion the earl had been riding in the park poked its head above the top of its stall and nickered at him softly.

Blackwood glanced at the horse and for an instant, his hard features softened. Then he clamped his scarred, hard jaw, and kept walking, tugging her along in his wake. He led her through a manicured garden with a fountain in the center and they entered what appeared to be his town house, a two-story brick building with white-painted shutters and little iron-enclosed balconies opening off rooms on the second floor.

He closed the door behind them but even the warmth of the house couldn't keep her from shivering. Blackwood tugged her down the hall to his study, hauled her in, and slammed the door.

Her head was spinning. She took a moment to collect herself, to assess her surroundings: a wood-paneled room with a fire in the marble-manteled hearth, floor-to-ceiling bookshelves overflowing with books, and French doors leading out to a manicured garden. A fine, masculine room, she thought in some obscure part of her mind.

For several moments Blackwood said nothing, just stood there staring down at her with those hard, nearly black eyes. He was standing so close she could feel the heat of his lean, powerful body.

"I must be insane," were the first words out of his mouth, and Jillian thought that perhaps they had both gone mad.

She couldn't really be a fugitive, running through dirty back alleys like a rat in a maze, trusting her life to a man she knew nothing about.

"This can't be happening," she whispered, beginning to tremble again. "Tell me this is all some incredibly horrible dream."

Blackwood eyed her a moment, then crossed the

room to the sideboard and poured liberal shots of brandy into twin crystal snifters. "You can be certain this is real. Believe me, I know the difference."

She had no idea what he meant, but this was far worse than any nightmare she had ever had. As she watched him striding toward her, cradling a glass in each of his long-fingered hands, she moistened her lips, which felt as parched as sand.

"Perhaps ... perhaps the earl was only wounded. I shouldn't have run. I should have stayed and—"

"I think we can assume your instincts were correct." He pressed the crystal snifter into her palm and wrapped her icy fingers around the bowl. "From the way the servants were behaving, I'd say there's every chance the Earl of Fenwick is dead."

"Oh, God." She started crying then. She couldn't help it. She turned away, fighting to stop the tears, but they ran in rivulets down her cheeks. Blackwood forced her down in a nearby chair and his handkerchief appeared at the edge of her vision. She accepted it without looking up, blew her nose, and wiped the moisture away.

She dragged in a shaky breath of air. "I know he could be gruff and overbearing at times, but he was terribly good to me and I ... I cared for him greatly. I don't know what I'm going to do without him."

At her reference to the earl, Blackwood's already erect bearing seemed to straighten even more. "At present, your biggest concern is proving you didn't kill him."

Her eyes slid closed. How could she possibly do that? "What am I going to do?"

The earl reached down and caught the hand imply holding the brandy snifter. He lifted the glass and pressed it against her lips, forcing her to take a swallow. She coughed and sputtered, tried to push the glass away, but he merely tipped it up again, making her take another drink.

"You'll feel better in a minute."

As much as she disapproved his technique, she had to admit she was beginning to feel better. The warmth of the liquid began to spread into her stomach and the trembling in her limbs began to ease.

When she looked up at him, he was staring at her skirt. Jillian followed his gaze to a red stain near the hem. "Oh, my God."

"I believe that is blood on your gown, madam. Perhaps you would care to explain how it got there."

At the chill in his voice, the trembling began again. Jillian swallowed, tried not to think of the surprised look frozen on poor Lord Fenwick's face. "When ... when I saw him lying there on the carpet, I knelt beside him to see if there was anything I could do. I must have got ... got the blood on my skirt when I did."

His hard gaze never softened. "So you heard the gunshot, ran into the study, found his lordship lying on the floor, and tried to determine whether or not he still lived?"

"Yes." Her mind felt so fuzzy it was hard to think. And she really didn't want to remember.

"Is there anything else, something you might have forgotten?"

She shook her head. She wasn't sure how far she could trust him and anything else she said might make her sound guilty. It occurred to her, perhaps for the very first time, how desperately she needed this man's help. She had to convince him to believe her.

"You can spend the night here," he said. "In the morning, I'll pay a visit to Lord Fenwick's home, find out as much as I can about what happened. If you're lucky, perhaps the constable will already have apprehended the man who committed the crime. If not . . ."

He didn't have to say what would happen. He would turn her over to the authorities and she would be locked away. "I-I can't possibly stay here."

A slashing black eyebrow arched up. "You would rather go back? Face the constable and his men?"

Her stomach knotted. "I-I can't go back. If I do, they'll put me in prison."

"Then it appears you have no choice."

She didn't want to stay, not with him. She didn't know anything about him, didn't know if she could trust him. Even if she could, she had endured enough censure living unchaperoned with poor, harmless Lord Fenwick. Imagine what would happen should she be discovered in a house belonging to the rakish Earl of Blackwood?

And yet, as he had said, with no money and no place to hide, she had no other choice.

Jillian forced herself to her feet. "I don't know why you've decided to help me. Whatever the reason, I am more than grateful."

A dark, sweeping glance assessed her from head to foot and her stomach twisted in an uneasy knot. She wasn't sure what that look meant and her mind was too foggy to speculate, but it didn't bode well.

"There's a room you may use at the top of the stairs," he said. "As the servants are all abed, I'll show you up myself."

She swallowed nervously and nodded, allowed

him to pass in front of her to open the study door, then followed him down the hall and up the stairs to the second floor.

He paused beside an ornately carved door. "We'll speak again on the morrow. Good night, Miss Whitney."

She swallowed. "Good night, my lord." Turning away from him, she went in and closed the door.

The room was elegantly furnished, with pale rose Aubusson carpets and draperies in cream and rose. As tired as she was, the big four-poster bed with its deep feather mattress looked incredibly appealing. Then she noticed the door connecting the room to the one next door, and her heart sank with despair. She knew the door led into the master's suite, occupied by the dark, forbidding earl.

She also knew without the slightest doubt that she wasn't going to get an hour's sleep.

The night dragged for Adam, endless hours of restless slumber marred not by visions of war, but dreams of a woman with dark copper hair and soft lips, her slender body spread like an offering beneath him. Knowing Jillian Whitney slept in the room next to his, Adam awakened hard and throbbing.

As he often did, he dressed without the help of his valet, Harley Smythe, but instead of his early morning ride, as soon as the sun was up, he climbed aboard his carriage and ordered the driver to head for Rathmore Hall.

He arrived not long after, dragging his friend from a warm bed and a pretty, accommodating wife with only a grumble or two. Adam hated to involve

Clay in the sordid business of murder, but he trusted the duke, and he needed a way to get into Lord Fenwick's study.

He wanted to speak to the servants, find out as much as he could about what had happened last night, and asking for Clay's help was the only way he could think of to do it.

Why he was involving himself in Jillian Whitney's troubles was another matter entirely, one he hadn't completely sorted out. He wanted her. Jillian was a beautiful woman and that undoubtedly was the root of it. And yet there was something more.

An image arose of her perched on the edge of the chair in his study last night, her auburn hair disheveled, her eyes, more blue than he had imagined, wide and frightened, making her look like a terrified child. He remembered their encounter in the alley just moments before, remembered the feel of her soft curves trembling against him.

Perhaps she had overstated her case and there had been no necessity for her to run. A simple explanation might have satisfied the authorities and led them in pursuit of someone else.

But Adam wasn't convinced.

His mind veered to Gordon Rimfield, a sergeant in his regiment, a man he had always respected. The sergeant had been accused of being a highwayman, a member of the Bart Robbins gang. In truth, the man had merely been in the wrong place at the wrong time. Unable to prove his innocence, Gordon had been sentenced to the gallows. Adam had watched him hang, along with three other men, for a crime he didn't commit.

Justice, Adam knew, wasn't always just.

And of course, there was Maria.

Unconsciously, he rubbed the scar along his jaw. The story of rape she had invented had followed him even after he had sold his commission and left the army. Fortunately, his newly inherited title and fortune had kept the gossip at bay, but still there were whispers. To some he would always be guilty.

Was Jillian Whitney an innocent victim as well? Perhaps for Gordon, or maybe for himself, he intended to find out. And of course there were other, more personal advantages to having her in his house.

"We're nearly there." Rathmore's deep voice rumbled toward him from the opposite side of the carriage. Clay lounged against the squabs with casual grace, his golden eyes fixed on the passing landscape. "You say you need to get into Fenwick's study?"

"If it's possible."

"We'll make it possible." Clay had only inherited the dukedom last year, but he had taken to the role as if he had been born to the part, which, as the former duke's bastard son, he definitely had not been.

Adam sat forward on the seat as the conveyance rolled to a halt in front of Fenwick's mansion in Grosvenor Square. A footman opened the carriage door and Adam stepped down to the paving stones leading up to the towering four-story structure. Clay followed and they climbed the front stairs to a broad stone porch stretching beneath a row of white Corinthian columns. Adam used the lion-head knocker, and a few minutes later, the butler opened one of the carved double doors.

Rathmore stepped forward, his smile only slight.

"Good morning, Atwater. I just heard the news about his lordship." Clay and Fenwick had been business associates, as well as friends, which was the reason Adam had sought him out.

"Yes, yes, terrible thing. Gossip already about, I suppose."

"Yes, I'm afraid it is."

"He was murdered, you know. I was the one who found him."

"Is that so?"

"Yes, yes, quite so."

"Lord Blackwood and I have come to see if there is anything we might do to help." Clay shouldered his way past the thin, beak-nosed man at the door. As large as Clay was, the butler stepped quickly out of his way.

"I don't know what you might be able to—"

But Rathmore was already walking down the hall toward the study. "Justice must be served, Atwater. Lord Blackwood was a major in His Majesty's Army. He has some very good sources of information. I take it you summoned the proper authorities last night."

Atwater raced along in Rathmore's wake, and Adam almost smiled as he followed the two of them into the study. "Yes, yes, of course. And his nephew and daughter-in-law were told as well."

Clay merely nodded. He swung his attention to the bloodstain on the carpet in front of the earl's rosewood desk. The room was stuffy and smelled of tobacco. A meerschaum pipe, the end darkened and dented with tooth marks from years of use, sat in a crystal dish on the desk.

"The constable asked that we not clean or move

anything for a few days yet," the butler said. Now that they were inside the study, Atwater seemed to accept the inevitable, that he wasn't getting rid of them until he had told them whatever it was they wanted to know. "One of the night watch took the gun—"

"Gun?" Adam's head came up. "You found the gun that was used to kill him?"

"Yes, my lord. The pistol was lying on the floor next to his lordship. She must have dropped it there before she ran."

Adam's gaze sharpened on the butler. "By *she*, you're referring to Miss Whitney, the woman who presumably shot him?"

"That is correct. I assumed you had heard that as well. Miss Whitney, she was his . . . I don't like to speak ill of the dead, but the earl, he kept Miss Whitney right here in this house. She was his doxy."

Adam's stomach clenched. Every time he thought of Jillian Whitney lying with the ancient Earl of Fenwick, he felt a wave of revulsion.

"Are you certain that is the case?" Rathmore asked mildly.

"Oh, she never behaved that way, not in front of us. But she was quite a lovely little bit of muslin and his lordship always had an eye for pretty things."

A harrumphing sound came from the open doorway. "Not a word of truth in it. Never has been." The housekeeper, a buxom woman wearing a mobcap and a starched white apron tied over her stiff black skirt, stood frowning just a few feet away. "The gel was good for 'is lordship and 'e loved 'er like the daughter 'e never 'ad."

"Glynis, you are still as naïve as the day you

started working here as a chambermaid," the butler said sourly.

Another harrumph and the housekeeper turned and stalked away.

"Tell us what happened," Adam pressed.

Atwater didn't hesitate, caught up as he was in the importance of being interviewed by a duke and an earl. "It was getting quite late, but his lordship and Miss Whitney had not yet retired. Most of the staff had already been dismissed, but I was feeling a little out of sorts. I thought I would enjoy a glass of warm milk before I hied myself off to bed. As I passed down the hall, I remember quite distinctly hearing Miss Whitney in the study in conversation with the earl. A few minutes later, I heard the shot. I raced down the hall and threw open the door and there he was, poor Lord Fenwick, lying in a pool of blood."

"Go on," Adam urged, trying to absorb the news that Jillian had been in the study *before* the shot was fired, not gone in *after,* as she had told him, and wondering if he had been duped by a woman yet again. Anger flooded through him. He calmly tamped it down, banking it until later.

"As I said, the earl was lying there covered in blood and Miss Whitney was standing beside him. It was obvious what had occurred."

"And that was . . . ?" Adam prodded.

"There is a set of stairs at the rear of his lordship's private library, just there." Atwater pointed toward an open door in the north wall of the study. "If I hadn't arrived when I did, Miss Whitney would have escaped upstairs to her room and no one would have been the wiser."

"But instead you rushed in and saw her standing over the body."

"That is correct."

"Was Miss Whitney holding the pistol?"

"No. She had dropped it on the floor a few feet away."

Perhaps she had. Since she hadn't bothered to mention the gun, it was more than possible she had been the one to use it. "Did you confront her at that time?"

He nodded. "I said, 'Oh, dear, what have you done?' She denied it, of course, said she had no part in the shooting. That's when I started shouting for help and Miss Whitney took off running. She ran out through the door at the back of the library, down the hall, and out through the garden."

Adam remembered it well. He could still feel her surprisingly full breasts pressing into his chest when he had captured her in the alley. Her struggles instantly aroused him and he'd been hard all the way back to the house.

Now, as he replayed the story she had told him, making no mention of the pistol or her presence in the study before the murder, fury at her deceit tightened a muscle in his jaw.

Clay spoke up just then. "Were the windows in the study kept locked?"

"Not usually. The earl always liked a bit of fresh air, especially in the evenings."

"So it's conceivable someone might have stood outside the open window, shot him, and tossed in the gun."

"In theory, I suppose that could have occurred."

"Did you check for footprints outside the study?" Adam asked.

"The beds beneath that window are gravel, and at any rate, it rained just before dawn."

"Can you think of any reason Miss Whitney might have wanted to see Lord Fenwick dead?" Clay asked.

The butler shrugged narrow, sloping shoulders. "Who can say? Perhaps it was a lovers' quarrel."

Adam ignored the rush of disgust brought on by those words. "Would you mind if we took a quick look around?"

He didn't wait for an answer, just strode toward the ornate door leading into Fenwick's private library. A brief perusal of the wood-paneled, book-lined room showed a mahogany table gleaming beneath a green glass reading lamp and two leather-seated chairs. A chessboard set up with exquisitely carved medieval ivory pieces sat in the corner. Noting the set of stairs at the back of the room, he returned to the study.

"You've been extremely helpful, Atwater." Adam passed him a sizable vowel for his trouble, the coins jingling as the butler curled his thin fingers around them.

"Thank you, my lord."

"Hopefully we'll see the villain—whomever it may be—arrested in very short order."

"Indeed," the butler said.

They left the house and returned to the carriage, Adam's anger building all the way.

"I take it that wasn't exactly the story you got from Miss Whitney," Clay drawled from the seat across from him.

"No."

"Then perhaps she is guilty, after all."

"Perhaps." But Adam couldn't quite convince himself. Not when every time he thought of her, he saw her feeding the ducks, her face etched into the softest, kindest smile he had ever seen.

He thought of the lies she had told and the image disappeared. By the time he had returned the duke to his home, Adam's anger had resurfaced. A memory of Jillian rose into his mind and unconsciously his hand balled into a fist.

3

❧

Jillian paced the floor of the drawing room. Like the rest of the town house, it was done in impeccable taste, from the cream brocade draperies and gold-striped wallpaper, to the ivory and gold brocade sofas in front of the sienna marbled hearth. Thick Oriental carpets covered finely inlaid parquet floors, but the most interesting items in the room were the Egyptian artifacts sitting on bookshelves and tables: stonework, jewel-encrusted beetles, magnificently carved figurines.

The study of ancient Egypt had been a passion of her father's. Over the years, he had become a rather well-known expert on the subject and some of his knowledge had, of course, seeped into her. Jillian recognized the stonework as coming from the Early Dynastic period, somewhere around 3000 B.C. The figurines were Middle Kingdom, believed to be some thousand years later.

She wondered if Lord Blackwood had collected the objects during his years in the army, surprised that a hard man like the earl was attracted to such fine, exquisitely crafted works of art.

Mostly, she wondered what he might find out at Lord Fenwick's mansion.

A noise sounded in the entry. Her heartbeat quickened at the rhythm of the earl's heavy footfalls pounding down the marble-floored hall. Then the door slammed open, Blackwood stood in the opening, and the dark look on his face told her all she needed to know.

"You lied to me."

She shook her head, unconsciously backing away. *Dear God, what had they told him?*

"You lied to me, Jillian," he repeated, striding toward her on long, powerful legs. "I want to know why."

She swallowed, kept on moving backward. Her shoulders came up against the wall and still he kept coming. "What . . . what did they say?"

"Why didn't you tell me about the pistol?" He was standing so close she had to tilt her head back to look at him and the fury in his face made her heart pound even harder.

"Pistol?" she repeated, then, for the first time, remembered the weapon she had seen on the floor next to the earl. "Oh, dear Lord, I forgot. Last night, I just . . . I didn't think to tell you. Everything was so muddled and I was so frightened that I . . . I could scarcely think."

A muscle tightened beneath the scar on his jaw, and she raced on, hoping to defuse some of his anger. "I noticed it when I knelt beside him . . . it was lying just a few feet away."

"And you saw it when you ran into the study—after you heard the shot."

"Yes . . . that's right."

"So you were outside in the hall?"

"Yes."

He reached out and caught her arms, pressed her up against the wall. He looked utterly ruthless, his anger barely contained, and suddenly she was afraid.

"You were in the study with Fenwick when it happened, Jillian."

"No!"

"The butler heard you talking to him just before the shot was fired."

Her throat closed up. Her eyes slid closed and her knees buckled. If he hadn't been holding her up, she would have slid into a puddle at his feet. She had prayed no one had seen her, that they would believe she had run into the study after she heard the shot. Obviously someone had known she was there.

His fingers tightened around the tops of her arms until it was almost painful. "Why did you kill him? Did you do it in self-defense? Had the earl done something—"

"I didn't kill him! W-we had just finished playing chess. He went over to sit by the fire and I-I went to fetch a book he wanted. The earl had trouble falling asleep so I often read to him before he retired. That night he sent me into his private library to retrieve a copy of a book by Lord Chesterfield. It wasn't his usual sort of reading, but he told me where to find it, and I had gone to fetch it when I heard the shot."

He studied her face for several long moments, then very slowly released her. Fortunately, her trembling legs decided to hold her up.

"If that is the truth, then why did you lie?"

Jillian moistened lips that felt as brittle as parchment. If the earl turned her over to the authorities . . . dear God, it didn't bear thinking about. "I was afraid if you knew I was there in the study, that you would react just as Atwater did. That you would be certain that I had . . . that I had killed the earl."

He assessed her for several moments more. Jillian kept her eyes on his face and her chin held high, praying that he would believe her. Another second passed before he took a step backward. Even with the few feet between them, she could feel the anger emanating from him and remember the imprint of his long, dark fingers on her arms.

"Tell me why I should believe you."

She straightened, fixed her eyes on his face. *Such a beautiful face,* she thought in some distant corner of her mind, *and so disconcerting.* "Because I am telling you the truth, and I believe that in some hidden corner of your heart you know it or you wouldn't have helped me in the first place."

The edge of his mouth barely curved. "What makes you think I have a heart?"

Why did she? Perhaps it was the affection he felt for his magnificent black stallion, or the beautiful Egyptian antiquities he displayed with such care, as if he respected their ancient wisdom.

And yet when she looked into those cold, forbidding eyes, she believed he might be every bit as unfeeling as he appeared.

"I'm telling you the truth. I didn't shoot the earl."

He said nothing to that, simply turned and walked away. He paused near a small round piecrust table near the hearth. "Let's assume for the present that I believe you."

Relief hit her so hard she swayed a little on her feet.

"If you expect me to help you, from now on you'll have to tell me the truth. All of it. No matter how painful, no matter how frightened you are. I'll accept nothing less, and should I discover again that you have deceived me, I will drag you down to the magistrate's office myself."

Jillian shivered, not doubting for a moment that he meant every word. "I've told you everything. At least all I remember. It happened so quickly and I was upset. But I didn't kill him. Whatever reason could I possibly have to harm that dear old man?"

One of his sleek black eyebrows went up. "That is how you saw him? Most of the *ton* viewed him as a miserly old fool, set in his ways, and impossibly self-indulgent."

Sadness tugged at her heart. "Perhaps to some extent he was a bit of those things, but he was always beyond generous with me."

Blackwood's deep voice hardened. "At what cost, Miss Whitney?"

Jillian frowned, uncertain what he meant.

"You took care of him, didn't you? Bent to his wishes . . . whatever they might be?"

An image of his dear, homely face appeared. "Whatever I did for him . . . it was a small price to pay."

Blackwood's mouth looked hard as he turned and walked to the door. "It would seem you'll be staying for a while. You'll need some things to wear."

Jillian looked down at the dark stain on the hem of her gown she had tried unsuccessfully to wash out that morning.

"I've a friend about your size," he said. "I'll see what I can do."

A friend her size. One of his mistresses, no doubt. A man as wealthy and attractive as the Earl of Blackwood would have any number of women. It wasn't a comforting thought.

"What about the servants? The authorities will be looking for me. By this afternoon your staff will all know about the murder."

"I've informed my staff that my cousin Jane Winslow has arrived unexpectedly from the country. They're all quite loyal. And used to my somewhat unusual endeavors, whatever they might be. They won't pursue the subject."

"There is one last thing," she said as he reached the door.

"Which is . . . ?"

"I need to know if you truly believe I am innocent of killing the earl."

He gave her a hard-edged smile. "For the present, let's just say my mind remains open. If you're innocent, there'll be a way to prove it. If you're not—" His eyes held a promise of retribution so dark she had to work to suppress a shiver. "But then, since you're telling me the truth, there is no need for concern."

So saying, he opened the door and strode off down the hall, leaving her alone.

Jillian sank down on the brocade sofa, Blackwood's handsome image still etched into her mind. There was something about him. Her heart beat faster the instant he appeared, and even with the ruthlessness stamped onto his features, he was the most attractive man she had ever met. And yet she didn't trust him. He was a member of the *ton,* another of the social elite who had shunned her from the moment of her arrival in London.

Why she was drawn to him she couldn't quite say and already, she was indebted to him far more than she would like. It occurred to her that in accepting the earl's assistance, she might be in more danger than if she had been captured and carted off to prison.

Adam strode into the drawing room of the Queen Elizabeth suite on the top floor of the Albemarle Hotel.

The suite was large and airy, with windows looking down on a small green park. The drawing room had been done in peach and gold, with darker peach draperies at the windows, a theme carried into the huge gold and peach bedchamber at the end of the hall. Adam knew because he had been there before—a number of times, in fact, during his days in the army.

The suite was kept for the exclusive use of the Countess of Melburn, a very old friend. Well, not really *old,* Adam mentally corrected, imagining the lady's lush curves and softly curling long blond hair just as she walked into the drawing room. She had recently turned thirty, he recalled, being a few months younger than he was himself.

"Adam! I can scarcely believe it. It's wonderful to see you." Lavender silk brushed her ankles as she gracefully floated toward him, extending pale, slender hands.

Adam captured both of them and drew her toward him, bent to kiss each cheek. "You're looking lovely as always, Arabella."

She smiled, used to men's flattery. "Where have you been hiding? I haven't seen you in . . . what's it been . . . ? At least six months or more."

"I spent the winter at Blackwood Manor." His country estate south of London, on the coast not far from Seaford. "As you know, I prefer the open spaces. I only just returned to the city a few weeks ago."

"Well, I'm glad you finally found time to drop by. The Season is just begun and already I grow bored. As I said, it's a pleasure to see you." She tossed him an intimate glance, though they were no longer lovers. "It always was."

Adam didn't respond to the entendre. The last he had heard, Arabella Saunders, widowed some nearly eight years, was involved with the Duke of Kerns. As enticing as she looked in the lavender gown that showed, for this hour of the day, a bit too much of her magnificent bosom, he realized he was no longer interested in anything beyond the friendship they had developed over the years.

"I wish this was a social call," he said to her, "but actually, I was hoping you might be able to help me."

"Of course, Adam dear, you know you only have to ask."

"A cousin of mine arrived unexpectedly from the country . . . a bit of a family problem, from what I gather. At any rate, she left home with only the clothes she was wearing. I was hoping you might be able to lend her something until we can muddle things out and she can go home."

"A cousin, is it?"

He gave her an unreadable smile, neither denying nor confirming her assumption that his "cousin" might be anything more. Whatever she believed, one thing he could count on: Arabella wasn't a gossip. She wouldn't mention his visit or the loan of her clothes.

"As I said, I'll be happy to help. I have a wardrobe full of things I should love to get rid of. It will give me an excuse to purchase something new."

"She won't need much," he said as she floated off down the hall. "She won't be staying all that long."

"Still, a woman needs to be well-dressed," she called over her shoulder, then disappeared out of sight into the bedchamber.

She was gone longer than he expected, returning with a footman in tow, carrying a stack of boxes so high the slim blond man couldn't see over them.

"These should do quite nicely. She may alter them if she wishes. I won't need them returned."

Adam bent and again kissed her cheek. "You're a jewel, Arabella."

She gave him a lighthearted smile. "You'll be sure to tell His Grace that, won't you?" She tossed her head. "On second thought, I don't think that would be wise a'tall. William is becoming quite jealous. A good sign, don't you think?"

"A very good sign," Adam said. "I wish you well, Arabella."

"Good luck with your . . . cousin."

Ignoring another of Arabella's not so subtle innuendos, Adam motioned for the footman to follow, then preceded him out the door of the suite. He loaded the boxes into his waiting carriage, settled himself inside, and rapped on the top.

As the carriage lurched into motion, Adam eyed the stack of boxes on the seat across from him, so tall they almost touched the ceiling. He imagined Jillian Whitney in the low-cut gowns Arabella always wore, and a cool smile pulled at his lips. It was followed by a tug of heat low in his groin.

First things first, he reminded himself, shoving the image away. He had to know for certain that Jillian Whitney was innocent. Though seducing her would be infinitely appealing and was undoubtedly part of his motivation for helping her, he didn't favor sleeping with a woman who might be involved in a murder, no matter how tempting she was.

He needed to discover the truth about the shooting and to do that he needed to get some answers. Leaning back against the tufted red leather seat, Adam went over his plan.

4

❧

Jillian tugged at the neckline of the fashionable plum silk gown she had found among the clothing Lord Blackwood had brought her. The dresses were a bit too short, the cut of the narrow skirts a little roomier in the hips than she needed, but aside from that, they fit almost perfectly. It irritated her to think how well acquainted with a woman's body the earl must be to gauge her proportions with merely a glance.

She studied herself in the full-length mirror, tugging on the bodice again. With Lord Fenwick dead, she felt as if she ought to be gowned in black from neck to toes. Instead, though the garment was styled à la mode, it was cut a little too low for day wear. If fact, there wasn't a gown in the lot that didn't reveal a little more of her cleavage than she would have liked.

Blackwood's *friend*, Jillian noted with no little annoyance, was obviously the sort she had imagined. Though it bothered her to wear his mistress's cast-off clothes—right down to chemise, silk stockings, and frilly blue satin garters—the notion of putting her dirty, bloodstained dress back on was far more repugnant.

Struggling to do up the last of the buttons without the help of a lady's maid, wishing she had a fichu to stuff into the bodice, and cursing the earl for his taste in women, Jillian descended the stairs, on her way to a meeting with his lordship to discuss her situation.

The door to the study was open when she got there. Seated behind a gleaming mahogany desk, the earl looked up from the stack of paperwork he had been perusing. Dark blue eyes surveyed the auburn curls swept up on her head, moved slowly down her plum silk gown. They lingered a moment on the swell of her breasts above the bodice of the too-low gown and Jillian found it hard to breathe.

His gaze moved lower, down to the toes of her brown kid slippers, the shoes she had been wearing last night.

"The matching slippers were too small," she said defensively. "Aside from that, everything fit very well." She cast him a disapproving glance. "Your *friend*, however, seemed to have a need to display her bosom. Perhaps the next time you are out, you might buy me a bit of lace or something."

Blackwood actually smiled. "I don't think so. You do the gown justice. And I like looking at you exactly as you are."

She flushed. She couldn't help it. He was studying her boldly and with obvious approval, and though she should have been angry, beneath the bodice of the gown, her nipples tightened, then went embarrassingly hard. Jillian felt a rush of heat to her cheeks and prayed he wouldn't notice.

She thought that he did, for an instant later, his usually guarded expression slid away. In the depths of those fierce dark eyes, something molten surfaced. It lingered only a heartbeat, then the shuttered look returned and his control settled firmly back in place.

Jillian ignored the weakness in her knees that sultry look had caused. She couldn't possibly be attracted to him—surely not. The man was cold and callous, and though he was helping her, she didn't trust his motives. Still, she was a normal, healthy woman and he was an extremely handsome man.

She moistened lips that felt drier than they had when she'd first walked into the study. "You said you wished to see me."

"Yes . . ." He rounded the desk and strode toward her. "There's a chill in the air. Have a seat in front of the fire and I'll have Reggie bring us tea."

"Reggie? That is your butler?"

"That's right. He served with me in the army."

"Tea sounds lovely. Thank you." Though she hardly noticed the chill. In fact, every time the earl's dark eyes drifted over her, she felt oddly warm. Still, as he tugged on the bell pull, she made her way over to the brown leather sofa in front of the hearth where a fire burned brightly. Flames in orange and gold licked the grate, spreading heat out into the study.

Jillian wandered toward the fire, trying not to be self-conscious in the dress. Her steps slowed as she noticed a gilt-framed piece of ancient Egyptian papyrus on the wall above the sideboard.

"That's a very nice piece," she said, her gaze on the ancient drawing of a man in profile wearing a headdress adorned with a serpent on the front. He was holding a hooked scepter and surrounded by boldly painted hieroglyphics. "Twentieth Dynasty, perhaps, somewhere around that time, I would say. Ramses III, if memory serves."

The look on his face was priceless. "I didn't realize you were a student of Egyptian history."

The smile she gave him was infinitely smug. "It's a fascinating period. But actually it was my father's passion, not mine. He was something of an expert on the subject. I learned a good deal from him, spending as much time with him as I did."

"God's blood—you're Giles Whitney's daughter. I never would have put the two of you together."

She turned, looked up at him. "You knew my father?"

"I knew *of* him. We never met. I've read a number of his papers. As you say, he was a respected authority on Egypt." He crossed the room and picked up a statue of a bird carved of dark gray stone. Between its claws stood the tiny figure of a man. "Do you recognize this?"

She nodded. "Horus Falcon." She walked closer, took the heavy statue from his hands. It felt smooth and cool, and there wasn't the least imperfection in the stone. She imagined it had been found in a tomb, where it had been well protected. "The man sheltered by the bird is probably Nectanebo II."

He cast her an assessing glance. "Probably. We think it's Thirtieth Dynasty. Somewhere around 300 B.C."

She studied him from beneath her lashes as she

set the statue down on the table. "You were there, weren't you? In Egypt. That's where you first got your interest in the subject."

His expression hardened. "I was there." But he added nothing more and an uncomfortable silence began to stretch between them.

At the butler's knock at the door, Blackwood seemed to collect himself. He walked over and pulled open the door, admitting the least likely butler she could imagine. "Reggie" was short and squat and looked a little like a bulldog, his nose smashed down as if it had been broken more than once.

"Wot can I get ye, Major?"

"Tea for Miss . . . Winslow and myself, if you wouldn't mind, Reggie."

"Right away, sir." He ducked back out and closed the door.

"Major? That was your rank in the cavalry?"

"Actually I declined a promotion to colonel when I decided to leave."

"I don't imagine you were sorry."

He paced over to the fire, held his hands toward the flames to warm them. "It might be hard to understand, but in some ways I *was* sorry to give it up. I liked the camaraderie. I liked the travel and living out of doors. As a matter of fact, that's the reason I was in front of Fenwick's house the night he was shot. I walk most every evening. It helps me get to sleep."

"You have trouble sleeping?"

"Unfortunately."

"So did Lord Fenwick."

One of his eyebrows went up. "Well, he is resting quite peacefully now."

She glanced away, swallowed against the lump in her throat. "Do you know when the funeral service is going to be held?"

His gaze found hers across the short distance between them. "Tomorrow morning at St. Katherine's."

"There are bound to be dozens of people. Perhaps if I arrived late and wore a veil, I could—"

"No. You'll have to do your grieving here. Someone might recognize you. If they do, you'll be arrested and taken straight to prison."

Jillian shivered, but she couldn't imagine not paying her respects to a man who had been like a father.

"Speaking of prison brings us to the business at hand." Adam paced over to where she sat on the sofa. "If I'm going to assume you aren't the one who shot his lordship, then we need to find out who did. To do that, we need to know why someone would want the earl dead. There is the obvious reason, of course, that Fenwick's heir will come into the title and fortune a few years prematurely."

"That would be the earl's nephew, Howard Telford. But he is already the Viscount Mayfield and as far as I know, in no immediate need of funds."

Blackwood walked over to his desk, took up the quill pen, and scratched something down on a piece of paper. "Wouldn't hurt to make certain of that."

"Even if he did need money, I can't imagine him killing his uncle." She realized she was twisting a fold of her skirt and began to smooth out the wrinkle. "But then I can't credit anyone killing a harmless old man."

"If it wasn't a matter of greed, then it had to be

something else. Did Fenwick have any enemies you knew of?"

She worried her lip, trying to remember, trying to think if there was anyone in particular who might have been angry enough with the earl to want him dead.

"Let me see," she said, stalling for time, desperate to think of someone. She finally gave up and shook her head. "I realize his lordship wasn't the most popular man in London, but I can't say there were many who out-and-out loathed him."

"Come now, Miss Whitney. The earl was hardly known for his diplomacy. As I heard it, he was outspoken to a fault. There must have been any number of people he offended."

Blackwood was right, of course. Lord Fenwick often said the most outrageous things. Now he was dead. Someone had certainly been displeased with him. Her mind raced backward, searching for someone—anyone she could think of—who might have been unhappy with the earl.

"Well, as you said, Lord Fenwick often made comments that were unusually blunt. Several weeks ago, a gentleman named Barton Witherspoon came to the house demanding to see the earl. He said that if—"

A knock at the door interrupted her. Blackwood's improbable butler shoved a tea cart through the door of the study. Gold-rimmed porcelain cups and saucers rattled as he pushed it over to the leather sofa.

"Thank you, Reggie."

"Anything else, Major?"

"Not at present."

Reggie the bulldog butler closed the door and Jillian turned to the earl. "Are you on a first-name basis with all of your servants?" It amazed her, made her wonder if perhaps there was more to the man than she had thought.

"Just the ones I knew before I left the army. Will you pour, Miss Whitney?"

She did so with ease, having learned all the niceties at Mrs. Davenport's very expensive finishing school, which, she now knew, had cost her father the last of his savings.

Seating himself in the chair next to the sofa, the earl took the cup and saucer she offered, his hand large and dark against the white of the fine porcelain, and yet they were elegant hands, strong, long-boned, and lean.

"You were talking about Mr. Witherspoon," Blackwood reminded her.

"Yes . . . as I was saying, Mr. Witherspoon came to the house a couple of weeks ago. I was in Lord Fenwick's library when he walked into the study. I saw Mr. Witherspoon's face and I could tell he was furious with the earl. He said that if Lord Fenwick didn't retract what he had said at the Collingwood soiree about his daughter Hermione looking like an underfed crane, there was going to be hell to pay."

Blackwood surprised her by laughing out loud. It was such a rich, masculine sound and it transformed his face so completely, for a moment she forgot what she was going to say.

He set his teacup down in the saucer he held in one hand. "Fenwick said Hermione Witherspoon looked like an underfed crane?"

"Yes, I'm afraid he did."

He chuckled, and wings seemed to flutter in her stomach. "I'll admit the earl wasn't far off the mark," he said, "though saying so wasn't quite the thing." He looked at her, his eyes still crinkled at the corners. "The question is, do you actually believe Barton Witherspoon was angry enough to kill him?"

She wanted to say yes. She desperately wanted to find someone who might be to blame. Instead she sighed and shook her head. "No. I don't believe the man would shoot the earl for comparing his daughter to a crane."

Blackwood set his cup and saucer down on a marble-topped table and came to his feet. "If Witherspoon is the best you can do, we're going to need some help. I'll send a note to Rathmore, ask him to stop by as soon as he is available."

"Rathmore!" Jillian surged to her feet so quickly she nearly knocked her teacup off its saucer. "How do you know we can trust him? What if he goes to the authorities? What if—"

"Apparently I forgot to mention Rathmore went with me to Lord Fenwick's house."

"Rathmore went with you?"

"He's known the earl for quite some years. It was the easiest way to get in."

She swallowed, her eyes flicking toward the door as if the constable's men might burst through at any moment.

"You needn't worry. The duke is completely trustworthy. Perhaps between the two of you, you can come up with something that will help."

But Jillian remained uneasy. Dear God, she would be putting her very life in Rathmore's hands.

Blackwood must have sensed her fears, for he

reached out and caught her chin. "If you want my help, Miss Whitney, you'll have to do as I say." She bit down on her lip. "Trust me, Jillian. I have your best interest at heart."

She wanted to believe him. He was the only one willing to help her. She nodded very faintly.

"Good. In the meantime, I'll speak to Howard Telford and the late earl's daughter-in-law, Madeleine. And I'm hiring a runner. In fact, I've an appointment in Bow Street this afternoon."

Jillian's stomach tightened. "But that is bound to be expensive. I haven't a farthing. How shall I ever repay you?"

Blackwood casually started walking toward the door. "You needn't worry." He cast an unreadable glance over his shoulder as he stepped out into the hall. "I'm sure we'll work out something."

Jillian awakened early the following morning, the day of Lord Fenwick's funeral. She had spent a restless night thinking about him, remembering the awful way he had died and how much she had come to love him. She needed to be there—or at least somewhere nearby—when he was laid to rest.

The funeral at St. Katherine's was scheduled to take place at ten o'clock that morning, she had read in the *Evening Post*, but as Lord Blackwood had rightly said, she couldn't possibly attend. Both Madeleine Telford, the earl's daughter-in-law, and his nephew, Howard, would be among the mourners, not to mention myriad other *ton* members, many of whom she had met.

Which meant, as his lordship had said, there was every chance she would be spotted the moment she stepped inside the church.

But a service would take place in the graveyard as well, and there she could pay her respects from a place among the headstones where she would not be seen.

Digging through her limited, borrowed wardrobe, Jillian chose a dove-gray gown with tiny pearl buttons up the front—the only thing vaguely suitable for a visit to a graveyard—drew on a cashmere shawl, and concealed herself in the long, hooded cloak she had worn the night of the murder. She wouldn't go near the graveside service, just remain hidden among the shadowy granite columns some distance away.

As the minutes ticked past, her nerves began to build. She checked the ormolu clock above the mantel, saw that it was time to leave, dragged in a steadying breath, and opened the door. Knowing the butler had probably been instructed not to let her leave, she carefully checked to be certain no one was about. The halls were empty, just a few chambermaids working in one of the guest rooms at the opposite end of the wing.

Jillian stepped into the corridor, quietly closed the door, and headed for the servants' stairs at the rear of the town house.

No one was in the hall when she reached the bottom of the narrow staircase. With a cautious glance around, she stepped out of the shadows and hurried for the door. She had almost made it when strong fingers clamped around her wrist, halting her flight and spinning her around. Her face went pale at the dark look on Blackwood's face.

"Going somewhere?"

Dear God, she thought he had already left for the service! Jillian lifted her chin and hoped it didn't tremble. "I am on my way to his lordship's funeral. I am honor-bound to pay my respects."

His eyes ran over her and she realized he thought she might be running away.

"Lord Fenwick was my dearest friend," she continued, trying to make him understand. "More than a friend. I owe him at least this much."

His features seemed to harden even more. "Whatever your *friendship* with the earl, it isn't worth being imprisoned."

A chill feathered down her spine. "I'm not going into the church, only the graveyard. I'll stay in the distance, pretend to be visiting another grave, but I have to be there to bid him farewell." She realized he still held onto her wrist and beneath his hand her skin began to tingle.

"I appreciate your feelings in the matter, but the fact remains, you're not going. The risk is simply too great."

"The risk is mine to take, not yours, and at any rate, why should you care? I still don't understand why you are helping me."

He shrugged those wide shoulders. "Perhaps I'm not sure either. Whatever the reason, it appears as though I am, and as long as that is the case, I won't let you foolishly put yourself in danger."

Angry heat rushed into her cheeks. What he thought of as foolish, she thought of as duty and love. Blackwood didn't move, didn't release his hold on her wrist. She could feel his iron resolve and her temper began to fade.

He was trying to keep her safe when no one else seemed to care. She should be grateful, not angry.

"If the earl was the man you believe," he said a

little more gently, finally releasing his hold, "surely he would understand."

Jillian swallowed past the tightness in her throat. Perhaps he was right. The earl had loved her. He wouldn't want her life endangered because of him. Reluctantly, she nodded. "Perhaps he would."

"Come," he said, settling a hand at her waist. "I'll have Reggie fetch you a cup of tea."

With a sigh of resignation, Jillian let him guide her down the hall. Inwardly, she gave up a prayer that the earl would know she was there in spirit if not in body.

The hours dragged past. Blackwood had departed for the funeral a few minutes after their encounter. He was tense and brooding by the time he got back, giving her only a brief rendition of the service then shutting himself away in his study.

Part of her was glad. Their earlier meeting in the hall had left her nerves on edge. The evening loomed ahead, a thought that unsettled her even more. As it happened, Jillian soon discovered she would be spending the evening alone, news that should have made her happy. Instead she felt oddly disgruntled.

The devil take Blackwood, she silently vowed in a show of temper she didn't quite understand. Determined to blot him from her thoughts, she enjoyed a light supper of vermicelli soup and lamb cutlets in a small, less extravagant salon at the rear of the town house, then left to retire to her bedchamber for the night.

Unfortunately, as she made her way toward the staircase, Blackwood appeared at the top of the stairs. Resplendent in snug black breeches, blue and silver waistcoat, and a dark blue tailcoat that perfectly fit his broad-shouldered frame, he looked impossibly handsome.

Jillian ignored the odd little clutch in her chest and stepped back into the shadows of the hall, hoping to remain out of sight.

No such luck, of course. When he reached the bottom of the staircase, Blackwood spotted her in the light of the sconces, turned, and started toward her.

"I see you are about to retire. I'm on my way out for the evening. I've instructed Maude Flynn, one of the chambermaids, to act as your lady's maid while you're here." His eyes swept over her, pausing an extra moment on the pale flesh rising above the low-cut bodice of her gown. "I know how difficult it is for a lady to undo all of those buttons by herself."

The faintly sensuous curve of his lips made her breath catch. She wished her heart would stop that infernal pounding.

"That's kind of you, my lord."

"Sleep well, Miss Whitney."

"Enjoy your evening, my lord." She tried to keep the censure out of her voice, but it crept in all the same. She couldn't help wondering where he was going, whether or not he might be visiting the woman who had lent him the dresses.

His lips curved even more. He was so damnably attractive. "I promise to do my very best." Accepting his satin-lined cape from Reggie, he whirled it around his shoulders, turned, and walked out the door.

Jillian watched him disappear into the darkness outside the house and felt a sharp pinch in her breast. She wasn't all that experienced with men, yet she was smart enough to know what that little pinch was. She had never been jealous of a man before and she certainly had no reason to harbor those feelings for this one. Aside from an occasional heated glance, Adam Hawthorne had shown little more than a passing interest in Lord Fenwick's penniless ward.

And she still couldn't fathom his reasons for helping her. Even he didn't seem to know and she was so desperately in need of his assistance that she was afraid to press him.

With a weary sigh at the terrible situation she found herself in, Jillian climbed the stairs. As the earl had promised, when she stepped into her room, Maude Flynn waited beside the bed.

"Good evenin' to ya, Mistress Winslow."

Mistress Winslow. For a moment she had forgotten whom she was masquerading as. "Good evening, Maude." The woman was short and stout, black-haired and fair-skinned, Irish, by the lilt in her voice, a broad-hipped woman in her thirties. As she helped Jillian undress, she rattled on about every subject, from the rise in bread prices to the navy blockade. She talked about her cousin's recent employment in the cotton factory, and finally began to chatter about the earl.

"Sure'n he's a fine man, is the major. Me late husband, Tommy, was in his regiment, ya know. I was one of the lucky ones what got to go along with their menfolk—only a few of us did, ya know." She shook her head, moving a curl of black hair that escaped from her mobcap. "I was only there barely two years. Cannon misfired and killed me poor, dear Tommy."

"I'm sorry," Jillian said.

"Major Hawthorne, he come to the tent himself ta bring me the news. 'Twas several years back, ya understand, and I never heard much about him after I got back to England. Six months ago, me mother passed on, and I come to London lookin' for work. The major—his lordship—he give me a job when no one else would."

Fascinated, Jillian sat down on the tapestry stool in front of the dresser and listened as Maude pulled the pins from her hair.

" 'Course, bein' his cousin and all, ya already know the sort of man he is."

"Actually, we're very distant cousins." Lying didn't sit well, but since she was forced to play the part, she might as well learn something useful. "I really don't know much about him at all." But she would like to, and perhaps this was her chance.

"Well, one thing's fer certain—whatever they say about him—sure as the king keeps raisin' taxes, there ain't a word a truth to it."

Jillian fidgeted as Maude ran the brush through her hair, determined now to find out all she could. "I'm glad to know that, Maude. I've heard the rumors, of course." Another bald-faced lie. "I wasn't sure whether or not to believe them."

"Sure'n that's just what they are, lass, rumors, nothin' more. The ladies flock to the major's bed, always have. He's hardly a man what needs to use force. The colonel's wife, the little tart, seduced him, she did. Seen her come to his quarters with me own two eyes. Then when her husband finds out, she turns on the major, says he took her against her will. Don't see how the fool coulda believed it, her all the time pantin' after the major the way she was."

By the time Maude left, Jillian had more questions about the earl than she had answers. And her curiosity continued to build. Lying in bed in the room next to his, she found herself listening for his return, wondering again where he was and if he would come back before morning.

The clock struck midnight. One o'clock chimed before she heard the tread of his footfalls on the stairs. She relaxed a little as he entered his room, then a new thought surfaced and she was wide-awake again.

But the door between their rooms didn't open and eventually her heartbeat returned to normal. Perhaps she could finally fall asleep.

5

∼◦∼

Another hour passed. Jillian punched her feather pillow, but sleep still refused to come. Too many thoughts swirled through her head, too many questions about the earl. Most of all, too many fears of what might lie ahead.

Dear God, if they didn't find out who the real killer was, she could yet wind up in prison!

The minutes ticked past, but her eyes remained open. In the room next to hers, noises began creeping in. First the restless shifting of covers, then the creaking of the mattress. The sounds grew louder, turned into quiet moans that seeped through the wall between the rooms.

Ignoring the fact she wore only a borrowed cotton night rail, Jillian swung her legs to the edge of the bed and walked over to the door. She pressed her ear against the wood.

Through the ornate paneling, she could hear the sounds more clearly. Blackwood, apparently in the throes of a nightmare, the moans so tortured, so filled with pain, she simply couldn't let them continue.

Steeling herself, calling herself a fool, she reached for the silver doorknob. Almost hoping the door was locked, she turned the knob and quietly eased it open. Blackwood's big four-poster bed lay in shadow, but a shaft of moonlight streamed in through a high, partially open window, and she could clearly see the earl's broad-shouldered figure on the mattress.

The covers were shoved below his waist and she saw that he wore no nightshirt. His body was slick with sweat, perspiration gleaming on smooth dark skin corded with ridges of muscle. His chest was wide and muscled and covered with a mat of black curly hair that formed a thin line down his flat stomach and disappeared beneath the sheets.

She told herself to look away, to turn round, walk back into her room, and simply close the door. But fascination held her rooted beside the bed. Aside from her father when he was ill, she had never seen a man's bare torso before, and her father's gray-haired chest surely didn't look like this one.

Blackwood's arms were roped with muscle, and as he shifted restlessly on the mattress, his biceps flexed and knotted. A long, crescent-shaped scar slashed across his side and, like the one along his jaw, she wondered where it had come from.

The earl moaned again and Jillian froze. *Go,* shouted the voice inside her head. *Turn round and leave before he sees you.* And she might have, if he hadn't cried out so pitifully just then.

Jillian moved closer. Leaning forward, she tentatively touched him. "Lord Blackwood?"

"No . . ." he whispered, tossing his head from side to side. "Forgodsake, no . . . not . . . not so many . . . men."

Jillian reached down and gripped his shoulder, very gently tried to shake him awake. "My lord?"

His hands shot out and a startled shriek escaped as long fingers wrapped around her shoulders. The next thing she knew, she was flat on her back in his bed, the earl's hard body pressing her down in the deep feather mattress. His eyes were glazed as if he still didn't see her, his muscles so taut they quivered.

"Adam . . . ?" she whispered, the name coming out of nowhere, bringing his eyes to her face. The glazed look remained as he focused on her lips. She saw heat and need the instant before his mouth crushed down over hers.

Jillian's lips parted on a startled gasp and his tongue slid into her mouth. It was hot and wet and it fired little tremors of heat that crawled over her skin. Her breasts flattened out beneath the heavy weight of his chest and her nipples tightened. The dampness of his sweat-slick skin seeped through her thin cotton nightgown, and something warm curled low in her belly. Lean hips pinned her to the mattress, and she could feel the sinews flexing in his long, powerful legs. Her eyes widened as she realized the heavy, hot hardness nestled so intimately between her legs was his arousal.

Oh, dear God! The knowledge set her in motion. Frantically, she shoved at his chest, trying to push him off her, Maude's words ringing in her head. *The colonel's wife . . . she says he took her against her will.*

Fear sank into her stomach—the instant before he let her go.

Jillian scrambled up from the bed, breathing hard and fast, her whole body trembling.

Blackwood swore foully. "What the hell are you doing in here?" Sitting up in the bed, he raked a hand through his damp black hair, shoving it back from his forehead. The scar along his jaw glinted in the moonlight, making his features appear almost brutal.

"You were . . . you were having a nightmare. I was trying to awaken you."

"God's blood." He started to get up, realized he was naked, reached over and grabbed his burgundy silk dressing gown off the back of a nearby chair. Jillian turned away as he shrugged it onto his broad shoulders. "I didn't hurt you, did I?"

She thought of his punishing kiss and tried not to remember the heat that had flooded her stomach. "Not really. Were you . . . were you dreaming about the war?"

His gaze swung to hers. For a moment he didn't answer. Finally, he nodded. "The memories aren't pleasant."

She wondered exactly what those memories were, but she didn't ask. It was clear he wouldn't tell her. "Last night I dreamt of the earl, lying there in his study, his chest covered in blood, but the dream soon changed and we were sharing the good times again."

"You were lucky." He turned away from her, roamed with restless grace toward the dresser along the wall. Pouring water from the porcelain pitcher into the bowl, he splashed his face, raked water through his wavy black hair, then blotted the droplets with a white linen towel.

His gaze returned to where she hovered near the door as if she meant to escape, which was close to what she was thinking.

"I didn't mean to hurt you. You startled me. Then you called me Adam and I . . . I thought you were someone else."

Color rose in her cheeks as she remembered the passionate kiss. "The woman who lent me the dresses?"

"No."

Her chin inched up. "Perhaps, then, you dreamt of the colonel's wife."

A hard glint appeared in eyes so blue they looked black. "What do you know of Maria?"

She shrugged, tried to appear nonchalant. "Nothing much. I know she made accusations . . . falsely perhaps. I know you may have suffered unjustly at her hands. I wonder if that is the reason you decided to help me."

He ranged toward her, his strides long and pantherlike. He stopped directly in front of her. "Perhaps it is."

She tilted her head to look up at him. "I give you my word your faith in me is not misplaced."

Blackwood flicked a glance at the bed. His mouth barely curved. "Perhaps, in time, you'll give me more than your word, Miss Whitney."

Jillian swallowed, tried not to tremble. "I-I believe it is past time I returned to my room." She turned and started walking in that direction and Blackwood made no move to stop her.

"Thank you for your concern tonight," he said softly as she reached the door. "But perhaps next time you should consider the consequences."

Jillian barely nodded. Continuing into the room, she hurriedly closed the door.

Adam paced the study, waiting for Rathmore, and the woman who had invaded his life like an enemy force. Since she'd come into his room the night before, he couldn't seem to get her out of his mind, and discovering her part—or lack of it—in Lord Fenwick's murder was fast becoming an obsession.

He told himself it was simply that he wanted her so badly and he couldn't pursue that course until he knew for sure she was innocent of the crime.

It was late afternoon. Adam walked over to the sideboard and poured himself a brandy. Ever since Jillian's appearance in his room last night, he'd been edgy and out of sorts. He could still remember the feel of her body beneath him, the softness of her breasts against his chest, the delicate curve of her hip bones, the feminine vee of her thighs as they cradled his arousal. The wanting had been so fierce it made him ache to think of it. He'd wanted to lift her nightgown, spread her shapely legs, and bury himself inside her.

He wanted that still.

Dammit to hell, what he needed was a woman, a female who would satisfy his lust with no strings attached, and he knew the very one. Lavinia Dandridge, Marchioness of Walencourt, was a wicked little morsel whose needs ran as hot as his own. Her husband remained in the country for the Season, blissfully unaware of Lavinia's proclivities, or perhaps too exhausted from his futile efforts to satisfy his wife to care.

Adam took a sip of his brandy, mentally reminding himself to send Lavinia a note as soon as his meeting with Rathmore was concluded. Perhaps the lady would be free for the evening. After a few hours at the theater—if they left her house at all—he could enjoy a night of debauchery in her more than willing arms.

A corner of his mouth edged up just thinking about it, then a firm knock sounded at the door and more serious matters intruded. Reggie showed Clay into the study, preceded by Jillian Whitney, whose worried blue eyes and obvious fatigue sent a shaft of guilt straight through him—and immediately shot his plans for tupping Lavinia straight to hell.

Bloody damn.

"I don't believe Miss Whitney is all that happy to see me," Rathmore drawled as he closed the door and moved farther into the room.

Adam felt the pull of a smile. "She isn't convinced you're as trustworthy as I am. Must be something in those shifty brown eyes of yours."

Rathmore laughed. He turned his attention to Jillian, who stood straight-backed a few feet away. "Lord Blackwood has vowed to help you prove your innocence. He asked for my help as he once helped me, and I gladly agreed. It is really as simple as that."

"Then please, Your Grace, know that I had nothing to do with Lord Fenwick's murder. His lordship was very good to me and I would never have done anything to harm him. In fact, now that he is gone, I find myself in very difficult circumstances. That alone should prove my innocence, for I gained no benefit from his demise."

"It certainly speaks to the issue of motive," the duke agreed.

Jillian seemed to relax. She tucked a strand of dark copper hair back into the thick coil at the nape of her neck and Adam noted the weariness in her movements. Her face was pale, turning her eyes an even more striking shade of blue. Even tired and worried, she was lovely.

Adam felt the same pull of attraction he had felt from the moment he had spied her at the duck pond, and yet there was something else, something more than her fine features and delectable little body, that drew him. He wished to God he knew what it was.

He walked over to the sideboard, poured Clay a snifter of brandy and Jillian a sherry.

"Establishing a motive is the reason I asked you to come," he said to Clay. "Jillian couldn't think of anyone who might want old Fenwick dead." He glanced at her and couldn't stop a smile. "Except for Barton Witherspoon, of course, who may have been sent into a homicidal fit when the late earl compared his daughter to a crane."

Clay laughed as he accepted the snifter of brandy. "Fenwick said Hermione Witherspoon looked like a crane?"

"An underfed crane, to be exact." Adam flicked a glance at Jillian, who did not look amused. "But we've agreed the notion is rather far-fetched, so perhaps you can help us come up with a more likely candidate." He handed the glass of sherry to Jillian, and they all sat down on the sofa and chairs in front of the hearth to begin their discussion in earnest.

"I'd like to begin by telling Miss Whitney that I knew Lord Fenwick for quite some years." Rathmore took a sip of his brandy. "Since the shooting,

I've been trying to think of anyone who might have wanted him dead."

"And?" Adam prompted.

"Actually, a couple of people came to mind. Theodore Boswell, Lord Eldridge, is one of them."

"Eldridge?" Adam swirled the brandy in his glass. "How does the marquess fit in?"

"Eldridge and Fenwick were in business together. A West Indies trading venture the earl recommended. Unfortunately, the deal went sour. The company went broke, and since Eldridge had invested far more heavily than Fenwick, he lost nearly everything."

Jillian sat forward on the sofa. "Good heavens—I should have remembered. Mrs. Madigan, Lord Fenwick's housekeeper, told me a couple of weeks ago that Lord Eldridge came to the house in a violent temper. She said he threatened the earl, that he stood right there in the entry and said he would never forgive him for the damage he had done."

Adam scratched a note on the piece of paper he had set in front of him to have the runner he had hired, a man named Peter Fraser, check on Eldridge's whereabouts the night of the murder. Of course, the marquess could have paid someone to kill the earl, a more likely scenario and more difficult to prove, but there was always the hope that Eldridge might have wanted the satisfaction of killing the earl himself.

"All right, we've got Eldridge to consider. Who else?"

Clay sipped his brandy, set the glass back down on the marble-topped table. "His solicitor, Colin Norton, had reason to kill him."

"I thought Norton left town."

"He did. And Fenwick was the reason. Apparently Norton was mishandling the old man's funds and a goodly sum came up missing. No charges were filed—as I recall, Norton was caring for an invalid wife at the time—but after the incident, his reputation was in shambles. His business was ruined, of course, and he was forced to leave London. I have no idea what happened to him after that, but the last I heard, he blamed Fenwick for all of his troubles."

Jillian set her sherry glass down on the table. "If the man stole the earl's money, he's lucky Lord Fenwick didn't send him to prison."

"True enough," Clay said, "but there are always people who refuse to accept responsibility for their actions."

Adam penned himself a few more notes. "Anyone else?"

"There are a number of others like Barton Witherspoon, people the earl offended, but I don't think they were outraged enough to kill him. Howard Telford, of course, had a motive. With Oswald Telford's death, he has gained the Fenwick title and fortune. And Ozzie's daughter-in-law is undoubtedly named in the will."

Jillian straightened. "I hadn't thought of Madeleine. Surely she wouldn't have killed him. The earl seemed to think very highly of her."

Adam knew little about the woman, except that she had been married to Lord Fenwick's only son. Early last year, Henry Telford, for reasons only Henry knew, had committed suicide. Word was Fenwick had been devastated by the loss. He had taken his daughter-in-law under his financial wing, though she remained at her late husband's estate on Hampstead Heath near the outskirts of the city.

"How much money was Madeleine due to inherit?" Adam asked.

"Quite a tidy sum, I imagine." Clay took a sip of his brandy. "As Miss Whitney said, Fenwick seemed to hold her in high esteem."

Adam turned to Jillian. "Did you know her?"

"A little. She came to the house a couple of times."

"How did the two of you get along?"

Jillian's eyes strayed toward the fire. "She was cordial. I'm not sure she really approved of me, but she was always courteous. As I said, I only saw her a very few times."

Adam had tried to pay a call on the woman but apparently as soon as the funeral was over she had left London to visit relatives in the country. He jotted down a reminder to pay a call on Howard Telford on the morrow and stuck the plumed pen back into its holder.

It wasn't much, but unless the constable turned up something else, it was all they had for now and more than they'd had before.

Adam stood up and so did Clay. "Thanks for coming."

"I'm happy to help." He turned a look of scrutiny on Jillian. "I'll do a little digging on my own. Perhaps I can come up with something we've missed."

She summoned a smile, but it was obvious she was worried. "Thank you, Your Grace."

Adam walked Clay to the door. Once they were out of earshot, Rathmore drew Adam aside. "Sooner or later they're going to find out she's here."

He nodded. "Hopefully by then we'll have found some sort of proof that she's innocent."

Clay nodded, but didn't look convinced.

"You haven't mentioned this to Kassandra, I gather."

Clay shook his head. "I think she's beginning to harbor suspicions that I haven't been entirely forthright, but so far I've been able to dodge her questions. I don't want her involved in a murder, and for Jillian's sake, the fewer people who know, the better."

"I appreciate all you've done, Clay."

"You still believe she's innocent?"

"What she says is true; she doesn't have a motive."

"That we've discovered so far."

"No, not so far. But if she were guilty, she would have tried to run, and she hasn't done that."

"Not yet, at any rate."

Unless she had planned to run the morning of the funeral. Adam sighed. "I realize Fenwick's entire household believes she's guilty, but my instincts tell me she isn't the one who shot him."

"Well, you've always had good instincts."

His mouth tightened. "Unfortunately, not when it comes to women."

Clay chuckled. "By the way, I heard Howard Telford has posted a reward for her capture."

"Christ."

"As I said, I'll do a little digging, see what I can find out. If I learn anything new, I'll let you know." Clay clapped a big hand on Adam's shoulder. "Take care, my friend."

Adam watched him leave, then returned to the

study. Sitting in front of the fire, Jillian stood up when he walked in.

"You were right about Rathmore," she said. "I believe he's a man of honor."

"He'll do what he can to help."

"Because the two of you are friends?"

"Yes. And because he wants to see the earl's murderer brought to justice."

"The same reason, then, that you are helping me."

That and his growing determination to have her in his bed. His eyes moved over her in a slow, thorough perusal. "Among other things, yes."

Jillian made no reply, but a hint of color crept into her cheeks. Good. He wanted her to know he wanted her. As soon as he was sure she wasn't in any way involved in the murder, he meant to have her.

"I need to get started on this," he said, reaching over to pick up the sheet of foolscap that contained his notes. He was headed for Bow Street to speak to Peter Fraser. He wanted this matter ended and Jillian freed from suspicion.

Most of all—he wanted her in his bed.

6

⚜

Another restless night, dreams of war and erotic dreams of the woman asleep in the room next door. He needed to get out of the house, Adam thought the following morning, needed to get away from his turbulent thoughts for a while.

As he strode down the hall toward the stairs, he cast only the briefest glance at Jillian's bedchamber door. He was on his way to the stable. He had missed his early morning rides, and even his late night strolls had fallen prey to his preoccupation with the mystery of Fenwick's murder. He needed to get out, and riding was the best way he knew.

He had almost reached the bottom of the stairs when he spotted Maude Flynn hurrying toward him. His senses went on alert at the worried look on her face.

"What is it, Maude?"

" 'Tis your cousin, milord . . . Mistress Winslow.

The lass is nowhere ta be found. She's not in her room, nor anywheres about. Ya don't think maybe she decided to go back to the country without lettin' ya know she was leavin'?"

The muscles across his shoulders went tense. "Are you sure she's not here? My . . . cousin is an early riser. Perhaps she's in the library. Or maybe she is out in the garden."

"I've looked, milord. Sure as there'll be hell to pay if the Little Corporal wins the war, the lass is gone."

Adam clamped hard on his jaw. Maude was right. If she wasn't in the house, she very likely *had* taken off for the country. Leaving the city was the best chance she had of escaping the gallows. Clay had suggested she might run and it looked as though she finally had.

Fenwick's lying little doxy would have known, sooner or later, he would find out she was the one who'd committed the murder.

Adam's hand unconsciously fisted. He'd sworn he would never be duped by a pretty face again, yet it appeared that was exactly what had happened. Anger surged through him, so hot it made the heat rise at the back of his neck. Storming up the stairs, he slammed open the door to her bed-chamber, not quite sure what he would find, think-ing of the morning of the funeral when she had tried to leave, wondering if she had meant to run even then.

His gaze searched the room. She wouldn't be able to take much with her, but surely she wouldn't go without a change of clothes and something she could sell, a silver candlestick, perhaps, or a small brass lamp, since as far as he knew, she had no money of her own.

But the room looked surprisingly normal, the rose silk counterpane turned back, the bed unmade but obviously slept in, her night rail draped over the tufted velvet bench at the foot of the bed. If she meant to run, why had she waited until morning? Or perhaps she had mussed the bed to make it look as though she had slept there when in truth she had left the house hours ago.

Barely able to control the fury sweeping through him, Adam left the room, trying to decide which way she might have gone, determined to bring her back to face the consequences of what she had done. No matter how much he might want her in his bed, if she had murdered poor old Fenwick, he was honor bound to see that she paid for the crime.

He had almost reached the stable when an odd thought crept in. Adam slowed for a moment, his mind whirling, grasping at the faint ray of hope. He shook his head at the ridiculous notion. The woman was guilty. She had run because she knew sooner or later the truth of her crime would come out. But the nagging thought remained, and as he approached the stable, waited while Angus saddled Ramses, then swung himself up in the saddle, he found himself turning away from the road out of town and riding toward the park instead.

Dammit, when he got there he was going to feel like a fool all over again, but he kept on riding, trying to ignore the heaviness in his chest and the ridiculous hope that he would find her there by the duck pond.

At the bottom of the knoll, he drew Ram to a halt for a moment before making the assent to the top, unwilling to face the disappointment he was certain lay ahead.

You're a fool, Major, he thought. Then he urged the animal forward, up to the top of the hill. When he looked down at the placid, glistening water and the little iron bench beside it, a wave of relief hit him so hard he felt dizzy.

Jillian sat on the bench, calm as you please, feeding the ducks as if she hadn't a care in the world.

His relief slid away, followed by a jolt of blazing anger. Adam nudged Ram off the knoll, down through the deep green grasses, toward the woman carelessly relaxed on the wrought-iron bench.

Jillian listened to Esmerelda's familiar quacking and tossed another bit of bread to the hen and her string of ducklings. After days of being confined in Blackwood's town house, she had awakened tired and disturbed, thinking about him, confused in a way she never had been before. She had to get out of the house and knowing it was a foolish, dangerous thing to do wasn't going to stop her.

Still, she wasn't a complete and utter harebrain. For weeks she had been up and about at this early hour, traveling the dew-slick streets, and she felt fairly certain that no one of consequence would be around to notice her. An image of Blackwood on his tall black horse flitted briefly through her mind, but she didn't think he had been going to the park of late and even if he did, there wasn't any reason to believe he would turn up at the duck pond.

Jillian smiled at Esmeralda, already feeling better, and tossed her another piece of bread. The hen's small, feathered head came up at the same instant Jillian heard the pounding of hoofbeats.

Oh, dear God! She jumped to her feet at the sight of the tall, dark earl swinging down from his horse, swearing an oath as he strode toward her. There was no mistaking the fury distorting his features, making him look utterly ruthless.

Unconsciously she took a step backward, then another and another, until the trunk of a sycamore came up behind her and she couldn't go any farther. Blackwood reached her in a few more strides, his mouth thinning into a hard, unforgiving line. His fingers gripped her shoulders and he hauled her toward him, glaring down at her from inches away.

"What the hell do you think you're doing?"

Her own temper flared. She tipped her head back to look up at him, and the hood of her cloak fell back. Who did he think he was? He didn't own her. He was helping her—that was all!

"What does it look like I'm doing? I'm feeding the ducks."

"Feeding the ducks?" He seemed incredulous. "You could be captured and thrown into prison at any moment and you are out here feeding the ducks!" His eyes were nearly black, his jaw clamped so hard the scar along the edge stood out in relief.

She tried to pull away but the tree blocked her escape. There was nowhere to go and his hold was unshakable. "I'm not your prisoner, no matter what you think."

His hard mouth barely curved. "Are you not?

Don't delude yourself, Miss Whitney. If you think for a moment you are leaving my house before I know the truth of Fenwick's murder, you had better think again."

Her temper spiraled higher. "I wasn't trying to leave, you . . . you jackanapes! I was only going for a walk. That is hardly a criminal offense!"

He stared at her in disbelief that she had dared to speak to him that way. Then his mouth edged up at one corner and some of the harshness seeped from his features. His hands fell away from her shoulders. Even with the distance between them, she could feel the heat of his body, and a curl of warmth slid into her stomach.

"No, taking a walk is not a criminal offense, but what if someone sees you out here? Do you know there is a bounty on your head?"

Jillian swallowed, tried to control the shudder that rippled through her. "All right—it was a stupid thing to do. I know you don't understand, but I simply couldn't stay in that house a moment longer. I needed to breathe. I needed a place to think, to figure out what I'm going to do."

His features softened. He no longer looked angry and she thought as she had before how impossibly handsome he was.

"Perhaps I do understand. I was coming here this morning myself. There are times God's green earth and good fresh air are the only tonics that work. But it's dangerous for you to be here, Jillian. If someone sees you, they might figure out who you are. The authorities could discover where to find you and if they do, they'll haul you off to prison. That, I assure you, is not a place you wish to be."

He didn't say more, but he didn't back away, just stood there looking into her face. Her pulse hitched into an even faster pace, only this time she wasn't angry. Very slowly his gaze moved down until it fixed on her mouth. Jillian nervously moistened her lips and for an instant something flared in his eyes. Insanely, she thought he was going to kiss her. Instead, he straightened, turned, and took a step away.

She couldn't believe she felt disappointed.

"It is past time we returned to the house," he said, his voice a little rough. "I'd take you back on Ramses, but the two of us riding that way might draw attention and it's imperative you remain unnoticed."

"I got here on my own. I can find my own way back."

He nodded. "You leave first. I'll follow a little behind you."

Grateful to be away from the unsettling feelings he stirred, Jillian turned and started walking. She couldn't resist a last glance over her shoulder. Blackwood's eyes remained fixed on her, and for the first time it occurred to her that he might have been worried about her. Or perhaps, he merely intended to see justice done—one way or the other.

The thought put an end to the rising spirits she had felt as she'd fed Esmerelda and her babies at the pond.

It was nearly dark, the sky a purplish gray, a low layer of clouds hanging over the city when Adam returned to the town house after another futile day. First his meeting with the runner he had hired, Peter Fraser, disappointingly had turned up nothing new.

"It takes time, my lord, to ferret these things out," Fraser had said. "You must try to be patient."

But he wasn't a patient man, especially when a woman's life hung in the balance.

Clay's efforts had also been in vain, though he remained optimistic. "Eventually, something will surface. I spoke to Justin this morning." The Earl of Greville was Clay's best friend. "He and Fenwick were in several business ventures together. I thought he might be able to help."

Adam paced over to the window of his study, looked out at the wind beating through the plants in the garden. He returned his attention to the duke. "For Greville's sake, I hope his ventures with Fenwick were more profitable than the ones the earl convinced Lord Eldridge to invest in."

Clay flashed a smile. "Far more profitable. Everything Justin does makes money, I'm happy to say. The man has always had the Midas touch."

"You didn't tell him that Jillian was staying with me?"

"No. I said I had my doubts that the woman under suspicion was guilty of the murder and I wanted to find out who was. Justin isn't the sort to press for information he hasn't been offered. He volunteered to see what he could do."

Adam didn't particularly like the idea of involving Greville in this, but if he was going to clear Jillian's name, he needed the help of people he could trust and he knew the earl was one of them.

After Adam's meeting with Clay, he had gone to see Howard Telford. The newly titled earl had retired to Fenwick Park, his country estate in Hampshire County, Atwater, the butler had said, to "sort things out and grieve for his murdered uncle."

All in all it had been a useless, frustrating day, and Adam was glad to be home.

Stepping into the foyer, he handed his greatcoat to Reggie, who hung it on the hook beside the door, then he wearily made his way down the corridor to his study. The London *Times* rested on the arm of the sofa. As he shrugged out of his tailcoat and draped it over the back of a chair, he absently picked up the newspaper and flipped it open. One look at the front page and his eyebrows slammed down.

Every day another article about the murder appeared, repetitious accounts of the incident with all the gory details and a description of Jillian Whitney, the woman suspected of the crime. There was nothing new in the case, the paper said, and the woman remained a fugitive.

But today, an addition had been made to the piece. An etching of Jillian's likeness appeared on the front page of the *Times.*

Bloody hell.

The servants would have to be deaf, dumb, and blind not to see the resemblance to his "cousin" Jane Winslow, then piece together the date of her arrival, his call at Fenwick's mansion the morning after the murder, and the trips he had made to Bow Street.

And yet they were a loyal bunch. He wasn't too sure Reggie and Maude, with the help of ex-corporal Lance Whitehead, his coachman, hadn't figured it out that first day and simply kept their silence.

A knock at the door interrupted his train of

thought. Jillian walked in looking pale and shaken, her hands trembling as she held up a copy of the *Evening Post.* "Have you seen this?"

He nodded, held up the *Times.*

"What am I going to do?"

He damned well wished he knew. "Considering your face is in every paper in the city, along with information on the reward the new earl has offered, it's only a matter of time until someone figures out who you are and that you're here. Instead of hiding, perhaps it's time you came forward. I've a friend who's a first class barrister. I could try to arrange—"

Jillian whirled away and bolted for the door. Adam caught up with her before she could escape and spun her around to face him.

"You can't run from this, Jillian."

"I have to run—can't you see?" Her incredible blue eyes were round as teacups. "I don't have any choice. I can't possibly go to the authorities—they won't believe a word I have to say. I've got to leave the city." She looked up at him, blinked against a well of tears. "Please . . . I'm not trying to escape. I simply need to find somewhere safe until the authorities can discover the person who is guilty."

Adam caught her chin, forcing her to look at him. "Listen to me, Jillian. We've been through all this before. You've nowhere to go and it isn't safe for you to simply wander the streets."

She swallowed, turned her face away. "You won't let me leave because you think I'm guilty."

"I won't let you leave because sooner or later they'll find you, no matter where you hide. The only way you're going to escape is to prove that you didn't kill Fenwick."

Her shoulders sagged. When he let her go, she walked over to the French doors leading out to the garden looking so forlorn he felt an unexpected pang in his chest. For a moment she simply stood there, then she pulled one of the glass doors open and stepped out into the night.

Adam followed, stopping on the terrace to watch her. By the light of the torches along the gravel paths, she wandered aimlessly over to the marble fountain in the center of the garden and sat down on one of the curved stone benches.

Clouds drifted across the sky, but glimpses of a full moon slanted down between the branches of the trees and he could see her features clearly, tense at first, her indrawn breaths shaky. Little by little her troubled expression began to ease.

She turned toward the fountain, trailed a hand through the water, let the tiny droplets trickle from her fingers. She tipped her head to gaze up at the sky, and just watching her, some of his own tension faded. She looked as she had when he'd found her this morning at the duck pond, quiet and serene, as she had appeared the first time he had seen her.

"Feeling better?" he asked.

She rose at his approach. "I always feel better when I am out of doors. And the water is soothing. It sounds like tiny crystal beads breaking on a mirror."

Her gaze remained on the gentle spray of the fountain. The statue in the center was Egyptian, a Greco-Roman period piece he had purchased just last month, the head of a man, his face tilted toward the sky, water spraying out of his mouth.

"There's more to it than simply being out of the house. What is it?"

Jillian's lips curved into a smile, and he noticed the hint of a dimple beside her mouth. His groin tightened. He wanted to press his lips against the spot, wanted to see if it deepened when he kissed her.

"Out here I'm able to think more clearly, put things in perspective. It's true that I'm frightened, more than I've ever been before. But in life there is always something to be afraid of. I learned that when my father died. His death was completely unexpected. I had no one to turn to, no one to help me, but somehow I knew I'd be all right."

She turned toward him, bathing her features in moonlight. "The truth is, I'm not guilty of murdering Lord Fenwick. Whatever happens, no matter what anyone says, I know in my heart I've done nothing to be ashamed of. As long as I am true to myself, no one can ever really hurt me."

Her gaze returned to the fountain and he wanted to reach out and touch her, to draw her into his arms and absorb her sense of peace, a tranquillity that continued to elude him.

He thought about Aboukir and the men in his command who had died there. He had done his duty at Aboukir, fought side by side with the soldiers who were killed. He had nothing to be ashamed of, yet the nightmares persisted, forcing him to fight the gruesome battle again and again.

But Jillian was different. Unlike the turmoil that raged inside him, with every breath, every smile, she exuded an inner peace that seemed to radiate out through her skin.

"I'll be glad when all of this is over." She looked into his face and he thought that her eyes were the bluest he had ever seen.

"What happened after your father died?"

"I had very little family, just a few distant cousins. I moved in with my great aunt Gertie. She hadn't much money so I tutored some of the village children and tried to make what little my father had left last as long as I could. But one of my students went off to boarding school and the other moved away. Then Aunt Gertie died. I couldn't stay in the cottage alone."

"That's when you came to London?"

She nodded. "My father always told me that if I ever needed help I should go to the Earl of Fenwick, as they had been best chums in school. I was desperate. I went to the earl and he was kind enough to take me in."

His muscles went tense. He didn't want to talk about Fenwick. Not now. Not here in the peacefulness of the garden.

"It looks like a storm's blowing in." He gazed up at the clouds drifting across the moon, beginning to stack up over the city.

Jillian's gaze followed his. "I've always loved storms. The sky seems to come alive and the next day everything looks fresh and clean."

She would see it that way, he supposed, but to him, the thunder sounded like the rumble of cannon, the lightning sparked like the muzzle flashes of a gun.

The truth must have shown in his face.

"Does the storm . . . ? Do the nightmares come with the wind and the rain?"

He didn't answer. He didn't have to. He felt her fingers like a brand against his cheek and something shifted in the air between them. He didn't know exactly how it happened, only that one instant she was there beside him and the next he had pulled her into his arms.

He kissed her harder than he meant to, taking what he had wanted from the start. Like the storm she spoke of, his body came to life, and for an instant, he nearly lost control. He forced himself to soften the kiss, to taste her, savor the sweetness of her lips. He battled the heat but it was there, simmering beneath the surface, ready any second to explode into his blood.

He felt her tremble, felt her hands slide up to his shoulders, and held on to his control by force of will. His tongue teased her lips, urging her to open for him, and invaded the dark, moist cavern of her mouth. She stiffened a little, a faint tension invading her body. Vaguely he realized she had never been kissed this way before.

Perhaps the aging earl had simply crept into her bed, lifted her night rail, and taken his pleasure in the darkness. Adam's pulse leapt to think that though she had been desperate enough to share the old man's bed, much of her innocence remained.

He kissed her again and this time she kissed him back, swaying toward him, unconsciously pressing her soft curves into his arousal. Fire ripped into his groin and he heard himself groan.

The kiss grew more fierce. He took her deeply with his tongue and some of his control slipped. He wanted her and he meant to have her, but he wasn't ready for this to go further. Not yet. He had to be sure she was innocent of the murder but his body seemed to have a will of its own.

His palm found her breast, cupped it, tested the

softness, the weight. His thumb rubbed over her nipple, and a faint moan rose in her throat. He kissed her deeply one last time, his shaft so hard it hurt. Damn, he wanted her. Wanted to feel her softness all around him, wanted to be inside her.

Jillian must have sensed his growing desire. He felt her stiffen, then she pulled away. She stood there trembling, looking dazed and shaken and wary.

"That . . . that shouldn't have happened."

He surveyed the lovely blush in her cheeks. "There is little doubt of that."

"I-I realize some of the blame lies with me, but it shan't happen again."

His mouth edged up, but he made no reply. It would happen again—he intended to ensure that it did.

Jillian seemed to have regained her composure, though her cheeks still carried the faint blush of embarrassment.

" 'Tis past time I went in," she said. "Good night, my lord."

She started walking away and though his body still throbbed with need, he made no move to stop her. He refused to be duped again, and Jillian's soft kisses and seemingly innocent responses warned him to beware.

He watched her escape back into the house, walking a little faster than she usually did. From the corner of his eye, he caught the distant flash of lightning, heard the roar of thunder, and knew that for him the night would be a long one.

Instead of retiring to his room, he strode through the house to the entry. Grabbing his greatcoat from its hook on the wall, he opened the heavy front door and stepped out into the darkness. Perhaps a walk would help him sleep. Perhaps if he were tired enough, he could forget the tantalizing sweetness of Jillian's lips, forget that she lay sleeping just beyond his bedchamber door.

Perhaps, if he were lucky, he might dream of her small, lithe body and surprisingly full breasts instead of the long-ago battle that still raged inside his head.

7

A harsh spring wind rattled through the branches of the trees the following day. A dense rain had fallen overnight, and a sullen sky hung above the London streets.

Standing beside the rose silk draperies in her bedchamber, Jillian watched a coal cart roll past on the street below, the vendor calling out as he pushed his heavy load. She watched him disappear, then closed the window she left partially open each night, wishing it wasn't too cold to be out of doors.

Dressed in peach muslin, the bodice and hem heavily embroidered in a Grecian design, Jillian crossed the bedchamber, catching sight of her reflection in the looking glass. Peach was usually one of her best colors but today it did nothing to improve the pallor of her face. Though her dark copper hair, braided and wound in a coronet atop her head, looked shiny and well cared for, shadows lingered beneath her eyes and her cheeks were sunken in.

She hadn't slept well. She wondered if she'd ever

have a peaceful night's sleep again. But it wasn't her nebulous future, it was Blackwood who plundered her restless thoughts last night.

She had known he was attractive, that the harsh, almost ruthless angles of his face gave him an uncommon appeal few men possessed. Still, a lot of men were handsome. It was the self-confidence, the air of command accompanying those attractive features that set the earl apart from other men. And the carefully hidden need she sensed in him, the restlessness he couldn't quite contain.

Last night, she had discovered how powerful a force it could be.

Jillian trembled to think of it. She could still feel the heat of his palm on her breast, muted by the fabric of her gown, the pleasure that swept through her when his fingers stroked over her nipple. His mouth wasn't hard, as it often appeared, but soft and warm and encompassing, like heated silk moving over her lips.

She didn't even know people kissed the way he did, his slick, hot tongue finding its way into her mouth. She'd felt invaded, plundered—and on fire. In those few brief moments, she had completely lost the power to think. It was beyond disconcerting—it was terrifying to imagine what might have occurred.

Fortunately, at the very last instant, her senses had returned and she had ended the kiss. Though his eyes remained hot, Blackwood had returned to his role as gentleman and ended his pursuit. She couldn't help a certain curiosity as to what might have occurred if he hadn't played the gentleman quite so well.

At any rate, the encounter was over and she had

other, more pressing matters to consider than her first and only, very brief experience with desire.

Turning toward the door, preparing herself to face the earl, and determined not to blush when she saw him, Jillian left the room and made her way to the head of the stairs. A commotion stirred in the entry.

Jillian froze in horror as two uniformed watchmen caught sight of her standing at the railing and bolted toward her up the stairs.

Oh, dear God!

They reached her before she could think to run. "Jillian Alistair Whitney?" the taller man said, taking a firm grip on her arm.

She opened her mouth to reply, but no sound came out.

"In the name of the Crown," said the second man, thick-shouldered, with badly scarred hands. He captured her other arm. "You are under arrest for the murder of the Earl of Fenwick."

"Nooo!" The plaintive wail erupted from deep in her throat. She wanted to break free, wanted to run, but she could see how useless it would be.

"Ye'd best come peacefully, Miss," the first man said.

" 'Twill only go the worse for ye if ye don't."

Two more watchmen waited at the bottom of the stairs. Maude stood a few feet away, her eyes red-rimmed with tears. Straight-backed, like the soldier he once was, Reggie let his bulldog face betray little emotion, but his chin thrust forward at a belligerent angle and she thought that he had done his best not to let the men in.

As they started down the stairs, one on each side,

boxing her in, she glanced frantically around for the earl. "Wh-where is Lord Blackwood?"

"Gone out, Miss," Reggie said. "Soon as he comes back, I'll tell 'im what's happened. He'll come for ye, Miss. The major stands by his friends."

So they knew she wasn't his cousin. She wondered if they had known from the start, wondered if one of them had turned her in for the reward. She didn't think it was Reggie or Maude.

As they started across the entry, her legs shaking nearly uncontrollably, she realized someone was knocking on the door. Reggie hurriedly yanked it open, clearly hoping that it was the earl. Instead, a small, red-haired woman swept in.

"Good morning. Please tell Lord Blackwood that the Duchess of Rathmore is here to see him." She was petite but not slim, with lovely green eyes that widened as she took in the scene in the entry. "For heaven's sake—what on earth is going on?"

One of the watchmen stepped forward. "Official business, Your Grace. We've just apprehended a fugitive. This woman—Jillian Whitney—is wanted for the murder of Oswald Telford, the late Earl of Fenwick."

Jillian wildly shook her head. "It isn't true! I didn't do it! I didn't kill him!"

"Where is Lord Blackwood?" the duchess asked, glancing around for the earl, her pretty face filled with concern.

"Gone out, Your Grace," Reggie answered. "He won't like the turn of this. Not one bit."

"I see. In fact, I'm beginning to understand quite a lot of things." She turned to Jillian, who stood a few feet away, trembling in the grip of the watchmen.

The duchess approached and Jillian felt the woman's small hand on her arm. "Take heart, Miss Whitney. Apparently Lord Blackwood believes in your innocence or you wouldn't be here. My husband, I believe, though he's done everything in his power to keep silent on the matter, has been helping in the earl's campaign to clear your name."

Jillian swallowed. "Tell him I am grateful for all he has done." The watchmen started hauling her toward the door and the duchess followed them down the front porch steps.

"Blackwood is loyal to his friends," the duchess said. "He won't abandon you. And he isn't a man to fail at what he sets out to do."

They were the last words Jillian heard as the watchmen shoved her into their waiting carriage and two of them followed her in. The tall man and the one with scarred hands climbed up on the driver's seat. One of them released the brake and the horses set off at a clatter down the cobbled street.

Dear God, they were taking her to prison, just as the earl had said.

Inside the airless, bad-smelling carriage, Jillian shivered. *Dear Lord*, she prayed, *please let him come for me.*

But she wasn't all that certain that he would.

Kitt Barclay, Duchess of Rathmore, paced the entry of Lord Blackwood's town house, waiting for his return. Dammit, where was he? It had been two very long hours. She was saying something of that nature to Reggie when she heard the doorknob turn and Blackwood finally strode in.

His head came up when he saw her, sensing from

her face that something was wrong. "Kassandra. To what do I owe the pleasure?"

"Originally, I came here to discover what you and my husband were up to with your mysterious visits, but finding four watchmen in your entry with a very lovely, very frightened young woman in tow, I believe I've found the answer to that."

Beneath his high cheekbones, his face went utterly pale. He turned to the butler, who hovered just a few feet away. "They took Jillian? How long ago were they here?"

"About two hours, Major. There weren't a thing we could do. I told 'em if they harmed a hair on her pretty head, they'd have to answer to you."

Grim-faced, Blackwood nodded. "Thank you, Reggie."

His attention swung back to Kitt. "I'm afraid you'll have to excuse me, Your Grace. I've a rather pressing matter to attend." Blackwood started walking and Kitt raced along at his side.

"I know you're in a hurry. I just wanted you to know that if your . . . if Miss Whitney needs a place to stay until this is all straightened out, she is welcome at Rathmore Hall."

His flashed her a look of gratitude but firmly shook his head. "I appreciate the offer, but it won't be necessary."

"Meaning Clay wouldn't approve of a possible murderer in the same house with his wife, and you are not about to gainsay him on the matter."

He almost smiled. "Close enough."

"But you *are* going to get her out?"

He was striding toward the rear of the house, heading to the stable to summon his carriage, Kitt trailing along in his wake. "Jillian's innocent. She doesn't belong in prison."

"You may need support in gaining her release," Kitt told him, hurrying to keep up with his long strides. "Tell them the Duke and Duchess of Rathmore stand firmly behind you in this."

He stopped and turned back to her, caught her shoulders, leaned over, and kissed her cheek. "Thank you, Duchess. Your husband is a very lucky man."

She blushed. She wasn't sure how he managed to accomplish that, since she was a happily married woman. "Good luck with your lady," she called after him.

He opened his mouth to deny it, but simply nodded instead. Once she had been a little afraid of him. In the past few months, she had come to admire his strength and courage and to sense the deep well of loneliness he carried inside. She hoped the woman, Jillian Whitney, would somehow ease the emptiness he so skillfully worked to hide.

And she prayed that Jillian was innocent of the murder.

For three long hours, Jillian paced the inside of the damp, gray stone-walled chamber. It was only a temporary holding cell, the warden had said. By nightfall, she would be assigned a permanent place in the prison.

Jillian swallowed a wave of fear but couldn't suppress a shiver. She tried not to notice how cold it was in the small, confining compartment, how damp and stifling the air, how the straw on the icy stone floor was soggy and smelled of urine. And yet it would get worse. If Blackwood did not come.

On the other side of the door, she could hear the

moans of the prisoners deeper inside the prison. Some wept as if they could not stop, others made terrible keening noises, some shouted endless obscenities.

And then there were the guards. Remembering the way they had looked at her made her flesh crawl. Sooner or later they would have her, their cold, unsympathetic eyes said. They would take her no matter how hard she fought them.

If Blackwood did not come.

Dear God, what if he didn't? He had never promised to intercede for her if she were arrested, never vowed to connect his name with hers and see it also dragged through the mud.

Dear Lord, let him come, she prayed for the hundredth time.

But even if he did, there was no guarantee he could free her. She might have to stay in prison and if she did . . . ? If she did, she wasn't sure she could endure it.

Footsteps echoed on the stones in the corridor and she raced to look through the tiny barred square in the heavy oak plank door. The two guards who had brought her to the cell were passing down the dimly lit passageway. They paused when they saw her face through the tiny opening.

" 'Tis the new one," the bigger man said, and she remembered his rotten teeth and foul breath that morning. "Fetchin' lit'le baggage, ain't she, Clive? Can't wait to put me whorepipe in that tight, sweet little passage."

"I get her first," the other man argued, a thick-lipped, sullen-looking guard with blunt fingers and dirty nails. "You was first with the last one and she were a virgin."

Jillian fought down a wave of nausea.

"She was a tasty little morsel, for sure and certain. I guess it's only fair." He grinned, exposing the blackened stumps of his teeth. " 'Sides, you ain't big enough to spoil 'er. She'll still be tighter than a fist when I get inside."

"Get away from that door." The third voice was cold and edged with steel, and Jillian knew in an instant it was the earl. "Now."

Relief made her eyes fill with tears. Blackwood was here. Everything was going to be all right.

Another guard was with him, she saw as the man slid a long brass key into the lock, turned it, and opened the heavy wooden door, this one wearing clean clothes, his hair neatly trimmed, his manner a little more refined.

"Are you all right?" the earl said, brushing past the guard and striding toward her.

She nodded, tried to be stoic, but a lump formed in her throat. Tears welled and began to slide down her cheeks. Blackwood came forward and wrapped her in his arms.

"It's all right. Don't cry." She could smell the starch in his shirt, feel his heart beating more rapidly that it should have been. "They've released you into my custody. I'm taking you out of here."

Jillian clung to him, her knees threatening to give way any minute. He reached out, smoothed back a long strand of hair, tucked it behind an ear. "They didn't hurt you?"

She shook her head. "I was just . . . I was just so frightened."

He watched with eyes full of turbulence and something else she couldn't quite read. "Come on. Let's get out of here." The formidable look on his face gave her the strength she needed. With his hand wrapped firmly around her waist, they started forward. When she walked out of the cell, she saw a small square of light at the end of the passage, and with every step toward it, more of her courage returned.

By the time they emerged from the prison and walked out into the courtyard, she was steady on her feet. They didn't stop until they passed through the heavy iron gates and crossed the cobblestone street out in front, and she spotted the Blackwood crest on the earl's expensive black carriage.

"Thank you for coming." Her legs felt shaky as he helped her inside. She settled herself on the seat but instead of seating himself across from her, Blackwood sat down beside her. He handed her a handkerchief and she used it to wipe her eyes and blow her nose. "I wasn't sure you would."

A black brow arched. "Weren't you?"

She swallowed. Perhaps in her heart she *had* known he would come. She wasn't quite sure why. Perhaps it had to do with duty and honor and being a military man used to fighting for those less able.

"What am I going to do?"

He glanced down at the hands fiercely clasped in her lap. "Nothing for the present. I've hired a barrister. A friend of mine. His name is Garth Dutton. He accompanied me to the magistrates' office and helped arrange for your release into my care. You may thank the Duke and Duchess of Rathmore, as well. I'm not sure we would have succeeded without their support."

"The duchess was there when they came for me. She was ... very kind."

His mouth faintly curved. "Kassandra is any number of things. I suppose kind is one of them."

"You like her."

"I like both of them. I'm fortunate to call them friends."

"It would seem I am also fortunate, having made a friend in you."

His eyes locked on her face. "Perhaps in time, Jillian, we'll be far more than that."

She refused to think what the words implied. Certainly, he didn't speak of marriage. Not to the impoverished former ward of the Earl of Fenwick, now under suspicion of murder.

He reached over and took her hand. His was long-boned and elegant and she remembered the heat of it, curved round her breast.

"Garth has asked that the trial be postponed and since you've the support of a duke and an earl, they've agreed. Also, I've done as Howard Telford did and posted a reward—this one for any information leading to the man who murdered the earl."

"But I can't afford—"

"Consider it a loan," he said, interrupting her protest. A dark glint appeared in his eyes. "We'll work out repayment when all of this is over. In the meantime, I'll send a footman to Fenwick's to fetch your things. I'm sure you'd prefer your own clothes."

She stiffened at the reminder that the clothes she now wore belonged to his mistress. "Yes, most assuredly."

His gaze slid down to her breasts where they rose above the immodest neckline of her gown. "Of course, there are certain . . . advantages . . . to the ones you've been wearing."

She flushed, felt the heat spread out until she was certain her breasts were flushed as well. The heat in his eyes said it was true, and she quickly glanced away. Blackwood settled back against the seat, studying her with heavy-lidded eyes that made her distinctly uneasy.

Jillian glanced away from his disturbing gaze and stared out the window. A fancy high-seat phaeton whipped past, a young dandy dressed outrageously in black stock and bottle green tailcoat tugging on the reins. They had returned to the fashionable West End, yet memories of Newgate lingered.

Suppressing a shudder, Jillian leaned back against the seat, grateful for the earl's intervention yet worried about the swelling debt she owed him.

Dear God, she had no money. Even should they succeed in clearing her name, how would she ever repay him? She thought of the hunger in his eyes as his gaze ran over her breasts, and the worry she was feeling continued to build.

8

❧

Adam slept little that night. He kept remembering Newgate, hearing the jailers' filthy threats, seeing the look of utter despair on Jillian's lovely face. For a single instant, he had believed with certainty that she hadn't killed the earl, could not possibly have done it, and in that same instant, it wouldn't have mattered if she had.

Protecting her was all he could think of, getting her out of that disgusting place, taking her somewhere warm and safe. Now that she was out of harm's way, his sanity seemed to have returned. He wanted Jillian in his bed, but in order to have her there he had to know the truth.

He was tired as he descended the stairs, later that morning than usual, and went to work in his study. A few minutes later, he heard Reggie's knock at the door.

"A note has arrived, milord." He walked over and handed Adam a folded slip of paper. "It's from a Mr. Fraser."

Seated behind his desk, Adam quickly scanned the words and rose from his chair. "Thank you, Reggie."

Grabbing his coat off the rack beside the door, he headed down the hall. He considered taking Jillian with him, but he wanted to hear what Fraser had to say and he wasn't sure the man would be as forthright if Jillian were along.

The Bow Street runner was waiting when he got there. "Good afternoon, my lord." A lanky, red-haired man in his late twenties, Peter Fraser wore a simple brown tailcoat, shiny at the elbows, and a pair of spectacles he seemed to have forgotten he had on. He stripped them quickly away as he led Adam into a small, orderly office where stacks of paperwork sat in tidy bundles on the floor.

Adam took a seat in a straight-backed wooden chair while Fraser sat down behind his battered oak desk.

"I came as soon as I received your message," Adam said without preamble. "What have you learned?"

Fraser scooted his chair a little closer to his desk. "To begin with, in the matter of Lord Eldridge, the man who had unfortunate financial dealings with the earl, the marquess claims to have been at his club, Brooks in St. James's, the night of the murder. I am working to corroborate his story."

"I'll take care of that. I'm a member of Brooks's, as well." Eldridge loved to wager, though he never bet all that much. Perhaps someone would remember whether he had been gaming there that night. And there was always the chance his name would be scrawled beside that date in the betting book. "I'll let you know what I find out."

Fraser nodded. "As regards the late earl's former solicitor, Colin Norton, it seems his ailing wife passed away a week before the murder and Norton disappeared shortly thereafter."

Adam leaned forward, alert to the first possible suspect they had encountered. "Perhaps he blamed Fenwick for the death of his wife. Have you sent men in search of him?"

"Yes, my lord. But so far there's been no sign of him."

"Hire more runners if you need to. I want this man found, and soon."

"Yes, my lord." Fraser looked down at the file on his desk. "And now to the reason I sent for you." He flipped open the file. "Early this morning, I spoke to Benjamin Morrison."

"The man who took over Colin Norton's duties as solicitor. I spoke to him briefly myself."

"So Morrison said. Apparently, there was something he didn't mention. Perhaps he felt the information was privileged, I don't know. I reminded him he had a duty to the late earl. I told him you had been working very diligently with the authorities to solve the earl's murder and asked if there was anything he knew that might be of help."

"What did he say?"

"He said that he had information that might be useful, but he would discuss it only with you."

Adam's pulse accelerated. "Anything else I should know?"

"Not at present. Perhaps your conversation with

Mr. Morrison will provide new information. Unfortunately, the man is out of town for the next several days."

Disappointment filtered through Adam but only for a moment. Morrison had information. It was more than they'd had before. He shoved back his chair and came to his feet. "Let's hope Morrison will be of help. We certainly need something new to go on."

Fraser walked him to the door of his office. "I'll keep after this, my lord. I won't rest until we've dealt with every possibility."

"Thank you, Fraser. I'll let you know if Morrison gives us anything we can use."

Adam left the office and climbed aboard his phaeton, turning his fine-blooded, dappled gray gelding back toward his town house. He had stacks of paperwork sitting on his desk and more waiting at his solicitor's. Being an earl, he had discovered, came at no little cost.

He was thinking of Jillian and what Morrison might have to say when he walked into the house and Reggie informed him he had a visitor. Howard Telford, newly titled Earl of Fenwick, waited for him in the Gold Room.

"Where is Miss Whitney?" Adam asked.

"She has gone for a walk in the park, milord. She said to tell you she took some bread with her. Said you would know what it meant."

His mouth faintly curved. He was only a little concerned she would run. With no place to go and no money, she was growing more dependent upon him every day.

Which was exactly what he wanted.

"Telford's in the Gold Drawing Room?"

"Right ye are, Major."

Curious and a little surprised, Adam paused in the doorway to survey the blond man pacing in front of the mullioned window. Howard Telford was average in height, early thirties, with a body that was slowly going to fat. He wasn't bad-looking, yet there had always been a certain depth of character that Howard seemed to be lacking.

"Sorry if I kept you waiting," Adam said blandly. "I must have forgotten our appointment." He walked past Telford over to the sideboard. "Care for a brandy?"

"No. And I didn't have an appointment. I've been in the country. I only just got back to town."

Adam lifted the stopper from a cut glass decanter, filled a snifter with brandy, then slid the stopper back into place with a sharp, crystalline ring.

"So why the haste?" He swirled the brandy in his glass. "Your visit obviously isn't social. What can I do for you?"

The thick folds beneath Howard's chin slightly lifted. "It's been brought to my attention that you've become involved with a woman named Jillian Whitney. As she is guilty of murdering my uncle, I should like to know why it is that you are standing between her and the gallows."

Adam sipped his brandy. "Are you well acquainted with Miss Whitney?"

"Well enough."

"And you're completely certain Miss Whitney is the one who shot him?"

Telford's blunt hands fisted. "How can you doubt

it? There were witnesses, forgodsake. My uncle's butler, Nigel Atwater, heard them conversing just minutes before the shot rang out. She was standing over the man's body when the butler walked in and she ran when he accused her of the murder. What more proof do you need?"

"Perhaps she was frightened, afraid no one would believe she was innocent."

"Innocent? I don't know what that woman has told you, but she came into my uncle's home on the pretext of needing his help and seduced the poor man. She openly lived there as his mistress! A woman with that sort of low moral character is certainly capable of murder."

Adam took another drink. He had wanted to speak to Howard Telford. He had expected the man's animosity where Jillian was concerned—after all, many of the earl's own servants were convinced she was guilty. But Adam had always believed the late, aging earl had taken advantage of Jillian's innocence and vulnerability. He didn't like hearing she had seduced the old man.

"Your uncle was obviously Miss Whitney's protector," he said with careful control. "What motive would she have to kill him?"

"I don't know. Perhaps he'd grown tired of her. Perhaps he was weary of the gossip she wrought on his family and his own good name and told her he wanted her to leave. Whatever the reason, the fact remains that my uncle is dead and Jillian Whitney is the woman who shot him. I want you to withdraw your support and let justice take its course."

"And if by chance you're wrong and Miss Whitney is innocent?"

"The woman is a murderer. I realize she is beautiful and she can be quite charming, but as they say, beauty only runs skin deep. And a clever actress can fool even a jaded man like you. Don't delude yourself, my lord. Don't fall prey to Jillian Whitney's charms or you may end up exactly like my poor dead uncle."

Adam made no reply. He didn't know how much of what Howard Telford said was true, but his fingers unconsciously tightened around the bowl of his snifter.

Howard said no more, simply turned and started walking toward the door.

"One last thing," Adam said, halting the man's departure.

"Yes . . . ?"

"Where were you the night of the murder?"

Howard's face turned crimson. "Surely you are not accusing me!"

"I'm not accusing anyone. You are, however, the person with the most to gain from your uncle's untimely demise."

Howard's lips went thin. "I was attending a soiree given by Lord and Lady Foxmoor. If you doubt my word, I'm sure you can find any number of people who saw me, as I was there until well past two in the morning."

Adam watched the earl storm out of the drawing room. A glance at the ormolu clock on the mantel told him it was nearly five. The afternoon was slipping away. He thought of Jillian and wondered how much of what Fenwick had said was true. *A clever actress can fool even a jaded man like you.*

His meeting with Benjamin Morrison was set for tomorrow night, but instead of the eagerness he had felt when he left Peter Fraser's, Adam found himself dreading the encounter.

9

Something was wrong. Jillian could sense it. All day, the earl had been moody and out of sorts, locking himself up in his study, coming out only briefly when Reggie had fetched him in to supper.

The meal had been a stiff, uncomfortable affair. Adam said little, just stared at her with dark, brooding eyes that made her want to shift uneasily in her chair. She wanted to ask if something had happened earlier in the day, but he seemed oddly remote and she didn't think he would tell her. Instead, he excused himself and retired to his study.

For a while, Jillian wandered around the town house, stopping here and there to examine an interesting artifact from the earl's collection, still too restless to think of sleep. The threat of Newgate hung over her head and now that she had been there, the horrors she had seen would not leave her.

She carried her embroidery into a small salon at the rear of the town house, but her hands were unsteady and she kept missing stitches. With a sigh of frustration, she set the embroidery aside and went in search of the earl.

She found him standing in front of the hearth in his study, his long legs splayed, a half-empty snifter of brandy in his hand.

"I thought you had gone to bed."

With the firelight glinting on the magnificent bones in his face, he looked impossibly handsome, and warning bells went off in her head.

Jillian paid no attention. "I don't feel like sleeping. Time is rushing past and I am sitting here doing nothing. I need to formulate a plan of some kind. I need to do something useful."

He eyed her in that way he had of making her feel uncomfortable. "What exactly did you have in mind?"

"I-I don't exactly know. I thought that perhaps you might help me."

Blackwood took a sip of his brandy, set the snifter down on a Hepplewhite table. "I am helping you, Jillian." He started walking toward her, his strides long and graceful, pantheresque, she had mentally dubbed them. "I'm doing everything in my power."

His mouth held a slightly sensual curve, and in the light of the fire the narrow scar formed a thin dark shadow along his jaw. His eyes glinted with heat and intensity, and she wondered for a moment what insanity had driven her to seek him out.

"The truth will eventually surface," he said. "I won't stop until I know what it is." Why did those words make her more nervous than she was before? "You just have to trust me."

Did she? There were moments she trusted him completely and other times, like now, when she didn't trust him at all.

Or herself.

"You're worried. I don't blame you." Adam reached out and touched her cheek. "But are you sure you didn't come here for something else?"

Why *had* she come? She was restless and fearful, but the truth was, she had simply wanted to see him.

"I-I wanted to do something useful." She moistened her lips, hoping he wouldn't realize how nervous she had become. He was standing closer than she thought, looking at her now with predatory dark eyes that warned of danger.

She realized what that danger was when his hands encircled her waist and he slowly drew her toward him. Her rose silk gown brushed his thighs. She could feel the warmth of his body, smell his cologne.

He was dark and male and standing this close sent a flood of heat rushing into her stomach. Adam tilted her head back and Jillian closed her eyes as firm, warm lips descended over hers. Blackwood nibbled and tasted, sank himself farther into her mouth. His assault was sensual and so erotic her fingers curled into the lapels of his coat.

The fire cast shadowy angles on his starkly beautiful face, and she remembered how he had looked that night in his room. She wanted to touch him, wanted to run her fingers over his smooth dark skin, to feel the ridges of muscle on his chest. She wanted him to kiss her as he was doing now.

His mouth slid over hers, hot and wet and arousing, taking her more intimately, sending little shivers into her stomach. She could feel the slick heat of his tongue as he took her more deeply, claiming her in some way, and the wild heat rushing through her blood left her trembling.

Unconsciously, her hands slid up to twine around his neck, which was as corded and strong as the rest of him. She found herself pressing against him, searching for the promise of that lean, powerful body.

Too many layers of clothing were in the way. She wanted to tear them off, wanted to drink in the sight of his hard bare torso as she had done that night.

The thought was so erotic—and terrifying—she started to pull away, but Blackwood caught her face between his hands and kissed her deeply again. Jillian moaned.

"We ... have to ... stop, my lord."

"Adam," he said softly, kissing her again, first one way, then the other. " 'We have to stop, Adam.' "

"Adam ..." she whispered, but she didn't ask him to stop. She didn't want these incredible feelings to end.

He must have read her mind. She felt a series of tugs on the buttons at the back of her dress and the front of her gown yawned open. He slid the sleeves off her shoulders, eased down the straps of her chemise, pushed the fabric to her waist, and long, dark fingers curled round her breast.

Jillian's stomach contracted so swiftly she sucked in a breath. Dear God, nothing had ever felt so good. She had told herself she wouldn't do this again, that succumbing to the charms of a man like the earl could only bring disaster, but the danger he posed only made it more exciting.

As he bent to capture her lips, he gently kneaded her breast. His thumb stroked over her nipple and it hardened into his palm. What they were doing was completely and utterly improper. It was the most outrageous thing she had ever allowed to happen.

And she didn't want it to end.

His tongue tangled with hers and hers entwined with his. His mouth slid down, moved along her jaw, touched the skin behind her ear, and each moist kiss felt like a brand on her flesh. Her head fell back, giving him better access. She gasped as his dark head dipped down, his lips took the place of his hand, and strong white teeth closed over her nipple.

Oh, dear God!

She was going to incinerate, to simply burst into flames. She wanted to tear off his crisp white stock, to tug his shirt out of his breeches so that she could touch him, press her mouth against his skin as he was doing to hers. She longed to gaze at that hard, masculine body, drink in the erotic, male scent of him. Instead, she trembled and clung to his shoulders while funny little moans escaped from her throat.

"Do you know how badly I want you?" he whispered near her ear, his voice a sensual caress.

She could guess. Dear God, she was beginning to understand what passion was all about. She lusted after the Earl of Blackwood. Just days ago, she wouldn't have believed herself capable of an emotion so foreign to her until now.

"I want to be inside you," he said, and she could feel that part of him pressing like a stiff, hot rod against her belly. "I need you, Jillian. Let me make love—" He stopped midsentence, his brows slashing down, his eyes going fierce and dark.

Stepping backward, he jerked away from her as if someone had dumped scalding water over his head.

"Goddammit! This isn't going to happen. I'm not going down this road again!"

Jillian swayed, a little shocked at the profanity, trying to collect her muddled senses. "What . . . what are you talking about?" She held her dress up over her breasts with shaking hands and tried not to let him see how flustered and embarrassed she was.

His face looked granite-hard as he stepped behind her, tugged the straps of her chemise back into place with sharp, jerky motions, then pulled up her gown and began to refasten the buttons down the back.

When he was finished, he turned away and simply started walking. At the door, he paused.

"Good night, Jillian." He didn't look back, just stepped into the hall and firmly closed the door.

Adam couldn't sleep. Not with his body hard and aching, his mind troubled by thoughts of the woman sleeping in the room next door. He shouldn't have kissed her. He should have known where it would lead and that ultimately he would be the one to suffer.

But she had looked so damned lovely standing there in the light of the fire, so vulnerable and uncertain. So damned desirable.

He wouldn't bed her, no matter how rampant his lust. If she had killed Fenwick . . .

Adam refused to let his thoughts drift that way. Instead, he dressed in evening clothes and left the house. He had promised Peter Fraser he would find out if Lord Eldridge's alibi would hold, and to do that, he needed to pay a visit to his club.

Afterward, he would make a long overdue stop at Madame Charbonnet's House of Pleasure. It was a favorite of Clay's before he had married, and Adam knew the women there were beautiful and well-skilled. It wasn't his usual sort of place, since he preferred a slightly more personal encounter, but this time he wanted a woman he could take without restraint. He wanted to pound out his frustrations until he was free of the ache that had been with him since the day he had first seen Jillian in the park.

As he climbed aboard his carriage and Lance drove the conveyance away, he envisioned several hours of mindless, physically exhausting sex. He was trying to decide whether to choose a fiery little blonde or a tall, sultry redhead when the carriage turned onto St. James's and pulled up in front of his gentleman's club.

He only meant to drop in, try to obtain the information he needed, and leave, but Clayton Barclay was there in the card room, embroiled in a game with Ford Constantine, the Marquess of Landen, and Clay's friend, the Earl of Greville. After checking the betting book in a futile search for Lord Eldridge's name, Adam found himself joining the game.

It was sometime near midnight that Sir Hubert Tinsley walked into the club and took over Landen's seat. As Tinsley and Eldridge were friends, Adam casually asked if he and the marquess had been gaming the evening of April second, the night Lord Fenwick was killed.

"Actually we were here for quite some time that

night," Sir Hubert said. "I remember distinctly because Theodore trounced me soundly." He grinned with obvious relish. "Afterward he made amends by treating me to a night with a delicious little lady bird he knew in Covent Garden."

Disheartened by Eldridge's alibi and what appeared to be another dead end, Adam leaned back in his chair and tried to concentrate on the game. He told himself the news wasn't important, that even if the marquess was in Brooks's Club during the time of the shooting, there was still the possibility the man had hired someone to avenge him against the aging earl.

But Adam's mood didn't improve and eventually he tossed in his hand and left the club. He considered the stop he intended to make at Madame Charbonnet's but couldn't muster the interest.

Instead of the night of debauchery he had planned, Adam simply went home. He wondered if he'd be able to fall asleep and knew that if he did, it would be Jillian who haunted his dreams.

Dressed in a prim white night rail, Jillian sat at the window of her bedchamber. The hour was late. She had awakened at the sound of the earl's footfalls coming up the stairs and had been unable to return to sleep.

If she closed her eyes, she could still see him standing in front of the hearth, long legs splayed, wearing that sensual expression. She could scarcely believe what had happened downstairs. The man had very nearly seduced her, and she had very nearly let him. Once again, it was he who had stopped.

Embarrassment washed over her. Sweet God,

what must he think? She wished she could leave his house, get as far away from the Earl of Blackwood as she possibly could—before she made a complete and utter fool of herself. Or worse.

She thought again of the way he had kissed her, the way he had touched her, and her embarrassment began to fade, replaced with a shot of anger.

True, she probably should have stopped him, but she wasn't entirely to blame. She was a novice at passion while he, no doubt, was an expert. She was the person who'd gone into his study, but he was the one who had initiated the encounter. It was hardly *her* fault she had succumbed to his superior skill. She still didn't understand why he hadn't continued his seduction, but for the second time she was glad.

Or at least she thought she was.

In the room next door she heard movement. Blackwood shifting about, preparing himself for bed. She knew he had left the house and tried not to think where he might have been or whom he had been with. Wherever he had gone, he was returned now and in minutes, he would be lying in his big four-poster bed, his chest bare and rippling with muscle, the sheet shoved down to his hips.

Jillian swallowed past the dryness in her throat and ignored the rush of heat that curled in the pit of her stomach.

By the time dusk arrived the following day, the fog had begun to roll in. Adam ignored the cold evening drizzle that turned the cobbled streets slick and sank into his dark blue tailcoat and arrived at Knowles, Glenridge, and Morrison precisely at seven in the evening.

Benjamin Morrison, a sophisticated man with salt-and-pepper hair and a pale complexion, led Adam into his office. It was paneled in richly grained cherry wood, with a polished rosewood desk and pictures of hunting scenes in gilded frames hung on the walls.

"I spoke to your man, Peter Fraser," Morrison said as he closed the door. "I've been expecting to hear from you." He motioned for Adam to take a seat on a dark green velvet overstuffed sofa, then sat down in one of the two matching side chairs.

"I know you're a busy man, Mr. Morrison," Adam began, "so why don't we dispense with formality. You represent the late Lord Fenwick's legal interests. I'm hoping there's something you can tell me that will help establish a motive for his murder."

Morrison crossed one leg over the other and adjusted a wrinkle in his pants. "I'm not sure I can do that, my lord. I can tell you what I know and trust you to use the information with discretion."

Adam gave a brief nod. "You have my word."

"As the late Lord Fenwick's solicitor, I've given a great deal of thought as to why the earl might have been killed. I don't know what bearing it might have, but . . ."

"Go on," Adam prodded.

"A week before the murder, Lord Fenwick came to see me. He wanted to make some changes in his will. As you may know, most of the late earl's fortune came to him through industry and investments, not the inheritance he received with the title. In fact, the Fenwick entailment itself is fairly meager, barely enough to provide a decent standard of living and maintain his ancestral estate."

"I'd heard rumors. Since Fenwick had so few relatives, I presumed his personal fortune would go to the heir along with the entailment."

"Yes. Originally, with his son, Henry, deceased, his brother's son, Howard, became heir to the title, and aside from a few bequests to other family members, the fortune, in total, was left to him."

"And Fenwick wanted that to change?"

"That's right. The week before he died, the earl instructed me to rewrite the document I had previously drawn. He ordered that upon his death, his entire estate, excluding, of course, the entailed income and properties that would by law go to the heir, be granted to Jillian Whitney."

Shock rolled through him, followed by a clenching in his stomach. The motive for her involvement in the old man's murder had suddenly appeared. Upon the earl's death, Jillian became one of the richest women in England.

"I can see by the look on your face the direction your mind has taken. Before your thoughts stray too far, let me tell you that his lordship never signed the new will. The day he was due in my office, a messenger arrived in his stead. His gout was acting up and he wanted to reschedule his appointment. Two days later, the earl was dead."

Adam's jaw hardened as a thousand different suspicions ran through his head. "Very unfortunate for Miss Whitney."

"Yes, very bad timing on the earl's part."

But Adam couldn't help wondering if Jillian had believed the document had already been signed. Perhaps she hadn't known about the missed appointment. Perhaps she had killed the old man thinking, as the butler had claimed, that she could escape to the safety of her room upstairs and no one would ever suspect she was the culprit.

He knew how smart she was. Her father had been brilliant, but he had also left his daughter a pauper and at the mercy of the aging earl. If Jillian's plan had succeeded and she had gotten away undetected, she would have remedied that situation. She would have been wealthy in the extreme.

He returned his attention to Benjamin Morrison. "Did Miss Whitney know about the changes the earl was making in his will?" *Had she seduced him into making those changes? Had she killed him thinking he had already done so?*

"I'm afraid I don't know the answer to that. He never said anything, one way or the other."

Adam's thoughts whirled as he rose from his chair. "Thank you, Mr. Morrison. I appreciate your help."

"I don't know how much help I've actually been. I just hope the murderer is apprehended."

So did he, and the more he thought about Jillian's possible role in the crime, the angrier he got. He'd been duped by Caroline Harding. He'd been made to look like a villain by the passionate, exotic Maria Barrett. He wasn't going to play the fool for a penniless waif with big blue eyes and a guileless smile that probably wasn't any such thing.

As Adam climbed aboard his carriage, he replayed Jillian's hysterical state the night of the murder. She'd been terrified that no one would believe

her and she would be thrown into prison, but perhaps her plan had simply gone wrong and she had
run because she knew she was going to hang.

By the time he reached his town house, he was
seething, and determined to shake the truth from Jillian's soft, deceitful lips.

10

Seated in an overstuffed chair in the Garden Room, a small salon she favored at the rear of the town house, Jillian pored over notes she had made in regard to the murder. It was dark outside, a damp, chilly wind beginning to howl through the trees.

Eventually, the letters on the page began to blur and no new thoughts came into her head—not that the ones she'd scratched down had been the least bit useful. Jillian set the portable writing desk aside and tipped her head toward the sound of muted voices in the entry. Adam had gone out early in the day and in the black mood he had been in, she didn't expect him home until late in the evening. She wondered who the visitor could be and her pulse took a leap.

Dear God, what if the authorities had changed their minds and come to take her back to prison? Jillian rose from her chair, her legs beginning to tremble as the sound of heavy footfalls echoed down the hall. Somewhere in the back of her mind, she recognized the familiar thump of Adam's boots, the swift, determined cadence, and her fear began to recede. She was only a little surprised when the salon doors slid open and the Earl of Blackwood strode in.

She came to her feet at the dark scowl on his face. "What is it? What's happened?"

His stock was slightly askew, his coat unbuttoned and hanging open. The scar on his jaw stood out as it always did when he was angry.

"I spoke with Benjamin Morrison. That is what's happened."

"Benjamin Morrison?" She frowned, trying to recall exactly who that was.

"Fenwick's solicitor." Blackwood stared at her so hard it took a good deal of control not to flinch.

"Why are you so angry? What did Mr. Morrison say?"

"Why don't you tell me?"

She stiffened, disliking his tone of voice even more than his thunderous expression. "I've never met the man. I haven't the foggiest notion what he might have had to say."

Blackwood strode toward her, his eyes hot with challenge. "Then you also had no way of knowing that the Earl of Fenwick intended to change his will." He drilled her with an angry stare. "That he had arranged to leave the vast majority of his land and fortune to *you.*"

Jillian's breath froze. Her chest seemed to be clamping down on the last lungful of air she had taken.

"Unfortunately for you," the earl continued, "the old man canceled his appointment to sign the documents two days before he was killed. His gout was acting up, you see. He meant to reschedule but he died before he completed the task."

He strolled toward her, his movements restrained, but the muscles along his jaw were so tight a cord flexed in his cheek. "Perhaps you didn't know that part. Perhaps you hadn't yet realized how badly your plan had failed. Perhaps that is the reason for the current pallor of your lovely, treacherous face."

Jillian dropped down on the sofa, her legs so boneless they refused to hold her up. Her lips were trembling. She pressed them together a moment before she was able to speak.

"The earl never mentioned anything about a will," she said. "We never even discussed it."

"So you didn't know dear old Fenwick was worth a fortune and most of it money he earned, rather than inherited with the title. Money he could freely have left to you."

She only shook her head. She couldn't breathe. The charming little room that overlooked the garden now seemed airless and overly warm.

"His nephew, Howard, was the heir," she said. "There was never any question about that. We never spoke of money. It was none of my business. The subject never even came up."

He moved closer, wrapped his fingers around her shoulders, and hauled her up from the sofa. "None of your business? I don't think Lord Fenwick would have agreed—since it was his most fervent wish that the fortune he had amassed over the years should belong in its entirety to you!" The sardonic look on his face twisted a knot in her stomach. "Not a bad reward for spending a few months in the old man's bed."

Jillian swayed on her feet, her shock so great, for an instant she simply stood there, staring into his furious features. Then she jerked away, her own anger boiling out of control.

"That is what you think? You believe that I was Lord Fenwick's mistress?"

He didn't answer, but his expression said that was exactly what he thought—just like the rest of the *ton*. The same as the gossipmongers who for months had made her life nearly unbearable. All this time, she had thought the Earl of Blackwood was a man she could trust.

All that time he believed she was a whore.

And now he was convinced she had killed the earl.

Blinking against the sudden sting of tears, she lifted her chin. "When I met you that first day in the park, I thought that perhaps you had heard the rumors. Later, when you decided to help me, I assumed that you had not, or that even if you had you didn't believe them."

She straightened her spine, squared her shoulders. "That is the reason you decided to help me. You thought that if you did, I would be grateful enough to ... to ... that I would repay your generosity by ... by ..."

"I've never had to blackmail a woman into my bed. I didn't intend to start with you."

"But you did intend to seduce me."

He shrugged as if he had no doubt that it would happen. "When the time was right, I believed you would come willingly to my bed."

She swallowed, glanced away. "If that was what you wanted, why did you stop last night?"

"I don't sleep with murderers, Jillian, no matter how desirable they might be."

Her throat closed up. She forced her eyes back to his face. "I'm not a murderer. And I wasn't Lord Fenwick's mistress."

His eyes remained hard on her face.

"Lord Fenwick took me in because it was my father's dearest wish. He was kind and generous to a fault. Where I was concerned, he never behaved as anything other than a gentlemen and he never would have. I loved him like the father I lost, and he loved me like the daughter he never had. I've missed him every day since his death, and I would never have done anything to hurt him."

The earl made no reply but she could see the wheels turning in his head. "You never slept with the earl?"

Her face flushed. "No." She glanced down at the toes of the shoes sticking out beneath the hem of her skirt. "I'm an unmarried woman. I've always behaved as such. Lord Fenwick was old enough to be my grandfather. How those silly rumors got started, I can't begin to imagine."

She glanced up at him, saw the way he watched her, as if somewhere in her face, he would find the truth.

The earl ran a hand through his windblown hair, but several thick black strands fell back across his forehead. "You're telling me that you're a virgin."

She fought down a rush of embarrassment. The conversation was too important for her to act missish. "The earl was a dear and loving friend. The only man who has ever touched me—is you."

A muscle tightened in his jaw, but he didn't speak.

"I don't know what more I can say to convince you. There comes a time when a person must look inside himself for answers. He must believe what his heart tells him to believe. I knew nothing about the changes in the will, and I swear to you upon my honor and my life that I did not kill the Earl of Fenwick." Several heartbeats passed. She could see the turmoil in his face, the thoughts being formed, examined, and discarded, the conclusions he was trying to reach.

"Do you believe I am telling the truth?"

Blackwood took a deep, shuddering breath. Eyes a piercing midnight blue stared hard into her face. "I admit I find it hard to imagine the woman I saw so kindly feeding the ducks murdering a man in cold blood."

"Does that mean you believe I am innocent?"

His eyes slid closed for an instant. "God help me, I know I shouldn't, but I do."

Tears started sliding down her cheeks. She wasn't quite sure how it happened, but she found herself in his arms. He was holding her and suddenly she didn't want him to ever let go.

They stood that way for several long moments. She could feel the heat of his body, the misty dampness of his clothes. At the nape of his neck, his hair felt slick and wet with rain and it curled enticingly around her fingers. Her pulse spun upward and her knees began to tremble. She moistened her lips and wished he would kiss her and because she did, she forced herself to move away.

Jillian brushed at the wetness on her cheeks and met his uncertain gaze.

"I assure you, my lord, if I were truly the schemer everyone believes, I would be smart enough to make sure the earl had signed the new will before I shot him."

Blackwood's mouth faintly curved. "Perhaps that is the reason I believe you. I think you're too intelligent to go to all that trouble without being certain of the outcome."

She relaxed a little. He believed her. She could see it in his eyes. "Yes, but perhaps there is a connection."

He nodded, his manner a little more at ease. "There certainly could be. You didn't know about the changes in the will, but perhaps someone else discovered what Fenwick intended."

One of her eyebrows arched. "You're not speaking of Howard Telford?"

"Howard had the most to gain. Telford would have had all the reason in the world to see Fenwick dead if he knew the earl meant to leave the majority of his fortune to you."

Her pulse took a hopeful leap. "How do we find out if he knew?"

"In the morning I'll send a message to Peter Fraser, ask him to see what he can discover." He looked down at his disheveled garments as if noticing them for the first time. "Aside from that, I've had a very long day. I'm bone-tired and I need time to sort all this out. If you'll excuse me, I'm going upstairs. We can talk again in the morning."

He took a step toward her and a lean hand reached out to cup her cheek. "Good night, Jillian." They were the same words he had said to her last night but tonight they were spoken softly, as if something had changed between them.

"Good night, my lord."

"Adam," he reminded her.

"Good night . . . Adam."

He nodded and turned away. He believed in her innocence, but he didn't look as pleased as he should have. She thought it might have something to do with her telling him that she was a virgin.

Remembering the way she had felt when he held her, Jillian wasn't so sure she was happy about it herself.

Sprawled in an overstuffed velvet chair in front of the fire in his bedchamber, Adam swirled the brandy in his glass and took a drink. Now that he had bathed and put on a burgundy silk dressing gown, he felt a little better. He took supper in his room, a meal of roast capon and oysters, and began to think like a calm, rational being.

Unfortunately every time he did, he kept seeing the blush in Jillian's cheeks as she told him that she was a virgin.

A virgin. *Christ.*

Adam swirled his brandy, stared past the glass into the flames. Caroline Harding had been a virgin the first time they had made love, but they had intended to marry, and in truth, the seduction was more her doing than his. Since then, he had never gone near a young, unmarried female. He had never really been tempted.

But Jillian tempted him sorely.

He took another deep drink, the liquid warming him and clearing his thoughts. The first time he had kissed her he had noticed her innocent responses. He should have known then, should have realized, but he simply hadn't been convinced.

He didn't trust women—almost none of them—
and it suited his purpose far better to believe she
was the bought-and-paid-for sort the gossipmongers
said. Fenwick's servants believed it about her—or at
least some of them did. Even the old man's nephew,
Howard Telford, believed Jillian had seduced the
aging earl.

But what he had said tonight was true. Even
knowing that the late earl had intended to leave her
his fortune, he couldn't shake his belief that she had
no part in the murder. In fact, after hearing what
she'd had to say, his instincts told him even more
strongly that she was innocent of the crime and he
was committed to helping her prove it.

Why that commitment remained so fierce he
couldn't explain. Perhaps he did it for Sergeant Rimfield. Or perhaps because of the false accusations
Maria had made.

Noticing his empty glass, Adam got up from his
chair and walked over to the silver tray on his
dresser where the brandy decanter sat. As tired as he
was, the alcohol ought to put him to sleep, though he
couldn't help wishing it were a different sort of seda-
tive that lured him into slumber. Instead of the
brandy, he envisioned a woman with hair the same
reddish hue and a body made for a man's pleasure.

An image returned of Jillian's naked breasts and
he remembered how much fuller they were than he
had expected, how they were heavier and more
rounded at the bottom, tilting her nipples slightly
upward.

Adam cursed as he went hard beneath the robe,
reminding him that he had missed his chance last
night for a female to ease his needs. He had hoped

that Jillian would soon be sharing his bed. It was the reason he had installed her in the room next to his. Instead, the matter of her innocence put another barrier between them, and he wasn't exactly sure what he intended to do about it.

Adam tilted his head back, draining his freshly poured drink in a single swallow, then set the glass down and padded over to the big four-poster bed. Tomorrow he'd be able to think more clearly, decide what course he should take.

Tomorrow, he thought as he shrugged out of his robe and tossed it across the foot of the bed. But he didn't think tomorrow would bring an end to the disturbing lust he felt for Jillian Whitney, or ease the hard flesh that throbbed every night beneath the sheets.

11

~~

Jillian swung her pelisse around her shoulders and fastened the clasp. She was going to see Peter Fraser, the runner the earl had hired. She wanted to find out for herself what progress he was making. She needed to know exactly what was going on.

Besides, she was about to go insane staying in the house all the time.

She had reached the bottom of the stairs when she spotted Adam striding toward her, brandishing the morning *Times*. The dark look on his face sent her pulse into a spin.

"Telford's demanding you be brought back to Newgate until the trial."

"Oh God."

"He's set up a howl, accused me of impropriety and you of licentious conduct and God knows what else. We need to remedy the situation before it gets out of control. We're leaving London this afternoon."

"What!" She wadded the hem of her pelisse in her

palm. "I can't leave London. I have to find out who killed the earl."

"You don't have any choice. Staying here, living unchaperoned under the same roof with me, is making your situation worse."

"I have to stay. I have to prove my innocence."

"Staying here isn't going to help you do that. You're a pariah in this town. Howard Telford has seen to that. No one is going to talk to you. They won't even let you through the front door."

"I won't go. I simply can't."

His eyes turned an icy dark blue. "I'm not giving you a choice. You've been released into my custody until this is over. That means you will do what I say."

She seethed but didn't argue. She knew that look, knew that he wouldn't change his mind.

"We leave for Blackwood Manor as soon as our bags are packed. My mother is in residence at the dower house. That makes your stay respectable enough to calm the wagging tongues."

"Your mother? How can you possibly expect the Countess of Blackwood to take in a murder suspect?"

"My mother won't know. Several years back, she suffered a stroke. There are times she is lucid, but much of the time she makes little sense."

Some of her temper faded. "I'm sorry. I can only imagine how hard that must be for you."

"Like your father, my mother had children late in life. She's lived a number of fruitful years and she's happy in whatever world she lives in. She's still a kind and generous woman. I think you will like her."

"I don't think this is a good idea. It isn't fair to

embroil your family in this. Surely there is someplace else you could take me."

He cast her an unrelenting glance. "Tempers are
running high. I want you somewhere safe. You'll be
out of harm's way at Blackwood Manor."

"And your family?"

"Once you're proved innocent, the murder scandal will fade."

And even if it didn't, he was giving her no choice.

As the earl commanded, Jillian was packed and
ready to leave by noon, her leather trunks filled with
the clothes the footman had retrieved from Mrs.
Madigan, Lord Fenwick's housekeeper, lovely garments the dear old earl had insisted she purchase.

Blackwood's fine black, four-horse traveling
coach waited downstairs, and though she wanted to
stay, the law had placed her under his control and
she had no choice but to obey.

The thought left her irritable and out of sorts as
she paced the floor of her bedchamber. At least she
would be free of the city, out in the open green
fields, enjoying clear blue skies untainted by soot
and fog.

She should be grateful, she told herself. He was
offering his assistance when no one else had. Her
stomach knotted. He had offered to help her, but
now she knew the price he expected in return.

It wouldn't happen, she told herself. The earl was
a reasonable man—most of the time. Once the cloud
of suspicion no longer hung over her head, she
would find a way to repay him—and not with the
use of her body.

Perhaps he would help her to secure a position as
a governess somewhere. She loved children and she

had been very good at teaching them. These past few months, she had missed the sound of their laughter, the joy in their young faces when they had earned her praise.

She glanced at the clock on the wall. Nearly noon. Time to leave. Dear Lord, she didn't want to go.

Feeling caged and ill-tempered, she descended the stairs to the entry. Reggie and Maude waited at the door. She had almost reached them when she saw Lord Blackwood step out of his study and start down the hall in her direction. His coat and waistcoat were missing, his cravat carelessly untied and his sleeves rolled up, showing suntanned, corded forearms. She couldn't help a quick, indrawn breath at the handsome sight he made, and her irritation crept up a notch.

He rolled down his sleeves as he approached. "Sorry. I had some paperwork to do before we left. I didn't expect it would take quite so long."

"I've changed my mind," she said just to be annoying. "I've decided to stay in London. Perhaps if I am here, I can find something that will help clear my name."

Hard blue eyes bored into her. "I don't think you understand. I have linked my name to yours and until this is over, you go where I go. Make no mistake, Miss Whitney. I am leaving the city and so are you."

She watched him climb the stairs in knee-high riding boots, snug black breeches, and a full-sleeved white lawn shirt, and wished he didn't look so blasted good.

Jillian shook her head, annoyed with her thoughts. So what if she found him attractive? So what if his kisses were utterly delicious? The earl was obviously a virile man and her brief experiences with desire had shown her what a potent force that could be.

He was attractive, yes, but he was also arrogant and far too domineering.

Whatever happened, one thing was clear—the Earl of Blackwood would scarcely have a serious interest in a penniless female embroiled in scandal and under suspicion of murder.

No matter how handsome he was, no matter how stirring his kisses, there could never be anything serious between them. She had to remember that.

Jillian turned as he pounded back down the stairs a few minutes later, followed by his valet, Harley Smythe. Harley was an ancient, white-haired man, bone-thin, who walked so straight his spine bowed slightly backward. Obviously another of the earl's acquaintances from the army.

Harley creaked over to the door and looked out at the heavily loaded conveyances. "Everything appears to be ready, milord." He carried a small leather satchel, the last of the earl's baggage—all he could possibly manage.

"All right. Let's get out of here." The earl took Jillian's arm and firmly guided her out the door.

A little after noon, a procession of three Blackwood-crested carriages bowled out of the city, Ramses, the earl's black stallion, tied to the last. One carried baggage. Reggie, Maude, and Harley occupied another. And riding in the lead conveyance, Jillian sat across from the earl.

As soon as they escaped the traffic, the vehicles set off at a fast clip for the tiny village of Black's

Woods, near Seaford, and the earl's estate, Blackwood Manor.

The journey fast became tiring. His lordship had
decided they should travel as far as they possibly
could. Jillian, he said, might be recognized, and he
didn't want to chance an ugly scene if she were.

With that in mind, they traveled the sixty-odd
miles in two days, stopping overnight at the Hare &
Thistle. Adam spent little time in the coach, prefer-
ring to ride his stallion, Ramses, and enjoy the fresh
air. Jillian tried to ignore how handsome he looked
astride his big black horse and the ease with which
he rode. She tried not to notice his straight-
shouldered, military bearing or the long, powerful
muscles in his legs as they flexed in the saddle.

She was exhausted by the time they arrived at
their destination at dusk the following evening. Still,
her breath caught at the first sight of Blackwood
Manor, perched on a cliff above the sea, an incredible array of round stone towers, red clay chimney
pots, and assorted spires. The setting sun washed the
house in blazing gold. With the sea below the cliffs
shadowed to a rich deep blue, the effect was daz-
zling. As tired as she was, the sight was so rousing
her fatigue fell away.

"What do you think of it?" There was pride in the
earl's deep voice as he gazed at the sprawling estate
that was his home. Standing at the bottom of the carriage stairs, they gazed out at the green lawns
stretching from the cliffs to the front of the house,
the verdant, rolling hills spread out around it.

"It's breathtaking. It looks as if it's been here for
hundreds of years."

"The house was originally built around twelve

hundred as an abbey. King John made a gift of it to the Cistercian monks, but in the early sixteenth century most of the building was destroyed by fire. The first Earl of Blackwood bought the land—a little over eight thousand acres, and what was left of the abbey. But much of what you see is Elizabethan, built by the third earl in the early seventeenth century."

There were windows everywhere and the way the house perched on the knoll the entire front overlooked the sea.

"It's like something out of a fairy tale." Her mouth tightened. "Quite luxurious . . . for a prison."

The earl cast her a forbidding glance. "If that is the way you see it, you might as well enjoy your stay. As you pointed out, you won't be leaving—at least not until I say."

She stiffened her spine and started walking up the path to the massive carved front door. They stepped into the entry, and try as she might, she couldn't ignore the breathtaking beauty of the interior.

"Your home is lovely." Polished wood paneling shimmered beneath the light of a wrought-iron chandelier that hung from a white plaster and thick-timbered ceiling. Intricately inlaid wooden floors gleamed beneath her kid slippers.

"We've an estate in Kent called Woodlands that my brother and sister preferred, but I've always been partial to this place."

Surprise had her turning to face him. "You have a sister?"

"Margaret. Maggie, we call her. She's twelve years younger than I, only just eighteen, staying with an aunt in Tunbridge Wells at present."

"Unmarried, then?"

He nodded. "She made her come-out last year, but Maggie is quite the romantic. She is determined to marry for love, and apparently so far that hasn't occurred. I'm sure in time she'll come round to a more sensible way of thinking."

Sensible or not, Jillian agreed with Maggie on the subject of marriage, and she thought that she would certainly like the earl's younger sister.

A fresh shaft of guilt skittered through her. "Oh, dear. This is bound to affect your sister's marriage prospects. Even if she does fall in love, no man wishes to marry a woman marked by scandal." She shook her head. "I knew coming here was a mistake. Now your sister is likely to suffer and—"

"Maggie is an heiress and the sister of an earl. On top of that, she is lovely in the extreme. She has never wanted for suitors and I doubt she ever will."

"It's still a problem—you know it is. At this stage of her life, any sort of gossip can cause serious repercussions."

His look held an edge of warning. "The problem will disappear—once you're proved innocent."

"With your help, I shall be."

His hard mouth barely curved. "In that case, Maggie has nothing to worry about."

But it wasn't quite the truth. There remained the gossip that she had been Lord Fenwick's mistress. Unfortunately, his association with a woman the *ton* considered scarlet would not be good for his sister.

And yet she had no choice but to do as he commanded. The court had seen to that.

She waited in the entry as the earl tossed out orders, surveying her surroundings once again. It was a strong, masculine house, the halls lined with ancient iron sconces and even more wood, and yet the warm yellow glow of the lamps and the gleam of the polished dark wood softened the effect, rendering it elegant and somehow even graceful.

As much as it annoyed her, she thought that it perfectly suited the earl.

"This is Mrs. Finley," Blackwood said when an austere, brown-haired woman appeared in the doorway. "She'll show you up to your room."

Jillian simply nodded, the grueling journey beginning to take its toll. "Thank you." She followed the fortyish female up the carved wooden staircase past the master's suite to an adjoining room on the opposite side and wondered if he worried that she might try to escape.

"The room is lovely." As she gazed into the bedchamber, she was surprised to discover that none of the age or masculine design of the house appeared in the room, which was done in a soft sea green with ivory gilt furniture. Bed hangings of sea green silk enclosed a big four-poster bed. There were draperies and carpets of the same soft hue, and an exquisite white marble hearth set into one wall, an elegant sitting area in front of it.

"Most of the upstairs rooms in this wing were redone by his lordship's mother," Mrs. Finley explained. "She always had beautiful taste." This was said somewhat wistfully, and Jillian thought of the Countess of Blackwood, no longer the woman she had been, living now in the dower house.

"Her ladyship did a marvelous job."

Mrs. Finley nodded, seemingly pleased by Jillian's

words. "If there's anything you need, just let me know."

"Thank you, I'm sure I'll be fine." The room was elegant but comfortable. So comfortable, in fact, that she declined supper and had a tray sent up instead. The minute Maude helped her undress, Jillian climbed under the covers and fell asleep.

She awakened just after sunrise, restless again, wishing she were back in London where she might be able to do something useful. And yet she felt surprisingly refreshed. Choosing a yellow muslin day dress, she made her way downstairs, encountering the earl at the sideboard in the breakfast parlor.

"I didn't expect you up so early," he said, filling a plate from the silver chafing dishes arrayed on white linen. "But then I should be used to your early morning exploits by now." He gave her a long perusal that took in the yellow gown and the upsweep of her hair. Setting his plate aside, he seated her, then returned to his task at the sideboard, filling a second plate for her.

He was dressed in riding clothes this morning, his jacket draped over the back of a high-backed chair. His hair was still damp and it gleamed in the sunlight slanting in through the window. Jillian watched the graceful way he moved, watched the way the soft white fabric clung to the muscles across his chest, the small vee of dark skin that showed at the base of his throat, and her mouth went suddenly dry.

She remembered the night she had gone into his room, remembered the naked, beautifully sculpted body that had pressed her down in the mattress, and a flush rose into her cheeks.

She turned away before he could see, forced her

mind in a safer direction. "Perhaps it's the fresh sea air, or simply this lovely house, but I feel completely marvelous this morning, as if I hadn't a care in the world." It was a lie, of course. She was worried and edgy. She didn't want to be there, didn't want to be with him.

One of his fine black eyebrows cocked up. Blackwood set a porcelain plate in front of her, filled with the same eggs and kidneys he had taken for himself, along with fresh baked bread and warm applesauce. "How about some coffee? That's usually your preference, as I recall."

"Coffee, yes. Thank you." He motioned to a footman who disappeared for a moment and returned a few minutes later with a shiny silver pot.

"When we're finished, I'll show you around the house, then introduce you to my mother." He waited for the footman to fill her cup, took a sip from his own, then picked up his fork and began to eat.

Delicious smells wafted toward her. Jillian nibbled but she was no longer hungry. She would be meeting his mother, the Countess of Blackwood. It didn't seem right, somehow, given the cloud of suspicion that hung over her head.

They finished their repast, and he took her on a tour of the house, which had been elegantly furnished and meticulously maintained over the years. Most of the salons on the main floor had been recently refurbished, just before his mother's stroke, he told her.

"She always had a special knack for color and style. It took a good deal of effort on her part, but she managed to keep the charm of the older parts of the house, yet see the bedchambers made modern and comfortable."

"Yes, my room is very nice, elegant yet livable." Her steps slowed as they walked by the open door leading into a drawing room at the back of the house done in dark woods, ruby flocked paper, and heavily carved furniture.

The richly paneled walls were lined with bookshelves that held a number of artifacts from the earl's Egyptian collection. "You have some very nice pieces," she said, peering at them through the open door. "My father would have enjoyed seeing them."

"Professor Whitney was a brilliant man. I wish I'd met him."

She cast him a speculative glance, wondering if the two men would have got along.

She felt his hand at her waist. "Come. It's time you met my mother."

Jillian ignored a twinge of nerves as he urged her toward the rear of the house, passing a modern, well-lit, slightly steamy kitchen smelling of cinnamon and yeast. They stepped out the back door and traveled a meandering, flower-lined walkway off toward the two-story structure, its high slate roof appearing in the distance behind a row of yew trees.

"After my father died, Mother insisted on moving out to the dower house. She thought Carter should have the main house to himself, but I think the place held too many memories."

Her interest stirred. "Their marriage was a love match?"

He shrugged. "They cared for each other. More than that, I couldn't say."

She could read by his expression the words he hadn't spoken. "Meaning your father kept mistresses."

His gaze strayed off toward the dower house, which loomed larger as they climbed the low hill in that direction. "That is the way of the world, is it not?"

"Not in my family. I'm afraid I'm old-fashioned enough to believe a man should be true to the woman he marries."

His eyes swung to her face. "I believe our mutual acquaintance, the Duchess of Rathmore, would agree."

"Good for her. I knew I liked that woman."

A slight smile tugged at the edges of his mouth. They stopped in front of the door to the dower house, and he rapped his knuckles briefly. When no one answered, he turned the knob, shoved it open, and simply walked in. A gray-haired butler hurried to where they stood in the entry.

"I'm terribly sorry, milord. I didn't hear your knock. Please, do come in."

"Good morning, Patterson. It's good to see you."

The older man beamed with pleasure. "Mrs. Finley told us you had returned. Your mother will be delighted to see you."

"How is she?"

"The same. Your timing is good, though. She is quite lucid this morning."

"Where will I find her?"

"Out in the garden, my lord."

"Thank you, Patterson." She felt Blackwood's hand at her waist, guiding her in that direction, past a series of beautifully styled salons, all of them a testament to his mother's impeccable taste.

And so she was surprised when they entered the garden behind the house to see the Countess of

Blackwood, down on her hands and knees, dirt smudging her cheek, her gray hair mussed and coming undone from its pins, planting pansies in one of the flower beds.

Blackwood seemed not to notice. "Good morning, Mother," he said softly, as if he feared he might frighten her away.

She turned, watched him walking toward her. "Carter?"

"It's me, Mother, Adam."

A smile bloomed over her face, erasing some of the wrinkles, making her appear years younger. She was tall and reed thin, perhaps a woman of sixty, with once-strong features that had softened with age, and blue eyes that appeared slightly cloudy.

"Adam!" She reached up to hug him and he wrapped his arms around her, holding her with a warmth that Jillian found surprising.

An image of Newgate returned, of Blackwood in her cell, holding her as she cried against his shoulder. He had rescued her, and though he'd made it clear she couldn't leave, brought her to a refuge of sunlight and flowers.

Maybe not so surprising, after all.

"There is someone I'd like you to meet, Mother." He turned and Jillian stepped forward. "This is Miss Whitney. She'll be staying with us for a while."

"Oh, dear. You should have warned me. I must look a fright."

"You look as if you've been working in the garden," Jillian said with a smile. "Since I love to garden myself, it's a pleasure to meet someone who also enjoys it."

His mother looked pleased. "It's lovely to meet

you, my dear. Adam says you'll be staying for a while. Perhaps you could come by sometime and I could show you my roses. I do so love roses."

"I love roses, too. I'd like very much to see them."

The countess looked from one to the other and the smile returned to her face. "I have so longed for grandchildren. I shall rest easier now, knowing my son has finally taken a wife."

Jillian's cheeks went scarlet. She tried not to look at the earl, but her gaze found his of its own accord. His jaw was set, his expression hard.

"Miss Whitney is merely a friend, Mother. You'll have to look to Maggie for the grandchildren you want."

She had known he would never consider her for a wife, but it surprised her he didn't plan to have children. She couldn't help wondering why.

"Grandchildren?" his mother said, looking suddenly fragile and more and more confused. "I have grandchildren?"

Blackwood's expression changed to one of regret. "No, Mother. Not until Maggie weds. Why don't we finish the pansies you were planting?" He knelt beside her, heedless of the dirt grinding into the knees of his breeches, dug a hole into the earth, reached over and took a cluster of flowers from the tray sitting on the ground. His mother joined him, and in minutes was immersed once more in her gardening.

Blackwood silently stepped away but his mother kept on working, humming a soft tune as she dug in the rich, black soil.

With a hand at her waist, the earl led Jillian out of the garden.

"For a while she seemed her old self," he said on

their way back to the house. "I always find myself
hoping . . ."

"Your mother is charming."

"I know. I just wish . . ." He took a deep breath.
"With my father and Carter gone, I am fortunate to
have her at all."

They walked back to the house and Jillian
thought of the woman in the garden and the love
and respect her son had shown her. The man Jillian
had once considered hard and unfeeling had consid-
erably more depth than she had believed.

She felt his eyes on her and a little tremor ran
through her. He was so unbelievably handsome. And
more and more appealing. Jillian warned herself to
beware. She knew what he wanted, what he still undoubtedly planned to collect as payment for his
help.

Ignoring the heat in his eyes as he opened the
door, and the corresponding warmth creeping into
her stomach, she let him guide her inside the house.

12

Adam paced the masculine Falcon Room, a salon done in dark red and heavy wood that was one of his favorites. It was dark outside, the sky a spray of diamond-white stars. After a supper of roast quail and oysters, Jillian had disappeared upstairs, leaving him alone.

All afternoon he'd been thinking about her, thinking of the kindness she had shown his mother, remembering her interest in his antiquities. She was intelligent as well as lovely, an interesting combination—especially in bed.

Through the French doors, he could see her out on the terrace, gowned in pale yellow silk. Unlike her borrowed, more revealing dresses that had helped to convince him she was an old man's whore, this one made her look young and innocent, and reminded him that she was likely a virgin.

His body reacted to the knowledge with startling force and instantly he went hard. *Bloody hell.* He couldn't remember wanting a woman so badly.

He could see her outline, Jillian staring up at the faint circle of moonlight glowing through the clouds. The light of the torches glinted on her auburn hair, and a throbbing began in his groin. Beneath the circle of light, he could see the rise and fall of her breasts, tantalizing him with memories of their weight in his hands. Her eyes were a brilliant, cornflower blue, so vivid a man could drown in them.

He wanted to open the doors and walk out to her. If he did, he would kiss her. He would cup her breast as he had before, test the weight of it, tease her nipple until it hardened into his hand. But he wasn't sure he could stop with heated kisses and a few brief caresses, and if Jillian was a virgin. . . .

To say nothing of the matter of the murder.

He believed she was telling him the truth, that she had no part in the crime.

Experience told him to beware.

He had trusted Caroline Harding. He had even thought he loved her, naïve fool that he was. He'd been twenty-one years old, looking at life through the unspoiled eyes of early manhood. He hadn't really decided what he would do with his life, but he had a small inheritance from his grandmother and he thought that perhaps the Church would suit, the vicar of some small country parish, perhaps.

A vicar. Thinking of the carnage he had seen and wrought, it seemed almost funny now.

But he had been different then. Bursting with plans, eager to share them with his future bride, he had gone to her home unannounced. Since she lived near Seaford, the trip took only an hour.

Caroline wasn't there when he arrived. He knew she enjoyed raising flowers as he did and often spent time in the old stone cottage her family had set up as a nursery and potting shed. A white-stockinged bay grazed in the shadows of the lean-to out back, but he didn't think that odd.

It was the sounds he heard as he approached the front door, the guttural moans and sweet cries of passion that twisted his guts up inside. In the cottage two weeks before, those same sweet sounds, combined with soft words and laughter, had come from him and Caroline making love. Adam didn't stop to knock, just slammed open the door and walked in.

Caroline was lying on one of the rough wood plank tables, her apple green skirt shoved up to her waist, her pale legs spread wide. His cousin, Robert Hawthorne, rutted between her thighs, a tall man with dark brown hair and the same lean, broad-shouldered Blackwood build. Adam paused only long enough to let them know he had seen them, to let them see his loathing, then he turned and walked away.

The next day he challenged Robert to a duel, but his cousin refused to meet him. Robert said that he was sorry, that he never meant for it to happen and he couldn't possibly duel with a member of the family. Adam thought he was a coward.

Since Robert never offered marriage, simply took off for his family home in York, leaving Caroline to face the scandal, undoubtedly he was.

The knowledge wasn't enough to satisfy Adam. He ached with disillusionment and betrayal. Two weeks later he joined the army. Anything, just to get away.

Adam shook his head, forcing the painful memories aside. Through the French doors, he watched Jillian with a mixture of desire and something else, something he refused to explore.

The night before they'd left London, his body strung taut with sexual need, he had contemplated again a night with Lavinia Dandridge. In the end, he hadn't gone to her. He didn't want Lavinia. He wanted Jillian Whitney.

As he watched her cross the terrace and slip quietly back inside the house, he reminded himself that she was untouched.

He wondered if the knowledge would be enough to stop him.

Jillian couldn't sleep. She had always been a person who could fall asleep without a problem, but since the night of the murder, sleep had become elusive. She sighed as she set aside the book she had borrowed from the library, *Thaddeus,* a Jane Porter historical novel, and swung her legs over the side. Perhaps a glass of warm milk would do the trick. Or maybe a few sips of sherry.

Drawing her robe over her long white cotton night rail, she crossed the rich Aubusson carpet to the door. She had just stepped into the hall when she heard a noise in the room next to hers.

Adam's room. She caught the sound of his deep, familiar voice mumbling incoherent words, then a harsh, pain-filled moan. He was dreaming again, another of his torturous nightmares.

Just keep walking, said the voice inside her head. *Remember what happened the last time.* Even as she remembered how easily he had pinned her beneath him, how his lean, hard-muscled body had pressed her down into the mattress, her skin flushed and soft heat unfurled in her stomach.

Jillian bit her lip, wanting to erase the memory.

Wanting to savor it.

He mumbled again and the sound drew her toward the door. Her braid fell over her shoulder as she crept closer, bent down, and pressed her ear against the panel. Even through the heavy wood, she could hear him thrashing restlessly in his bed.

She should summon his valet, Harley Smythe, she knew, but poor old Harley was scarcely in shape to wrestle with the earl if it came to that—and Jillian knew firsthand that it could. She would be careful this time, she vowed, as she turned the silver doorknob and stepped into the master's suite.

Just as before, she could see him lying in his bed, his wide chest bare, the sheet shoved down, lower this time, to a point below his hip bones. A thin line of inky black hair trailed down from the thatch on his chest to a point just above the freshly ironed sheet. She could see his flat belly and the taut ridges across it.

Lean muscle rippled as he twisted on the bed, lost somewhere in his painful past. His skin was smooth and dark, and there was that intriguing, crescent-shaped scar across his ribs that she remembered from her last visit to his room. As his head moved back and forth, wavy black hair curled against the stark white pillow and the scar on his jaw stood out. But his nose was perfectly straight, his lips sensuously curved.

Her stomach contracted. Lord, he was beautiful. Her nipples tightened at the memory of his long, elegant fingers molding her breast, of his dark head bending to take the pink bud into his mouth. Just thinking about it made her feel light-headed.

It occurred to her that now that he knew she hadn't been Lord Fenwick's mistress, he probably wouldn't touch her like that again. In his own way, the earl was quite gallant, though he didn't seem to know it. He was a hard man, perhaps even ruthless at times, but she didn't believe he was the sort to take advantage.

Not unless she wanted him to.

The covers slipped lower, exposing a faint glimpse of black curly hair surrounding his sex. When she'd read about the male member in one of her father's anatomy books, she had thought it sounded disgusting. Instead, gazing at Blackwood's magnificent body, she had the oddest urge to pull the sheet even lower, see what those dark, intriguing curls protected. She wanted to see what he looked like—all over.

That was the instant Jillian realized that taking advantage of her was exactly what she wanted the earl to do. She wanted him to kiss her until her knees turned to jelly. She wanted him to touch her until she was hot and breathless and couldn't find the words to speak. She wanted him to make love to her.

Her heart began an erratic thudding and she suddenly felt hot all over. For an instant, she could almost feel his hands skimming over her body, his mouth moving over her shoulders down to her breast. Then he moaned and thrashed on the bed, and she shoved the erotic thoughts away.

"Adam," she said softly, moving a little closer. "Adam, it's Jillian. You need to wake up. You're having another bad dream."

She was almost disappointed when his eyes instantly snapped open and he shot bolt upright in bed. He blinked several times as if he tried to regain his bearings, then let out a long, shuddering breath.

"Sorry," he said, running a dark hand over his face. "I didn't mean to wake you."

She turned her back as he swung his legs to the edge of the mattress and started to climb out of bed. She heard him moving behind her, heard the rustle of fabric, then the sound of his footfalls as he padded toward the dresser and poured water into the basin.

When she turned she found him dressed in a pair of black breeches, his chest still bare—no shirt, no shoes—his feet long and slim, as elegant as his hands. He plunged his cupped palms into the water, then splashed the liquid over his face. He rinsed his mouth and drove wet fingers through his sleep-tousled hair, shoving heavy black waves back from his forehead.

He glanced up, saw her standing as she had been, just a few feet away from the bed, and frowned. "I thought you'd gone."

She should have left. She should be back in her room by now, lying in her own bed. But she simply could not leave. Now was her chance, the only chance she might ever have. She was ruined by scandal, her reputation in tatters. She would never marry, never have a husband. She would never know the joys of a man and woman—not unless she threw caution to the wind and took the chance.

She swallowed, forced the words she had only realized she was thinking past her lips. "You said once that you wanted me. Tonight, when I came into your room, I discovered how much I want you."

Something flashed in the depths of his eyes. "I don't think you know what you're saying."

"I know exactly what I'm saying. After everything that's happened, marriage for me is out of the question. I'll never know what it's like to make love with a man I desire . . . not unless you show me."

He shook his head. "I don't know, Jillian. I'm not sure you really understand—"

"I understand enough. I want to know what it feels like to be a woman."

A long moment passed. His gaze remained on her face as he started toward her, his strides long and rangy, a panther on the prowl. He stopped just inches away and his eyes seemed to burn. "Are you sure this is what you want?" His mouth was set, his jaw hard, his expression hinting at wildness and danger.

Was she sure? She wasn't certain of anything anymore, not since the night she had been accused of murder. She only knew that her heart crumbled when she thought he had lost his belief in her, that her body ached when he touched her.

"Neither of us knows what's going to happen on the morrow. If you want me, then I want you. I want us to spend this time we have together."

Perhaps a heartbeat passed before he reached for her, slid an arm around her waist, and drew her against him. She could feel the heat of his naked skin, the tension in the long bands of muscle across his shoulders. Her palms pressed flat against his chest, and short, curly black hair wrapped around the tips of her fingers.

Adam caught her chin and tilted her head back, forcing her eyes to his face. "I want you," he said. "I have since the first time I saw you. I can't remember anything I've wanted more than to make love to you."

Lowering his head, he brushed his mouth over hers, once, twice, a slow, gentle exploration of lips. A soft meeting of mouths that deepened into something more. Jillian opened for him and his tongue slid in, hot, wet, and hungry, incredibly exciting. Her own tongue curled around it and she heard him groan.

He kissed her even more deeply, taking his time, his lips so much softer than they appeared, first teasing, then demanding. Her senses filled with him: the scent of him, the taste of him, the texture of his skin. She didn't notice when he slipped off her robe, barely heard the whoosh of it pooling at her feet. He tugged the pink ribbon at the front of her night rail and slid it off her shoulders, letting it fall on top of the robe.

Standing naked in front of him, she fought an urge to cover herself. The notion slid away at the hot look in his eyes.

"Beautiful," he said. "All sweet curves and high, luscious breasts." He took her hand, pressed it against the front of his breeches. She could feel his hardness, long and thick and heavy, bigger than she'd thought a man would be. He was hot and pulsing and she was the cause, a knowledge that filled her with a sense of power unlike anything she had known.

"I ache for you, Jillian. I have since that first day."

He cupped her face between his hands and kissed her, took her deeply with his tongue. A tiny moan escaped as her arms slid up around his neck and damp black hair curled around her fingers. Her heart was thudding. Her skin felt stretched tight, and the place between her legs throbbed and burned.

Adam caught her braid, slid off the ribbon that held it in place, then combed his fingers through her hair and spread it around her shoulders.

"Like fire," he said softly. "Cool silk fire."

Bending a little, he slipped an arm beneath her knees and lifted her up, carried her over to his big four-poster bed. Laying her down in the deep feather mattress, he kissed her again, nibbling the corners of her mouth, molding their lips together, sending little tremors of gooseflesh over her skin. He stopped only long enough to strip away his breeches, then he joined her naked on the bed.

In the moonlight streaming in through the mullioned windows, she could see the heavy male part of him, straining upward against his flat belly.

"Don't be afraid," he said at the very same instant that notion occurred. "We'll take our time. I'm not going to hurt you."

Her eyes moved over his broad chest, the sinews in his arms and shoulders. She wasn't frightened. Not when she heard the concern in his voice. "I want to touch you," she said, surprising him, surprising even herself. "I want to feel the way your skin curves over your ribs, the way your muscles tighten when you move." It was a bold thing to say, but the future was uncertain. Their time together could end at any moment. "I want to know what it feels like when you're inside me."

She knew only what little she had read, that his hard length would somehow fit inside her. That it was God's plan for men's and women's bodies to be joined.

"Jillian . . ." Adam kissed her as she reached out to touch him, tentatively ran a finger over a flat copper nipple, discovering the ridges, the way it puckered and tightened. His muscles contracted. "God, you're driving me insane."

Then his mouth moved along her neck and across her shoulders, down to capture a breast. He tasted each one, licking the tips, making them harden, sending jolts of pleasure shooting through her. All the while, her hands skimmed over his body, exploring the muscles and tendons that flexed and moved, the smoothness of his skin, the scar over his ribs. Adam made a sound low in his throat.

Jillian trembled at the feel of his dark hand sifting through the curls between her legs, sliding lower, a long finger probing, then easing gently inside.

Her body arched upward. Dear God, she was so hot. Adam knew exactly where to touch her, how hard to press, when to go softly. Little waves of heat slid out through her limbs; delicious jolts of pleasure rushed into her stomach. By the time he settled himself between her legs, she felt ready to explode. She was writhing and moaning, begging him for . . . what? She wasn't exactly sure.

"Easy. We don't have to hurry."

Oh, but she did. She was in a hurry for something. She just couldn't figure out what it was. She felt the thick hard length of him probing the entrance to her passage, felt him begin to slide himself inside.

He paused when he reached her maidenhead and for a moment, he stilled. It occurred to her that until that moment, he hadn't completely believed her, hadn't believed she had told him the truth about the earl, but she shoved the vague feeling of betrayal aside.

"I'll do my best not to hurt you." He kissed her deeply again. "If it happens, it will only be just this once."

She could feel the tension in his body, feel how much control it took to hold himself back. His mouth moved hotly over hers, renewing the hunger, then he drove himself through the fragile barrier of her maidenhead. A sharp stinging pain had her sucking in a breath and grinding her teeth. Braced on his elbows, Adam came to a shuddering, softly swearing halt.

"Dammit, I tried not to hurt you. I—"

She stilled his words with a finger over his lips. "The pain is fading. I like the way you feel, the way you fill me up inside. As if some part of me was missing and now it isn't anymore."

He stared into her face and there was something in his eyes . . . something she wished desperately to read. Then he lowered his head and kissed her. It was a deep, drugging, sensual kiss that filled her almost as completely as his body.

The room grew hotter as he began to move, slowly at first, then faster. The air caught in her lungs. Her body began to tremble, to coil and tighten, closing around the hard male part of him that continued to stroke the walls of her passage. The rhythm grew faster, deeper, harder, until she was whimpering his name, clinging to his shoulders, raking her nails down his back.

"God . . ." he whispered, driving into her deeper still. "You feel so . . . I don't know how much longer I can last."

She wasn't sure what he meant. It was impossible to concentrate when her entire body was flaming out of control. Each thrust tightened the knot in her belly, building to a point where she couldn't catch her breath.

She moaned as a wave of sensation rocked her, the force so strong she cried out his name. Bright lights flashed behind her eyes and a sweet taste rose on her tongue. Her body shook, tightened, then seemed to float away. Dear God, it felt better than anything in her wildest dreams and unlike anything she had ever felt before.

She was breathing hard, clutching him so tightly she barely noticed when his muscles went rigid and his body began to shudder. His skin felt warm and damp beneath her hands as he slowly relaxed on top of her, and still she held on tight.

He didn't move for several long seconds. The last thing she expected was the sound of his laughter, muffled against the pillow. Adam gently took her arms and unwound them from around his neck and she realized she had been squeezing him so hard he couldn't get free.

Her face went warm with the first rush of embarrassment she had felt since they had started making love. "I'm sorry. I didn't realize . . ."

He smiled into her face. Such a beautiful smile. She wished he would smile that way more often.

"It's all right. I can still breathe. I don't think you hurt me." He was teasing. It was such a rare occurrence, her embarrassment slid away.

"I never thought it would feel that way . . . like stepping off the earth and flying through the stars. I guess it frightened me a little."

Lying on his side, he propped himself up on an elbow, his lips curved with amusement. "I don't think I've ever sent anyone to the stars before. I guess that could be a little bit frightening."

"It was also quite marvelous. For the first time in my life I understand the attraction between a man and a woman. I never really did until now."

Adam flashed that rare smile again, revealing a flash of beautiful teeth. Then the smile slowly faded. "You were a virgin. It wasn't fair, the things they said about you. You deserved a husband and family."

Now you'll never have them, were his unspoken words. She ignored the quick sting in her heart. There was nothing she could do to change the past, and even to avoid the gossip she wouldn't have missed those months she had spent with her father's dearest friend.

"Life is hardly ever fair. As a man of the world, you ought to know that by now."

He reached toward her, lifted a strand of her hair away from her cheek. "You're right. I know that better than anyone."

The way he looked at her set her heart to pounding again. It was desire, she now knew. She hadn't realized it would return again so soon. "Do men make love more than once a night?"

His eyes instantly darkened. He came up over her with his usual easy grace, his gaze once more intense. "This man does," and he softly kissed her lips. "Why don't we see if I can send you on another trip to the stars."

13

Adam studied the woman lying next to him in his bed. It was nearly dawn, faint gray light sliding in between the velvet curtains. He had awakened half an hour ago from an amazingly peaceful slumber. He would have to wake Jillian soon so that she could return to her room before the servants discovered her missing.

Just days ago it wouldn't have mattered. He'd believed her a fallen woman and he meant to take advantage of the fact. Now, knowing firsthand that she had been an innocent, her life destroyed by malicious untruths, he wanted to protect her from any further pain.

Adam lifted a strand of dark copper hair away from her cheek and thought of the incredible night they had shared. He had made her a woman last night, yet always she had seemed so. She made love unashamedly, with a sort of greedy abandon he found nearly irresistible. She was amazingly responsive, demanding as well as giving, with a need clearly matching his own.

I want to touch you, she had said. *I want to know what it feels like when you're inside me.* Her innocent bravado inflamed him in a way he hadn't expected. He'd made love to her three times last night and would have taken her again this morning if she hadn't been a novice. He couldn't seem to get enough of her. He enjoyed her body and admired her intelligence.

Yet he held no notion of marriage.

That thought had died years ago, when Caroline had betrayed him with Robert. When the women he had known were those like Lavinia Dandridge, ladies who cuckolded their husbands without the least remorse; or more recently Maria Barrett, a woman who had appealed to his darker nature and very nearly destroyed him.

Of course there were a number of good women, too. His mother and sister were angels, as far as he was concerned. But those sorts of women were few and far between and he had long ago given up finding one for himself.

Adam glanced over at Jillian. He wanted her in his bed, wanted to enjoy her intellect and her passion, but he still didn't trust her. Not completely. She was a woman and that in itself was enough to make him wary.

Still, he wanted her. He imagined peeling down the covers and replacing their warmth with the heat of his body. He imagined sliding himself deeply inside her, and instantly went rock hard.

There wasn't time, he knew, not with the gray light turning a soft pinkish gold, a harbinger of the sun that would soon be rising. Instead, he concentrated on the dilemma he faced where Jillian was concerned and thought that he had found the solution.

With her father and the old earl dead, except for a few distant cousins she had long ago lost touch with, Jillian was alone. She needed a protector, someone to treat her with care and see to her financial needs. Adam believed he was exactly the man.

Once the murder was solved and she was cleared of the crime, he would set her up as his mistress. Jillian would want for nothing and he would have what he wanted as well—a beautiful, intelligent, passionate woman in his bed. He wasn't sure how long his desire for her would last, months at least, perhaps even years. Once the affair was over, he would make her an equitable settlement and she could live in comfort wherever she wished.

And if there were children—well, he wouldn't shirk his duties there either. It would work out perfectly for both of them.

The mattress shifted. Adam turned to find Jillian watching him from beneath a fringe of dark auburn lashes. He thought she might be embarrassed, but it was concern he read in her face.

"Last night when I came into your room, you were having another nightmare. Will you tell me about your dream?"

It wasn't the question he had expected. There was nothing of guilt or accusations, only concern. He took a steadying breath. He had never talked about the nightmares that plagued him. There wasn't any point. And yet he found himself thinking of Aboukir, feeling the memories pour into his head. And speaking them aloud seemed the only way to get them out.

"I'd been in the cavalry four years by the time my regiment sailed for Egypt."

Jillian scooted backward, pulling the sheet up with her to cover her breasts, propping herself against the headboard.

"I'd seen action by then, of course. We'd lost some damn fine men, but it was nothing like what happened at Aboukir."

He could still see the great stretches of sand interrupted by a few straggly date trees, the landscape sterile and parched, like the bottom of a barren riverbed that seemed to have no end. The ship arrived at dusk and it took all night to land the men and horses, hampered as they were by heavy artillery fire from the fort at Aboukir where the French were entrenched. Overloaded with heavy packs, sabers, and muskets, some of the soldiers lost their lives when they stepped into water over their heads, others were shot as they hit the beach, their bodies floating facedown in the tide at the edge of the sand.

"It was March, but when the sun came up the following day, the heat grinding down was unbearable. We were short of water almost from the start. Pretty soon, it was all we could think of. In the dreams, my throat is swollen and I feel like I'm choking to death."

He shook his head at the memory, plunged ahead, a flow once started that could not be stopped. "There was fighting nearly every day. But it wasn't till nearly three weeks later that the main battle began."

Not until the night twelve thousand French soldiers left Fort Aboukir in secret and attacked British forces. If he closed his eyes he could still hear the rumble of cannon, the whine of gunfire, the thud of lead balls slamming into the bodies of the men. He recalled a soldier on his left, standing one moment, falling over like a toppled tree the next, beneath the heavy weight of a cannonball careening across the earth.

"The grapeshot was murderous," he said, his voice devoid of emotion, the pain locked carefully behind the protective wall of his mind. "Everywhere I looked, I saw men being blown apart and horses screaming in pain, falling beneath a deadly barrage of hot, tearing metal. A group of French cavalry swept down on the Ninetieth Foot, a regiment of infantry. In a matter of minutes, a thousand fighting men were reduced to six hundred. Those that survived cheered at the even higher losses of the French. Men who had fallen out of their saddles dangled from the stirrups, beaten to death as their terrified horses raced madly back and forth along the line."

Adam swallowed. "My brigade made a sweeping charge from the left and engaged the enemy with sabers. I remember a young lieutenant. I could see how frightened he was by the erratic movements of his blade. He swung at a French cavalry officer, missed and slashed into his horse. The poor animal reared over backward and crushed the lieutenant beneath the weight of its body." He ran a shaking hand over his face, telling himself to stop, but the words just kept spewing out.

"There were thirty-five hundred casualties that night. I can still see them lying on the battlefield, their blood soaking into the sand for as far as the eye could see. So many men. God, we lost so many good men."

So lost was he in the memories, he might have gone on if he hadn't heard the soft little mewling sounds Jillian was making beside him. Forcing the awful memories away, he turned to see her fist pressed over her mouth and her cheeks streaked with tears.

"God, I'm sorry." Leaning over, he pulled her into his arms. "I don't know why I told you that. I shouldn't have. It isn't something a woman should ever have to hear."

She simply held on, her arms around his neck, holding him as if she could somehow help him erase what he had seen. It made a lump rise in his throat.

"I'm glad you told me. No one should have to keep such terrible memories locked up inside them."

He only shook his head. Outside the window the sky was getting lighter. He needed to get her out of there before it was too late. She reached toward him, smoothed her hand over the scar across his ribs.

"Is that where you got this? At Aboukir?"

He nodded. "A saber cut. Lucky for me it wasn't too deep."

"There's another scar on your thigh. I noticed it last night."

"Nothing so heroic. A practice maneuver went wrong while I was training some new men."

"And the one along your jaw?"

His mouth thinned, tightened. "A personal matter. Nothing to do with the war." She ran a finger along the thin line, then rested her hand against his cheek. He felt the soft brush of her lips against his, inhaled a delicate, lingering trace of her perfume mingled with the musky scent of sex, and all rational thought flew out of his head.

He knew what she was offering and in that moment he needed to be inside her more than he needed to breathe. He was already hard and throbbing. He eased her beneath him, parted her legs with his knee, and slid himself into her welcoming heat. He tried to take her slowly, to make sure she reached her peak, but in the end he couldn't hold back. He pounded into her, driving hard, her soft cries muted by his kisses.

His release came swift and hard and left him a little bit shaken. He didn't apologize for his roughness when he eased himself off her, just reached out and caught her hand, linked his fingers with hers and carried them to his lips. The next time they made love, he would make it up to her, see her pleasured as she should have been this morning.

The next time they made love.

Though his growing need for her worried him a little, Adam thought about the pleasures he had only begun to show her. Once he cleared her name, he would set her up in a small but elegant town house where he could visit her often. He had never kept a mistress, never wanted even that small degree of commitment. But Jillian was different and he meant to enjoy her. Surely something would break soon on her case and once it did, he would tell her, ease some of her worry about the future.

With that thought in mind, Adam climbed out of bed.

Jillian took chocolate and toast in her bedchamber that morning, unwilling to face the earl after what had happened last night. She could still hear the pain in his voice as he described the battle that raged in his nightmares, but mostly she thought of the hours they had spent making love.

She told herself she wasn't sorry, and in most ways she wasn't. She had given herself to him freely and the night had been incredible.

But Adam was an earl and even if she were proved innocent of Lord Fenwick's murder, he had no plans for marriage and he wouldn't choose her if he did. What they shared would be a brief affair at best.

As Jillian descended the carved wooden staircase and crossed the paneled entry, the thought sat like a lead weight on her chest.

"Good mornin', Miss."

"Good morning, Reggie."

"Lord Blackwood left word for ye. He wants ye to join him in the greenhouse."

Her stomach contracted. Sweet God, she didn't want to face him—not yet.

She took a steadying breath. "I don't believe I know where the greenhouse is."

"I'm sure ye've seen it. 'Tis that big domed buildin' behind the trees at the back of the garden. That's where the major—I mean, his lordship—raises his orchidaceous plants."

Orchidaceous plants?

"Thank you, Reggie." As Lord Blackwood often did, Jillian found herself calling the servants by their given names. She was beginning to like the informality that made them seem less like employees and more like friends.

Leaving Reggie to his butlering tasks, she made

her way to the rear of the house, thinking of the earl, more nervous by the minute but also intrigued. She couldn't imagine the dark, masculine earl in a room full of orchids. The image was a lure in itself.

As she walked toward the greenhouse, she caught a glimpse of the nearby dower house, a reminder of the promise she had made to the countess, Adam's mother, but after what had happened with the lady's son last night, Jillian wasn't ready to face her.

Instead, she continued along the path until the greenhouse appeared in the distance, a two-story structure built of the same smooth stone as the house. Paned windows formed the walls, supporting an oblong, dome-shaped roof fashioned of large glass panels. The panels were set in copper frames gone green with age, giving the place a whimsical appearance.

Jillian took a breath to steady her nerves and walked into the warm, humid interior, catching the scent of rich, black peat and the lighter, more delicate fragrance of orange blossoms. Passing a row of miniature citrus trees, she caught a flash of white and black and spotted the earl's full-sleeved shirt and dark breeches.

Damp with sweat, the shirt clung to the muscles between his shoulder blades and Jillian remembered running her hands over those muscles last night. She remembered his lean, naked body pressing her down in the deep feather bed, and her mouth went dry. His sleeves were rolled up to the elbows, exposing the long sinews in his forearms. Dark hands covered with earth moved gracefully as he bent over to repot one of his orchidaceous plants.

In contrast to the delicate ruffled white flower, he looked impossibly dark and male, and Jillian felt a shivery sensation in the pit of her stomach. Silently, she noted his unhurried movements, the gentleness with which he handled the orchid, and remembered the care he had taken with her last night.

He must have sensed her presence, there by a row of purple iris, for he turned, set the orchid aside, and slowly rose to his feet—a considerable height by anyone's standards. Washing his hands in a nearby bucket of water, he dried them on a linen towel, then started walking toward her.

Jillian forced her own feet forward. There was nothing in his features that said what he was thinking, and her heart set up a nervous clatter. Perhaps he regretted last night. Perhaps his already uncertain opinion of her had changed for the worse. Her footsteps slowed. Suddenly she wished she were anywhere but there.

"Good morning." His smile was slow and so sensuous her insides turned to butter.

"Good morning, my lord."

"I thought you might enjoy the orchids. I find peace here when it seems to elude me everywhere else. I've been meaning to show you." His gaze ran over her, an intimate perusal that made her think of the things he had done to her last night. "Other matters kept intruding."

Other matters? Like murder and prison—or making love to her for hours on end? But she saw no censure in his features, only a trace of the heat she had seen in his eyes last night.

Jillian moistened her lips, more than a little disconcerted. "I-I'm afraid I don't know much about orchids. In truth, I've seen very few of them."

"Then showing them to you will be my pleasure."

There was an almost imperceptible pause on the final word and her stomach swept up. *Pleasure.* Adam Hawthorne knew the true meaning of the word. It terrified her to realize how badly she wanted him to make love to her again.

Adam seemed unaware of her thoughts.

He took her hand and began to lead her down a row of variegated white-and-purple orchids, pausing in front of a pot that contained smaller cream-colored, smooth-petaled orchids with burgundy spots growing from a long, single stem.

"Cymbidium ensifolium. They're from China. They go back nearly three thousand years." He led her down another row. "These are from South America." Astonishingly bright yellow. "Oncidium, they're called." He pointed to a group of magnificent broad-petaled purple plants. "These are called Orchis mascula. Shakespeare wrote about them." There were orange ones, pink ones, lavender, and white; star shapes, triangles, and hearts, all of them exquisitely lovely.

"They're beautiful." But as she watched Adam gazing at them with pride and an odd sort of tenderness, she couldn't take her eyes off his face. She forced her attention back to the plant. "Difficult to grow, I imagine."

His smile turned brilliant and it transformed his features. "And therein lies the challenge. No one knows much about raising them. A friend of mine from the army brought some plants back from the West Indies. That's how I got interested in the first place."

"Rather like your interest in Egyptian antiquities."

"Yes." His gaze flicked over her and she knew he was thinking of Egypt and the dream that had brought her into his room last night. "Aboukir was a nightmare. It still is. But afterward . . . I don't know . . . there is something compelling about Egypt, the power and majesty of a culture that lasted for thousands of years."

Returning his attention to the orchids, he paused beside a basket filled with moss. "I keep a coal fire burning under this section of the greenhouse, and warm air vented in. We pump water into the room in open trenches to keep enough moisture in the air. I've been thinking of writing a paper on it for the London Horticultural Society."

One of her eyebrows went up. "The London Horticultural Society? Why, Major Hawthorne, who would have guessed?"

"You're laughing at me," he said, but he looked faintly amused.

"It doesn't exactly fit your image. You're supposed to be mysterious and dangerous." *Then again,* she thought, assessing the hard, handsome lines of his face, *dangerous is exactly what he is.*

Adam's eyes locked with hers. He caught her wrist and drew her toward him. "You have no idea, Miss Whitney, just how dangerous I can be." Lean hands framed her face. "But I intend to show you." He tilted her head back, his mouth came down over hers, and a wave of heat washed through her.

"I'd like to make love to you right here," he whispered against her ear. "I'd like to lay you down among the orchids. I'd like to unbutton your dress and peel it away, to fill my hands with those lovely pale breasts."

Jillian moaned as his long fingers slid over the bodice of her gown, purposely grazing her nipple.

Firm lips moved to the side of her neck. "I'd like to lift your skirts and—"

"Carter? Carter, is that you?"

Adam swore softly at the sound of the countess's voice. Jillian flushed, and both of them stepped away at the same instant his mother poked her head around a row of orchids.

"Carter?"

"It's me, Mother, Adam."

"Adam!" She always seemed surprised—and overjoyed. Jillian thought that perhaps it was because her second son had been gone for so long in the army.

She continued walking toward them. "I thought I might find you out here among your lovely flowers." She was wearing a simple beige muslin gown, her hair pulled back in a tidy gray bun. She looked more like a governess than a countess.

Adam reached for Jillian's hand and drew her forward. "You remember Miss Whitney?"

"Why, yes, of course. She's coming to see my rose garden."

Jillian managed a smile. "I could stop by this afternoon ... if that wouldn't be inconvenient."

"No, no, of course not. But perhaps you'd like to see it now. It's beautiful this time of day, with a trace of dew still clinging to the petals."

Jillian latched onto the chance for escape. "I should like that very much." She tossed Adam a glance. "With your permission, my lord."

He made a slight inclination of his head, his dark gaze warning he meant to take up where he had left off. "Enjoy the roses."

Oblivious to the swirling currents around them, Lady Blackwood linked her arm with Jillian's and the two women walked to the door. They talked of flowers and planting as they left the greenhouse, but Jillian found it hard to concentrate.

Her mind kept returning to the earl, and every time it did, her worry kicked up another notch.

It was nearly an hour later that Jillian said farewell to the countess and returned to the house. As they had strolled among the roses, Lady Blackwood had spoken of Adam, regaling her with humorous tales of his misspent youth. It was just before she departed that Jillian learned the story of Adam's betrothal to Caroline Harding.

"Adam was in love with her," the countess had said.

Jillian had the feeling the woman wouldn't have uttered a word of something so private before she'd had her stroke, but her mind worked differently now.

"I suppose Caroline convinced him that she was in love with him, too. At any rate, I didn't discover the truth of her betrayal until after my son joined the army. Then I heard the gossip that poor dear Adam had discovered his beloved Caroline in a compromising situation with his cousin Robert." She glanced up. "*Extremely* compromising. It must have been terrible for Adam."

Terrible indeed. To fall deeply in love and then find your betrothed making love with another man. It occurred to her that Caroline Harding was probably the reason he had joined the army. In a way, the nightmares he suffered were a result of Caroline's deceit.

"But all of that is behind him now," the countess finished as they walked among the roses. "I couldn't be more thrilled with his choice of bride. You'll give him beautiful sons and strong, intelligent daughters. I can scarcely wait to see them."

Jillian swallowed. "Please understand, Lady Blackwood, your son and I are merely friends." *Friends?* Adam was her lover. And even that tenuous bond would be brief. Jillian felt a painful twist in her heart.

The countess started fanning herself as if she had walked several miles. "You'll have to excuse me, my dear. These old bones simply aren't what they used to be. Tell Carter I'd like to see him whenever he can manage to get away, and don't worry, dear. I'm sure Adam will be back from Egypt very soon."

It was sad, Jillian thought as she watched the woman walk away. At least Lady Blackwood had enjoyed a fruitful life and the joy of having a family. It was something Jillian would never experience. Even the number of years the countess had lived might be denied her. In truth, if she didn't find a way to prove her innocence, she might yet hang.

Jillian ignored a shiver as she walked back to the house.

14

❦

She didn't see Adam for the rest of the day. He had been working in his study, the task of being an earl more demanding than most people knew. There were properties to manage, tenants to look after, family matters that required hours of time and attention.

In fact, just before supper, one of those family matters appeared on Adam's doorstep.

"Sorry to interrupt ye, Major, but your sister, Lady Margaret, just arrived." They were finishing a meal of creamed salmon and perigord pie that Jillian mostly shoved around on her plate. She was worried, and not just about the search that was going on in London.

It was her growing attraction to the earl that had her stomach tied in knots. The man exuded power and sexual appeal and whenever he looked at her, the hunger in his eyes was unmistakable. She knew what he was thinking, knew he meant to come to her tonight.

Then Reggie stepped into the dining room and whatever plans Adam might have had disappeared like smoke in the wind.

"Ye've company, milord," Reggie said. "I told Lady Margaret I was supposed to announce her but—"

"But I told him he needn't bother. I am perfectly capable of announcing myself." Margaret Hawthorne entered the room like a beautiful, raven-haired whirlwind. Dressed in a ruby velvet riding skirt with a short matching jacket cut in the military style and a matching top hat cocked at a saucy angle, she had refined, perfect features and skin as pale as cream.

Though Adam was darker, the resemblance between them was unmistakable, as well as Adam's affection for her.

"Maggie!" He shoved back his chair and came to his feet. "I thought you and Aunt Sophie were in Tunbridge Wells. What in God's name are you doing here?"

Lady Margaret threw her arms around her brother's neck and gave him a hug Adam warmly returned. "Aunt Sophie's been giving me fits. I had to get away before I went insane." She flicked a glance at Jillian. "Besides, I heard you were embroiled in a marvelous new scandal, and I had to see for myself the woman who had lured you into yet another bout of intrigue."

Another bout of intrigue. Jillian's stomach tightened even as the whirlwind turned in her direction, flashing a bright, seemingly guileless smile.

"I'm Margaret Hawthorne," she said before her brother had a chance to introduce them. "Everyone calls me Maggie. You must be Jillian Whitney."

Jillian stood up from her chair. Maggie was several inches taller and she already felt at a disadvantage. "It's a pleasure to meet you, my lady."

"Now that you've interrupted our supper," Adam said, "and made Jillian wonder at your sanity, perhaps you'd like to join us for something to eat?"

Lady Margaret smiled. It was the same magnificent smile her brother used so rarely. It seemed to come naturally to Maggie. "I ate at the George and Dragon, just outside the village. I'm as full as an overstuffed feather bed."

Adam chuckled, took in her velvet riding outfit, and frowned. "How did you get here? Tell me you didn't ride all this way by yourself."

"Of course not. Winifred, my maid, is in the carriage, along with a driver and a footman. They should be arriving any moment."

Adam cursed softly. "You should have stayed with them. How many times have I warned you about the danger of riding off on your own?"

Maggie waved away his concern. "Oh, don't be such a toad, Adam. I daresay, nothing happened. I hate riding inside that stuffy old coach and you know it. Besides, I told you, I only came ahead the last few miles."

Jillian fought a smile at the dark look on Adam's face. He glanced from his sister to Jillian, imagining, perhaps, what might have occurred between them if his sister hadn't arrived, and frustration flashed for a moment in his eyes.

"I think we're through with supper," he said. "Why don't we adjourn to the drawing room? Maggie can regale us with tales of her journey."

She flicked a sideways glance at Jillian. "I should

rather hear what is happening with the murder investigation you are involved in. Perhaps there is something I might do to help."

Adam sighed. "How did you know I was conducting an investigation?" He offered his sister one arm and Jillian the other and guided both women out of the dining room.

"It was mentioned in the *Times*. And on every wagging tongue in London. I swear, brother dear, you have a knack for stirring up trouble, even when it isn't your own."

"And you, young lady, have a knack for sticking your nose into other people's business."

"You're my brother." She aimed a pointed glance at Jillian. "That makes it my business." With those words, Jillian realized that Maggie Hawthorne was far more than the flighty, outspoken young woman she appeared. She had come to assess the situation her brother had got himself involved in and perhaps do something to protect him. Jillian was beginning to like Margaret Hawthorne.

It would be interesting to see how the evening progressed.

As it happened, the night developed quite differently than Jillian expected. In the beginning, it was rather a sparring match, with Adam irritated at his sister's none too subtle probing and Jillian deciding the best approach to Margaret Hawthorne's interest was an honest one, which meant giving the girl the answers she had come to get.

"So the butler accused you of murdering Lord Fenwick," Lady Margaret said, repeating the explanation she had been given thus far. "You were afraid no one would believe your side of the story so you ran away."

"Yes, that is exactly what happened. And as it turned out, no one did ... except your brother."

Adam filled in the part about confronting Jillian in the alley, adding, "Much of the gossip you've heard about Miss Whitney is wrong. She was Lord Fenwick's ward, nothing more. And she had no reason to kill him. In fact, if the earl had lived just a few days longer, Miss Whitney would have become an extremely wealthy woman."

By the end of the evening, miraculously, the women wound up on a first-name basis, Jillian apparently having won Maggie Hawthorne's support.

"I wasn't sure I was going to like you," Maggie said with her usual candor during a moment Adam had briefly departed the room. "My brother's taste in women isn't known to be particularly good, but I think perhaps on this occasion he has stumbled upon a different sort."

"Thank you—I think." Both women laughed. They were still grinning when Adam returned to the drawing room.

"It's getting late," he said with a heated glance in Jillian's direction. "Since you both seem to be in such good humor, perhaps now is a good time to take yourselves off to bed."

"Good idea." Maggie came to her feet. "It's been quite a long day." She smiled at her brother. "I'm sure you two would like a moment. If you'll excuse me." She brushed past them on her way out the door, leaving them alone in the drawing room.

Apparently Jillian had been right about the younger woman's support, and it made her feel guilty for bringing such a terrible scandal down on her head.

"I hate what this is doing to your family," Jillian said. "Your sister is so very young and lovely. She should be able to choose from the most eligible bachelors in London, but with the scandal I've embroiled you all in—"

"Maggie's a little too outspoken for a good many of those men, no matter how lovely she is. Besides, it's too late to worry about that now. Once this is settled, I'll do what I can to repair the damage."

She swallowed, nodded. What other choice did she have?

Adam walked her up the stairs to her room and she could feel the tension in his body. All evening, he had watched her with hot, hungry eyes, a banked fire waiting to burst into flame.

By the time they reached the door to her bedchamber, that fire had blazed to life. The air seemed to heat and thicken around them. Adam's mouth held a sensuous twist as he bent his head and brushed her lips with a feather-soft kiss, then moved to the side of her neck.

"Leave your door unlocked," he whispered, his warm breath feathering the hair at her temple. "I'll come to you as soon as the household falls asleep."

Part of her wanted to, the wild, wanton part of her that had led her into his room last night. With the servants abed and just the two of them in the house, she had been brave enough to take what she wanted. Tonight, knowing his sister slept just down the hall and no decent woman would behave in such a manner, welcoming the earl was impossible to do.

Jillian looked up at him. "I realize after last night

what you must expect from me, but your sister is in the house and I just . . . I cannot feel right about . . . about . . ."

For a moment his jaw went tight. Then he sighed and made a faint nod of his head. "You're right. I shouldn't have pressed you, not with Maggie in the house. And in a strange way, I'm glad you feel as you do." He smiled and stepped back, very gallantly lifted her hand, and pressed his lips against the back. "Good night, Miss Whitney. Sweet dreams."

Three days passed. A cool breeze blew clouds in from the coast and only a weak sun shined through the high arched windows. Across from Adam in the Green Drawing Room, Jillian sat next to Maggie on the sofa, while Garth Dutton, the barrister he had hired, sat in an overstuffed chair in front of a malachite hearth.

"I wish I'd brought better news," Garth said to the small company sharing the warmth of the slow-burning fire. "I know you were hoping to discover that Howard Telford had a motive for murdering his uncle—aside from the obvious fact it would hasten his acquisition of the title. But according to Benjamin Morrison, Telford had no idea his uncle meant to change the will."

Garth was taller than average, an attractive blond man of thirty Adam had known at Oxford. Garth had been among the most brilliant students in his class. He was loyal, trustworthy, and determined, already a powerful force in the legal profession. Exactly the reason Adam had hired him.

"Morrison says he never talked to anyone about the will and particularly not the late earl's nephew or his daughter-in-law, since they were beneficiaries.

"I need to speak to them myself. I'd like them to recount their last few conversations with the earl. I talked to Howard briefly, but I haven't spoken to Madeleine. I wish I'd had time before we left London."

Adam glanced at Jillian, obviously worried by Garth's less than optimistic news. Maggie reached over and squeezed her hand.

"Let me speak to Howard and Madeleine," Garth offered. "At the moment, you're not exactly high on either of their popularity lists—not with the chief suspect staying here under your protection." He turned clear green eyes on Jillian. "Excuse my frankness, Miss Whitney, but we don't have time to mince words."

Her chin lifted in that way Adam was coming to know. "It's quite all right, Mr. Dutton, I prefer your candor. In fact, it is extremely important to me, considering it is my life that is at risk."

He nodded his approval, and went on with what he had been saying. "I shouldn't have any trouble getting in to see them. Howard is a fairly close acquaintance and I've known Madeleine Telford for several years. The way things stand, they're far more likely to disclose something useful to me than they would be to you."

Adam sighed. "Perhaps you're right. I just wish we had something more to go on."

"Fraser has high hopes of finding his lordship's thieving ex-solicitor, Colin Norton. With luck, that could happen very soon. In the meantime, I've some questions I'd like to ask Miss Whitney. If this matter does go to trial, I need to know what to expect from my client."

Jillian's face drained of color.

Damn, he wished he could spare her this, but Garth was right. There was a good possibility Jillian would be tried for murder. If that circumstance occurred, Garth was the best chance she had.

They spent the next two hours going over Jillian's story, Garth covering every small detail from the moment she stepped into Lord Fenwick's study till she raced out the back door and down the alley, straight into Adam's arms—where he wished she were right now. But of course he didn't say that.

"I hope it doesn't happen," Garth was saying, "but if you do have to face a trial, I think you'll make a very good witness, Miss Whitney. Besides being composed, you give a strong impression of credibility."

She straightened a little on the green-striped sofa. "It isn't difficult to seem credible, Mr. Dutton, when one is telling the truth."

The lawyer's mouth curved. He nodded, pleased with her conviction.

"You'll spend the night, won't you?" Adam asked. "You've come a good distance. You deserve a good night's sleep. You can head back in the morning."

"As you say, I have a great deal to do, but yes, if you don't mind, I think I'll stay." His glance strayed to where Maggie sat on the sofa. "I could use a decent meal and a good night's rest."

But something told Adam that Garth might also be interested in spending an evening in his sister Maggie's company. *Interesting.* Garth rarely had time for women. In his youth, he'd been too driven to succeed in his studies. As a man, his career seemed to take precedence over any sort of social life. Adam wondered what Maggie would say if she knew.

But Garth's attention seemed fixed once more on Jillian and the matter at hand. Perhaps he had been mistaken.

Maggie Hawthorne wandered out on the terrace. From where she stood near the balustrade, she could see the ocean below the cliffs. Beneath a waxing moon, the tide rushed in against the rocky shore and she could hear the crash of waves churning up the sand.

It was growing late. She had excused herself and wandered away from the others, desperate for a breath of fresh air and a chance to be alone.

She was worried about her brother, worried at his involvement with Jillian Whitney.

Though she was coming to like Jillian more and more and beginning to believe, as her brother did, that she was innocent of Lord Fenwick's murder, she didn't want Adam hurt, and that could certainly happen.

If something went wrong, if Jillian were arrested and brought to trial—if they were wrong and Jillian was actually guilty of the crime—Adam was bound to suffer.

Though it was highly unlikely, considering his mistrust of women, there was even a chance he might fall in love with her. The way things stood, that was the very last thing he should do.

Maggie sighed as she stared out over the moon-touched, midnight-blue water. As tough as Adam had taught himself to be during his years in the army, inside he was sensitive, perhaps even gentle. Though he had known scores of women, he had loved only two, and the pain he had suffered at their betrayal had left him hurting for years.

"I thought I might find you out here." Garth Dutton's deep baritone, perfect, she imagined, for the courtroom, swept toward her out of the darkness. "Mind if I join you?"

Actually, she did. She had come out here to be alone. "I don't suppose you're going to give me a choice."

His lips slightly curved. "Not really, no. I wanted to speak to you. I thought now might be a good time."

Her interest stirred. Most men did exactly what she wanted. If she dropped the least hint that they should leave, they would. It was refreshing when a man stood up to her. "Well, we're both here now. What did you want to talk about?"

"Why don't we start with Miss Whitney? She's my client, after all. I'd like to know what you think of her."

She shrugged noncommittally. "I find it hard to believe my opinion matters, but the truth is, I like her. I don't like that she has involved my brother in another ugly scandal. I don't like that he obviously has an interest in her that goes beyond friendship. But as a person, I like her."

"Do you think she is capable of murder?"

Maggie considered that a moment. "Under the right set of circumstances anyone is capable of murder."

One of his blond eyebrows lifted. "Even you?"

He was handsome and self-possessed; she had noticed that more than once during the course of the evening—attractive qualities in a man. "I'd kill to protect my family or the people I care about. To save myself, if I had to. Though that would be a different sort of murder, I suppose."

"Do you think it's possible Jillian Whitney killed Lord Fenwick for one of those reasons?"

"Perhaps. Somehow I don't think so. I don't think she did it at all."

He moved closer, till he stood just inches away. She caught the scent of pipe tobacco and the faint spice of his cologne. "I don't think so, either." There was something in his manner . . . something that heightened her awareness of him as a man. It occurred to her suddenly that he wasn't there for the reasons he had said.

"I don't think you came here to ask my opinion of Miss Whitney."

"No? Well, you're right, though I find what you had to say extremely astute."

"What is it you want?"

"I could tell you the truth, but then I would just be lumped among your dozens of admirers who want exactly that same thing, so I'll merely say I'd like to get to know you a little, and that is also the truth."

He was staring at her mouth. His eyes were green and there was something about the frank way they studied her that increased the beating of her heart.

"Why? Why would you want to know me?"

A corner of his mouth edged up. It was nicely curved, his lips subtly sensual. "Because you're intelligent and straightforward. I like both of those qualities in a woman. You're beautiful—but then, you already know that." He reached out, caught a loose strand of wavy black hair next to her temple and looped it over an ear. "Perhaps it is merely that you have the most kissable mouth I've ever seen."

She couldn't move. No one ever spoke to her in quite so forward a manner. Her "admirers," as Garth Dutton called them, spouted endless poetry about her beauty. They said that she was as lovely as a flower in spring, that her eyes were limpid blue pools. Complete drivel—all of it. She secretly laughed at every word.

"What's the matter? You like plain speaking, don't you? At supper, you had an opinion on everything from the British blockade to wartime taxation."

She found herself stepping backward and realized that whenever she did, Garth Dutton followed. She felt like a hare pursued by a fox. It was ridiculous. Since she refused to play the terrified rabbit a moment more, she stood her ground, which meant when she stopped, he loomed above her.

"I'm sure your brother would highly disapprove of my kissing you. The question is how would you feel about it?"

She swallowed. She had been kissed before, of course, more often than she should have allowed. Boring, drymouthed kisses nothing at all like she had imagined a kiss should be. Now, looking into Garth Dutton's handsome face, thinking about his beautifully shaped mouth pressing down on hers made her slightly breathless.

Her temper shot up. Garth Dutton was just a man and she refused to allow *any* man to affect her in such a way. Shoving against his chest, she pushed him away and started walking. She was astonished to discover that her legs were trembling. She couldn't believe he had made that happen with only a few brief words.

She paused at the doors leading into the drawing room and turned to look back at him. Even in the darkness, she could see the gleam of his yellow hair.

"You're right," she said. "My brother would scarcely approve of your kissing me. As for myself, I'm not quite certain how I feel about it. You're a barrister. Perhaps in time you can convince me to give it a try."

He said nothing for a moment, then soft laughter rumbled in the darkness. Maggie found herself thinking about that deep male sound as she turned and walked back into the house.

Two more long, frustrating days later, Adam strode toward the stable behind the house. Garth had returned to the city, nothing new had turned up in the murder investigation, and out of respect for both of the women residing in his house, he had made no effort to seduce Jillian back into his bed. He had kept himself away, no matter how much his blood thickened whenever he saw her, no matter how his body ached at night.

Adam was sure if he didn't make love to her soon, he was going to go stark raving mad.

He had almost reached the stable door when he spotted the manor's head groom, an Irishman named Jamie O'Connell, walking toward him leading a pair of horses.

"I've saddled Ramses and Cocoa, milord. Cocoa's a darlin'. She'll do fine for a novice."

A sure-footed sorrel gelding with two white-stockinged feet. Adam didn't know exactly how much of a novice Jillian was. She had said that she could ride, but not all that well. It didn't matter. All he needed her to do was stay in the saddle until they had descended the trail to the bottom of the cliffs and ridden a ways down the beach.

He felt a surge of heat as he thought of the different sort of riding he meant for her to do once they got to the place he meant to take her.

"My lord?"

He turned at the sound of her voice, saw Jillian standing just outside the open barn door. She was dressed for an outing, as he had instructed, in a simple habit of worsted gray wool edged with black piping, her lovely auburn hair pinned up beneath a small black top hat. She looked uneasy as he started walking toward her, her riding crop tapping unconsciously against her boot.

"You're right on time. I thought women were supposed to keep men waiting."

"It's something of a waste, don't you think? And rather childish, too."

"Absolutely." And Jillian was hardly a child. He allowed his gaze to roam over her, remembering her lovely curves. Her hips were narrow, yet her bottom was round and her breasts amazingly plump for a woman so slightly built. His groin tightened with the urge to feel their soft weight in his hands.

He lifted her up on the sidesaddle and waited till she took the reins. "Just for today, I want you to forget all the troubles swirling around in your pretty little head. I want you to relax and enjoy yourself."

Some of the tension she was feeling seemed to ease. "That sounds like a marvelous notion."

"Good, then it's time we were off."

Adam tied a blanket on behind his saddle and the basket Cook had prepared beside his knee. None of the servants seemed concerned that Jillian was unmarried and accompanying him without a chaperon, but then his mother was officially in residence, if some distance away, and now his sister had arrived for a visit.

Still, it bothered him. Bringing one's mistress into the family home simply was not done. And there remained the question of the murder. The crime had not yet been solved and as strong as his belief was in Jillian's innocence, it wouldn't be the first time he had been wrong.

His sister and his mistress.

God, what a coil he had managed to get himself into.

Adam exhaled a breath, ridding himself of the unpleasant thought, determined to take his own advice and enjoy the afternoon.

The breeze had come up by the time they reached the path leading down from the top of the chalk-white cliffs to the beach. The day was warm, the sky a brilliant blue and almost perfectly clear, just a few fluffy clouds floating by overhead. From where they sat their horses, the bay formed a crescent-shaped cove and foamy waves washed up on the beach.

They descended the trail without a problem and galloped along the edge of the surf. Jillian rode better than she had said, not an expert by any means, but certainly capable of staying in the saddle. And she was obviously enjoying herself, laughing when she pulled her horse to a halt, her little black top hat tilting over at a slightly crooked angle.

"Oh, Adam, this is such fun. Thank you so much for inviting me."

He simply nodded. She seemed carefree in a way he had never seen her, smiling at him with so much warmth it made his chest feel tight. It occurred to him he hadn't seen her smile that way since he had come upon her at the duck pond. He wondered if she had been more carefree before her father died, before she had been faced with trying to survive on her own.

"Are you hungry yet?" she shouted above the thunder of the surf.

"Starving!" he shouted back. He was hungry, all right, but not for food. Jillian was radiant with life and energy, happy as he had never seen her. He wanted to drag her off the horse and tumble her down into the sand. He wanted to shove up her skirts, open his breeches, and take her with the surf running over them and sea gulls screeching above their heads.

"I know a place," he said as she rode up beside him. "My brother Carter and I used to go there when we were boys." It was their secret, special place and he had never brought a woman there before—had never wanted to before.

He tethered the horses at the far end of the cove and took Jillian's hand. Climbing a narrow trail that led up into the rocks, he steered her out of the breeze.

Inside the cave, she glanced around in wonder. "How can it be so light in here?"

He pointed toward a chimney-like opening with a

view of the crystal blue sky. "There's a hole in the ceiling. The water carved this place out over hundreds of years, but the tide only gets high enough to reach it during a very bad storm."

"It smells like salt and sunshine. The perfect place for a picnic. Oh, I can't remember when I've enjoyed myself so much."

Adam smiled. Now that he thought of it, neither could he. Jillian kicked off her shoes and sat down on the blanket he spread beneath the rock chimney. Following her lead, he tugged off his boots and stockings. God, he couldn't remember the last time that he had gone barefoot, but it felt amazingly good to sift his toes through the fine white sand in the bottom of the cave.

Jillian helped him set out the items in the lunch basket: mutton pasties and Cheshire cheese; cold chicken and warm, freshly baked bread; candied fruit and cherry tarts for dessert. Adam leaned over and picked up a pasty, only mildly hungry, but Jillian began tearing into the food with such gusto he found himself laughing out loud.

"When you said you were hungry, you really meant it."

She took a bite of cold chicken and made a purring sound in her throat. "Everything tastes delicious. Do you think it's because we're eating at the beach?"

He smiled. He'd been doing that all day. He had brought her here to seduce her. Now he discovered it was he who was being seduced, in a completely different manner.

"I imagine that could be part of it." Damn, he wanted to kiss her, to lick the crumbs from the corners of her mouth, to taste the sweet, dark cavern inside.

His body tightened. He took a last bite of pasty and tried to ignore the clench of desire in his belly.

Jillian sighed and leaned back against the wall of the cave. "This is wonderful. I can't remember when I've felt so content."

The words zinged into him with the force of an arrow. She was smiling softly, slightly windblown and utterly lovely. For months she had been gossiped about and shunned. She'd been accused of murder, forced to hide in the house of a stranger, and ultimately thrown into prison. She'd lost her innocence to a man who had no intention of marriage, and even now she faced a future that might see her hanged.

Adam closed his eyes, his conscience eating away at him, his plans for seduction eroding like sand beneath the waves rushing up on the beach. Jillian deserved a carefree afternoon—without any strings attached. She deserved it, and suddenly he wanted more than anything in the world to see that she got it.

"Could I please have a little more wine?" She came away from the wall on her hands and knees, holding out her empty pewter goblet. She looked into his face. "Your smile is gone. We said we wouldn't think about anything bad today."

He forced his mouth to curve, lifted the flagon, and refilled her cup. "So we did."

They drank a little more wine, but the conversation that had come so easily in the beginning seemed to grow stilted and strained. They folded the blanket in silence as they prepared to leave the cave. Accidentally, their shoulders brushed and both of them turned. Jillian didn't move away, just stood there looking at him with those incredible blue eyes, and lust curled like smoke through his veins.

It ran hot in his blood, sank its claws into his loins. He had to get out of there before he did what his body demanded and dragged her down on the floor of the cave.

"You want to kiss me," she said softly. "Why don't you?"

He wasn't an easy man to read. As an officer in command of hundreds of men, he prided himself on keeping his emotions well-hidden. "Because if I kiss you, I won't want to stop."

Jillian's gaze remained on his face. "If you kissed me, I wouldn't want you to stop."

His blood pumped, throbbed in his groin. He was already hard, pressing uncomfortably against the front of his breeches. For several long seconds, his eyes remained locked with hers.

He let out a shuddering breath. "Ah, God . . ." Cupping the nape of her neck, he slid his fingers into her hair, scattering the pins, dislodging the weighty mass, and knocking off her silly little top hat. Soft curls tumbled around her shoulders as his mouth crushed down over hers.

The kiss was long and deep, a taking, demanding kiss he couldn't seem to turn into anything gentle. He absorbed the softness of her lips, trailed kisses over her jaw and along her throat, then kissed her deeply again.

He could feel her arms around his neck, feel her slender body arching against him. Jillian kissed him back with the same hot need that pulsed through his blood and he heard himself groan.

"Jillian . . ." He kissed her as he stepped forward,

urging her backward up against the wall, easing his knee between her legs. He lifted her a little, forcing her to ride his thigh, and a soft little whimper escaped from her lips.

"I want you," he said, his hands moving down to cup her bottom. It was round and firm and nicely filled his palms. He lifted her, pressed her softness into his painfully hard erection. "I want you so damned much."

He kissed her again, absorbing the taste of her, feeling her tremble, feeling the faint touch of her fingers at the back of his neck, sliding into his hair. God, she was so damned responsive. Her nipples formed tight little buds beneath the bodice of her gown, her tongue felt slick against his, and her legs were shaking as she tried to press herself even closer against him. Everywhere he touched her seemed to come alive.

Reaching down, he slid up the skirt of her riding habit and her chemise lifted with it. He found her softness, parted the warm, plump flesh, and began to stroke her. Jillian moaned and squirmed against his hand. She was wet and hot, so incredibly tempting it was nearly impossible to maintain control.

He fumbled with the buttons at the front of his breeches, cursed when one of them refused to come undone, and finally freed himself. Lifting her a little, he kissed her hard and drove himself deeply inside.

For several long seconds he simply stood there, her body sheathing him so hotly he didn't want to move, but the urge to have her was nearly unbearable, and his muscles flexed, driving him deeper still.

"Adam," she whispered as he wrapped her legs

around his waist, her body shifting restlessly against him. "I need . . ."

"It's all right, love, I've got what you need." Holding her hips immobile, he eased himself out, then thrust deeply into her again. Slow, steady strokes made the sweat break out on his forehead. Hard, demanding strokes had his jaw clenched so tightly pain shot into his temple. Still, he drove on, thrusting hard, harder, until he felt her tremble, felt her body tighten around him, and knew she had reached release. A sob tore from her throat and she clung to his shoulders while the rush of a pounding climax poured through him.

At the last possible moment, he withdrew, more careful this time than he had been before, spilling his seed in the sand on the floor of the cave.

He held her as they spiraled down, listening to the fast-beating rhythm of their hearts. With surprising reluctance, he released her, easing her down his body till her feet touched the sandy floor. Still, she clung to him, her arms wound tightly around his neck. Just as before, she seemed unaware of what she was doing, how fiercely she hung on, and he started to smile again.

"Easy, love. You're back from wherever you traveled, safely returned to English soil."

She blinked up at him and warm color flooded her cheeks. "Sorry."

He chuckled, and bent down to retrieve her top hat.

Jillian gazed down at the sandy floor. "Oh, dear, I've lost my pins. I'll look a fright when we get back."

"We've been riding. They'll think it was the wind."

She didn't look convinced. "There is . . . there is something I need to ask."

Wariness washed through him. Women always wanted something in return for their favors. "What is it?"

"The night I came into your room . . . I wanted to know what it was like to make love. I never really thought we would do it again." She glanced up at him. "What if I get with child?"

His wariness eased. Leaning over, he very gently kissed her. "Would that really be so bad?" He couldn't believe he had said that. He had never thought much about children. He knew almost nothing about them, and after his experience with Caroline, marriage and family held no appeal.

"I love children," she said. "But I wouldn't want a child if . . ." She broke off without completing the thought. She had no way to care for a child. Of course she would worry.

"It's all right. There are ways to keep it from happening. I was careful this time, but even if something like that should occur, I would take care of you and the child."

Some unreadable emotion passed over Jillian's face. She turned away from him, walked over to the entrance of the cave. "I should like to go back now," she said softly.

He nodded, though already he wanted to make love to her again. Watching her comb her fingers through her hair, a dozen erotic images popped into his head. Jillian astride him. Jillian on her hands and knees. Christ, he wanted to take her in a hundred different ways, a thousand.

It wasn't going to happen. He should have returned to London long before this. He had hired the very best people to prove Jillian's innocence, but it wasn't enough. There might be something he could do if he were there.

He would leave Jillian here as he had planned. Reggie and Maude could stay with her. She would be safe from Telford's threats and the vicious London gossip as long as she stayed at Blackwood Manor.

15

Jillian tried not to think of the murder. But the extension she had been granted by the courts would end in two short weeks. God alone knew what would happen if she failed to prove her innocence and they put her on trial. With so much evidence against her, she was sure to go to prison or perhaps even hang.

Time was running out. She couldn't bear sitting there doing nothing a moment more—she simply could not. Determined to speak to Adam, she encountered him in the hallway, apparently feeling the same frustration.

"I've been looking for you," he said. "I wanted to tell you I'm leaving."

"You're going back to London?"

"That's right. There are people I need to see, avenues I need to explore. I'll be leaving for London in the morning."

Jillian hoisted her chin. "I'm glad to hear it, my lord—as that is exactly when I plan to leave."

His jaw hardened. "Not chance. I brought you here

so that you would be safe. Dammit, if you go back to the city, Telford will discover your return and start clamoring to have you thrown back into prison."

"I have to go back," she said. "I was certain something would turn up by now, but it hasn't. It's my life that is at stake. If you won't take me, I shall wait until you leave and go back on my own."

Adam's eyes darkened. He reached out and gripped her arms. "In case it has slipped your mind, the magistrates have placed you in my custody. That means you do as I tell you. If I decide you will stay, then that is what you will do. I swear I'll lock you in your room, if that is what it takes."

She looked at him and her eyes filled with tears. "Adam, please. I'll go mad if I have to stay here. I have to do something. I have to try to help myself. Can't you understand that?"

For long moments, he stared into her face, then his hard grip softened. With a sigh, he stepped away. "How is it I commanded the obedience of hundreds of men, but can't seem to manage one stubborn slip of a woman?"

Jillian wisely made no comment.

Tomorrow they would return to London.

It was later in the afternoon when she answered his summons and joined him in his study, nervous as to what he might want. It was merely a report from Peter Fraser, rather elaborately informing them he had discovered nothing new. She was heartsick when Reggie rapped on the study door, afraid it was more disturbing news.

"Ye've visitors, milord," he said to the earl. "A Vicar Donnellson and a lad he called Christopher Derry. I've shown 'em into the Green Drawing Room."

Adam glanced at Jillian. "I don't know anyone by that name." He reached over and took her hand. "Why don't you come with me? We'll see what business they have."

Just the two of them were left again in the house. Earlier that morning, Maggie and her lady's maid had returned to Aunt Sophie's. Jillian had grown fond of Adam's spirited younger sister, and the thought of being alone with the earl left her nerves on edge.

Trying to ignore the warm dark hand encircling her fingers, she let him lead her down the corridor into the Green Drawing Room, one of the more lavish salons in the manor.

Vicar Donnellson and the boy, Christopher Derry, stood near the mullioned windows. The vicar made an appropriate bow when the earl walked in.

"I'm sorry to inconvenience you, my lord. But there is a matter of some importance we need to discuss."

Adam introduced Jillian as a friend of the family, then suggested they make themselves comfortable around the fire. "Our visitors will need some refreshments, Reggie," he told the butler.

"I'll see to it meself, Maj—milord." Reggie was doing his best to reform, but old habits died hard.

"That won't be necessary, my lord," the vicar said, still standing next to the child. "But perhaps, while we speak, Christopher might enjoy a chance to see the garden."

Adam's gaze sharpened on the boy. He was slender to the point of thin, but his shoulders were straight, and very wide for the rest of him. Wavy, dark brown hair hung over his eyes, which were a lovely shade of green in a face that would have been almost pretty if it hadn't been for his straight nose and sharply carved features.

"The garden is beautiful this time of year," Adam said to the child. "Reggie will show you the way."

The butler's thick paw wrapped around the boy's thin hand. Christopher Derry said nothing but he seemed relieved at the prospect of escaping the house.

Adam turned his attention to the vicar, a nondescript man perhaps in his forties with dark hair silvered at the temples and an air of solidarity that commanded respect.

"What can I do for you, Vicar Donnellson?"

"The matter is personal, my lord. Are you certain you wish your friend, Miss Whitney, to remain?"

"Personal in what way?"

"It involves a rather delicate matter between you and your former betrothed."

The muscles in his jaw went taut. "If this involves Caroline, it is hardly private. In fact, I should be glad for Miss Whitney to remain."

A little surprised, Jillian sat down beside him on the sofa while the vicar took a seat in a dark green brocade chair.

The older man nervously cleared his throat. "I've come to speak to you about the child."

Adam casually leaned back against the sofa. "What about him?"

"First, let me say that Christopher is not the usual sort of boy. He is intelligent, and though he is often rather too serious, there is a kindness in him that is rare among children. Chris is—"

"That is all well and good," Adam interrupted,

"but what has the child's disposition to do with me?"

The vicar frowned at being cut short in his speech, probably not a common occurrence in his line of work.

"Derry is not the lad's real name. It's the name of his adoptive parents in Borough Green. The child's real mother is Lady Caroline Harding—your former betrothed."

Adam leaned forward. "The boy is Caroline's?"

"That is correct. Christopher is your son."

The skin over Adam's cheekbones went pale as he surged to his feet. "That's insane."

"The night Christopher was born, he was given to a couple in Borough Green, Silas Derry and his wife Nancy. Nancy wanted a child and couldn't have one. When Silas agreed to take the boy, Caroline's father, the marquess, arranged it. She lived with a cousin in Sussex during her pregnancy. Almost no one knew about the birth."

Adam paced over to the hearth. "Even if the boy is Caroline's, what makes you think he is mine? And why have you come to me now, after all these years?"

"The child's adoptive parents both died, the father several years back, the mother just last week. Before she passed away, Nan Derry told me the truth about the boy. She asked me to bring him to you."

"I don't believe any of this. If Caroline had been carrying my child she would have told me. She would have come to me for help."

"She might have," he said, "but the two of you had parted badly and at the time you were soldiering on the Continent. Six months after the birth, she married Ashley Bingham, Lord Durnst. They have a family of their own now."

Adam raked a hand through his hair, shoving it back from his forehead. "How old is the boy?"

"He'll be eight the first of next month. He was born on May third in the year seventeen hundred and ninety-eight."

Jillian could almost see Adam's mind spinning, adding up the dates.

"I'll concede the boy might be Caroline's. He has her same green eyes. And they tilt up a little at the corners, just as hers did. But his hair is brown, not black like mine. Around the time the child would have been conceived, Caroline had an affair with my cousin Robert. It's obvious, the child belongs to him and not to me."

"But you were bedding her as well. As a matter of fact, as I understand it, she was a virgin when she came to you."

"I planned to marry her," Adam said defensively. "I'm not normally the sort to compromise an innocent young woman." For an instant, his gaze sliced toward Jillian and she thought she caught a flash of guilt.

"Mrs. Derry was very specific," Donnellson went on. "She said the child was yours and I believe she was telling the truth. Whether you wish to deny his parentage is a matter between you and God, but I won't thrust him onto your cousin because of what you refuse to believe. If you won't have him, I'll take him back to the parsonage with me. Chris is a very good worker. His father saw to that. I'm sure I can find someone who will take him in."

"What do you mean, his father saw to that? Was the boy mistreated?"

The vicar sighed. "I'm afraid the boy's circumstances weren't the best. Nancy wanted a child. Silas wanted a servant. The lad worked from dusk till dawn from the moment he was old enough to stay on his feet."

Adam's expression grew grim. It was obvious he believed the boy was his cousin's bastard son, yet his conscience couldn't stand the thought of the child being raised by strangers who might again mistreat him. Jillian's heart went out to him.

"Whatever the truth, the boy is apparently a Hawthorne," Adam said. "As I am the earl, that makes him my responsibility. Christopher may remain at Blackwood Manor."

The breath Jillian hadn't realized she was holding slowly seeped from her lungs.

The vicar nodded. "Thank you, my lord." He took his cue to leave and rose from his seat. "The boy knows nothing of his parentage. He believes he is the orphan son of Silas and Nancy Derry. Whatever you decide to tell him from here on out will be up to you."

The vicar took his leave, heading for the garden to make his farewells to Christopher and give him whatever few possessions he had brought with him. Jillian watched Adam make his way to the sideboard, pour himself a brandy, and take a hefty drink.

"Are you all right?" she asked.

"No." He tossed back the brandy and refilled his glass. "I've taken in my cousin's bastard. Every time I look at him, I'll think of the two of them the day I found them together in the cottage."

"The boy might be yours," Jillian softly reminded him. "He looks a great deal like you." It was true.

Tall for his age, with the same lean, broad-shouldered build. He was a beautiful child, just as Adam must have been.

"Robert is my cousin. We look somewhat alike."

As all of the Hawthorne men seemed to do, Jillian thought, remembering the portraits she had seen in the long gallery.

"I'll need to hire a governess," Adam went on, as if he spoke more to himself than to her. "He's going to need tutors as well. I'll look into it when we get back to London."

"I'm very good with children. Perhaps I can help with the boy until you have time to work things out."

He nodded, looked a little relieved. "I don't know much about children." Adam stared off toward the garden and it was obvious his thoughts were on Christopher Derry.

Jillian wondered if the boy could possibly be Adam's son, and if Adam's thoughts ran along the same lines.

The nursery at Blackwood Manor sat on the third floor of the huge stone house just below the servants' quarters. According to Fanny Dickens, the cook, all three Hawthorne offspring had occupied rooms up there from the time they were born, along with their governess and various nursemaids and tutors. The atmosphere had been warm and friendly, filled with the laughter of the siblings.

This evening as Jillian made her way along the dimly lit hall, she heard only the echoes of silence. Even as she paused in front of the door to Christopher Derry's room, she heard nothing but quiet.

Her heart squeezed. This wasn't the place for a

child. Not when the small boy who had come into the house just hours before must be feeling lonely and frightened. She made a mental note to speak to Adam, see if he would consent to moving the boy to a room downstairs, then determinedly rapped on the door.

When Christopher didn't respond, she rapped again. Still no reply. Worried now, she turned the knob and slowly shoved it open.

Christopher Derry stood with his feet braced apart and his fists knotted, facing the door as if he were prepared to take on some unknown enemy. He relaxed when he saw who it was.

"Why didn't you answer?" Jillian asked gently.

"I was afraid it was a haunt. I thought I heard one on the stairs."

"A ghost?"

He nodded. Her heart ached at the relief on his face as she walked toward him, a woman of real flesh and blood.

"I'm not a ghost, I promise you. My name is Miss Whitney. We met briefly in the drawing room downstairs."

He nodded but still looked uncertain and she was very glad she had come. The child was bound to be frightened. He was in a strange place, with strange people, and no family or friends. The house itself was huge and intimidating, a maze of corridors and empty rooms, and he was only a little boy.

"Do you really think you might have heard a ghost?" she asked. "That sounds rather exciting. So far, I haven't seen a thing. I keep hoping, but I guess I just haven't been lucky."

His eyes sought hers and interest sparkled in them. "You wouldn't be afraid if you saw one?"

She shook her head. "I don't think so. I've heard a lot of stories about them. I think I should like very much to see one."

He seemed surprised and not a little intrigued. "I wonder what they look like."

"I'm not sure. I've heard you can see right through them, rather like a foggy windowpane." She glanced round the room, which was pleasant enough, decorated in pale blue and peach, the countess's touch evident here as it was in the rest of the house. And yet a chill pervaded the air and the fabrics smelled musty, as if the place hadn't been used in years, which of course it hadn't.

Again she thought of Adam and hoped he would move the boy downstairs.

"How are you settling in? Did Reggie bring you something to eat?"

She knew the older man would have seen to it. One look at Christopher Derry and Reggie's bull-dog face seemed to soften. It was obvious Reginald Sanderstead, formerly a sergeant of the Royal Artillery, melted like taffy at the sight of a child's trembling lips.

"He brought me up a tray, but I wasn't hungry."

Jillian walked over to the big silver tray on the dresser, covered by a white linen cloth. "You know, I think I could use a bite of something. Why don't we see what Cook sent up?"

She lifted the napkin and inhaled the pungent odors of cheese, roast lamb, fresh baked bread, and assorted other goodies chosen with a child in mind. She picked up a silver spoon and took a bite of the custard, making a sound of delight as she swallowed. "This is delicious. Want to try some?"

He eyed her for a moment, then walked over and took the spoon she held out to him. He ate for a while in silence.

"I never had custard with gooseberries in it before."

Jillian imagined there were lots of things Christopher Derry never had. His plain brown twill breeches and homespun shirt reflected the simple life he had lived, yet the clothes were clean and he spoke fairly well.

In minutes the food had disappeared and Christopher gave her a shy, grateful smile that somehow made her think of Adam. Dear God, could the man really be so certain the boy wasn't his?

Just the thought of her own child being raised by strangers, mistreated, then orphaned made her stomach roll. And yet, if he were Robert Hawthorne's son, as Adam firmly believed, the reminder of what his cousin and beloved had done would be torture of the very worst sort.

Jillian spent the next half hour talking to the boy, assuring him the Earl of Blackwood wasn't the hard man he must have first seemed.

"Everything's going to be all right, Christopher. In time, this will all work out."

But the boy didn't look convinced.

And Jillian wasn't either.

The hour was late by the time Jillian left the nursery and went in search of Adam, determined to discuss the child she had left upstairs. She found the earl leaning back on the sofa in his study, his gaze focused on the flickering red and yellow flames in the hearth.

"How is the boy?" he said without glancing in her

direction. Long dark fingers cradled a half-full snifter of brandy, and she wondered if memories of Caroline had etched the harsh lines into his face.

"The child's all right, I suppose ... considering ..."

He turned toward her, arched a sleek black eyebrow. "Considering?"

"Considering he is up there on the third floor all by himself. Christopher is lonely and frightened, terrified there might be ghosts up there to haunt him."

Adam scoffed as he came to his feet. "There aren't any ghosts." He took a sip of his brandy and his heavy-lidded gaze said he had drunk more than he usually did. "At least not in that part of the house."

She cast him a glance he ignored.

"The room he is in was Carter's. It's a very nice room and *considering* the circumstances, he ought to be damned grateful for it."

Irritation trickled through her. "I'm sure he is. It's only ... I just thought that until you are able to hire someone to watch over him, you might give him a room on the second floor where there are other people about."

"No."

"Why not?"

"Because, dammit, I don't want to look at him. I don't want to think of Caroline and Robert and what a fool they made of me."

"That's a little selfish, don't you think? Whether the child is yours or Robert's, he is just a little boy. He shouldn't be punished for what they did to you."

Dark blue eyes assessed her. He swirled the brandy in his glass, tilted back his head, and took a long swallow. "I'll think about it."

"Thank you."

She watched him walk over to the sideboard and refill his glass. "Drink?"

She shook her head. "Since we're on the subject, there is something I've been wanting to speak to you about." It was probably bad timing, but she had already waited longer than she should have.

"The subject being children."

"In a round-about manner, yes. I was hoping that once this is over, you might help me find a position. I realize the scandal will hurt my chances of securing employment, but if by some miracle my name is cleared, surely I'll be able to find some kind of suitable work. I thought perhaps a governess—"

He laughed. It had a bitter ring. She knew he was still upset about the boy. She should have listened to her instincts and picked a better time to broach the subject.

"You're not serious. You want to be a governess?"

Her chin angled up. "What's wrong with that? As I said, I've tutored children before. I think I'd make a very good governess."

His gaze ran over the expensive plum silk gown that dear Lord Fenwick had purchased for her. "Governesses don't wear fancy dresses and fine silk stockings, Jillian."

She stiffened. "You think I need those things to be happy?"

He took a sip of his brandy. "It isn't a matter of need. You weren't raised to be a governess. You deserve better than that. Once this is over, I'll find a place for you in London, someplace discreet where we can be together. I'll see you have a carriage, fashionable clothes, anything you need. I'll take care of you, Jillian. You won't have to worry about a thing."

Her chest constricted into a knot so tight, for an instant she couldn't breathe. "You're . . . you're not suggesting that I become your mistress?"

He smiled but there was something hard-edged about it. "You're already my mistress, sweeting. We'll simply clarify the arrangement."

She was appalled. So aghast she actually felt dizzy. She swallowed, forced out the words. "Becoming your mistress was never . . . never my intention. I gave myself to you because I . . . because I desired you. I wanted to know what it was like to make love with you."

"Whatever your reasons, the result is the same. We have a very satisfying physical relationship—brief as it has been. We might as well make the most of it."

Jillian shook her head, feeling sick to her stomach. "I have no intention of becoming your mistress, Adam. Not now or any time in the future."

"Try to be realistic, sweetheart. You've got no family, no friends. What other choice do you have?"

Her throat ached. She had *chosen* to make love to him. She had given herself to him because she desired him. *Because she was in love with him.* She didn't expect anything in return and especially not the sordid financial arrangement he was proposing.

God, unless she got out of there now, this very minute, she was going to cry, and she refused to do that in front of him.

"I'm sorry. I believe I feel the beginnings of a headache. If you'll excuse me, I'd like to go up to my room." She didn't wait for his permission, just started walking toward the door.

Adam crossed the room, his long strides intercepting her, neatly cutting off her escape. "I don't know what you're thinking, but I'm not doing this to hurt you. You knew from the start marriage wasn't a possibility. I just want to make sure you're taken care of."

He had made it clear he never intended to marry and she had never considered the possibility of becoming his wife. But she wouldn't play the whore for him, either.

"You want to take care of me—like that poor little orphan boy upstairs? Well, I've had enough of your charity, *your lordship*. Your sister was kind enough to offer me the loan of some money, should I need it. As soon as we arrive in London, I'll find myself another place to stay."

Adam gripped her shoulders, his face a mask of steel. "You forget yourself, Miss Whitney. Until the matter of Lord Fenwick's murder is resolved, you'll stay exactly where I tell you. Which means—when we arrive in London, you'll be a guest in my town house, as you were before. Do I make myself clear?"

She clamped her jaw, fighting back tears. "Perfectly." Lifting her chin, she jerked free of his hold and swept past him out of the study.

She didn't start crying until she reached the second floor and escaped into the privacy of her bedchamber.

God, how could she have been such a fool?

16

Jillian's mood remained bleak as they prepared to depart for London. As if sensing the dismal atmosphere in the house, the weather had changed. Surly, metal-gray clouds threatened rain, and cold, damp air seeped into their traveling clothes. Before boarding the carriage, she and the earl each bid a separate farewell to the countess.

"You'll be returning soon, won't you?" the older woman had asked her, referring to Jillian as her "dearest daughter-in-law."

Jillian mustered a strained, weak smile, lied, and said, "Of course."

Her mood was grim, but the earl, she discovered, was in such a foul temper everyone tiptoed around as if they walked on eggshells. Even Reggie, who knew him better than anyone, seemed nervous.

"Wot . . . wot about the lad, milord?" he finally asked, forced to broach a clearly unwelcome subject.

"We'll have to bring him along, I suppose. Have

him collect his things. He can ride in the carriage
with you and Maude."

"Yes, milord."

She wondered what young Christopher thought
of the earl and if he had the slightest notion why he
had been brought to Blackwood Manor, for clearly
he had been placed in a home where he was not
wanted.

The trip to London was long and uncomfortably
silent. Seated across from Adam, Jillian tried to em-
broider but kept missing stitches. Adam pretended
to read, but time and again his turbulent gaze sliced
to hers. She was bone-weary and out of sorts by the
time they arrived at the George and Dragon, a comfortable little inn along the road.

Jillian stiffly declined the earl's invitation to supper and took her meal instead with Maude, Reggie,
and little Christopher Derry.

"Are we truly going to London?" the boy asked
excitedly.

Jillian smiled, thinking what a good-natured child
he was. "Have you never been there?"

"No, but Mum and Da used to live there. Mum
said there's some wondrous sights."

"Aye, lad," Maude agreed. " 'Tis wondrous they
are and no doubt. Perhaps the major will take ya to
Mrs. Salmon's Waxworks in Fleet Street. They got
the death masks there." She made an ugly face in im-
itation, and Christopher howled in delight.

He had the sweetest laugh, Jillian thought, so vi-
brant and compelling for such a little boy. Instantly
the memory of similar laughter rang in her ears. It
was a rare, glorious sound she remembered only too
well.

It belonged to Adam Hawthorne.

Christopher looked up at Maude. "Couldn't you take me, Mrs. Flynn? I don't think 'is lordship likes me."

Reggie cleared his throat. "A course he likes ye, boy. He just never had no children, is all. Once he comes to know ye, he's bound to like ye. Why, yer 'is own flesh and—"

"Why don't we have some dessert?" Jillian interrupted, flashing Reggie a warning glance. Apparently the servants had come to their own conclusions about Christopher Derry's relationship with the earl. "They have plum pudding tonight. I've heard it's very good."

"Oh, yes," the boy said. "I'd love to have plum puddin'."

And so dessert was ordered for everyone but Jillian, whose appetite had waned. She had too much on her mind: the trial, worry for the child who crept deeper and deeper into her heart, the quarrel she'd had with the earl.

Jillian ached to think of it. It wasn't as if she weren't grateful for all he had done. Adam had come to her rescue, fought for her when no one else would. But she didn't want to be his paid-for woman, the very sort she'd been accused of being before.

It didn't matter that she was in love with him. It didn't change the way she felt. She had no money, no life of her own. The only thing she had left in the world was her self-respect. It was precious to her, and she wasn't about to give it up.

Not for Adam Hawthorne or anyone else.

As soon as the meal was finished, the four of

them retired upstairs, Chris in a room with Reggie, Maude on a pallet at the foot of Jillian's bed. It was well past midnight when Jillian finally fell into a troubled sleep.

It was several hours later that she awakened to noises in the room next door. In an instant, she recognized the soft moans and curses, the earl dreaming of the terrible battle in Egypt that he had described. She wanted to go to him, to comfort him with her body, make him forget his awful memories as she had done before.

She knew what would happen if she did.

She was weak where Adam Hawthorne was concerned, and in this she had to be strong. Jillian dragged the pillow over her head to block the cries of Adam's pain-filled slumber.

But she didn't fall asleep until the sounds had faded and the room fell silent once more.

His first day back in London, Adam left the house early, his clash with Jillian brief.

"Take me with you," she demanded.

"Next time," he promised. "Today, I have things to do that are better done alone."

So saying, he climbed aboard his carriage for the trip to Chancery Lane. Thinking of his meeting with Garth Dutton, Adam leaned back against the tufted leather seat, glad to be returned to London where he hoped to move things forward. He only wished Jillian would have heeded his advice and remained in the country.

Adam thought of his clumsy attempt at making her his mistress. Since that night, Jillian had barely spoken to him. Damn, he'd made a mess of things.

He'd been half-foxed that night, immersed in dark memories of Caroline and Robert, angry at the arrival of the boy.

Christopher Derry wasn't his. He'd been careful when he made love to Caroline. Still, accidents happened. His sister, Maggie, was evidence of that, coming late in his parents' marriage when his father and mother had mostly lived apart.

Adam stared out the window of the carriage, his mind on the child and his newly undertaken responsibilities as the little boy's protector. The child was undoubtedly Robert's, and it galled him to have his cousin's bastard foisted off on him. The next time he spoke to Peter Fraser, he would ask the man to employ someone to look into the matter of the child's parentage—another mystery to be solved and unless he was careful, another round of scandal.

Sometimes it seemed as if it were his fate to continually be the focus of wagging tongues.

Not this time, Adam vowed, determined to keep the child's identity a secret. As much as he despised Caroline Harding, he knew she had also suffered at Robert's hand. She was married now, with children of her own, and he would do his best to protect both her son and the woman he once meant to marry.

No matter what he discovered, there was no question of locating Robert Hawthorne. His cousin was an adventurer, off to the Colonies, the last Adam had heard, and not the sort to accept the task of raising a seven-year-old boy. The child, no matter the sins of his father, was a Hawthorne. He deserved better than that.

Outside the window, a row of brick buildings appeared in Adam's line of vision, followed by a sign for Chancery Lane. Time was running out and it was obvious Jillian was as aware of it as he was. She'd grown distant since they'd left the country and much of the fault lay with him.

Adam sighed, angry with himself all over again. Dammit to hell, he had made his proposal sound sordid when he hadn't meant it to be that way at all. He should have explained things better, made Jillian understand that what he was doing was in both their best interests. She wanted him. He knew women well enough to be certain of that. It was only a matter of stating his case in a way that she would accept.

Adam stretched his long legs out in front of him as best he could in the carriage, restless as he thought of her, wanting her with the same fierce hunger he had felt since the first day he had seen her at the duck pond.

Tonight he would talk to her again, make her understand the way he felt. He cared for her. He should have told her that. It was the sort of thing women wanted to hear and though he was always careful to avoid any sort of commitment, in this case he meant the words.

In the meantime, proving her innocence was all-important. The moment the conveyance pulled up in front of Garth Dutton's office, Adam turned the silver doorknob and shoved open the carriage door.

"Blackwood." Garth's deep voice resonated into the reception area of the stately brick building that housed Selhurst and Dutton, Attorneys at Law. "You're right on time. Please come in."

"Thank you." Adam stepped into the lawyer's elegantly furnished private office. A huge cherry wood desk sat in the middle, surrounded by matching book-cases that ran floor-to-ceiling along the walls. Gold letters glittered on the backs of dozens of leather-bound volumes, and the far wall housed a marble-manteled hearth. The office spoke of success, but Garth was also the grandson of the wealthy Baron Schofield, with an impressive fortune of his own.

"Thank you for seeing me on such short notice. I wanted to discuss your progress on Jillian's case."

"Actually, I'm just on my way to see Madeleine Telford. She's been in the country, but she is returned. We've an appointment later this morning."

"I planned to pay her a call today myself."

Garth's thick blond eyebrows pulled together. "As I said before, there's a good possibility you won't be welcome."

"I'll have to take my chances."

"Or we could go together. Perhaps the lady will be more forthcoming if you are in company with me."

Adam nodded. "Good idea."

A few minutes later, they boarded Adam's carriage for the hour drive to Hampstead Heath, where Madeleine Telford, the late earl's widowed daughter-in-law, spent most of her time. If she was surprised to find the Earl of Blackwood accompanying her expected guest, she hid it well, cordially inviting both men into the domed, stained-glass foyer lit by a crystal chandelier.

"It's good to see you, Garth." She allowed him to take her hands and kiss her lightly on the cheek. "And you, as well, my lord, though I admit I'm a bit surprised—considering the reason for this visit and where you have placed your loyalties."

Madeleine was petite and attractive, with dark brown hair and brown eyes. She wore a fashionable high-waisted gown of pale blue silk and an expensive string of small, perfect pearls that seemed to match the pearly whiteness of her teeth. At five and twenty, she remained childless, her figure lush, her breasts full and high.

Adam bowed over her hand. "I assure you, madam, my first loyalty is to your former father-in-law, the late Lord Fenwick. No man deserves to be murdered in cold blood. Our only difference of opinion lies in the matter of whom we deem guilty of the crime."

Her smile held a faintly sharp edge. "I suppose that is fair enough."

Adam had become acquainted with Madeleine Telford before her marriage to Henry, Lord Fenwick's only son. Though Adam had found her attractive, she had been an innocent and well out of his reach. Now, as he recognized the intimate glances Madeleine cast at Garth, it was apparent that they were also well-acquainted.

"The drawing room is this way. Gentlemen, if you will please follow me." The salon she led them into looked newly refurbished, the gold-flocked wallpaper glittering as if it had recently been hung, the brocade sofas spotless, the cushions so stiff it appeared few visitors had yet sat on them.

It seemed Madeleine Telford had already begun to make use of the money the late earl had left her. Adam wondered how she would have taken the news that the old man had changed his will and Jillian was to inherit most of his money.

"I've already rung for tea," Madeleine said. "It

should be here any moment. In the meantime, why don't we sit down?"

They did so and moments later the tea cart rolled into the room. As Madeleine poured the steaming brew into gold-rimmed porcelain cups, Adam forced himself to relax. The last thing he wanted was to put the woman on guard before his questions had even been asked.

"Your note said you wished to speak to me about the late earl," Madeleine said to Garth as she set the teapot back down on the cart. "What is it you wished to know?"

Adam let Garth answer, keeping his attention on Madeleine's face.

"As you're undoubtedly aware, I represent Miss Whitney. Neither Lord Blackwood nor myself are convinced the lady is guilty of murdering the earl."

"But surely . . . I mean, nearly everyone who works at Fenwick House believes it was she. The butler saw her standing over my father-in-law's body."

"Miss Whitney doesn't deny she was in the room," Adam said, briefly explaining Jillian's side of the story.

"What was your relationship with Miss Whitney?" Garth asked when he had finished.

Madeleine sipped her tea. "We barely knew each other. In the beginning, when she first arrived at the house, I thought she would be good for the earl. He was terribly distraught after Henry's death. I thought she might help him recover. I actually hoped we might become friends. Then rumors began to circulate about her. My father-in-law denied them, of course. He was furious, in fact, when I asked him outright if he was having an affair with her. But men will be men and Miss Whitney is a very attractive young woman. I didn't really know what to believe, so I simply distanced myself."

"But you continued to visit the earl," Adam pressed.

"On occasion. My father-in-law was always very good to me. I was worried about his welfare."

"Did he tell you he meant to alter his will?"

"What?" She sat forward on the sofa, rustling her long silk skirt.

"Lord Fenwick had instructed his solicitor, Benjamin Morrison, to draw a new set of documents leaving the majority of his estate to Miss Whitney. He was killed before the papers could be signed."

"Oh, dear." Madeleine's teacup rattled against its saucer. "I never knew about the will. But I suspect, now that you've told me, that it must have been true about the earl and Miss Whitney. Why else would he have wished to make such a change?"

Why indeed? Whatever the reason, it wasn't because Jillian had seduced him into leaving the money to her, at least not with her lovely little body. Adam knew that firsthand. It was difficult to control an urge to say so, but if he did, it would only do more damage to her already tattered reputation.

Adam set his untouched cup of tea down on the table in front of her. "When was the last time you saw the earl?"

"On Wednesday, two days prior to the murder. I knew he had been feeling somewhat poorly. I wanted to be sure that he was all right."

"Did you see Miss Whitney that night?"

"Only briefly. She was cordial, as I recall, but she

didn't join us. I suppose she knew I was uncomfortable, being in the room with my father-in-law's mistress."

Adam's jaw clenched. "You would be wise not to make those kinds of presumptions, Mrs. Telford." He could hear the edge in his voice, but he no longer cared. "Not without some sort of proof."

She mustered a slightly embarrassed smile. "You're right, of course. I apologize. And of course, I do hope that all of us are wrong about who murdered poor dear Lord Fenwick, as well as the other accusations against Miss Whitney. It's obvious my father-in-law thought a great deal of her, whatever their relationship. If she is innocent, for his sake, I hope you are able to prove it."

Somewhat mollified, Adam waited while Garth asked a few more questions.

"One last thing," Adam said as the interview came to a close and both men rose to their feet. "On the night of the murder, can you tell us where you were?"

"Why, here, of course." She came up from the sofa with a rustle of silk, looking slightly affronted. "I had a headache that night and retired early to my room. I didn't come down until late the following morning. That is when I heard the dreadful news."

"Thank you, Mrs. Telford," Adam said. "That's all we need for the present."

Garth made a very proper bow over her hand. Adam didn't miss the look Madeleine gave him. "You've been extremely cooperative, my dear. Thank you for being so forthcoming."

Madeleine accompanied them to the door, then waited as the men took their leave. A few minutes later, they were back inside the carriage, bowling down the road back to the city.

Garth seemed exceptionally quiet. Adam thought he knew why. "Under different circumstances, I wouldn't bring this up, but unless I'm mistaken, you and Mrs. Telford are more than simply friends."

Seated on the opposite side of the carriage, Garth sighed. "I was afraid you'd pick up on that." He stared out the window at the passing landscape, the rolling green fields, the pony cart at the side of the road guided by a wrinkled old man in a threadbare tailcoat.

"It happened after Henry's suicide. A brief affair that lasted only a couple of weeks. Perhaps she was reacting to her husband's death, I don't know. We never really talked about it. The affair might have continued a little while longer, but Madeleine was extremely nervous that someone might find out, and for me, the feelings just weren't there. We parted friends and that is all we have been since. Until today, it never occurred to me that my brief association with Madeleine Telford might be a breach of ethics. If you wish to seek other counsel, I will certainly understand."

Adam studied the barrister for several long seconds, then shook his head. "I don't think bedding a desirable woman constitutes a breach of ethics. I trust this won't interfere with your judgment and you'll do your job to the best of your abilities."

Garth looked relieved. "You may count on it. I don't believe your lady is guilty of murder. And if her case goes to trial, I'll do everything in my power to see that she is found innocent of the crime."

Your lady. It was the second time Jillian had been

referred to as belonging to him. It wasn't true, especially not lately, and yet some part of him thought of her that way. "Thank you. That is all anyone can ask."

Adam said nothing more as the carriage rolled along, but his mind churned with worry. It was looking more certain every day that Jillian would be brought to trial for murder. If that happened, even with a brilliant barrister like Garth Dutton representing her, the evidence against her was daunting.

A memory returned of Sergeant Gordon Rimfield in his spotless red-and-white uniform, a hangman's noose around his neck, his big body swinging from the gallows in the icy morning breeze. The thought of Jillian marching up those same gallows stairs made his stomach roll with nausea.

It isn't going to happen, he vowed.

If all else failed, he would do the unthinkable—break his word to the authorities and ship her off somewhere safe. It was the first time he had given the notion serious consideration, but the more he mulled it over, the more he realized he was willing to do exactly that. It didn't matter that his reputation as a gentleman would be forever ruined.

He wasn't about to stand by and watch another innocent person hang.

17

~∞~

Are you insane? I won't run away!" Jillian stood in front of the hearth in Adam's study, her hands biting into her waist. It was late. Adam had been gone all day and she had been worried. Now he was home, and she couldn't miss the troubled look on his face.

"I'm sure it won't come to that. I just wanted you to know that if matters got worse—"

"You're telling me I'm going to have to stand trial."

"We don't know that for certain, but it's beginning to look like a definite possibility."

Her eyes closed for a heartbeat. "I'm going to have to stand trial and if I do I'll be convicted." She had prayed so hard it wouldn't come to this. Deep inside, she had never believed it would.

Adam took a step toward her. "That isn't going to happen—that's what I'm trying to tell you. You won't be convicted because you won't be in the country. You'll be on a ship, headed someplace they won't find you."

Jillian shook her head, dread sinking into her stomach. "I can't do that."

"Why not?"

She swallowed past the lump in her throat. "Because for months I've been accused of doing things I didn't do. When they said I was Lord Fenwick's mistress, I never tried to defend myself. I knew it wouldn't do any good and there was the earl to consider. Now I'm accused of murder. I'm innocent of that as well, but this time I'm not going to stand by and do nothing. I'm going to face my accusers. I'm going to tell them what happened the night the earl was killed and convince them I am not the one who shot him."

"What if they don't believe you?"

She studied the toes of her pale green kid slippers and remembered the day Lord Fenwick had helped her pick out the pretty muslin gown they matched. "In my heart, I believe they'll know I'm telling the truth and they will realize I am innocent of the crime."

"Jillian . . ."

"If they find me guilty, so be it. I would rather be dead than to steal away like a criminal in the night, to live the rest of my life with the whole world believing I'm a murderer."

Adam opened his mouth to argue. Jillian held up a trembling hand. "Please, don't say any more. I shall always be indebted to you for the things you have done, but nothing you can say is going to change my mind."

Adam closed the short distance between them and pulled her into his arms. "It's all right," he said beside her ear. "If you're that certain, we will simply have to find out who killed Lord Fenwick." And very gently he kissed her.

It was a brief, almost chaste sort of kiss she hadn't expected. "I'm sorry about the way I acted the other night," he said. "I drank too much, though that is certainly no excuse. Mostly, it was the arrival of the boy."

She gave him an uncertain glance, wishing she could block the distasteful memory of the night he had offered to become her protector. "I understand. I can imagine what a shock Christopher's appearance must have been."

He tipped her chin up. "I never meant to insult you. I care for you, Jillian. I only wanted what was best for us both."

She nodded, still uncomfortable with the topic.

Adam drew a little away. "The hour grows late and the day has been a difficult one. Perhaps you should get some sleep."

She knew that was exactly what she should do, that she should stay as far away from him as she possibly could. But as she looked up at him, as she saw the hunger in his eyes and remembered the heat of his hard body moving over hers, she wanted nothing so much as for him to make love to her, erase for a while the troubles that weighed her down.

Fortunately, her moment of weakness was ended by a firm knock at the door.

With a reluctant sigh, Adam walked over and pulled it open, then stepped back as the Duke and Duchess of Rathmore came rushing into the drawing room.

Rathmore was grinning, his little red-haired wife beaming with excitement. "Good news," Rathmore said. "They just arrested Colin Norton. He's been charged with suspicion of murder."

Adam flashed Jillian one of his rare bright smiles and Jillian's legs went weak with relief.

"Thank God," she said.

Adam gripped Clay's shoulder, then bent and kissed Kassandra Barclay's cheek. Catching Jillian's hand, he drew her into his arms and gave her a reassuring hug.

"Thank you for letting us know," he said to his friends. "How did you happen to find out?"

Clay chuckled, a rumble in his thick chest. "It's amazing what a bit of coin here and there will do. One of the jailers at Newgate was on duty when they brought Norton in. He saw the arrest papers and as soon as he got off duty, he came to me."

Adam's smile reappeared. "This calls for a celebration." He walked to the door and called for the butler, who on slightly bowed legs hurried toward him down the hall. "Champagne, Reggie. Our lady is about to be cleared of Lord Fenwick's murder."

"I say, Major, that is good news."

Adam turned back to the duke. "Are they certain they've the right person this time?"

"All I know is that someone came forward who heard Norton making threats against the earl and apparently he doesn't have an alibi for his whereabouts that night."

Adam turned to Jillian. "With Norton arrested and the support of the duke and duchess added to mine, it should be enough to clear your name."

Relief washed over her so strongly tears sprang into her eyes.

Adam eased her back into his arms. "It's all right,

love, the worst is over. Everything is going to be fine."

She nodded, dragged in a shaky breath of air. She accepted the initialed white handkerchief the duke handed over. "I'm sorry. I didn't mean to do that. It's just such a relief."

"Don't be silly." The duchess reached over and squeezed her hand. "You have every right to cry. You've been through a terrible ordeal. But all of that is behind you now. You can start to think of the future."

Kitt Barclay looked beautiful tonight, her fiery hair swept up in curls, her pretty green eyes flashing. She was gowned in emerald silk, obviously dressed for an evening out, and the duke looked magnificent in a russet tailcoat over a waistcoat of ivory and gold.

Jillian flashed a smile. "Thank you so much. You've both been incredibly kind. And Adam . . . Lord Blackwood has been wonderful."

The champagne arrived and they all toasted Jillian's innocence and the man—whoever he might be—who had apprehended Colin Norton.

"We know what you've been through since Lord Fenwick was killed," the duchess said to Jillian. "We thought that perhaps you might like to stay with us for a while . . . until you can decide what to do about your future."

"Thank you, that's very—"

"That's a very generous offer," Adam cut in before she could accept. "But it won't be necessary." The duchess took one look at the determined expression on his face and any argument she might have made stayed locked behind her lips.

"I believe what Adam is saying is that he intends to see to your welfare," the duke said diplomatically, casting a look at his friend. "As you already know, you're in very good hands, but if there's anything you need, we'll be happy to help in any way we can."

She managed to smile. She didn't like Adam's interference, but she owed him a very great deal. He had saved her life. She would respect his wishes in this—at least for a while.

"As Lord Blackwood said, your offer is extremely kind. I'm indebted to you both for your help and support and honored by your friendship."

The duke and duchess seemed pleased. They departed the house soon after, and the moment they were gone, Adam turned to face her.

"I know this isn't the time. You're obviously exhausted. But tomorrow, we need to talk."

Jillian nodded, though she wasn't looking forward to the conversation. She knew what the Earl of Blackwood wished to discuss. He might have apologized for his behavior, but he hadn't changed his mind. And in that regard, neither had she.

She refused to become his mistress, and no matter what the future might hold, she wasn't going to sell her soul to the devil. Even if this particular devil was handsome as sin and she was in love with him.

Though Rathmore's news had lifted a terrible weight from her shoulders, Jillian thought of Lord Blackwood and the battle he intended to wage and wearily trudged up the stairs.

*   *   *

Adam had departed on business. Jillian was in the breakfast room when Maggie Hawthorne arrived at the town house early the following morning. The *Times* contained the story of Lord Fenwick's murder and the arrest of his ex-solicitor, including the fact Colin Norton had been caught embezzling money from Lord Fenwick's accounts. Though the authorities hadn't officially ruled out Jillian as a suspect, it appeared likely they would do so very soon.

"It is simply wonderful news," Maggie said, taking a seat in a yellow damask chair across from her. A footman hurried to bring her a plate of teacakes and fill a silver-rimmed cup with hot cocoa. "I'm terribly happy for you, Jillian."

Though the hour was early, Maggie wore a fashionable high-waisted plum silk gown that complemented her flawless complexion and the braided black coronet of her hair. She was young and incredibly lovely, and Jillian prayed the scandal that had blackened her family name wouldn't destroy her future.

"Norton's arrest is a dreadful weight off my shoulders," Jillian told her, "though I am somewhat up in the air as to what I am going to do now that this is behind me."

"Yes, I imagine you are. I hadn't really given it much thought, but I don't believe my brother will abandon you. It simply isn't his nature."

"Actually, I was hoping that perhaps you could speak to him in my behalf. I'm going to need a means of supporting myself. Do you think you could convince your brother to help me find a suitable position?"

Maggie's sleek black eyebrow arched. "A suitable position? You mean you intend to seek employment?"

"After my father died, I tutored some of the children in the village. I thought perhaps I might find work as a governess."

"I've always supposed I would marry. I can't imagine what it might be like to control one's own destiny as you intend to do, but I believe in some ways I would like it. And I'm sure my brother would be happy to help. Why don't you simply ask him?"

"I have. He won't even consider it."

Maggie set her cup of cocoa back down in its saucer. "For heaven's sake, why not?"

Jillian looked down, saw that the hand on the napkin in her lap was fisted so tightly the skin was bleached white.

Maggie reached over and touched her arm. "You mustn't worry, Jillian. It's obvious my brother cares for you a very great deal. Surely he has something in mind—" She broke off at the pallor on Jillian's face. "Oh, my God."

Reading Maggie's too-perceptive thoughts, Jillian swallowed. "It isn't . . . isn't as bad as all that. I mean . . . your brother isn't . . . he isn't . . . it isn't as though I'm still . . ." She broke off, groping for a better choice of words.

"I think I know what you are trying very hard *not* to say. The two of you have already been lovers. That is it—isn't it?"

Jillian didn't answer.

"Adam said you were not Lord Fenwick's mistress, merely his ward. He knows that for a fact, doesn't he?"

Jillian looked away. "Yes." She couldn't believe she was having this conversation with the innocent young woman who was the earl's sister. "We shouldn't be talking about this. It's highly improper and I'm sure your brother would greatly disapprove."

"Oh, fiddle-faddle. My brother can go hang. He refuses to realize that I'm a grown woman and not nearly as naïve as he would like to believe." She sighed. "I should have expected this. Do you love him?"

As much as she might wish it weren't true, there was no reason to lie. "Yes."

"Oh, dear, I was afraid of that. He won't offer marriage, you know. That is the reason he has offered to act as your protector."

"I know the way he feels. He has never lied about his intentions. And even if he did wish to wed, I am hardly the sort of woman an earl would choose."

Maggie got up from her chair and began to move restlessly around the room. Pausing near a Hepplewhite table along the wall, she picked up a small Egyptian terra-cotta jar. "Adam says you're practically an expert on this stuff."

Jillian smiled. She walked over to where Maggie stood next to the table. "My father was the expert."

"Do you know how old this is?" Maggie held out the jar for Jillian's inspection.

"From the geometric patterns, I'd say it's Late Predynastic, somewhere around thirtieth century B.C. But the study of Egyptian history is only in its earliest stages and at this point much of it is guesswork."

"Adam has been collecting Egyptian antiquities ever since he traveled to Egypt with the army. My mother bought this for him from a dealer in the Strand." Maggie set the jar on the table.

She studied Jillian, her thoughts shifting again. "It's all Caroline's fault, you know. If it hadn't been for Caroline Harding, Adam wouldn't feel the way he does about women."

Jillian focused her attention on the jar, nervously adjusting it to its original position on the table. "Do you think he is still in love with her?"

Maggie released an unladylike snort. "Hardly. I'm not sure he ever really was. But I was young then, so I can't know for certain. I told you once my brother has never been lucky when it comes to women. Perhaps I should tell you about Maria Barrett."

Jillian's pulse accelerated. She remembered the night Maude had mentioned Adam's involvement with the woman. "Would you? I've heard whispers. I should like to hear the story very much."

"My brother won't like it, but sooner or later, you'll probably hear the whole of it anyway. The gossip was terrible when he first left the army. At least what I tell you will be the truth."

The two of them returned to the table and Maggie briefly relayed the tale of Colonel Barrett's beautiful, exotic, half-English, half-Spanish wife.

"She and Adam met when my brother was on the Continent, perhaps six months before he sold his commission and left the army for good. One of Adam's fellow officers, a friend of his named Anthony St. Regis, told me the story. He said it was better I knew the truth, and he didn't think Adam would tell me."

Jillian's heart thudded uncomfortably. "What did St. Regis say?"

"That Maria Barrett was nearly irresistible where men were concerned. Half the soldiers in the regiment fell in love with her the moment they saw her. She could have had any one of them, but it was Adam she wanted. Perhaps because, according to St. Regis, my brother was determined not to get involved with a fellow officer's wife."

Jillian almost smiled. "That sounds like Adam. He can be very gallant at times."

"Maria became obsessed with seducing him and apparently in the end, she succeeded. Adam was half in love with her by then, and according to St. Regis, she had convinced him that if he asked her, she would leave her husband and marry him."

"What happened?"

"St. Regis claims Maria never had the slightest intention of divorcing Colonel Barrett. He had money and social position far beyond what my brother had at the time. One night the colonel caught them in bed together. Maria claimed Adam had forced his way in and tried to rape her. The colonel called him out. They dueled with sabers, but Adam barely defended himself. That is where he got the scar along his jaw. I think he sees it as a reminder that he should never trust a woman—at least not completely. And that is the reason he has vowed never to wed."

The lump that had risen in Jillian's throat grew more painful as she thought of another betrayal Adam had suffered. "Thank you for telling me."

Maggie reached over and clasped her hand. "I know this may sound terrible, but perhaps you should consider my brother's offer. Even if things didn't work out, Adam would see you were well taken care of."

Jillian tried to smile. "I'm sure he would." But she still couldn't agree. She simply couldn't live with herself.

"I'd better be going." Maggie came to her feet, bent and kissed Jillian's cheek. "I know at times he can be difficult. He's stubborn and occasionally hot tempered, and far too used to being in command. But—"

"But he's a very good man," Jillian finished. It was the reason she had fallen so deeply in love with him.

She had to get out of his house, had to get away from the Earl of Blackwood before he convinced her to do something she would regret for the rest of her days.

Jillian walked Maggie into the foyer, her mind on the earl and her uncertain future. Reggie draped Maggie's quilted pelisse around her shoulders and Maggie bid her farewell. Unfortunately, that was the very moment little Christopher Derry came thundering down the stairs.

"I didn't realize Adam had company," Maggie said in surprise, gazing at the boy who had spotted them before he reached the bottom of the stairs and now looked as though he wanted to turn and run back up.

It was hardly the occasion Jillian would have chosen to introduce the child, but there was no help for it now.

"Do come down and join us, Chris." He did so shyly, staring up at Maggie with a mixture of interest and reluctance.

"Maggie, this is Christopher Derry. Christopher, this is Lady Margaret Hawthorne, Lord Blackwood's sister. You may address her as my lady."

Christopher attempted a shaky bow that made both women smile. He no longer wore the thread-bare garments he had arrived in but was dressed today in the fashionable clothes the earl had provided: tailored brown corduroy breeches, a white lawn shirt, and a darker brown tailcoat that set off his green eyes and wavy dark brown hair.

Jillian glanced from the boy to Maggie, who was studying him with far too much interest. Jillian didn't know exactly what to tell her and the silence began to lengthen.

"And Christopher is . . . a friend of the earl's?" Maggie prompted, urging her to say something more.

"Yes . . . yes, he is."

Maggie knelt beside the boy. "Are you here all by yourself, Christopher?" He nodded. "You're a very handsome boy. How old are you?"

"I'm gonna be eight next week. That's what Vicar Donnellson said."

"I see." And from the assessing look on Maggie's face, it appeared that she very well might.

Jillian took the boy's slim hand. "I think Cook has been baking sugar cookies this morning. Why don't you go and see?"

His solemn expression brightened, he smiled and raced off toward the kitchen. Jillian thought she recognized that smile. By the wide-eyed look on Maggie's face, apparently so did she.

"That little boy isn't . . . he isn't who I think he is . . . is he?"

Jillian sighed. "He might be. The vicar Christopher mentioned brought the child to Blackwood Manor. Adam thinks the boy is his cousin's illegitimate son."

Maggie stared down the hall toward the kitchen. "He does have Robert's brown hair, but he looks more like . . ." Maggie shook her head, unwilling to voice what each of them was thinking.

"Adam is determined to keep this quiet," Jillian warned. "He doesn't want any more scandal."

"Believe me, I couldn't agree with him more." As Maggie made her way out the front door and down the steps to her waiting carriage, Jillian thought of Adam, understanding him now in a way she hadn't before. It made her love him all the more—made him an even bigger danger.

Jillian shivered as she walked back into the house.

18

Garth Dutton surveyed the crowd in the Duke of Chester's lavish ballroom, his gaze skimming over the Season's crop of eligible young ladies available in the marriage mart. All evening he had been dodging hopeful mothers and their cloying offspring. Modesty aside, he knew he was considered a very good catch.

Garth lifted a glass of champagne off a passing silver tray and took a drink. A year ago, he would have refused to attend this sort of affair. He wasn't in the market for a wife—he didn't have time for one. But lately he'd grown restless, bored somehow with his bachelor existence. On top of that, six months ago, his uncle Frederick had died, leaving him in line for the Schofield barony, and his grandfather had been prodding him to marry.

They expected him to choose a woman without peer, a lady of flawless background and exceptional breeding. Though his grandfather was only a baron, the title had been passed down for hundreds of years. Garth's mother never failed to remind him that the Schofield title was one of the most respected in England.

Garth wondered what Eleanor Dutton would say if she knew the only woman who interested him was immersed in scandal up to her pretty little ears. Margaret Hawthorne's brother might be an earl, but in the past few years, he had managed to blacken the family name with one intrigue after another, and the latest—Blackwood's involvement with a woman believed to have been old Fenwick's mistress, a woman accused of murder—still titillated wagging tongues.

Knowing he shouldn't, that even considering such a match would raise the eyebrows of every Dutton in England and might well get him disinherited, Garth scanned the dance floor in search of her. He knew she was there. He had seen her earlier in company with her aunt, Lady Sophia Hawthorne, surrounded by her usual crush of simpering admirers.

He spotted her beneath a crystal chandelier on the far edge of the dance floor, laughing and flirting, sparkling more than the shimmering lights above her head, one of the most sought after young women in the room, though her family name was far from sterling. At first glance, Maggie appeared to be having a very good time, and yet he wondered . . .

His gaze met hers a little too boldly. He let her know he watched her, let her see a little of the heat she stirred inside him every time he saw her. Faint color crept into her cheeks, replacing an expression of insouciance, and inwardly he smiled, satisfied that he could unsettle her a little, as she very definitely unsettled him.

Garth started walking toward her.

Maggie tried to ignore the tall, remarkably handsome blond man who strode toward her. But there was something about Garth Dutton that refused to be ignored. The men who crowded around her parted like stalks of wheat in the wind, allowing him to enter their circle.

"Lady Margaret . . ." He made a very formal bow over her hand, his green eyes glinting with challenge. "I believe this is our dance."

It wasn't, of course. He knew it as well as she. She could embarrass him and refuse. Or she could ignore Randall Wiggs, the overblown dandy strolling over to claim her, and do what she really wished to do.

Why not? She flashed Garth Dutton an equally challenging smile and accepted the arm he offered. "Yes, I believe it is." He covered her gloved hand where it rested on his sleeve and led her straight past Randall Wiggs, who sputtered with indignation and pointed toward her dance card. Garth flashed him a look meant to cool his ardor and simply kept on walking.

"I would have preferred a waltz," Garth said, once they reached the floor, "but you hardly need any more raised eyebrows than you are getting already."

The reminder of the whispers drifting her way all evening did nothing to lighten Maggie's mood.

Her chin inched up. "If you're so concerned with your reputation, perhaps you'd be better off dancing with someone else."

Garth's mouth faintly curved. "That isn't possible. You see, I don't want to dance with anyone else."

Why that pleased her so inordinately Maggie couldn't say. Smiling, she gave Garth Dutton her hand and let him guide her in the first steps of the dance. He was graceful for a man his size and she thought that he was actually enjoying the rhythm and steps of the dance, making it more fun for her. As the music came to an end, he leaned toward her.

"It's warm in here. Perhaps you'd enjoy a breath of air."

She cast him a conspiratorial glance. "Yes, perhaps I would." They slipped out the door leading onto the terrace. Maggie gasped in surprise as he drew her into the shadows and straight into his arms.

"What do you think you're doing?"

"Nothing yet. It's what I'm going to do that you should be worrying about." Then he bent his head and kissed her.

Maggie's whole body tensed. She knew she should struggle. It was the ladylike, the proper thing to do, and just for an instant she did. Then the hands that shoved against his chest slid up around his neck and she started kissing him back.

Garth groaned and deepened the kiss, turning it hot and wild. The taste of him, the feel of his mouth and tongue, was sensuous and drugging. It was a kiss that turned her legs to jelly and her stomach to butter. The sort of kiss she had always dreamed of, and she didn't want it to end.

Maggie felt a shudder move through him just before he pulled away.

"I was afraid of that," he said, his hands still settled around her waist. In the light of the torches, eyes the color of emeralds gleamed with a hunger he didn't try to hide.

"Afraid of what?" she asked, hoping he wouldn't notice that she trembled.

"That once I tasted you, I would have to have you."

She stepped away from him then, frightened for the first time. "I-I have to go in."

"Yes, you do. It wouldn't do either of us any good to be discovered out here in the dark together."

And especially bad for her. Rumor and innuendo had swirled around her family ever since Adam's broken betrothal to Caroline Harding. Robert Hawthorne's name had also been dragged through the mud. Then came Maria Barrett and her unfounded accusations against Adam's character. Now her brother's involvement with Jillian Whitney blackened the family name once more.

Maggie had never really cared. But now she had met Garth Dutton, whose family sat at the opposite end of the spectrum, one of the oldest and most respected in England.

Which made the two of them a highly unsuitable match.

As she walked back into the ballroom, Maggie felt an unexpected rush of despair. It was ridiculous, she told herself. Why should she care what Garth Dutton's family thought of her? If she wanted a suitor, she could choose from a dozen different men.

Still, as she passed among the crush of people in the ballroom, her gaze wandered back to the attractive blond man whose head appeared in the doorway leading in from the terrace.

Maggie forced a too-bright smile and stepped back into her own personal circle of men.

The following day, seated at a cozy corner table in an intimate café in the Strand called À La Mode, Jillian was forced to listen to Adam's unwanted offer again. It was the first time in weeks that she had been out in a social situation, but with the news of Colin Norton's arrest, Adam felt it was safe.

"You know why I brought you here?" he said, reaching across the white linen tablecloth to clasp her hand. "It's time to think of the future. Let me take care of you."

Jillian stiffened. Insanely, she had hoped that perhaps he had brought her here to tell her that he understood her feelings and that he was willing to help her find the employment she so desperately needed.

"You know the way I feel. If you're truly concerned with my welfare, you'll help me find a way to support myself. Surely for a man with your connections that wouldn't be too difficult a task."

"It isn't a matter of how difficult it is. It's simply a matter of doing what is best."

The argument had escalated. In the end, they wound up leaving the restaurant before the meal was finished, both of their tempers heated. It was obvious the earl believed becoming her protector was the answer to her troubles. Jillian vastly disagreed. They returned to the town house, both of them angry, Jillian telling him she intended to accept the money his sister had offered to lend her and find a place of her own. Perhaps the Duke of Rathmore would help her find a position, she said.

Adam was furious, angry with his sister for offering to give her the money and with the duke and duchess for the unspeakable crime of offering their aid.

Supper was a strained affair. Adam's mood was dark and surly. He drank several glasses of wine then turned to brandy. When Jillian tried to retire upstairs, he commanded that she join him in the drawing room. She thought of pleading a headache, but she could see he wouldn't tolerate any excuse.

Back rigid, she followed him down the hall and walked past him into an intimate salon at the rear of the town house. The blue velvet draperies were drawn, the brass lamps turned low, and a small fire burned in the hearth. Adam closed the door and turned to face her, his arms crossed over his chest. Even in a temper, his face all sharp angles and dark, angry lines, he was so handsome her heart felt as if it might stop beating.

He crossed the room to the fire, began to pace back and forth in front of it, the muscles in his shoulders bunching beneath his dove-gray tailcoat when he turned. He paused for a moment, splaying his long legs, clasping his hands behind his back. Midnight eyes locked on her face, pinning her where she stood near the arm of the sofa.

Something shifted in his features and they seemed to harden with determination. His gaze remained on her face as he unbuttoned his coat and tossed it over a chair, removed his waistcoat, unwound his neckcloth and tossed it away, then stared striding toward her. If she hadn't known him so well, she might have been afraid.

As it was, the dangerous look he wore simply

made him more attractive. Jillian stiffened as he caught her shoulders, dragged her into his arms, and very thoroughly kissed her. She tried to pull away, determined to resist, but his mouth warmed hers with a sullen, angry heat and her pulse began pounding in her ears.

She turned her face away. "I won't let you do this."

Adam nibbled the corners of her mouth. "Won't you?"

"No, I—" He cut off her protest with a ravenous kiss and desire flooded into her core. She knew what he was doing, knew that he was using his body to seduce her to his will, and yet she felt powerless to stop him. She wanted him to touch her, make love to her, wanted the hot, demanding kisses that turned her body to liquid fire.

"I've tried to be patient," he said softly, kissing the side of her neck. "I've talked till I'm out of breath and still I can't make you see. I've had enough of talking. I think it's time I showed you what I can give you—what I can make you feel." Another hard, plundering kiss followed that made her knees feel weak.

When his tongue found its way into her mouth, heat enveloped her, fogging her brain until she felt dizzy. Her skin tingled and her stomach quivered.

Adam kissed her as if he couldn't get enough, taking her deeply with his tongue, capturing her face between his hands, kissing her first one way and then another. She felt his hands unbuttoning the back of her rose silk gown, shoving the small puffed sleeves off her shoulders, along with the straps of her chemise. The soft silk and fine lawn slid into a puddle at her feet, leaving her in garters and stockings and dainty rose kid slippers.

Hot need tightened in her belly. Fire seemed to bubble in her blood. "No," she said weakly, more of a plea than a protest.

Adam cupped her bare breast, caressed it, molded it in his hand. "You told me once that you gave yourself to me because you wanted to know what it was like to make love." He gently pinched her nipple, making it swell and distend. "I've only begun to show you. Tonight, I'm going to teach you more." He was completely clothed and fully erect. Somehow being naked in front of him aroused her like nothing else before.

"Teach me," she whispered, the words coming out against her will. Dear God, she knew she should stop him but she wanted this, wanted him to be the man to show her. With every touch, every caress, he was bending her more and more to his will, but Jillian no longer cared.

He kissed her again, even more deeply, cupping her breasts, his elegant, skillful hands sending little shivers of heat over her skin. His mouth moved along her neck and down to her breasts. He sucked her nipple between his teeth, bit down on the hardened tip, and flames leapt into her stomach.

Jillian whimpered. She felt his fingers smoothing over her stomach, burning a path to the place between her legs. He stroked her there even as he kissed her again, and Jillian whispered his name.

"Turn around," he said softly, his voice so deep and rough it sounded like a growl.

"Wh-what?" She wasn't sure she heard him correctly with her heart thundering so madly in her ears.

"You want to learn. Let me show you." His hands circled her waist and he turned her toward the arm of the sofa. She could feel his hardness pressing against her bottom as he bit the lobe of her ear, the back of her neck, then gently bent her over. "Part your legs for me."

She complied with his rough demand, opening for him, wanting the pleasure to continue. She felt greedy with need, hot and wet and on fire.

His hands smoothed over her bottom. He stroked between her legs and she knew he had discovered how moist and hot she was, how badly her body craved him. He made a sound of satisfaction in his throat, she heard the whisper of fabric as he unbuttoned the front of his breeches, then he found her softness again. Guiding himself into her passage, he caught her hips and thrust himself deeply inside. Pleasure tore through her, sweet and dark and forbidden. Jillian moaned as he started to move.

"I can give you pleasure, sweeting, unlike anything you've dreamed." He wasn't gentle, he gripped her hips to hold her in place, then thrust deeply inside.

He wasn't gentle and she realized, as her hips arched toward his, that gentle wasn't what she wanted. She bit down on her lip as Adam thrust into her again and again, heightening the pleasure until her knees threatened to give way beneath her.

As if he sensed her weakness, his hold tightened, steadying her and keeping her in place to receive him. She felt the heavy thrust and drag, felt the fullness of his arousal against the walls of her womb, and her body began to tighten. Her stomach coiled and contracted, and a wave of deep, saturating pleasure washed over her.

Her release struck hard, making her moan and tremble, but Adam didn't stop, just held her immobile and drove into her until a second climax shook her.

He had said he could give her pleasure. Dear God, the man defined the meaning of the word. Seconds later, his hard body tensed. Adam shuddered as he reached his own release and his rigid muscles slowly began to relax.

Time drifted. Adam eased her backward until she rested against his chest and his arms tightened around her. She didn't know how long they stood that way, Adam's presence surrounding her completely. A reluctant sigh seeped out when he finally pulled away.

A little embarrassed at the ease with which he'd aroused her, she retrieved her chemise and gown, holding the garments up over her breasts.

She expected to see smug satisfaction on his face. He had proven her need of him in the most elemental manner. He would be certain now that she would accept his proposal. Instead, when she looked at him, the dark centers of his eyes held a glimpse of desperation.

"You want me," he said softly. "Even now—after what we've just done—I can see it in your face." He reached for her, drew her toward him. "I can teach you more, give so much pleasure. Say you'll let me take care of you."

It was true—she *did* still want him. Just thinking of the wild rush of joy she had experienced had her trembling with need again. Yet the lure of sex was easy to refuse. It was one thing to make love to him, another matter entirely to become his kept woman.

She could resist her desire for him.

It was his eyes that she couldn't resist.

So dark, so turbulent. Intense blue eyes that had seen more suffering than any man should have to endure. They moved over her face and there was a yearning in them so powerful it seemed to touch her soul.

Dear God, she had never witnessed such need in another human being, and she realized in that moment that it wasn't merely her body that Adam wanted. He needed a woman to love him. He had enjoyed dozens of women, but none had ever truly loved him.

He needed her, and it was that need that cried out to her, destroying her resolve as if it had never existed.

"Say yes, my love . . . please. I promise you won't be sorry."

She reached up and cupped his cheek, felt the faint dark shadow of his late-evening beard and the thin line of his scar. She nodded and tears began to spill down her cheeks. She wanted to tell him that she loved him, for just as she had recognized his need, she had also recognized her own.

Adam Hawthorne had changed her, awakened something inside her. He had made her a different woman, and yet she felt more her true self than she ever had before.

And she didn't merely love him. She was wildly, passionately, madly in love with him, and she knew in her heart she would never love like this again.

"Please don't cry," he said, brushing the tears from her cheeks. "I'll make you happy. I promise you. You won't have to worry about anything."

She tried to smile, feebly managed. He didn't understand what she was feeling. How could he? He didn't realize what she had conceded, what part of herself she had agreed to give up.

She would never be his wife, never know which day he might tire of her.

He had no idea how terrified she really was.

Christopher Derry strolled through the garden early the following morning. The irises were blooming, and the daffodils. He loved daffodils. Loved just saying the word. Daf-fo-dil. It had a silly sound that made him laugh just to hear it. He leaned toward one, saw a butterfly of the same bright yellow hue land on one of the petals.

Chris stuck out a finger and the butterfly hopped up on the end of it. He watched the perfect wings descend, once, twice, then it lifted off and floated up among the trees.

Chris envied the butterfly. He wished he could lift himself up and simply float away. He would soar up into the air away from the city, go back to the country where the sky was blue instead of gray. He would leave this house where no one wanted him. Where people stared and whispered, and though Reggie and Maude were kind to him, they were careful to keep their distance, just like everyone else.

The lady, Miss Whitney, was the nicest. She came up to his room every night just to check on him. She hadn't seen a haunt yet, but she said that she was still looking. She was younger than his mother, and prettier. He felt kind of guilty for thinking that, though it was the truth.

He missed his mother. Not his father, though. Chris could never seem to please him, no matter how hard he tried. And lots of times Da drank too much and he could be awful mean when he did.

Chris kicked a piece of gravel as he walked along the path. He should be grateful to be here, he knew. With Mum and Da gone, he could be starving in the streets, or forced to climb up hot, smoky chimneys, burning off his fingers like some of the boys he'd seen in the alley.

And yet sometimes he thought he would rather be out there on his own than in this fancy house that belonged to a man who looked at him as if he weren't there whenever they happened to meet. Chris did his best to avoid him.

He had seen the earl ride off that morning, as he did most every day. Knowing he was gone, he decided to prowl around a bit, see what he could discover about the place.

That's how he stumbled onto the little glass shed at the far end of the stable. Through the steamy windows, he could see drops of mist formed along the panes and the hazy outline of plants inside. Glancing around to be sure no one saw him, Chris opened the door and sneaked in.

For a moment he just stood there, amazed at the bounty he had discovered. Pots overflowed with flowers—the most beautiful he had ever seen. Some had ruffly white and purple petals, others were a smooth dark pink. There was a yellow flower so bright it made his eyes hurt to look at it.

The room was warm and miserably damp, but the steamy feel was worth it. He had never seen anything so beautiful in all his life. He wondered if the petals of the flowers were as soft as they looked and couldn't resist reaching over to touch one.

"What the hell are you doing in here!" The earl's booming voice cut through him like a knife. Chris whirled away from the plant, but his foot caught on a brick and he jerked forward again. His hand snaked out to break his fall, landed on the beautiful white ruffled flower, and the pot toppled over. Chris scrambled away, backing into the corner, his stomach tied in knots.

"Now look what you've done!"

He was shaking as he watched the earl kneel down, very carefully scoop up the plant, set it back into its container, and tamp down the soil.

Unfortunately, one of the blooms had been broken in the fall. Chris knelt, carefully lifted the bloom up in his palm, and held it out to the earl. "I'm sorry. I didn't mean to break it."

Blackwood ignored the offering. "You should have thought of that before you came in here. It's ruined. You can't put it back now."

The flower trembled in Chris's hand. He set it down very carefully next to the earl's black boot.

"These plants are extremely delicate. Don't come in here again."

His stomach churned. He had hoped to come back and look at the flowers again. As he backed toward the door, Chris took a last glance around. "I never saw anythin' like 'em."

"That's because they don't grow in this country. They're orchids. They grow in tropical regions in other parts of the world."

"Orchids," Chris repeated with undisguised awe.

Blackwood glanced up from his survey of the

plants, one of his slashing black eyebrows going up. "You like flowers?"

He started to lie. His father had birched him more than once for being a sissy-boy. He said he was a real Miss Molly for liking the same stuff girls did, like flowers and butterflies and birds. He opened his mouth, remembered the way Lord Blackwood had handled the orchid, and found himself nodding instead.

"I love 'em. I like to watch things grow. Me Da didn't like it, though. He said that kind of stuff was for girls."

Blackwood frowned. Chris didn't know why. The earl made a sudden, unexpected movement and Chris's hands instinctively came up to ward off the blow.

The earl went very still. "I'm not going to hurt you," he said softly.

A lump swelled in Chris's throat. He didn't know why it had, or why his eyes were stinging like he might be going to cry. "I'm sorry about the flower. I wish I hadn't broke it."

The earl studied his face, then he reached down for the broken white blossom and held it out to Chris. "Here, you can have it."

Chris took the flower from Lord Blackwood's hand. "You think Miss Whitney would like it?"

For a second Chris thought the earl was going to smile, but he didn't. "I imagine she would."

Chris turned and started walking toward the door.

"I come out here in the mornings," Lord Blackwood called after him. "Maybe you'd like to help me with the plants sometime."

Chris blinked at a second unwelcome burning. "Yes—I would like that oh so much."

The earl said nothing more, just turned back to his flowers.

As Chris walked through the garden toward the house, he saw another yellow butterfly, but this time he didn't think of flying away. He wanted to learn about the orchids in the shed, and the earl had promised to teach him.

Chris looked down at the ruffled white flower he held in his hand, and he smiled.

19

Adam worked for another hour in the small glass shed he had built to house the plants he kept in London, separating and repotting several different varieties of orchids. He found solace in working with the plants, a peace he often found elusive. He'd been surprised to stumble across the boy.

Since his disastrous attempt at home and hearth with Caroline, he had given up any notion of family, and over the years had come to think it was probably for the best. He wasn't good with children. He had rarely been around them.

An image returned of little Christopher Derry holding the orchid blossom as if it were a precious gem. Was there a chance Christopher was *his* son and not Robert's? Surely, it couldn't be. He had to admit the child had the swarthy complexion and lean, wide-shouldered build of a Hawthorne, but Chris's hair was the same deep brown as Robert's. Then again, Adam's grandfather had also had brown hair.

Still, remembering the care he had taken to avoid an out of wedlock child, Adam discarded the notion. So what if the boy loved flowers just as he had when he was a child? It didn't mean a thing.

Adam frowned, thinking of the way Chris Derry had recoiled in fear, believing Adam had meant to strike him. Robert's son or not, it angered him to think what the boy might have suffered at his foster family's hands.

Adam carefully blocked the thought of how he would feel if the boy were truly his son.

Finished with the final planting, Adam left the greenhouse. As he traveled the gravel path, he glanced up at the wrought-iron railing around the balcony outside Jillian's bedchamber. This afternoon he would contact an agent, find a suitable place for her to live. In the meantime, with the boy in the house, he would have to stay away from her.

This morning, before he had come to the greenhouse, he had saddled Ramses and gone for a ride in the park. Something was bothering him, something about Jillian, but even the brisk spring air couldn't clear his mind enough to figure it out.

He had finally persuaded her to become his mistress. With Colin Norton in prison for murder, she could begin a new life. He wanted a place nearby where he could see her whenever he liked. Which, the way his body stirred to life every time he thought of her, would undoubtedly be often. Damn, he was glad he had finally convinced her.

And yet when he looked into her eyes, he saw something there that disturbed him, something he hadn't seen before. Adam was afraid he knew what it was. Though her father had been a professor, a man of little wealth, Jillian had been reared as a lady. If Professor Whitney had lived, she would have married. She would have had the husband and children every woman seemed to want.

With the scandal and the loss of her virtue, marriage was impossible for her now.

Unless he was the man she wed.

His stomach instantly knotted. It was the first time thoughts of marriage had entered his head in years and Adam quickly squashed them. He had traveled that road before and he knew, far better than most, exactly where it led. After the bloom wore off, most married couples had affairs. It was an accepted part of the world in which he lived. It wasn't the sort of marriage he had imagined sharing with Caroline Harding. Now he knew what a fool he had been.

Not this time, he vowed, as he had years ago.

And with those words set firmly in his mind, he continued up the path to the house, stepped inside, and firmly closed the door.

A light May rain pattered on the roof and the wind picked up, rattling the mullioned panes. Jillian felt restless, as if her life were on hold, waiting for something to happen, though she wasn't sure what it was.

Giving in to her need for escape, she left her room and headed for the library to return the book she had borrowed, *A Midsummer Night's Dream.* She was halfway down the stairs when she looked up to see Reggie speaking to Garth Dutton in the entry.

"Very good, sir," Reggie said to Garth. "I'll fetch 'im in all haste." He didn't look back as he rushed pell-mell off to Adam's study.

Jillian continued down the staircase, a queasy

feeling building in the pit of her stomach. She stopped in front of the barrister and her pulse kicked up at the grim look on his face. "What is it?"

"I was hoping to speak to Lord Blackwood first. The butler has gone to fetch him."

"It isn't . . . it isn't about the murder?" *Please God, anything but that.*

Garth carefully smoothed his features into a look of calm, the sort of expression he probably used to soothe hysterical clients. "I'm sorry, I'm afraid it is."

Her pulse jerked skyward. She started to ask what had happened, but Adam approached just then. One glance at Jillian's bloodless features and his smile of welcome faded.

"What is it?"

"I take it you haven't yet read the morning papers."

"No. By the look on your face, apparently I should have."

"Perhaps we should retire to your study."

"Yes, of course." Adam led the way down the hall and into the wood-paneled room that smelled faintly of leather and smoke. "I gather this visit isn't a social call," he said as soon as the door was closed.

"No, I'm afraid it isn't." Garth was dressed in a charcoal-gray morning coat and dove-gray breeches, his clothes perfectly fitted, but his blond hair looked slightly disheveled, as if he had run his fingers through it.

He cast a sympathetic glance at Jillian. "Yesterday, a woman came forward—the wife of a peer. She claims she was with Colin Norton the night of the murder."

Jillian's knees nearly buckled. She felt Adam's hand at her waist, holding her steady.

"Apparently the lady was worried about her husband discovering her relationship with Norton or she would have spoken sooner. Norton was released late last night."

Tension tightened the muscles beneath Adam's coat. "How will this affect Jillian?"

"I'm afraid she resumes her place as the prime suspect in the murder. The trial is officially set for the ninth of May."

Jillian swayed on her feet and Adam eased her down into a nearby chair. "Oh, God, I knew it was too good to be true." Tears sprang into her eyes. "I was afraid to believe, afraid something like this would happen." Garth handed her a handkerchief, and she dabbed at her eyes, determined not to cry.

Adam made his way to the sideboard and returned with a glass of brandy that he pressed into her hands. "Drink this."

She took a tiny swallow, but he brought the glass back up and she drank again, sputtering once before the liquor began to spread through her limbs.

"I'm sorry. I just . . . I wanted this so badly to be over."

"Apparently that isn't going to happen," Garth said gently, "at least not for a while."

"We've still got a week." Adam's deep voice rang with authority. "I never called Peter Fraser off the case. As soon as we're finished here, I'll go see him, go over everything again."

"I'm going with you." Jillian unconsciously knotted Garth's handkerchief. "I'm tired of doing nothing. I can't sit here a moment more. Perhaps if I am there while you go over the case, I'll think of something I might have missed."

She expected Adam to argue but he didn't. "All right. We'll start at the beginning, go back and look at every shred of evidence, every possible suspect."

Garth nodded his approval. "Good idea. We'll re-examine every possible venue. In the meantime, I'll continue working on your defense. When the time comes, we'll be ready."

Jillian swallowed, determined to be brave when all she wanted to do was run back upstairs and bury her head beneath the pillow. "I shan't give up." She forced a little stiffness into her spine. "I didn't kill Lord Fenwick. With all of us working together, somehow we'll find a way to prove it."

Adam's hand covered hers on the arm of the overstuffed chair. "The answer is there. All we have to do is find it." He straightened. "In that regard, we might as well get started."

Jillian mustered a smile and the courage to get back on her feet. "I'm ready whenever you are."

Dear Lord, how she wished it were true.

Peter Fraser's office in Bow Street turned out to be the second stop on their agenda. First, Adam ordered his coachman to drive them to Threadneedle Street.

"I never really considered Madeleine Telford a suspect," Adam said as he helped Jillian down from the carriage in front of the prestigious offices of Knowles, Glenridge, and Morrison. "I didn't think she had any sort of motive. But there are questions we need answered before we can rule her out completely."

Retying the strings on her plum silk bonnet, Jillian preceded Adam into the reception area. While he spoke to the young blond man at the desk, she sat down in a forest green leather chair, setting her reticule on an elegant mahogany table beside it.

On a matching sofa a few feet away, a well-dressed man and woman also sat waiting. The woman, blond and attractive, perhaps late twenties, in a stylish butter-yellow muslin gown, gave Jillian a brief perusal that took in her fashionable clothes and started to smile. Her lips wobbled and tightened, the smile sliding away as she realized Jillian was the woman in the newspapers.

The lady shot up from the sofa, her chin tipped regally upward. "The air has suddenly grown fetid in here, Charles. I believe I shall await you in the carriage."

Her husband eyed Jillian with speculation and rose in gentlemanly fashion. "As you wish, my dear. I won't be long." He watched his wife march out the door, slamming it a little harder than she needed.

Jillian ignored his knowing glances and the sick feeling in the pit of her stomach. She was a woman scorned. She might as well get used to it. Still, she was glad Adam hadn't witnessed her humiliation.

He turned her way as the young man motioned him forward. "Mr. Morrison says he'll be happy to speak to you," the assistant said. "Please follow me."

Ignoring the man on the sofa, Jillian crossed the room and accepted Adam's arm. He led her into the solicitor's office, which, she noticed, was as handsomely furnished as the rest of the building. Adam introduced her to Benjamin Morrison, an elegant-looking gentleman with a congenial expression and silver-flecked dark brown hair.

Adam declined the attorney's invitation to be seated. "This won't take long. I just have a couple of questions I'd like to ask."

"Of course, my lord."

"When I was here before, you told me Lord Fenwick planned to leave the majority of his estate to Miss Whitney. You mentioned there were a few bequests to other family members. I assume one of those bequests went to his daughter-in-law."

"As a matter of fact, that wasn't the case. Lord Fenwick removed the provisions he had made for Mrs. Telford in the new will we prepared for him."

Jillian felt a shiver roll down her spine. "Lord Fenwick meant to disinherit Madeleine? Surely you're mistaken."

"I assure you, Miss Whitney, I am not mistaken. The only other beneficiaries in the second will would have been the earl's spinster cousin—a woman named Harriett Telford—and a couple of the earl's lifelong servants."

"But why would he do such a thing?"

"I'm afraid I wasn't privy to Lord Fenwick's whims, Miss Whitney. All I can say for certain is that you were to receive Madeleine Telford's share of the fortune."

"Is there any way Mrs. Telford could have known about those changes?" Adam asked.

"Not that I'm aware of. Unless of course, the earl told her himself."

Adam seemed to ponder that. "Thank you, Mr. Morrison. I appreciate your time and candor."

"You're most welcome, my lord."

When they left the office and returned to the carriage, Adam sat back with a grim look on his face.

"You not seriously thinking Madeleine Telford killed the earl?"

"I'm thinking she had a very good reason to want him dead. As Henry's widow, Madeleine was under Lord Fenwick's protection. I assumed—as I'm certain everyone else did—that the earl would provide for her in his will. Without the income he provided, Madeleine would be forced into poverty. That is very good motivation for murder."

"Even if she killed him, how could we possibly prove it?"

Adam stared for a moment at the trees passing outside the carriage window. "Perhaps Peter Fraser can be of some assistance in that regard."

Peter Fraser's office in Bow Street was a far cry from Morrison's elegant establishment, being small but tidy, with stacks of paperwork in neat little piles on the floor.

Jillian sat down in a straight-backed chair, the only seat available opposite the red-haired man's battered desk, a fact that seemed to embarrass Mr. Fraser.

"Marcus!" he called to his assistant in the other room. "Fetch his lordship a chair—and be quick about it!"

"That isn't necessary." Adam stood behind her, his long fingers wrapped around the top ladder of the chair. "If you've read the morning papers, you know that Colin Norton has been released and that Jillian is once more under suspicion. That is what's important and the reason we are here."

Peter Fraser nodded. "Yes. I've rather been expecting you."

"To begin with, we'd like to reexamine the information you've collected so far, along with anything you might have come up with since Norton's arrest. Perhaps with Miss Whitney here, we'll uncover something we missed the first time round."

"Let me collect the files." Fraser cast a sympathetic glance at Jillian, leaned over, and scooped a stack of files off the floor.

He set them on top of the desk and she and Adam began to examine them. Behind her, she heard the door open and the grate of chair legs scraping the wooden floor as Fraser's assistant placed a chair for the earl next to hers and quietly left the room.

"In addition to the information you've already examined," Fraser said, "I've added a report outlining Howard Telford's alibi for the night of the murder."

"Then you've verified his attendance at the Foxmoor soiree." Adam sounded disappointed. In a way, so was she.

"According to a number of people—including Lord and Lady Foxmoor—the earl arrived early and didn't depart until late in the evening."

"I also need to verify that Madeleine Telford was home that night."

"I've a friend, a sheriff in Surrey who owes me a favor. The two of us will pay an official call on some of the servants who work for Mrs. Telford. We'll see what they have to say."

Jillian flipped through the papers, spotting information on Colin Norton as well as a file on Lord Eldridge. "Is there anything in here about the gun that was used to kill Lord Fenwick?"

Fraser plucked a pair of round gold spectacles off the desk and hooked them over his ears. "Indeed." He dug through the stack and pulled out a sheet that Jillian had missed. "According to the magistrate's records, the weapon was a double-barreled flintlock pistol, custom made here in London by a smith named Jonas Nock."

Adam picked up the sheet of paper. "Nock's work is well-respected and his guns don't come cheap. His customers include some of the wealthiest members of the *ton*."

"I remember it was very small," Jillian said, a painful memory surfacing of the pistol lying on the Oriental carpet next to the earl's lifeless body. "At the time, I remember thinking, 'surely that little gun couldn't kill him.' "

"Having a second barrel makes that 'little gun' capable of firing twice," Fraser pointed out. "The killer was prepared if the first shot didn't do the trick."

"And that small a gun could be easily concealed," Adam said. "Perhaps even in a woman's reticule."

"You're thinking of Mrs. Telford," Fraser said.

"It's possible. It's only an hour's ride from Hampstead Heath. She certainly knew her way around Fenwick's house and in which rooms she would most likely find the earl at that hour of the evening. And she freely admitted seeing him just two nights before he was murdered. He could have mentioned his intention to disinherit her."

Adam tapped the paper. "We need to get a list of Nock's customers, see who purchased this sort of weapon. Perhaps we'll turn up someone connected in some way to the earl."

"We've already attained a portion of the list, my lord." Fraser pulled out another sheet of foolscap and handed it to Adam. Jillian leaned over to read it.

"Unfortunately, Nock isn't good with records," Fraser said. "He's been compiling a second list for the magistrates' office, which means it will also be available to us."

The list wasn't lengthy. Jillian recognized the names of several wealthy members of the nobility, but none of them was a suspect or seemed connected to Lord Fenwick except as an acquaintance.

"Damn. No names here that strike a chord. Perhaps the additional list will give us something." Adam set the list back on the desk. "Several of these people live in London. We need to locate as many as possible. We need to find out whether they still have the weapon Nock made for them, or if they have sold it. If they did, I want to know to whom."

"Yes, my lord."

They reviewed the rest of the information, but nothing else leapt out at them. It was late in the afternoon by the time Jillian and Adam left Fraser's office. Jillian was exhausted, and with only seven days left till the trial, more discouraged than she had been since the night of the murder.

"I know what you're thinking." Adam's deep voice reached out to her from the opposite side of the carriage. The curtains had been drawn for privacy and the interior lamps were lit. They flickered against the dark red velvet draperies at the windows. "Come here, love."

A lump rose in her throat. He always seemed to know what she needed, and right now she desperately needed him to hold her. Adam opened his arms and her throat closed up as she went into them. He lifted her onto his lap and held her close against his chest.

"You mustn't lose hope," he said softly. "We're going to beat this."

"I know." But she didn't really believe it and she didn't think he did, either. She was very close to giving up and apparently Adam knew it.

"There's still a week left." He pressed a kiss against her temple. "We'll make use of every moment. Meanwhile, I'm going to book passage for you on a ship—"

"I told you before—I won't run away." Tears welled and her throat went tight. "I didn't kill him and I'm not leaving."

"You won't have to. We're going to find out who killed him. This is just a precaution in case we need more time."

She eased away from him, brushed at the tears on her cheeks. "I won't go, Adam. I won't leave here with the entire country believing I murdered the earl."

She thought that he would be angry. He was a major, after all. He didn't like his orders disobeyed. Instead, he eased her back into his arms and tightened his hold around her. She could hear the rhythmic clopping of the horses' hooves, feel the vibration of cobblestones beneath the wheels. As the minutes crept past, she imagined they must be close to reaching his town house and fresh tears burned.

"I don't want to go home," she said on a shaky breath. "Not yet. I don't want to talk to anyone, not even the servants. I just need . . . I don't know, I just need some time or . . ."

Adam rapped on the roof of the carriage and slid open the panel between the interior and the driver's box on top. "Keep driving, Lance. I don't care where. I'll let you know when we're ready to return to the house."

"Yes, milord."

Adam slid the panel closed and settled himself back on the seat. "Is that what you wanted?"

She nodded faintly. "Thank you."

"There's something else I think you need."

She looked up. "What?"

In answer, he cupped her face between his hands and very gently kissed her. "I'm going to make love to you, sweeting. For a while, at least, I'm going to make you forget all of this."

"In here?" The words came out with dismay, yet a surge of heat speared through her.

"It's a little crowded, but I assure you we'll accomplish the task." The glance he gave her could have scorched the inside of the carriage. "Consider it another learning experience."

Seated on his lap, she could feel his heavy arousal beneath the layers of her plum silk skirt. Adam kissed the side of her neck, then turned her a little to unbutton the back of her gown. He slid her skirt up, bunching it around her waist, and positioned her astride his thighs, propping her knees on the velvet seat on either side of him.

His kiss was soft yet fierce. The top of her gown gaped open. He eased it off her shoulders and began to feast on her breasts.

They made love in the back of the carriage, their clothes half on, half off, a sensual, erotic coupling that had her moaning his name. With her legs spread across his thighs, she was open and exposed and Adam made the most of her vulnerable position, his long fingers moving beneath her skirts, stroking her with such skill she forgot where she was, forgot the fear that wrapped around her every time she thought of what lay ahead.

Lifting her a little, he positioned his hardness at the entrance to her passage, and eased himself inside until he impaled her fully.

"Adam..."

"Hold on to me, sweeting. Hold on tight." Pleasure rolled through her as he began to move, the impact of his deep, rhythmic thrusts enhanced by the sway of the carriage and the potholes in the road.

It was an exquisite, deeply sensual mating, yet each touch, each skillful caress, held a tenderness he had never shown her before. After they reached release, he simply held her, as if they had all the time in the world, instead of just seven more days.

I love you, she thought. *I love you so much.*

But he wouldn't want to hear the words, wouldn't know what to say in return if she said them.

"I promised I would take care of you," he said softly. "That's what I'm going to do. Put your trust in me, Jillian. I won't fail you."

He wouldn't fail her. He would stand beside her no matter the outcome. It was one of the reasons she loved him so much. And she trusted him—with everything but her heart.

If she survived the trial, he would become her protector, she his kept woman. She would give up her dignity, abandon her self-respect because she loved him more than her own life.

Even if she won, she would lose.

20

May the third. With Colin Norton's release and the trial date officially set, Jillian had forgotten that today was little Christopher's birthday. Fortunately, Maude remembered. Maude, Reggie, and Fanny the cook had been planning something special.

At Reggie's invitation, Jillian arrived in the kitchen, a warm, cheery room that smelled of yeast and vanilla. The long oak table where the servants took their meals had been set with a white linen cloth and decorated with red and yellow paper flowers. A sign painted in big red letters hung on the wall, spelling out HAPPY BIRTHDAY CHRIS. At the end of the table, three gaily wrapped packages bore little white cards inscribed with Chris's name.

As she walked toward the table, Jillian's fingers tightened around the present she had purchased just yesterday with money she borrowed from Maggie, a small, exquisitely carved and painted wooden horse that she had discovered in a little shop in Bond Street.

Jillian smiled at the servants standing behind the

table. "Chris is going to be pleased. This is very nice of all of you."

"The lad deserves a bit o' somethin' on his special day." In the steamy kitchen, wisps of black hair escaped from Maude's mobcap and curled around her rosy cheeks. "I'm thinkin' the major won't be doin' nothing for 'im, though Lord knows he should, seein' as how the lad is his son."

Jillian stiffened, coming to the earl's defense though part of her thought it might be true. "It's a good thing the major—I mean Lord Blackwood—didn't hear you say that. He would scarcely approve your discussing his family affairs. I'm certain the matter provides some juicy gossip belowstairs, but there is no way to know for certain that Chris is Lord Blackwood's son."

"I got eyes in me head," Maude grumbled. "Saints alive, the lad looks just like 'im."

"That's enough, Maude," Reggie said, though Jillian knew he felt the same.

The patter of small feet coming down the hall ended the discussion. "Here comes Chris now. We had better get ready."

Fanny hurried over with her special dessert, a layered, custard-filled spice cake with Chris's name spelled out in little hard candies on the top. Then the swinging door shoved open and Chris walked in.

"Surprise!" they all shouted in unison.

Chris just stood there, staring. When no one said anything else and he still didn't move, Jillian rounded the table and walked over to where he stood.

"This is all for you, Chris." She gestured toward the cake and the presents and the three people grinning down at him. "Happy birthday."

The boy walked farther into the kitchen, staring at the packages as if he couldn't believe his eyes.

"Come on, lad." Reggie motioned him over to the chair at the head of the linen-draped table. "We 'aven't got all day."

The child didn't need more encouragement. "Mum always gave me a present on me birthday. I got a new pair of shoes once. Well, not exactly new but almost." He opened a package wrapped in blue-and-silver paper, carefully setting the ribbon aside to be used again.

"That's from me," Reggie said proudly as Chris drew out the little toy soldier he found in the box, examining the piece as if it were made of glass instead of wood.

"It's a cavalry officer from the major's old regiment," Reggie said, "Eleventh Light Dragoons."

"The major?" Chris looked up, his small fingers smoothing over every line of the soldier's blue uniform.

"Reggie means Lord Blackwood," Jillian explained from over Chris's shoulder.

"He was in the army?"

"One of the best officers in the regiment," Reggie said proudly.

" 'Tis wondrous," the little boy said. He was examining the wooden soldier, stroking it with reverent care, when the door swung open and the earl walked in.

Adam took in the scene in an instant and his slashing black eyebrows drew together. "The footman thought you had gone into the kitchen," he said to Jillian, but his eyes were fixed on the boy.

Myriad emotions crossed his face. Jillian would

have given her last shilling—if she'd had one of her own—to know what he was thinking.

Chris must have been wondering the same thing, because a faint tremor ran through him.

"Happy birthday, Christopher," Adam said softly.

Chris's mouth curved up, his smile so sweet Jillian's heart turned over. "Reggie gave me a soldier." He proudly held it up for Adam's inspection. "He said you were in the army."

Adam flicked a glance at Reggie, strode over to examine the wooden soldier in the uniform of his old regiment. "Yes, I was."

"I should like to be a soldier, I think. Would you tell me about it sometime?"

Adam's posture subtly straightened. "War is not for children." But he handed back the toy. "Enjoy your party, Chris." He returned his attention to Jillian. "May I see you a moment, Miss Whitney?"

"Of course." She excused herself, squeezing Chris's shoulder as she left the steamy kitchen. Out in the hall, she followed the earl down the corridor and into his study, where he firmly closed the door.

His jaw looked hard when he turned to face her. "The boy may or may not be my son, but one thing is certain. He is here under my protection. That means that he is not to be treated as a servant. If you wish to hold a party in his honor, from now on you will do so in the dining room."

He was angry, she saw, and she wondered if perhaps he felt guilty for the way he had been dealing with the boy.

Jillian lifted her chin. "It's difficult to know exactly how you wish the child to be treated. He remains up on the third floor all by himself. You ignore him most of the time, then you worry that he is being relegated to the status of a servant."

A muscle ticked in his cheek. "Very well. Ask Maude to remove his clothes to a room on the second floor."

Relief filtered through her but she kept her chin held high. "As you wish, my lord." She wasn't a servant either, and she didn't appreciate the earl's high-handedness, even if she was in love with him.

For an instant Adam stood rigid, then he sighed. "I'm sorry." He raked a hand through his hair. "This isn't your fault. I'm just not used to having a child in the house. I've never been very good with them."

She realized he felt bad that he had forgotten the little boy's birthday. In a way it surprised her that he cared. In another way, it surprised her that he had been able to ignore the boy even this long.

"I should have reminded you that today was Chris's birthday. I just . . . I wasn't sure it mattered."

Adam glanced away. "To tell you the truth, I'm a little surprised it does. My mother always made my birthday special. It's something every child deserves."

Jillian's heart swelled with love for him. "You're a good man, Adam."

He closed the distance between them and pulled her into his arms. "Will you help me with the boy?"

If only she could. In less than a week, there was every chance that she would be back in prison. Or worse. "I'll do anything I can to help."

She looked up at him, saw that his eyes were dark, and knew that he wanted to make love to her. As it was, they simply had too much to do.

"A note has arrived from Garth Dutton," Adam

said. "He wants to see both of us in his office. That's what I was coming to tell you."

Though she had been expecting the summons, her knees felt shaky as she thought of the six days left until the trial. "I'll get my shawl."

Adam opened the study door and Jillian walked past him into the hall. Knowing Garth wanted to discuss the trial, she mentally girded herself for the meeting. As she climbed the stairs to retrieve her wrap, she ignored the shudder that rippled down her spine.

A heavy layer of clouds rolled in to cover the stars. The air was damp and chilly, the ground slick with a layer of mist. Maggie drew the hood of her satin-lined cloak up over her head and followed her aunt, Lady Sophia Hawthorne, up the wide stone stairs leading into the Earl of Winston's town house.

Tonight they were attending the annual soiree given in honor of the earl and the countess's anniversary. With the endless toasts and toadying, it was usually a tedious affair that Maggie had earlier tried to escape. Her aunt, however, had been determined.

"Need I remind you," Aunt Sophie had said with a lift of her thin white eyebrows, "your second Season is well under way. It is beyond time you reined in that wild streak of yours and started thinking of marriage."

Sophie Hawthorne was a widow well past seventy and set in her ways, and she ruled her small corner of the world with an iron fist. That corner included Maggie Hawthorne. At least it had since she was fifteen, when Maggie's mother, the Countess of Blackwood, had suffered her terrible stroke.

"There's plenty of time for marriage, Aunt Sophie. And I told you—I refuse to marry a man I don't love."

"You will do as your brother and I tell you, young woman." Sitting in the sewing parlor of her Mayfair town house, her white hair drawn into a snug, no-nonsense coil at the nape of her neck, Sophie set her needlework down on the cream velvet sofa.

"*Love*," she sneered. "Balderdash—that's what it is. Marriages are made for any number of reasons and love is rarely among them."

Maggie made no reply, but for some strange reason Garth Dutton's face popped into her head. He would probably be working tonight, since Jillian's trial was so near. Maggie secretly wondered if perhaps that accounted for her lack of enthusiasm for tonight's affair.

Aunt Sophie sighed. "Well, for whatever reason, soon you will choose a husband or wind up on the shelf. And the only way to meet someone appropriate is to get out in Society. Therefore, you will take yourself upstairs right now and change into proper attire for Lord Winston's soiree."

Maggie grumbled, but did as she was told, choosing a high-waisted rose silk gown trimmed with bands of moss-green velvet accompanied by a matching velvet cloak. Winifred pinned her black hair up in curls, leaving wispy strands beside her cheeks, then tied a simple gold locket on a moss-green ribbon around her throat.

For all Aunt Sophie's idiosyncrasies, Maggie loved her dearly and usually tried to please her. She would not, however, under any circumstances, marry a man she didn't love.

Now, as Maggie followed her aunt through the crush of people making their way into the elegant drawing room of Lord Winston's town house, she thought of that vow and the monotonous evening ahead. The affair would undoubtedly be lengthy and dull, but as long as she was there, she might as well try to enjoy herself.

Noticing a friend, tall, statuesque Ariel Ross, the Countess of Greville, in conversation with two other women across the room, Maggie started in that direction. She had always liked the countess, who was only a year or two older than she.

"Lady Margaret!" Ariel motioned for her to join them. "It's wonderful to see you."

"I didn't realize you were back in London. I thought you and your husband remained at Greville Hall."

"Justin had some business in the city." She flashed the brightest smile Maggie had ever seen. "I have the most marvelous news—we're going to have a baby!"

Maggie grinned. "Ariel, that's wonderful! I'm so happy for you."

"Justin has been walking on air. I've never seen him so happy." She turned to one of the women she had been talking to before Maggie's arrival. "Oh, dear, I've forgotten my manners. I was just so excited. I believe you know Anna Constantine, Marchioness of Landen."

Blond and beautiful, the Italian contessa had married the handsome marquess just last year.

"Sì, sì, of course she knows me," Anna said before Maggie could answer. "She came to Landen Manor with that handsome brother of hers for the wedding."

"It's good to see you, Lady Landen." Maggie flashed a smile, having instantly fallen under Anna's spell, just like everyone else. The women chatted pleasantly for a while; then Maggie wandered away in search of other friends.

An attractive dark-haired man approached whom she didn't recognize at first. "Good evening, Lady Margaret. I don't know if you remember me. My name is Michael Aimes. We met at a ball last year, given by the Duke and Duchess of Rathmore."

"Actually, I do remember." Michael Aimes was the second son of the Marquess of Devlin. Michael, a lean, rather scholarly young man of perhaps five and twenty, was handsome in a bookish sort of way, and she remembered his rather nice smile.

"I was wondering . . . the woman, Miss Whitney, whom your brother has so bravely defended, is a friend of mine—or actually, her father was a friend. Dr. Whitney was a professor at the small college I attended. We shared a common interest in Egyptian antiquities."

"As does my brother, Adam."

"Yes, so I've heard. I've been concerned about Miss Whitney. I wondered if you might have some word as to how she fares."

How would anyone fare who faced imprisonment and possibly the gallows? "As you've probably read in the papers, her trial is set for next week. My brother hopes they will find the true culprit before then."

"I can't imagine Miss Whitney hurting anyone. I hope you will tell her I enquired after her well-being, and if there is anything I can do to help her, I hope she will let me know."

He handed Maggie a small, engraved white card

bearing his address, which she stuffed into her reticule with a mental reminder to see that Jillian received it. Michael Aimes made a polite farewell, and Maggie wandered away. She saw a number of familiar faces, but each time she started toward them, they seemed to drift away.

Across the Oriental carpet, she spotted Madeleine Telford in conversation with a woman named Lavinia Dandridge and Madeleine's cousin by marriage, Howard, the new Earl of Fenwick. The instant the group saw her standing near a piecrust table, they pointedly turned and walked away.

Maggie frowned, an uneasy feeling building in the bottom of her stomach. She started toward Katherine Mayborne, a young woman her age she had known in finishing school, but Katherine also walked away. Forcing herself to move casually toward the big silver punch bowl, Maggie ladled herself a cup of champagne punch and took a fortifying drink. Behind her she heard the faint sound of voices. Her whole body stiffened at the whisper of her name.

"Just look at her standing there as bold as you please. I can't believe she has the gall to come out in polite society while that brother of hers harbors a murderer."

"Yes, and the creature is living right there in his house!"

"Everyone knows the sort that Whitney woman is. She was sharing old Fenwick's bed—now she is blatantly sleeping with Adam Hawthorne under his very roof!"

"At least her taste in men has improved," one of the women snickered.

"The whole family is incorrigible." It was the voice of the Viscountess Wimbly, a patroness of Almack's and a notorious gossip. "Remember Blackwood's cousin, Robert? If he hadn't sneaked off to the Colonies, they would have tossed him into debtor's prison."

Maggie turned away, her stomach rolling with nausea. Her hands were shaking and her face felt completely drained of blood. She set the punch cup down, turned on trembling legs, and walked straight into Garth Dutton's chest.

Maggie bit back a sob. God in heaven, of all the people she didn't want to witness such a moment.

"Garth," she choked out, the familiarity slipping over the lump in her throat before she could stop it. His jaw looked granite-hard and his usually bright green eyes were as flat and hard as sea-washed jade. He had heard every word, she knew, and she couldn't stop the tears that sprang into her eyes.

"It's all right, love," he said gently. "There isn't one among them with the sense God gave a goose." He wrapped her stiff fingers around his arm and tucked her against his side. "Just hang on. I'll get you out of here."

Maggie managed a jerky nod and began to move woodenly along in the wake he created. She didn't care where he took her. She had to get out of there before she started to cry—or worse, told those three old biddies exactly what she thought of them. Blinking back the moisture in her eyes, she kept her head high as he led her out of the drawing room and down the hall to the entry.

She thought of Aunt Sophie and wondered if her aunt was also receiving the cut-direct, but Sophie was older and tougher, more used to the capricious nature of the *ton* and nearly impervious to its cruelties.

Maggie felt every brutal word like a barb jabbed under her skin.

She clung to Garth's arm and didn't let go until they were outside the house and standing at the bottom of the front porch stairs.

"Stay right here," Garth commanded. "I'll get your wrap." He returned a few minutes later, draped the rose velvet cloak around her shoulders, and lifted the hood up over her head.

Maggie looked at Garth and her eyes started stinging again. "Thank you," she whispered, praying she wouldn't cry in front of him. "It isn't far back to the town house. Would you mind telling my aunt I wasn't feeling well and I walked back to the house?"

"I already told your aunt that you were leaving, and that I would see you safely home."

She shook her head, her throat still aching. "You can't possibly. There is already so much gossip—"

"I'll be back here before there is time for any more tongues to start wagging." He took her arm again and, accepting defeat, she let him guide her down the brick path to the street.

They walked along the lane until they reached his carriage; then he helped her ascend the iron stairs. Settling back against the tufted red velvet seat, Maggie closed her eyes, wishing she could shut out the cruelties of the world with that same ease.

Instead of seating himself across from her, Garth sat down beside her, reached over, and gently took her hand. He cradled it between both of his, warming her icy fingers.

"The trial is just a few days away," he said gently. "The matter of the murder will come to an end, one way or another, and in time, all of the gossip will fade."

She nodded, but she knew it wasn't completely true. No matter what happened to Jillian, the Hawthorne name would always be slightly tainted. She refused to ask herself why it suddenly mattered so much.

"I asked your aunt if I might call on you tomorrow evening," Garth said, drawing her gaze back to his face.

"There is no need to concern yourself on my account. I'll be fine, I assure you."

"Well, I am concerned. But more than that, I would simply like to see you."

Her chest squeezed. She should refuse him. A match between them was impossible, as Garth must certainly know. She had no idea what his intentions might be, and yet, God in heaven, she wanted to see him. "What about the trial? Surely you're busy making preparations."

"I've been making preparations for weeks. Miss Whitney has been thoroughly schooled on what and what not to say, and I am as ready as I'm ever going to be. Which means I shall be free to call on you after supper tomorrow evening." His gaze slid down to her mouth and a hollow feeling crept into her stomach. "That is, if you would like for me to come."

Maggie stared into those green, green eyes and knew she was heading for disaster. "Yes," she said, her lips drawing into a wobbly smile that actually felt sincere. "I'd like that very much."

As the carriage rolled home, they talked about

the upcoming trial, the work he had done with Jillian and Adam that day, and some of the progress Adam had made in trying to discover the villain. All too soon the coach reached her aunt's Mayfair town house and pulled to the side of the street.

She waited for Garth to open the door, but instead, he reached up and caught her chin. "Don't let them upset you. Those women thrive on scandal, but soon the trial will be over and the gossip forgotten." Then very gently, he bent his head and kissed her. It was a soft, brief kiss, nothing like the time before, and yet she felt an unexpected jolt of heat.

"Until tomorrow night," Garth said, his voice a little deeper than before.

She let him help her down from the carriage, her mind still clinging to the kiss they had shared. A few minutes later she was back inside the town house, upstairs in the safety of her bedchamber. Tomorrow night Garth would come to call.

Maggie sat down on the tapestry stool in front of her mirror and tried not to think how futile it would be to let herself fall in love with him.

21

Peter Fraser listened to the echo of his scuffed leather shoes as he crossed the marble floor in the entry of the Earl of Blackwood's town house. It was ten o'clock in the morning, early yet for wealthy members of the *ton*, but instinctively he knew the earl would want this news no matter what time it arrived.

As he expected, as soon as his message was received, Peter had been summoned, and the squat, beefy man who looked nothing at all like a butler but apparently was one stood waiting to lead him down the hall to Blackwood's study.

"Come in, Fraser." The earl motioned him forward, into a masculine room lined with books and furnished with deep brown leather chairs. "I received your note. We've been expecting you."

The earl strode over to greet him but the woman, Jillian Whitney, remained seated, looking paler than she had the day she had come to his office. Worry lines marred a forehead that had been smooth that day beneath the upsweep of her fiery hair. And she was noticeably thinner, her startling blue eyes even more pronounced. Still, she was a beautiful woman. He wished he wasn't the bearer of such bad news.

"You said it was urgent," the earl said, not a man to waste words. "What have you found?"

"I've just received the balance of the names on Jonas Nock's list." Peter handed the sheet of foolscap to the earl. "A pistol of the very same size and caliber was purchased by Henry Telford six months before he killed himself."

"My God, then Henry's wife Madeleine must be the one who—"

"I'm sorry, my lord. The pistol was given as a gift to Henry's father, the late Lord Fenwick, on his sixty-sixth birthday three years ago. I've already verified the fact with several people who attended the party Henry gave in his father's honor."

Peter glanced at the woman, who had realized the implications of what he'd just told them and risen shakily to her feet. "Perhaps Lord Fenwick left it with his s-son for safekeeping."

Peter shook his head, wishing again that the news were not so grim, wondering if perhaps all of them were wrong and the woman had actually murdered the earl.

"According to his valet, the earl highly prized the weapon. He kept it in a velvet-lined box in the top drawer of the desk in his study. Apparently until the list was produced no one associated the murder weapon with the pistol Henry Telford had given to the earl."

Blackwood glanced over at Miss Whitney, who

looked even paler than before and had sagged down
into her chair.

"Anything else?" The earl's voice remained calm,
but his eyes looked dark and turbulent.

"That's all, I'm afraid. We're still trying to verify
that Madeleine Telford was at home the night of the
murder. We'll let you know as soon as we find out."

"Thank you, Peter." Blackwood walked him to
the door and waited till he left the study.

As he headed down the hall, he imagined what
the man must be thinking and wondered if the Whitney woman's staunchest defender had also begun to
have his doubts.

As soon as the door was closed, Adam strode to
the sideboard and poured himself a brandy. He took
a long, steadying drink, then turned to Jillian, who
sat woodenly in her chair. She looked pale and
shaken, as brittle as a leaf and ready to crumble at
any moment. He tried to harden his heart, tried to
be objective as he so badly needed to be.

She didn't look at him. Instead, her gaze fixed on
a row of leather-bound books sitting on a shelf along
the wall, but he doubted that she saw them.

"The gun belonged to the earl," she said dully, her
voice so faint he barely heard the words. "It was
right there in his study." She looked up at him and
her eyes were so bleak his heart pinched hard inside
his chest. "It was right there where I could reach it,
where I could take it out of his top drawer, aim it at
his heart, and pull the trigger."

His chest was aching. He looked her straight in
the face. "Did you?"

She moved her head slowly back and forth and

her lovely blue eyes filled with tears. "No." She glanced away. "I don't expect you to believe me. Not anymore. No one else will. Why should you be any different?"

But he did believe her. Now more than ever. He didn't know why. Every shred of evidence pointed to the fact that Jillian was guilty. His instincts where women were concerned had failed him time and again, and yet he believed she was innocent to the core of his soul.

Setting the brandy glass down on the sideboard, he started walking toward her. When he reached her chair, he caught her shoulders, drew her up and straight into his arms. Jillian started to shake. She felt small and fragile, her slender body stiff with her effort to remain in control.

"I believe you," he said into her hair, inhaling the faint scent of roses. "I know you didn't do it. I don't think you could ever hurt anyone."

She made a soft little sound in her throat and her arms slid up around his neck. Then she started to weep. Adam sank down in the chair and drew her gently onto his lap. Jillian cried as if she had lost all hope, cried all the tears she had been keeping locked away. He let her weep until the sobs turned into faint little hiccups, then he handed her his handkerchief.

"I'm sorry." She dabbed the moisture from her eyes and gave him a watery smile. "I've been saying that an awful lot lately."

"It's all right to cry. You've got more than your share of reasons."

She dragged in a shaky breath and blew her nose. "I just had such high hopes and now . . . now they have all turned to dust." Her eyes locked on his face. "No matter what happens, I'll never forget what you've done for me. The way you've stood by me when no one else would."

"We aren't giving up," he said, but he was thinking of the ship's departure he had found in the *Evening Post*. The *Madrigal* would be sailing for the Indies, leaving just before the trial was set to start. He wondered if it was too late for him to book passage.

"How can we possibly prove I didn't kill the earl when everywhere we look seems to point right back to me?"

"Yes, it does." He bent and pressed a kiss on her trembling lips. "And just a little too conveniently."

She wiped her eyes. "What do you mean?"

"I'm beginning to wonder if that wasn't exactly the plan. Perhaps whoever did this intended that the blame should fall on you. Did anyone know you would be in the earl's study the night he was killed?"

"Not specifically, I don't think, but it would probably be a good assumption. We had got in the habit of spending the evenings there together, and especially if the earl was feeling too poorly to go out. Usually we read or played chess. He was used to late hours, and even when his gout acted up, he rarely retired before midnight. I was always pleased to keep him company."

"Then the servants would have known. And a number of them would have had access to the gun the earl kept in his desk."

"But most of them were devoted to him and none of them had a reason to want him dead."

"Perhaps not. But whoever it was who killed him had to have been in the study at some point in time. Either Eldridge or Norton might have killed him for revenge, but neither of them had access to the pistol or knew you would be there that night. That leaves us with the new Lord Fenwick or Madeleine Telford or one of the old earl's servants. According to Peter Fraser, Howard was there earlier in the week. He could have taken the gun, but his alibi for the night of the murder has been confirmed. Madeleine told us she was there two nights before he died. Did she know the earl's habits?"

"I imagine she did. For a while after Henry died, she lived there in the house. She kept the earl company in the same manner I did."

"And she knew that he had been ill, that he would likely be home that night."

"But she was in Hampstead Heath the night of the murder. Unless she slipped away without being seen, made the long ride into London, then returned—again without being seen—she didn't do it. And we still don't know if either of them knew about the changes in the will. If they didn't know, they had no reason to want him dead."

Her shoulders slumped. "Which brings us right back to where we were when we started."

"Unless we can find a crack in the alibi either of them gave us. If we can prove one of them lied about his whereabouts that night, it's a pretty fair assumption he knew he was about to lose his share of the Fenwick fortune."

He caught a faint flicker of hope in her eyes. "What can we do?"

"Hire more men. Have them question the servants in Madeleine Telford's house and as many of the guests at the Foxmoors' soiree as they can track down. I'll ask Rathmore and Greville to help. They know most of the people who were there that night. If we're lucky, perhaps someone will remember seeing something that might have been overlooked."

"And if each of them is where he has said?"

"There is always the chance one of them hired someone to kill him, but in some ways that would be even more risky."

"Because the person who shot him couldn't be trusted to keep his silence."

"Exactly. Which is why we're going to up the reward we've offered. Maybe this time greed will take over and someone will come forward with the information we need."

Jillian said nothing more and neither did Adam. They were down to their very last options and there were only four days left until the trial.

Adam thought of the chance for escape Jillian had refused and prayed she wouldn't be sorry.

Freight wagons, coaches, and hackney carriages clogged the cobbled streets, making Garth's after-work journey home seem to take an eternity. Eventually, his driver drew up on the reins and the barouche pulled over in front of his town house in Portman Square.

With its tall, Corinthian columns and impressive domed entry, the residence was elegant by anyone's standards. Garth was proud it had been purchased with money he had earned from his profession and not his rather substantial inheritance.

Wearily climbing the stairs, he stepped through the door and handed his high beaver hat to the butler. "Good evening, Pims."

Edward Pims, tall and regal and far too staid for his mere thirty years, made a very proper bow. "Good evening, sir. Your grandfather, the baron, is here. He awaits you in the drawing room."

Garth sighed. God's teeth, hadn't his day already been trying enough? First, the Marquess of Simington's stepson had been tossed into jail for debauching a tavern wench in full view of a half-dozen patrons. Then Sally Weatherby, the married daughter of a wealthy merchant Garth had known for years, had come to him for help when Sally's husband had taken a bat to her after a night of drunken carousing.

The rest of his day hadn't been any better: hours combing over his notes for the Whitney trial, a trial it looked as if he might very well lose. The only thing that made the miserable day bearable was thoughts of the evening he planned to spend with Maggie.

In that regard, the person he least wished to see was his grandfather, the baron.

Garth steeled himself. "Thank you, Pims." As he strode down the hall and slid open the doors to the drawing room, he could smell the pickled herring, Wilton cheese, and freshly baked bread his grandfather loved and Cook generally kept for the old man's all too frequent visits.

"Good evening, Grandfather. You're looking well."

Tall and only slightly stoop-shouldered, with once-blond hair turned silver and the same green eyes Garth had inherited, at five and seventy, Avery Dutton was still a vital man.

"I am hardly well," he grumbled as he always did, forcing Garth to hide a smile. "I am coming down with an ague and the ache in my back has flared up again. Worse than that, there's a rumor going round that you've been carrying on with the Hawthorne gel."

Garth had wondered how long it would take for the old man to get word. Apparently, not nearly long enough.

"If you're speaking of Lady Margaret, I saw her home from Lord Winston's anniversary party after she came down with a headache. If that is carrying on in your estimation, then I suppose I am guilty."

Avery drew himself up. "Don't patronize me, you young stallion. The gel's a beauty and no doubt, but she is young and well into the marriage mart, and you, sir, have a different sort of match to make."

"Is that so?"

"You know well enough that it is. You'll be taking my place all too soon. 'Tis well past the time that you wed and started siring offspring. And Margaret Hawthorne is not the wife for you."

Garth walked over and casually picked up a slice of bread from the silver tray next to where his grandfather sat, pretending a nonchalance he didn't really feel. He held the bread under his nose, inhaling the yeasty scent. "And just why is that?"

His grandfather's wrinkled face turned red. "You know very well why 'tis. The gel's a Hawthorne. That is reason enough. Rumors swirl around Blackwood and his family like fog through a London street. I won't have our family name connected to his. I won't have the Dutton line mongrelized by a match between you and that young woman."

Garth's fingers unconsciously tightened around the bread, crumbling bits of the crust onto the carpet. "Margaret Hawthorne has intelligence, courage, and beauty. She has more spirit than a dozen of those simpering young misses you consider 'suitable' all put together. If I were lucky enough to win Maggie Hawthorne's hand in marriage, I would consider her strength an asset to our lineage, not a liability."

The baron thumped the end of his silver-headed cane on the floor and rose to his feet. "There was a time I might have seen some merit in what you're saying. Lord knows Adam Hawthorne doesn't deserve half the maligning of his character he has received over the years, but this, his latest adventure—involving himself with a woman suspected of murder—simply goes beyond the pale. I warn you, Grandson, should you involve yourself with his sister in any way, the title shall go to your younger brother and no one in this family will have anything more to do with either one of you."

Garth ground his jaw to keep from making a reply he would regret. He watched the old man thump his way out the door and stomp off down the hall, not the least surprised at the baron's reaction to an involvement with Maggie, yet actually hearing the words was like a blade stabbed into his chest.

He loved his grandfather. The old man might be

cantankerous, but in most ways he had a good heart and he was dedicated to his family.

Garth sighed as he left the drawing room and climbed the stairs to his bedchamber to bathe and change. Until his encounter with the baron, he hadn't actually acknowledged his interest in marrying Margaret Hawthorne. Now that she was forbidden to him, he realized that he was considering exactly that. He had thought of her and little else since the night he had kissed her on the terrace.

But pursuing thoughts of marriage wouldn't be fair to Maggie, not if his family refused to accept her.

Maggie deserved far better than that.

Wearily, Garth sat down in the chair in front of the writing desk in the corner of his bedchamber and drew out a blank sheet of foolscap. Dipping the pen into the inkwell, he began to scratch out a note, making his excuses for the evening he wouldn't be spending with her tonight. He was almost finished when he noticed the sluggish beating of his heart and the tightness in his chest. The pen stilled in his hand.

Dammit to hell, he had to see her. Perhaps if he did, he could convince himself they didn't suit. His mouth grimly set, Garth wadded up the paper, tossed it into the waste bin, and called for his valet.

Another day passed. Standing in the entry, Adam took the box from the delivery boy and flipped him a coin for his trouble. He knew what was in the package. He had bought the statue from an antiquities dealer in Bond Street over a month ago, before his mind was consumed with thoughts of murder and his body on fire for a slender, blue-eyed beauty with thick, dark copper hair.

Cradling the package in his hands, Adam strode down the hall to the drawing room, set the box down on a small mahogany Hepplewhite table, and carefully opened the box. The statue was carved of marble and about six inches high. It was probably late Ptolemaic, the figure of a goddess named Isis holding the child, Horus.

Unconsciously, Adam's hands moved over the smooth lines and indentations in the stone, appreciating the workmanship, wondering why the piece had moved him so strongly the moment he had seen it in the drawing that had advertised it for sale.

Perhaps it was the way the seated figure of the woman seemed to be slightly bent over, protecting the child.

"It's ... beautiful."

Adam's head jerked up at the sound of Christopher Derry's voice. The boy had appeared several mornings in the makeshift greenhouse, but their conversation had been limited, a discussion of orchids and the most successful ways to grow them. Aside from those encounters, Adam continued to keep his distance from the child.

"Yes, it is. There seems to be something special about it." He kept telling himself he would make time for the boy, that it wasn't fair to simply ignore him, but every time he looked at Chris, he remembered Robert and Caroline and the ugliness of their betrayal. He couldn't help thinking that if Caroline had been faithful, perhaps they would have a child that same age, an intelligent, curious little boy like Christopher Derry.

And lately it had begun to bother him that Caroline had simply thrown her child away.

"She loves her baby," Chris said, his gaze fixed squarely on the statue. "She wants to keep him safe."

Something squeezed inside his chest. "Yes, I think she does." And it was extremely astute of the boy to notice.

"Me mother was like that," Christopher said, still staring at the statue. "I miss her sometimes."

Adam felt an unwanted tug at his heart. "Sometimes life is painful, Chris, but not always. Good things happen, too."

Chris made no reply. So far the child had little reason to believe him. Adam studied the boy, whose coloring, features, and build so boldly carried the stamp of a Hawthorne male. Was there the slightest chance the boy could be his?

The notion made him uneasy. He was Caroline's son. Caroline and Robert's. If the boy were his and Caroline hadn't told him . . . if his own son had been tossed aside like so much rubbish . . . it simply didn't bear thinking about.

"Was there something you wanted, Chris?"

The boy glanced up, and Adam read the worry in his face. "I heard Maude and Reggie talking. They said people think Miss Whitney killed a man. They said she might have to go to prison."

Adam set the statue aside and went down on one knee beside the boy. "Sometimes people make mistakes, Chris. Sometimes they accuse the wrong person of doing something bad."

"I don't think Miss Whitney would ever hurt anyone."

Adam reached down and smoothed back the little boy's hair. "I don't think she would ever hurt anyone, either."

Christopher looked at him with big, moist, solemn green eyes. "You won't let them take her away?"

Emotion coiled inside him. God, he couldn't stand to think that might happen and yet he knew it could. "No, Chris. I won't let them take her away."

But unless something happened soon he wouldn't be able to stop them.

He watched Chris Derry leave the drawing room and thought again of the *Madrigal*, leaving on the morning tide. Bloody hell, it was time they both faced reality. Jillian had to get away before it was too late.

With grim determination, Adam strode out of the drawing room. He would make her leave, dammit. As soon as it was dark, he would take her aboard the ship himself—if he had to tie her up and drag her there.

She was upstairs resting. She had grown more wan with each passing day and he worried for her health. He climbed the stairs to her bedchamber and banged on the door, then strode in without permission.

"Adam!" Jillian sat curled up in the window seat, her feet tucked under her, the novel she had borrowed from the library clutched in one hand. In the sunlight slanting into the room, her breasts were outlined beneath the slick pink satin of her dressing gown and his body went instantly hard.

"What is it?" Nervously, she straightened in the window seat. "Has something happened?"

Adam continued walking toward her, wishing he could forget the reason he was there and act on the desire that hummed through him. "No, but it's about to. I want you to call Maude and tell her to pack your things. You're sailing for the Indies on the morning tide."

"The Indies?" She set the book aside and slowly came to her feet. "I told you, I'm not leaving."

Adam caught her arms. "Yes, you are. You're sailing on that ship if I have to tie you up and carry you there myself. I'll be damned if I'll stand by and watch them throw you into prison." *Or hang you.*

She thrust out her chin. "That isn't your decision to make—it's mine. And I refuse to run away!"

Worry sent his temper up a notch. He shook her a little, as if the sheer force of his will might pass through his fingers. "Listen to me, dammit! Once you're safely away, we'll have time to find out who the real killer is. I'll send for you as soon as we catch him."

Emotion flickered in her eyes. "Is that what you want? Is it really so easy for you to send me away?"

Was it easy? As much as he knew it was exactly the right thing to do, the idea of losing her ached like a boulder on his chest. Before he had met her, his days had been bleak and empty, his nights filled with painful memories of the war. Since then, even with the murder hanging over her head, Jillian had brought light and joy into his world. He couldn't imagine what it might be like to see that light snuffed out.

His hold on her arms grew gentle. "Sending you away would be the hardest thing I've ever had to do." He cupped her face between his hands and tipped her chin up. "Whatever my feelings might be, you have to go. You have to get away while you still can."

She blinked back a film of moisture, turned her

head, and pressed a kiss into his palm. "My father taught me that running from a problem only makes it worse. I can't run from something as important as this. I'm innocent. I have to prove it, no matter how difficult that might be. I'm going to stay, Adam. I don't have any other choice."

He wanted to argue. He wanted her safe and the only way he could be sure of that was for her to leave England. But another, deeper part of him thanked God that she would stay. If she went to the Indies it could be months, perhaps even years, before he saw her again. He knew the emptiness, the starkness of his life, would be unbearable.

Adam looked into her eyes, saw the strength there, the quiet determination, and in that moment knew with crystal clarity that he was in love with her.

The notion hit him so hard, for an instant he simply stood there staring. After Caroline, he had gone out of his way to avoid romantic entanglements. Even Maria couldn't completely reach him. Jillian had done it with ease.

The thought made his stomach clench. Only his fear for Jillian's life overrode his need to turn and run. He inhaled a steadying breath, worked to slow the pounding of his heart and infuse an even tone into his voice.

"We've three days left until the trial. There is still a chance we'll find the guilty party. We won't give up until we do."

Jillian's lips trembled. "Thank you."

He simply nodded. He had to escape. He needed time to deal with his astonishing newfound knowledge and decide what to do. At the back of his mind, he imagined falling under another woman's spell and his stomach squeezed harder.

"Try to get some rest," he said. "I've a couple of matters to attend. I'll meet you downstairs in a couple of hours. We'll go over everything again, see if there is something we might have missed."

Ignoring the seductive picture Jillian made in her pink satin robe, Adam quit the bedchamber.

22

Resting was out of the question. She had tried to read, but the print seemed to blur and she had finally given up. Jillian paced over to the window of her bedchamber, watched the harsh May wind tear at the newborn leaves on the branches of the trees. She felt restless and caged. She had to do something, had to get out of the house, at least for a while.

After dressing in a warm gray woolen gown and a simple gray bonnet, she pulled her pelisse from the rosewood armoire, draped it around her shoulders, and fastened the clasp. Knowing Adam wouldn't approve, she took the back stairs and left through the rear of the town house, heading off to the park.

As cold as it was, there were few pedestrians on the street. She hadn't got far when she noticed a tall, brown-haired man striding toward her along the street. He was dressed simply in trousers of nankeen twill and a dark brown tailcoat, an attractive man, she saw as he drew near, and there was something familiar about him.

"Michael!"

He paused in front of her, surprised to find her walking along the street. "Jillian. Believe it or not, I was just on my way to see you."

She remembered the card Lady Margaret had passed along to her after the Winstons' anniversary party. Michael Aimes, second son of the Marquess of Devlin, had been one of her father's students, a handsome young man four years her senior when she had met him at just sixteen.

"Time has been good to you, Michael. How long has it been?"

"More than two years. I didn't learn of your father's death until only just recently. You have my sincerest condolences."

"Thank you. Lady Margaret mentioned seeing you. She relayed your very kind offer of assistance and gave me your calling card."

"Actually, that is the reason I was coming to see you." He glanced back down the block. "There is a little café just round the corner. Perhaps you would join me for a cup of tea and we could get in out of the wind?"

Grateful for such an offer from a man who had once been a close family friend, she accepted his arm and he led her down the block to a cozy little neighborhood café called the Crown.

The smell of rich brewed coffee and fresh baked buns filled the air as they sat down at one of the small round tables in front of the window. Jillian ordered coffee and Michael ordered tea. It was good to see a friend again when she thought she hadn't any left.

"Your father meant a lot to me," Michael began,

stirring a lump of sugar into his steaming cup. "The two of you befriended me at a time in my life when I wasn't sure which way to turn. Mother had only just died and Father was grieving. I owe you both a very great deal."

"You don't owe us anything. You were one of my father's favorite students—more than that, you were his friend and he cared about you greatly."

Michael reached over and took her hand. "I've been reading about the murder in the papers. I can only imagine what you must be going through. I don't believe a word of what they're saying. Is there anything I can do?"

She dragged in a trembly breath. "I wish there were, Michael. Unless you know who killed the Earl of Fenwick, I don't see how you can."

"You mustn't give up hope. Mr. Dutton, your attorney, is one of the finest in England. A number of members of the peerage have shown their support— Rathmore and Greville, and of course, Lord Blackwood."

She nervously stirred her coffee, hoping he wouldn't guess the true nature of her relationship with Adam, though half the *ton* gossiped about it daily.

"At the trial," he went on, "you will tell your side of the story. You must believe they'll know you are telling the truth, that they will find you innocent of the murder."

Jillian took heart from his words. "I shall make them believe me. I intend to walk away cleared of all the charges."

He gave her an encouraging smile. "And after it's over, then what will you do?"

It was a question she wished he hadn't asked, words that forced her to admit the truth she had been trying to deny for the past several days. She couldn't become Adam's mistress. No matter how much he needed her. No matter how much she loved him. She couldn't live with herself if she did.

"I've been afraid to think about it. Afraid to hope, I suppose." She gazed into his kind brown eyes. "I was thinking that perhaps if my name is cleared, I might find a position as governess. I know it wouldn't be easy, but—"

"Perhaps, then, there is a way I can repay you. My father is a powerful man. He also greatly respected Professor Whitney. We've discussed your circumstances and he believes as I do, that you are not guilty. Once you are cleared of the charges, I'm sure I could persuade him to use his influence to help you."

Jillian felt a shot of hope she hadn't felt in weeks. "Oh, Michael, would you?"

"You've my word on it. I promise I shall do all I can."

They finished their refreshment speaking of more pleasant things, memories of his days at university, happy times the three of them had shared when her father was alive. She left him on the paving stones not far from the town house.

If she could somehow win her freedom, with Michael's help she could start a new life. She refused to think of Adam. Refused to think how much she loved him and how empty her life would be without him. But perhaps it wouldn't matter.

Jillian tried not to think of the threat hanging over her head.

*   *   *

It was late that afternoon, the wind still bitterly cold and kicking up dust in the street, when Jillian stepped into the study.

"Where have you been?" Adam's voice held a note of anger. "Maude said you'd left the house."

Jillian brushed past him and continued toward the fire. "I went for a walk. I had to get out for a while."

Adam raked a hand through his hair. "I was worried. I was afraid something might have happened."

"Actually, I ran into a friend of my father's. He only recently learned of Father's death. He was on his way here to offer his condolences and ask if there were anything he could do to help."

Some of the tension seeped from his shoulders. "I'm sorry. I guess my nerves are a bit on edge." He held up a piece of foolscap. "This just arrived. It's a note from Peter Fraser."

Her stomach instantly knotted. "What does it say?"

"The servants confirmed Madeleine Telford's presence at her home in Hampstead Heath the night of the murder."

Adam crumpled the note, crushed it in his fist, and tossed it into the fire. "Dammit!"

He looked at Jillian and she saw the turbulence in his expression. And there was something more, something she couldn't quite read.

"We never really thought it was Madeleine," she reminded him gently.

"It could have been. She had every reason to want him dead before he could cut her out of the will."

"If she knew he meant to change it."

He glanced away, a muscle throbbing beneath the fine scar along his jaw. He didn't say more and left the house a little while later, heading for Rathmore Hall to speak to the duke. It was a futile trip, Jillian was sure, but at least it gave Adam something to do.

She tried to keep her own fears tucked away, stored in neat little boxes in her mind, a trick her father had taught her. As she sat down on the sofa in the drawing room, she closed the lid on the box filled with painful thoughts of her upcoming trial and picked up her embroidery hoop, determined to do something to occupy her mind. A few minutes later, she glanced up to see Reggie at the door of the drawing room.

"His lordship, the Earl of Greville is here, Miss. Come to see the major. He says it's important. I thought it might be somethin' about the trial."

"Ask him if he would consider speaking to me."

Reggie nodded and disappeared, returning a few minutes later with Justin Ross, the tall, imposing Earl of Greville.

Jillian greeted him at the door of the drawing room. "I'm afraid Lord Blackwood has stepped out." He was even taller than Adam, with cool gray eyes that never missed a thing. "He shouldn't be long. Is there anything I can do for you in the meantime?"

"Perhaps there is something I can do for you," Greville said.

Her pulse kicked up as he stepped farther into the drawing room, then waited while Reggie closed the doors, making them private.

Her nerves pulled taut at the earl's serious expression. "Shall I ring for tea?" she asked.

"Thank you, no. What I've come to tell you won't take long."

Jillian indicated a seat opposite the sofa and both of them sat down.

"I believe I may have uncovered something useful in regard to the murder."

Jillian nervously sat forward on the gold brocade sofa. "Useful in what way?"

"As you probably know, the night of the murder, Howard Telford attended the Foxmoor soiree."

"I'm aware of that."

"What you don't know is that Howard wasn't there the whole of the evening."

"What?"

"About an hour before midnight, Lord Richard Maxwell and his wife took a walk out to the gazebo. They are recently wed and I suppose they wanted a moment alone."

"I believe I heard it was a love match."

He nodded and she wondered if he were thinking of Ariel, of whom he was so obviously enamored.

"While they were sitting there in the darkness," he went on, "they happened to see Howard Telford walking through the garden. Lord Richard saw him go out the gate leading into the alley behind the mews. Maxwell says Howard didn't return for quite some time and when he did, he came in through that same back gate."

Her heart was thundering, pounding so hard she jumped at the sound of Adam's voice as he walked into the drawing room. "And it is only a four block walk to his uncle's house in Grosvenor Square," he said, having heard the last of the convesation.

"Exactly so," said Greville. "If Maxwell hadn't

chanced to see him leave, he would have had the perfect alibi. As it is, I believe Howard Telford has some very hard questions to answer."

Jillian's heart raced. She looked at Adam and saw the same bright glimmer of hope that was burning in her. Silently, she said a little prayer.

They spent the rest of the day and into the evening planning their strategy. Greville had given them their first real lead and they needed to use it well. Adam sent notes to Peter Fraser and Garth Dutton, and both men were seated in the study when Kitt and Clayton Barclay unexpectedly arrived at the house.

"We've got news," Kitt said excitedly, hugging Jillian briefly and receiving a kiss on the cheek from Adam.

"Very interesting news," Clay drawled. His golden eyes surveyed the room, taking in the study's occupants. "I see you're all hard at work. Perhaps this will help."

With Adam's encouragement, Clay guided his petite wife to a chair near the sofa, then perched on the padded leather arm and dangled a long leg off the end. "As you recall, after the late earl's funeral, both Howard and Madeleine Telford were out of the city."

"That's right," Adam agreed. "I wanted to ask them some questions about the murder but Madeleine had gone to visit relatives in the country and Howard was at Fenwick Park, the estate he inherited in Hampshire."

Rathmore smiled. "Not quite. Neither Madeleine nor Howard was where they claimed to be the week after the funeral."

Jillian's pulse quickened. "Where did they go?"

"I'm afraid I don't know that, but it's rather an amazing coincidence that both of them would lie."

Peter Fraser spoke up. "You're suggesting they might have been together."

"I'm saying there's a very good chance that the two of them are romantically involved. Kitt did a little digging on her own and turned up a rumor to that effect. Word is Howard and Madeleine are having an affair."

"Good heavens."

"If that's the case," Adam said, "perhaps Fenwick found out and that is the reason he cut them out of the will."

Jillian shook her head. "That doesn't make sense. He wanted Madeleine to remarry. He would have been glad the two of them had found each other."

Jillian got up from the sofa and started moving around the room. "Ever since the murder, I've replayed that night a thousand times. Each time I do, I recall how distracted the earl seemed that evening. I beat him badly at chess, which was nearly impossible to do, and then there was the book he sent me to fetch just before the shot was fired."

"How was that unusual?" Adam asked.

"It was the book itself that was odd, a volume by Lord Chesterfield, something about gentlemanly conduct. It was a strange choice, even for the earl." She bit down on her bottom lip. "The entire evening was odd somehow, though I can't exactly put my finger on it."

Adam gazed at her intently from across the room. All evening he had been distant, more withdrawn than usual, and she wondered at the cause.

"All right," he said, "so now we've caught Madeleine in one lie and Howard in two. What do we do about it?"

"Perhaps we should try to get back inside the old man's study," Clay suggested, "see if there is something there that's been overlooked."

"I'm not sure I should hear this," Garth said from his place on the sofa.

"You're right," Adam agreed. "I suspect this could get a little disconcerting for a member of the Inns of Court."

Garth got up from his chair. "If there is anything you need from me, I'll be in my office all day tomorrow." He turned to look at Jillian. "Whatever they're planning, I wish you the very best of luck."

Adam turned his attention to Peter Fraser. "It appears we need to be private."

The slender man rose to leave. "I'll see if I can discover the whereabouts of our errant suspects after the funeral." With a brief bow, Fraser also left the study and Adam returned his attention to the duke.

"You're not serious about breaking into Fenwick's house?"

"I realize," Rathmore drawled, "that as a military man, breaking and entering goes against your principles, but it seems to me that if you wish to prove your lady's innocence, you are rapidly running out of options."

Adam flicked an unreadable glance at Jillian, but didn't hesitate. "How do you suggest I get in?"

"There's an entrance at the rear of the house. That is the way I left the night of the murder." Jillian walked over to where Adam stood next to his desk.

"The door is partly overgrown with ivy and very rarely used, but it leads to the study and I know where to find the key."

"All right. Tomorrow night, sometime after midnight, I'll break into the house and—"

"*We*," two voices corrected in unison.

"It was my idea," Clay said, "and if you do find something, you'll need a credible witness to testify to its authenticity."

"I'm going, too," Jillian said firmly. "I'm the one who knows the way."

"Not a chance." A dangerous glint appeared in Adam's eyes. "You're staying here where you'll be safe."

"I'm going. I know every inch of that study— even the hidden drawer in the bottom of Lord Fenwick's desk. I have a far better chance of finding something useful than you do, and it's my life that's at risk."

Adam softly cursed.

Sitting next to her big handsome husband, Kassandra Barclay sighed. "I hate to miss all the fun, but I imagine three people trying to sneak in without being seen will be difficult enough."

Clay kissed the top of her head. "All too true, my love." He grinned. "Besides, we'll need you to help us if something goes wrong and we all wind up in jail."

It was later that same night that Garth arrived as promised at Maggie's house. The hour was late, the traffic on the street mostly gone as she walked beside him in the garden. Aunt Sophie had been sitting with them in the drawing room, but she had fallen asleep, slumped down against the arm of the sofa, and they had escaped for a moment alone.

In deference to the chilly May evening, Maggie wore a cashmere shawl over her blue silk gown, but instead of being cold, every time she looked into the strong lines of Garth's face, every time she caught the glint of moonlight on his golden hair, her body felt overly warm.

Garth had called on her every night since he had rescued her from Lord Winston's anniversary party. He had been charming and solicitous, regaling her and Aunt Sophie with stories of his childhood and interesting cases that he had represented. Aunt Sophie was beaming, heady with thoughts of the offer she was certain the wealthy lawyer, heir to Baron Schofield, intended to make.

Maggie was equally certain her aunt was wrong. It was obvious Garth found her attractive. He made no effort to hide the desire in his eyes whenever he looked at her, but his intentions where she was concerned were a subject he had never broached, and several times Maggie had caught his troubled expression when he thought she couldn't see.

His family would scarcely approve of a match between a Dutton and a Hawthorne, no matter that Maggie's brother was an earl. With another man, she would simply have come out and asked, but if she did that with Garth, he might admit that he only wanted her in his bed, and if his intention was other than marriage, she would have to refuse to see him.

The thought made her heart squeeze.

Garth paused in the middle of the gravel path. "Your mind is wandering, love. Do you really find my company so tedious?"

Startled, she glanced up at him, into those bright green eyes. "You know I don't."

"What were you thinking?"

If only she could tell him, admit that she was afraid she was falling in love with him, that if she did, her heart was bound to be broken.

"I was thinking about my brother and the trial," she lied, though earlier it had been true.

Garth reached toward a little yellow marigold, plucked the blossom, and absently twirled the stem. "Your brother is in love with Miss Whitney, you know."

Maggie's stomach contracted. "Adam has always had a protective streak. He's been fighting for the underdog since he was a boy. It doesn't mean he loves her."

And Maggie prayed he didn't. If Adam truly loved a woman, he would want her to be happy. He wouldn't consider keeping her as his mistress; he would want her to be his wife. As much as Maggie adored her brother and wanted him to be happy, as much as she had come to like Jillian, she prayed it wasn't the truth.

Even if Jillian's innocence was proved, Adam's reputation would never recover, and Maggie's own would be blackened right along with it. If there were the slightest chance Garth intended to offer marriage, that chance would disappear.

"You disapprove of Miss Whitney?" Garth held out the marigold and Maggie accepted it with a hand that only faintly trembled.

"No. I like her. Very much, in fact. I just . . . I'm not sure my brother is capable of falling in love." That was the truth, or at least it had been true until

Jillian had appeared. Maggie couldn't help wondering if perhaps Garth was right and her brother was falling in love.

In the moonlight, Garth's eyes seemed to caress her. "What about you, Lady Margaret? Do you think you could ever fall in love?"

Maggie stared up at him, her pulse taking a leap. "That depends. I suppose I could . . . if the right man came along."

He brushed a finger along her cheek and a little ripple ran over her skin. "This man . . . what would he be like?"

Like you, she wanted to say. *Strong and solid, handsome as sin. The kind of man who takes my breath away.* "He would have to be honest and sincere." She twirled the stem of the marigold between her gloved fingers. "I'd want him to be gentle, but also a man of strength, someone I could count on."

"What about passion?" Garth asked softly, his gaze steady on her face.

Maggie moistened lips that suddenly felt too dry. "Yes . . . that would certainly be important. A strong, passionate man—a man who makes me feel like a woman."

Garth's hand pressed into the small of her back as he drew her into his arms. "Do I make you feel like a woman, Maggie?" She didn't have time to answer before his mouth descended over hers.

What started as a gentle exploration of lips grew hotter in an instant. Maggie trembled. She opened for him, allowing the invasion of his tongue, then entangled it with her own and heard him groan. She found herself clinging to his shoulders, pressing herself against him, straining to get even closer. She could feel his arousal, a solid ridge pressing hard against her belly. Instead of being frightened, she felt her heartbeat quicken and the blood begin to pulse in her ears.

Garth shifted, deepened the kiss, and Maggie clutched his neck, going up on her toes to press into the hot rod that seemed to promise respite from the heat he created. She was trembling, whispering his name when Garth turned away, bringing the kiss to an end.

"We have to stop," he said gruffly, "before I take you right here." He held her close, one big hand cupping the nape of her neck, cradling her head against his shoulder.

Maggie made a faint sound in her throat, whether of protest or gratitude she couldn't be sure. She only knew she wanted him to hold her forever and she knew that he could not.

"You're shivering. It's time we went in." But his eyes, a smoky shade of green in the moonlight, said he didn't want to leave and neither did Maggie.

Reluctantly she released him and took a step away. "My aunt will be furious if she wakes up and finds us gone."

"I know." His thumb brushed over her kiss-swollen lips. He opened his mouth as if he wanted to say something more, and her heart swelled with hope. Instead, he shook his head and his lips seemed to tighten. Resting a hand at her waist, he guided her back to the house.

They passed the drawing room, saw that her aunt still slept on the sofa, and kept on walking. In the entry, he paused.

"I'll be busy for a while. The trial begins soon and I've got things to do."

She nodded, but her throat felt tight. She wondered if he had come to his senses and decided not to see her again. She started to ask him, but couldn't seem to force out the words.

"Good night, love."

"Good night, Garth."

He didn't kiss her again and she knew a moment of disappointment. Her heart felt swollen and tender. She was no longer worried about falling in love with Garth.

As she watched him descend the front porch stairs on the way to his carriage, Maggie knew it had already happened.

23

The rattle of harness and the whir of iron wheels echoed against the brick walls in the alley behind the late Lord Fenwick's mansion. The vehicle pulled to a halt in the shadows and Adam swung open the door.

Dressed completely in black, he descended the narrow iron stairs, followed by Clay, also dressed in black, then reached up to help Jillian alight. In her simple dark gray gown, her auburn hair pulled into a knot at the nape of her neck, she blended with the men into the moonless night that was the answer to the first of their prayers.

The air was cold and damp, the city submerged in a thick gray mist that obscured visibility. A sheen of dew softened the earth, helping to muffle their footsteps as Adam followed Jillian toward a vine-covered gate at the rear of the mansion. Crickets stilled as they walked past, replaced by the hoot of an owl and the flap of wings just over their heads.

Adam barely noticed. His mind was fixed on his

mission, undertaken with the same cold precision he had exercised in the army. They had decided to enter the house shortly after midnight in hopes that Howard would either be out for the evening or asleep upstairs in his room. The servants would be abed and the lower floors deserted, allowing them to get in and out without being seen.

Or at least that was the plan.

As Adam watched Jillian moving silently along in front of him, the muscles across his shoulders tightened. He didn't want her there, didn't want to put her in danger, but her arguments had been persuasive. She knew the house, knew the best way in and out—and no other options remained.

She paused at a small door obscured by ivy clinging to the weathered wood. He watched her search the mossy bed of a big clay flowerpot until she located a heavy iron key. Holding up the key in triumph, she inserted it into the lock, opened the door, and motioned for him to follow her into the house. Clay walked in behind them.

"This way," Jillian whispered, once they stood in the darkened hallway. Silently, Adam followed her down a narrow corridor that bisected another hall. One path led off to the left toward the kitchens while the second corridor turned right. They headed in that direction until another door appeared. Jillian turned the handle, quietly shoved it open, and they stepped into a small, windowless room.

"We're in the earl's private library," she said softly, fumbling in the darkness for the brass whale oil lamp that sat on a long mahogany table. Clay lit the lamp, casting light and eerie shadows along the book-lined walls; then they proceeded toward the door to the main part of the study.

Unlike the library, it was a large, less formal room. Evidence of the late earl remained in the worn leather sofas and chairs, the etching of his long-dead wife over the hearth. With the lamp turned low, they moved to the windows and closed the heavy damask draperies, then Adam lit a second lamp and Clay turned up the wick on the first.

He heard Jillian's sigh of relief. At least they had made it this far.

In the soft yellow light, he could see her face, paler than it should have been, the lines around her mouth tight with nerves. She glanced down at the carpet, stretched out on the polished wooden floors, the place where the old earl had lain after he had been killed, and her face paled even more.

Dammit, he shouldn't have let her come, should have found some other way. He had known the memories would surface, and with them the grief.

He was in love with her. Sometime during the long, sleepless night, he had come to grips with the knowledge. Now he wanted to protect her, to hold her, soothe the sorrow he read in her face.

Now was not the time. Her life depended on finding something useful and he intended to make the most of each second they remained in the study.

He moved closer, slid an arm around her waist. "Show me the hidden compartment," he said to her, purposely drawing her thoughts from memories of the past. She nodded and they walked over to the big rosewood desk in front of the window. Seating herself in the high-backed leather chair, Jillian reached beneath the desk and pulled a tiny concealed lever. When she opened the middle drawer, another hidden drawer popped open behind it.

Unfortunately, the drawer was empty.

"You go to work in the library," he said, ignoring the disappointment on her face. "Clay and I will search in here."

"All right." She turned to leave, but he caught her wrist and pulled her back, gave her a swift, hard kiss. "If anything goes wrong, get out of here as fast as you can. Go back to the carriage. Lance will get you home."

Her gaze grew more disturbed, but she didn't argue, just kissed him one last time and hurried away. He prayed if things went bad, she would do as he had told her.

Returning his attention to the desk, Adam began searching through drawers while Clay went through a small bookcase next to the door.

They worked in silence for perhaps twenty minutes, Adam carefully examining each drawer, rifling through stacks of papers, making a cursory review of each one. Nothing looked the least bit hopeful, mostly tenant leasehold papers, stock certificates, and insurance forms. He was immersed in a document that appeared to be a record of income received from one of the Fenwick estates when the door slammed open and Howard Telford walked in.

Adam's gaze locked on the pistol Howard held in a pale, blunt-fingered hand and silently he cursed.

"Well, well, well." In a black-and-gold silk dressing gown, his sandy hair rumpled as if he had just got out of bed, Howard tilted his weak chin at an arrogant angle. "Look what we have here."

Adam willed himself not to glance at the door to the room where Jillian was. He prayed she had heard Howard's entrance and escaped outside to the carriage. Instead, she walked in just then, her head down as she skimmed the pages of a book.

"Adam—you won't believe what I've found." She glanced up, stopped dead at the sight of Howard, and her eyes went round with shock.

Howard's expression grew even more smug. "Isn't this cozy. I'm only slightly surprised to see you here, Jillian, considering how desperate you must be." He shifted his gaze to Adam. "But I'm astonished that a man of your position—an earl, no less—would lower himself to the level of a common thief."

Adam flicked a glance toward the bookcases Clay had been searching, but the duke had disappeared out of sight behind the door Howard had come in through.

"Thievery was never my intention, as I'm certain you know. But even if I were a thief, it would be preferable to being a murderer."

Howard's fleshy face turned red. "You have some nerve accusing me." But he swallowed as he walked farther into the room and quietly closed the door. From the corner of his eye, Adam saw Clay move into the shadows behind Howard's back, a small pocket pistol in his hand.

"I think you know very well what I'm talking about," Adam continued. "If not, considering your alibi for the night of the murder has recently been torn to shreds, perhaps you can guess."

Howard's thick fingers imperceptibly tightened on the pistol. "That's insane. I was attending the Fox-moor soiree that evening. Half the *ton* saw me there."

"Yes, they did," Jillian added. "And two of them also saw you leave."

"She's right." Adam drew Howard's attention back to him. "You were gone just long enough to walk the four blocks back to this house, shoot the earl through the study window, toss the gun into the room, and return to the soiree. It would have been the perfect murder if you hadn't been seen."

Something stirred in Howard's features, a tautness that made his fleshy face look harsh. "You always did think you were smarter than the rest of us. *A major in His Majesty's Army.* Well, so what if I left the party and went for a walk? Do you really believe that is grounds to accuse me of murder?"

"You also lied about your whereabouts after your uncle's funeral. Two lies, Howard, and people begin to get suspicious."

"I don't think so. I think your precious Jillian is going to hang for murder."

"She isn't guilty," Adam said, casting a look her way. "But then you know that firsthand."

Howard's mouth thinned. The corners faintly curved and Adam caught the gleam of teeth in a smile that looked almost feral. "What if I do? What if I told you I knew the old man and the girl would both be here in the study that night, as they had been every night that week? What if I told you I came into the yard through the garden, that I watched them through the window, and when Jillian went into the library, I shot that selfish old bastard and tossed the gun onto the floor next to his body?"

Adam heard Jillian's gasp.

"What difference would it make?" Howard gloated.

"With your reputation and your involvement with the girl, who do you think would believe you?"

"I would." The Duke of Rathmore's powerful voice swept across the dimly lit study. The pistol in his hand glinted in the lamplight as he stepped out of the shadows. "And I would suggest, *my lord*, that the best chance you have of saving your miserable life is to confess your crime and throw yourself on the mercy of the court."

Howard's hand shook. At Clay's appearance he had begun to sweat, but he kept the gun pointed at Adam's chest. "They won't believe you. They know you've both been against me from the start."

It was very possibly true, but it was obvious Howard wasn't sure and panic flared in his eyes. Howard turned the pistol, focusing it on Jillian, and Adam's blood ran cold.

Moving behind her, Howard wrapped a thick arm around her neck and jerked her back against his chest. "Drop the gun," he said to Clay.

Adam's heart thundered. This was his fault. He shouldn't have let her come, no matter how convincing she was. Fear for her made it hard to think.

"Drop it!" Howard demanded. "Now!"

Very carefully, Clay placed the weapon on the floor in front of him.

"Very good. Now kick it over here."

Clay used the side of his foot to send the pistol sliding across the polished wood. It disappeared through the door to the library.

"The gun is gone. Let her go," Adam commanded, his voice hard with the fury he fought to control.

Howard shook his head. "I'm afraid that isn't possible. You see, Miss Whitney and I are leaving. If you wish her to remain alive, you will stay exactly where you are until we are safely away."

Jillian's fingers dug into Howard's arm as he dragged her backward, heading for the library and the door leading out to the garden.

Unconsciously, Adam took a step toward them. He instantly stilled when Howard lifted the pistol and pressed it against the side of Jillian's head.

"I wouldn't do that if I were you." One step at a time, Howard continued backing away, and Adam's muscles tensed with every step.

Easy, he told himself. *Let the enemy get into your sights before you make your move.* But with Jillian's life at stake, his patience was wearing thin. He couldn't let Howard leave the house or he might never see her again.

The moment Howard disappeared into the library, Adam moved and so did Clay. They had almost reached the door when a shot rang out.

Fear—more savage than he had known on the battlefield—ripped through him like red-hot grape shot. Adam burst through the library door, breathing hard, his mouth so dry he couldn't swallow.

Instead of finding Jillian wounded and lying on the floor, it was Howard, facedown at her feet, the back of his dark blue tailcoat covered in blood. On the opposite side of the room, Madeleine Telford stood pale and shaken, Clay's pistol hanging loosely from her hand.

"I-I didn't mean to shoot him. We . . . we were together up in his room. He thought he heard noises in the study. When he came down to see, I-I left by the servants' stairs. I heard . . . heard him say he killed Lord Fenwick. I saw him threaten

Lord Blackwood and Miss Whitney and I-I picked up the gun . . ."

Madeleine swallowed, then started to cry. As Clay drew the gun from her fingers, Adam wrapped Jillian in his arms. He could feel her trembling, and a shudder ran through him. He would never forget the terror he had felt when he thought that she had been killed.

"I didn't mean to kill him," Madeleine repeated softly. "I just aimed and somehow the gun went off." She continued to weep, and Clay urged her down into a nearby chair.

"You probably saved Miss Whitney's life," Clay said.

The butler, Atwater, burst into the library just then and saw the earl on the floor. With a glance at Adam and the duke, he turned and raced off to summon the needed authorities.

A movement on the floor drew their attention to Howard.

"He's still alive," the duke said, kneeling beside the wounded man.

Adam moved next to him and together they gently turned Howard over. His pain-filled eyes searched for Madeleine Telford across the room.

"I loved you," he said. "I always . . . loved you." He was breathing hard, blood oozing out of a small hole in his chest where the lead ball had exited his body. "But you never . . . really . . . cared about me at all . . . did you?"

Madeleine's face turned a ghostly shade of white.

Adam shrugged out of his coat, wadded it up, and shoved it under Howard's head. "Save your strength. Atwater has gone for help. A surgeon will be here any moment."

Howard's glassy eyes swung to his face. "It . . . it was her idea . . . not mine."

Madeleine came swiftly to her feet. "I don't know what he's talking about."

"The night she came to . . . see him . . . the old man told her he was . . . changing his will. She knew where he . . . kept his pistol. She took it out of his . . . drawer and . . . brought it to me . . . said we had to . . . kill him."

"He's lying!" Madeleine nearly shouted. "I didn't have anything to do with it!"

Howard's lips thinned, barely curved. "He found out about us . . . a couple of weeks ago. Found out that . . . Madeleine had been . . . cheating on Henry. That is the reason . . . he was going to change the will. He thought Madeleine's infidelity was the reason Henry . . . killed himself." Howard fixed his gaze on the woman he had loved. "He never knew the truth."

"Shut up, Howard. Please . . . if you ever really loved me—"

"Keep quiet, Madeleine," Rathmore warned.

"What truth, Howard?" Jillian gently prodded.

Howard coughed, wheezed in a breath, and moistened his dry, trembling lips. "Madeleine made it look like . . . Henry killed himself . . . but it wasn't the truth. Madeleine . . . shot him."

Madeleine jumped up from the sofa and raced toward the door at the back of the library, but Clay's long strides cut off her escape. He caught her easily, sliding an arm around her waist, hauling her back into the room, and dumping her down into the chair.

"You aren't going anywhere, Madeleine. Not just yet, at any rate."

Howard gazed dully at Jillian. "She started . . . those rumors about you."

Jillian made a soft little sound in her throat and Adam felt a tightness in his chest for all she had suffered at Howard and Madeleine's hands.

Then the door burst open and half a dozen watchmen rushed in. When Adam looked at Howard, his eyes were closed and his chest no longer moved up and down.

The recently titled Earl of Fenwick was dead.

Adam strode to Jillian and pulled her into his arms.

The next two hours passed in a blur. Jillian barely remembered watching the uniformed officers dragging a hysterical Madeleine off to their battered carriage for transportation to Newgate prison. She only faintly recalled picking up the book she had found in the library, and showing it to Adam.

"This is the what the earl sent me to get the night he was killed. It's Chesterfield's *Letters to His Son on How a Gentleman Should Behave*. I thought it odd at the time. Tonight I found what the earl had actually sent me to retrieve."

Her hand shook as she held out the small, leatherbound volume she had discovered behind Lord Chesterfield's book. "It's his son Henry's journal."

"So that's how he knew," Clay said.

"I only read the last several pages, but it mentions Madeleine's betrayal and how much it hurt him. Henry said he loved her too much to share her with another man. He said when he told her, she laughed. He wrote that he was going to divorce her."

Adam released a weary sigh. "Then that is the reason she killed him."

"Madeleine would have lost everything," Clay said.

"Yes, but with Henry dead, Howard Telford became next in line for the title—and if Madeleine played her cards right, she would still become a countess, just as she had planned."

It was almost two in the morning when the carriage pulled away from the mansion, heading first to Rathmore Hall. Exhaustion kept them silent along the way, weariness mingled with relief. It didn't take long to reach the ducal mansion. As Clay reached for the door, Adam caught his shoulder.

"That invitation you and Kassandra extended to Jillian . . . is that still open?"

Clay cast him a glance. "You know it is."

"Good. Then if it's agreeable with you and the duchess, she'll be arriving tomorrow afternoon."

"Of course." The duke turned to Jillian. "We'll look forward to your visit." Stepping down from the coach, he headed up the path to his house. As the carriage rocked forward, Jillian caught a glimpse of the duchess flying down the steps into her husband's arms.

Jillian glanced at Adam. Brass lanterns next to the velvet curtains reflected on his raven black hair, but his face remained in shadow.

"What will they do to Madeleine?" she asked softly, remembering all too clearly the horrors of Newgate prison.

"There is no way to prove Henry was murdered. She'll have to face charges for conspiracy, but in Howard's death, she can claim she was only trying to protect you. Perhaps she'll be transported. Madeleine's always been a survivor. Whatever happens, I imagine she'll land on her feet."

Darkness hid the sharp planes and angles of his face, but she could hear the bitterness in his voice. He was thinking of Caroline, she knew, and the betrayal he had suffered. Jillian felt the sharp sting of tears. Her ordeal was over, the danger past, but the future remained nebulous, even more uncertain than it was before.

She would put her trust in Michael Aimes, pray he and his father would help her make a new life somewhere else.

"It's over," she said, more to herself than to him.

Adam wrapped his arms around her. "Yes. . . . You're free, Jillian. No trial, no prison, no threat of the gallows over your head. Nothing more to worry about."

But it wasn't that simple. Not for her. She was in love with the Earl of Blackwood. Just looking at him made her heart swell almost painfully.

And yet they had no future. She wouldn't become his mistress and that was all he had to offer.

"I'm going to be staying with the duke?"

His eyes looked bluer than she had ever seen them. He pressed his lips against her temple. "Just for a while, my love."

Jillian didn't say anything more. She didn't understand why he had suddenly decided to send her away but as much as it hurt to leave him, she knew it was the right thing to do.

The wind came up, making the carriage shudder as it rolled toward his town house. She could hear the clatter of the rain on the roof and the splash of water beneath the iron wheels.

She must have fallen asleep. It was sometime later that she awakened in her bedchamber dressed in a clean white night rail. In the light of a freshly stoked fire, she saw the tall, shadowy figure of the earl on his way out the door.

"Adam?"

At the sound of her voice, he stopped and turned. "Yes, love . . . ?"

She was leaving on the morrow. Their time together was over. Though she knew it would only make things harder, she couldn't stop the words. "Don't go."

She was in love with him. Wildly, desperately, and she was going to lose him.

He returned to the side of the bed and his hand brushed gently against her cheek. "Are you certain?"

She was sure it was the wrong thing to do and even more certain it was exactly what she wanted. "I need you. I don't want to be alone. Not tonight."

Adam sat down on the edge of the bed and for several long moments simply held her. He left her only long enough to strip away his clothes and return to the bed. Thunder rumbled, rattling the windows as he reached for her, his elegant hands drawing off her simple white night rail.

She thought how much she loved him, how much she would miss him. The pins were gone from her hair and he fanned the heavy auburn curls around her shoulders.

"I've always loved your hair," he said softly, running his fingers through it as he kissed the side of her neck, trailed moist kisses over her bare shoulders. Lightning flashed outside the window, illuminating the little wrought-iron balcony that overlooked the garden and Adam's lean, muscular body. Reaching out, she ran her fingers over the long hard muscles across his shoulders, the sinews on his chest. Adam kissed her deeply and pleasure streaked through her, as wild as the storm outside. He kissed her eyes, her nose, her mouth, kissed her deeply again.

Her hands trembled as she touched him, explored a flat copper nipple, felt the shudder that rippled through him. Very gently he cupped a breast, his fingers warm where they rubbed across her nipple. Very thoroughly, he kissed her. A slow, erotic, sensual kiss, and yet it was achingly tender.

He kissed his way down her neck, pressed his lips against her collarbone, trailed kisses lower, and took the weight of her breast into his mouth. The small bud at the crest puckered and tightened. She trembled at the feel of his lips and teeth, at the slickness of his tongue circling her nipple. Heat enveloped her, swelled inside her like the building storm.

He moved lower. His tongue ringed her navel and she shifted restlessly on the mattress. Her body felt hot, her skin tight and flushed. He moved down her body, eased her legs apart, and settled himself between them. He kissed her belly, found the soft thatch of dark red curls at the juncture of her legs, and kissed her there, slowly kissed the insides of her thighs.

She moaned as his hands slid under her bottom and he lifted her, pressed his mouth against her softness. Her hands slid into his hair and heavy black curls wrapped around her fingers. She trembled as he parted the folds of her sex with his tongue and she couldn't believe what he was doing, couldn't believe it could feel so impossibly good. Need encompassed her. Her thighs fell open and her hips arched up. She fisted the sheets and bit down on her lip to keep from crying out at the sheer, sweet pleasure pouring through her.

He took her with tenderness and endless determination, using his mouth and hands, making the need swell until she could no longer control it. Her climax came swift and hard, flooding her with a deep, drenching pleasure. Her flesh pulsed and heat sliced through her like lightning.

In the flickering orange glow of the fire, his eyes looked nearly black as he came up over her. Her fingers dug into his shoulders and she felt the muscles bunch as he surged inside her, filling her with a single deep thrust.

She moaned at the fresh heat stirring to life inside her. Muscles that were limp and sated coiled and tightened with renewed desire. Lightning flashed and thunder rumbled. Her hands smoothed over the wide, sleek muscles in his back as he began to move and she thought that nothing had ever felt so good, so right. She loved him completely and forever, and tomorrow she would lose him.

The tempo of his movements increased, the deep thrust and drag of his shaft, the powerful drive of his long, lean body. She could feel his muscles tightening, rippling, straining for control. His rhythm increased, carrying her toward the pinnacle that she had reached before. Adam drove faster, deeper, harder.

"Come with me," he whispered, and the rough, erotic cadence of his voice spun her over the edge.

I love you, she thought. *I love you so much.*

Afterward, they lay together. After all they had

been through these past terrible weeks, exhaustion claimed them and they slept for a while. Near dawn, cradled spoon-fashion against him, she felt him stir, felt the growing hardness of his arousal. He made love to her slowly, with great care and tenderness, and so thoroughly that when he was finished she slept again and didn't hear him leave.

By the time she awakened late in the morning, Adam was gone.

24

Jillian's heart felt leaden as she tossed back the covers and eased from the bed. Her body ached in places it never had before and a slight headache pounded at her temples. She flicked a glance at the bed, wondering when Adam had left her, missing him already. She barely heard the knock at the door before Maude bustled in and threw open the curtains.

Outside the window, the rain had stopped but sullen gray clouds hung over the city and a heavy mist hung in the air.

" 'Tis time to be packin' yer things," the Irishwoman said, scurrying toward the armoire. " 'Tisn't every day a lady gets invited ta stay with a duke."

Jillian suppressed a twinge of despair. She was leaving the home that had been her place of refuge for the past four weeks. She thought of little Christopher and how much she had come to love him. She remembered Adam's heated lovemaking last night.

She thought of how much she loved him, thought

of all she was leaving behind, and a cold knot formed in the pit of her stomach. She was free again, cleared of the charges against her. But as Maude continued to pack her things, sadness settled like a heavy black cloak around Jillian's heart.

Maggie Hawthorne shoved open the door to Adam's greenhouse the following morning and stepped into the warm, humid interior. Through the leafy foliage, she caught a glimpse of Adam's hair, the same raven black as her own, as he bent over a purple ruffled orchid.

"Good morning," she said, walking toward him. He turned at the sound of her voice. "Reggie told me you were out here."

He smiled as he came to his feet—a wide, full, generous flash of white, the kind of smile she hadn't seen on her brother's face since he was a dashing young student at Oxford.

He brushed the rich black soil off his hands. "You're looking lovely this morning. To what do I owe the pleasure?"

Maggie sighed. "The gossip in town is rampant. The *Chronicle* says Howard Telford shot the Earl of Fenwick, that he admitted it just before he died."

"Yes, thank God."

"The article said you were there with Rathmore and Jillian when Madeleine Telford shot him."

"I'm afraid that's also true."

God, she'd been praying it was a mistake, that Adam hadn't been anywhere near this latest scandal.

"Does that mean Jillian no longer faces charges?"

As he finished washing his hands, Adam flashed

another winning smile. "She's been completely exonerated of any involvement in Fenwick's murder."

"I never believed she did it. She simply isn't the sort."

Adam's features held a longing Maggie had never seen before. "I'm going to marry her, Maggie."

Dear God. The blood in her face completely drained away. Sweet Jesus, this couldn't be happening. "Then you must . . . must be in love with her."

His eyes sparkled, seemed a brighter shade of blue. "I didn't realize it at first. But Jillian's different, gentle and loving, courageous and loyal. When I'm with her . . ." He shook his head. "I don't know . . . she makes me feel like the man I was before I went to war."

Maggie's heart tugged. She loved her brother. During his years in the army, he had suffered more than his share of pain. She wanted him to be happy.

She had never imagined that happiness would come at the cost of her own.

She pasted on a smile and walked toward him, went into his arms, and gave him a long, warm hug. "I'm happy for you, Adam. I'm so glad you finally found someone to love."

He let go of her, his mood a little pensive. "I never really thought I would. Not after Caroline."

Maggie kept her smile in place, though her heart was beating with a rhythm that was almost painful. She refused to think of Garth and what his family would say about the Earl of Blackwood marrying a woman of Jillian's reputation. She knew any hope she had of marrying Garth would disappear the day her brother wed.

"Where is Jillian? I didn't see her when I came in. Have you asked her yet?"

"She's staying with Kassandra and Clay. The gossip has been vicious enough already. This afternoon, I'm going to look for a ring. I thought on Saturday night the four of us would go out for a very proper evening. I want to take her somewhere special. A private room at the Golden Chalice, perhaps. She's never been properly courted. I want her to have a night she'll remember. I thought I would ask her afterward, in the gardens at Rathmore Hall."

She caught the edge of nervousness in Adam's voice. Did he actually believe Jillian might refuse? It was obvious she was in love with him, and the evening he planned sounded wonderfully romantic.

Garth's golden-haired image popped into her head. She could almost hear his deep laughter, feel the heat of his mouth moving over hers. Maggie blinked back a sudden sheen of tears.

Adam tilted her chin up. "You're not crying, are you?"

She forced her lips to curve. "I'm just so happy. Be sure to tell Jillian how very pleased I am."

And part of her was. She had worried about Adam for years. She had seen his loneliness and the hard protective shell he had built around himself. She had hoped one day he would find someone who could break through that shell and bring his loneliness to an end. And she liked Jillian, she really did. Under different circumstances, she would have been overjoyed at her brother's choice of wife.

Leaning toward him, she kissed his lean cheek and hoped he didn't notice that her lips were trembling.

"I know you're going to be very happy, Adam.

Now, I'm afraid I've got to run. I expect to hear all the details after everything is official."

Adam nodded, smiled again. She couldn't remember ever seeing him smile so often. As Maggie climbed into her waiting carriage, she thought of Garth and fought not to cry.

He hadn't been to see her. Undoubtedly, he was aware of the shooting and that Jillian and Adam had been there that night. Every tongue in London was wagging and it was bound to go on for years.

And Madeleine Telford's trial still lay ahead. Adam would have to testify, perhaps Jillian as well. For generations, the Dutton family had kept itself aloof from any sort of scandal. If there had ever been a chance that Garth would want her for his wife, that chance was over now.

Once the coach arrived home, she managed to make it upstairs before she started to cry, but the minute she closed the door, a flood of tears erupted. She pulled the strings on her blue silk bonnet and tossed it aside, then crumpled down on her big feather bed.

She wanted her brother to be happy—she did—but dear God in heaven, she hadn't expected his happiness would destroy her own. She swallowed past the tight knot in her throat, thinking of Garth, thinking how desperately she had come to love him.

Wishing that she had never met him.

How could she have been stupid enough to fall in love?

"Margaret?" The sound of her niece's bitter sobs echoed across the bedchamber. Sophie felt a jolt of alarm. "Margaret, whatever is the matter?"

Curled in the middle of her big feather bed, her niece sat up on the bed. She madly wiped her eyes but they looked red-rimmed and damp. There was simply no way to mistake Maggie's misery, and worry hastened Sophie across the room.

"Come, dear one, tell me what is wrong."

Maggie dragged in a shuddering breath. "Oh, Aunt Sophie, I feel so absolutely wretched!" She started weeping again and Sophie opened her arms.

"There, there, dear," she said as the girl accepted her embrace. "Surely it can't be as bad as all that."

"It's worse than that, Aunt Sophie."

"Come now. We'll sit down in front of the fire and you can tell me all about it." Sophie led her to a settee and chairs grouped around the hearth, then went over and tugged on the bell pull. In seconds, a chambermaid appeared with a silver tea tray. As soon as the maid left the room, Sophie poured them each a cup.

"Now. Tell me what is wrong." She handed the cup and saucer to Maggie, who grasped it with trembling hands.

"What's wrong is that I'm a stupid, silly fool. I've fallen in love with Garth Dutton and there is no way on God's green earth he is ever going to marry me."

"That is completely ridiculous. The man is obviously smitten. It is only a matter of time before he makes an offer."

Maggie's eyes filled with tears and Sophie handed her a handkerchief. "Even if he wanted to, his family would forbid it. You know how well-respected the Dutton name is. Garth is in line for the barony. He'll be expected to marry someone with a name as old and revered as his own."

Seated in a blue velvet chair across from her niece, Sophie steadied the cup and saucer in her lap. "I realize our family has suffered a bit of scandal over the years. Your brother's involvement with that woman—Miss Whitney—certainly didn't do us any good, but at least she has been cleared of the murder. Allowing her into his house was in the worst possible taste, but I'm sure he'll move her out now that this is over."

"He already has. She is staying at Rathmore Hall with the duke and duchess."

"There, you see? Matters are improving already. Men are always allowed their little indiscretions, and even should the affair continue, you know the way your brother is. It won't be long before he grows tired of her."

Maggie's eyes filled with tears. "Adam's going to marry her, Aunt Sophie."

Sophie's hand shook, rattling her cup. "Good Lord, you can't be serious."

"He's going to ask her on Saturday night." Her niece looked even more miserable. "Jillian's going to be the next Countess of Blackwood."

"Oh, dear, oh, dear."

Maggie sniffed back tears. "I like her, Aunt Sophie, and I want Adam to be happy. I just wish I didn't have to lose Garth."

Sophie straightened her spine. "Garth is a strong, independent man. Perhaps this won't make any difference."

But they both knew it would, that the chances of an offer had dwindled the moment this latest story had hit the papers. They would dissolve completely the day Adam and his latest mistress wed.

"I wish I didn't love him," Maggie said softly. "I tried not to. I don't know how it happened."

But Sophie knew. Garth Dutton was handsome, intelligent, and charming. And Sophie believed he was equally enamored of her niece. She glanced toward the small settee where Maggie sat with her feet curled beneath her and her lovely face streaked with tears. Setting her teacup aside, Sophie walked behind the settee and began to pull the pins from her niece's long black hair.

"Sometimes things work out," Sophie said. "You mustn't give up hope just yet." She spread Maggie's hair out over the arm of the settee. "Why don't you try to rest? Perhaps later, you will feel better."

And Sophie was going to make certain that she did. She was going to make sure that Adam didn't go through with his ridiculous notion of marrying a scandal-ridden woman like Jillian Whitney.

Adam meandered around the house, missing Jillian, feeling moody and out of sorts. Early hours spent at Tattersall's, bidding on a fresh crop of horses, had helped ease his restlessness, but now that he was home, he'd begun to feel edgy again. Jillian was gone and the house seemed empty without her.

He couldn't believe it had been only days since he'd discovered that he was in love with her. Until the heart-stopping moment he had thought he would lose her, he hadn't realized how deeply he cared. He was passionately, hopelessly in love with her but perhaps equally important, he trusted her. In Jillian, he had found a woman he admired and respected, one who could give him back his long ago dream of having a family.

He smiled as he thought of the shopping he meant to do that afternoon and the wedding ring he meant to purchase. As he walked out of the drawing room, his thoughts were so far away he almost ran into little Christopher Derry.

"Chris! I didn't see you." He smiled. "I guess my mind was somewhere else."

Christopher smiled back a little shyly. "Did you plant your new orchid yet? I was hoping . . . I thought maybe I could see it."

Adam had mentioned the arrival of an orchid he had been expecting from India. Now he studied the small, brown-haired boy, marveling at the fact a child Chris's age would have an interest in flowers. Oddly, at about the same age, Adam had already planted a small garden of his own.

"I suppose it wouldn't take long for you to have a look." Together they walked outside to the greenhouse and over to the newly repotted purple ruffled orchid.

"They're supposed to be kept cool and dry in the winter after they bloom. I guess we'll have to try it and see."

The boy looked up at him, his eyes big and solemn. "Will I still be living with you when winter comes?"

Adam didn't like the worry in the little boy's face. He knelt beside him. "We may be back at Blackwood Manor by then, but wherever we are, you'll have a home with us, Chris. You don't have to worry about that."

Chris's gaze still seemed troubled. "Will Miss Whitney be there, too?"

Something tightened in his chest. "I hope so, Chris." But he wasn't completely certain. He was in love with Jillian, but he wasn't exactly sure of Jillian's feelings for him. She desired him, yes. But love? Adam had learned well enough that love and passion were two very different things.

"She isn't mad at us, is she?"

"No, son. She's just off visiting friends. With any luck at all, she'll be living with us again very soon."

Christopher Derry grinned and Adam blinked. For an instant, it was like looking at a reflection in the mirror. An uneasy feeling swept over him. What if Christopher were truly his son?

He imagined the years the boy had lived with a father who abused him, when Chris didn't have enough to eat. Adam reached down and took Christopher's hand. It felt small and warm, and something loosened inside him. Soon he would be married. In time, he would have a child of his own. Memories of Caroline and Robert no longer plagued him as they had for so many years.

Thinking of Jillian and the future he hoped lay ahead, somehow it seemed less important that Christopher Derry was Robert Hawthorne's son.

Jillian walked down the long marble corridor of Rathmore Hall toward the elegant Persian Salon. It was early afternoon. The sun was shining for the first time in days, and yet she felt uneasy, as she had since her arrival.

The wariness heightened as she continued along the hall toward the woman who awaited. Only a few minutes had passed since the butler, a bald, bushy-eyebrowed man named Henderson, had summoned her to the drawing room, informing her that Lady Sophia Hawthorne had arrived to see her. It was a matter, Henderson said, that appeared to be of some importance.

Jillian's heartbeat kicked into a faster rhythm, her intuition telling her something was wrong, yet she couldn't for the life of her imagine the reason the woman wished to see her.

Silently Jillian stepped into the beautiful Persian Salon, a high-ceilinged room with walls and columns of black-and-gold marble. "Lady Sophia?"

The silver-haired woman turned to face her. "Yes, dear. I know I should have sent word that I wished to see you, but one of the benefits of old age is being humored in small breaches of etiquette such as this."

"It's very nice to meet you. Henderson is bringing tea. Would you like to sit down?"

Spine-straight though she had probably shrunk several inches over the years, Lady Sophia sat down on the sofa and Jillian took a seat across from her. Tea arrived a few minutes later. Jillian poured each of them a cup, then sat back down in her chair.

"Henderson said the matter you wished to discuss was of some importance."

"And so it is." Lady Sophia took a sip of her tea. "I've come to speak to you about an affair of the heart." She set her porcelain cup and saucer down on the black lacquer table beside her chair. "You've met my niece, Lady Margaret?"

"Yes. I like her very much."

"She likes you, too. Margaret is a wonderful girl. Not merely beautiful and intelligent but also kind and thoughtful. Margaret is the sort of child who looks out for everyone's happiness but her own."

Jillian sipped her tea, hoping it would ease her

nervousness. "I'm afraid I don't understand where all of this is leading."

"Then perhaps you aren't yet aware that my nephew is planning to ask you to marry him."

Jillian's knees trembled beneath her blue silk skirt, rattling her teacup against its saucer. It couldn't be true. But she couldn't stop a rush of hope so fierce it made her giddy.

"I can see by the look on your face that you hadn't considered the possibility."

"No. No, I hadn't."

"And rightly so. Because in your deepest heart you realize it cannot possibly happen."

Jillian said nothing.

"Surely you can see that it wouldn't be fair to Adam. Whether or not the gossip about you is true—and considering my nephew's infatuation I'm inclined to believe it is not—everyone in the *ton* is convinced that you are something of a scarlet woman. That impression is not going to change. Should you become the Countess of Blackwood, Adam's already tarnished reputation will fall into utter ruin. And that would be completely unfair to Margaret."

An ache lodged in Jillian's throat.

"You're a young, unmarried woman yourself," Lady Sophia continued. "Surely you can understand what such a union would mean. Adam is the Earl of Blackwood. As such, he is the head of our family and being so, his responsibilities extend to all those under his protection, particularly his younger sister."

Shrewd blue eyes, a far paler hue than Adam's, remained steady on Jillian's face. "Margaret has fallen in love with a man with whom you've recently become acquainted—a barrister named Garth Dutton. Garth comes from an old, aristocratic family that is extremely well-respected and Garth is now the heir. Neither Baron Schofield nor members of the Dutton family will ever approve a match between Margaret and Garth should a woman of your reputation become Margaret's sister-in-law."

Jillian just sat there. In less than two minutes her fondest dream had turned into her greatest despair. Her heart just simply shattered.

"What about Adam?" she said softly. "If he asks me to marry him and I refuse, he'll want to know why. He'll think I never really cared for him. He'll believe I betrayed him just like Caroline Harding."

Lady Sophia stood up from her chair. "I'll leave that to you, my dear. You're obviously an intelligent young woman or my nephew wouldn't be so enamored of you. I'm sure you can think of a way to let him down without hurting him."

Jillian swallowed past the ache in her throat and also rose to her feet. She tried to speak, but couldn't form the words.

"I shall take your silence as agreement. If you truly love my nephew, you will do what is best for him and his family."

Jillian steeled herself against the pain eating into her and made a faint nod of her head. Her despair must have shown on her face, for Lady Sophia paused at the door and cast her a sympathetic glance.

"I'm sorry, my dear. For your sake as well as my nephew's, I wish things could have been different." Turning, she continued out the door of the drawing room and wandered off down the hall.

As her footsteps faded, Jillian sank down into a

chair beside the door. She felt drained and numb, sick to her very soul. Since her arrival at Rathmore Hall, she had been uneasy and uncertain. Kitt and Clay had tried to reassure her. They'd said that Adam cared for her greatly. That she shouldn't worry, that things would work out.

Now she knew things would never work out. Lady Sophia was right. She couldn't put her happiness before Maggie's. It simply wouldn't be fair. She had come to Adam a scarlet woman. The *ton* still viewed her that way. Madeleine's trial would make matters worse and even after it ended, Jillian's reputation wouldn't change.

Leaving the salon, she climbed the stairs to her room, her feet moving as if they were made of lead. She thought of Adam and how much she loved him. Though she had never imagined he might offer marriage, it was her most fervent dream.

Now if Adam asked to marry her, she would have to refuse him. She would have to pretend she didn't love him and do it in a way that wouldn't leave him even more embittered than he was before she met him.

Dear God, she loved him. She didn't want to hurt him.

Whatever it took, she vowed, she would have to find a way.

25

⟡

Jillian received a note from Adam the following day requesting the pleasure of her company, along with that of Kitt and Clay, at a restaurant called the Golden Chalice. Though Jillian had never been there, she had heard of the place. It was considered one of London's finest establishments, very expensive and exclusive, with a chef whose reputation was renowned.

Jillian recognized immediately that Adam was planning something special and must have already received agreement from his friends.

Dear God, Lady Sophia was right—Adam was going to ask her to marry him!

Jillian's eyes slid closed against a shot of pain. She was in love with him. She wanted to marry him more than anything in the world.

Instead, she spent all the next day frantically trying to figure out how to refuse his offer without hurting him, hiding away most of the time upstairs in her room. Kitt had come up to see her, excited about the dinner Adam had invited them to and worried that something was wrong.

Instead of declining supper that night as Jillian had planned, she was forced to paste on a smile she didn't feel and join Kitt and her husband in the dining room.

"Are you sure you're feeling all right?" Kitt asked during a meal of roast partridge with oyster stuffing that Jillian barely tasted.

Her smile felt so brittle she feared her lips would crack. "I'm a little tired, is all. Probably just relief after all the excitement."

"If it's Adam," Clay said gently, "you needn't worry. I saw him at Tattersall's this morning. All he talked about was you and the evening he has planned." Clay didn't elaborate but it was obvious by the knowing glance that passed between him and his wife that they suspected Adam intended to offer marriage, probably in the garden after they returned to the house.

Lord, what would they think of her when she refused his offer? Kitt and the duke had surely guessed that they had been lovers. They would see her as the worst sort of ingrate and harlot. And Adam would think so, too. She had to stop him before he ever said the words.

Shoving away the pain of what she must do, Jillian finished the meal and returned upstairs to her room, declining a game of cards she simply could not endure.

The following day, she left the house to implement the first step in the desperate plan she had conceived. She had sent a note to Michael Aimes in the matter of his promise to help her find employment. Now she had a far graver favor to ask.

Jillian perched nervously on the carriage seat all the way to Bond Street, where the coachman dropped her off in front of Madame Joyce's Millinery Shop with a promise to return two hours hence. As soon as the conveyance rolled out of sight, she walked to the nearest hack stand and hired a vehicle to carry her to Michael's bachelor quarters in Roderick Lane.

Having received the message one of Rathmore's linkboys had carried, he was waiting when she got there. They spoke of Howard Telford, of the night he'd been killed, and Michael's relief that she had been cleared of the crime. He told her he had already started making inquiries into the matter of her employment.

"I hate to ask more of you, Michael, but there is another favor I need." Michael's dark brown eyes grew wider by the moment as she explained the situation, praying that he would agree.

Michael got up from the sofa in his parlor and began to pace the floor. "I said I would help you in any way I could, but . . ."

"I know it's a lot to ask." Jillian nervously toyed with the finger of her glove. "If you are worried about your reputation—"

"I'll be leaving London in less than a week. Besides, I'm a man and merely a second son. As unfair as it may seem, it won't be a problem for me."

"What, then?"

"Are you certain this is what you want?"

She swallowed. "I have to do this, Michael." She told him that she had no other choice. She loved Adam Hawthorne and because she did, she refused to be the cause of the ruination of his family.

Michael had argued, but in the end, he had agreed.

By the time she had reboarded the waiting hack, her meeting had reached a successful conclusion. Michael would provide the excuse she needed to refuse Adam's offer of marriage. Later, he could simply pretend things hadn't worked out between them.

Her plan was set and by Saturday morning she was ready. Standing in front of the armoire, Jillian tried to calm the queasiness in her stomach. Her nerves were frayed, her eyes ringed with fatigue, her heart a shredded, bloody lump inside her chest. But she was prepared to do as she had promised Lady Sophia.

Swallowing against the painful ache in her throat, Jillian set off for Adam's town house, determined to play the hardest role of her life.

Adam finished cataloging his most recent acquisition, a mask from the time of Amenhotep III done in gold leaf with geometric patterns in brilliant reds and blues. Shoving his plumed pen back into the inkwell, he closed the heavy leather volume that documented the pieces he had acquired over the years and leaned back in his chair.

He could feel the small, square lump in the pocket of his navy blue tailcoat. Reaching down, he lifted the flap and pulled out an elegantly carved wooden box inlaid with mother of pearl and lifted the lid.

On a bed of white satin rested the diamond and ruby ring he had purchased from one of the half-dozen shops he had visited in the last several days. Until yesterday afternoon, he had almost given up hope of finding such a ring. Nothing had seemed quite right. The stones were either too large or too small, or the cut just didn't seem correct.

He wanted a ring that would reflect Jillian's beauty, a strong, clear stone that symbolized her courage and strength.

The ring he had found in the little shop Clay recommended in Ludgate Hill seemed perfect: a large, flawless, square-cut diamond, surrounded by smaller, perfectly faceted rubies that reminded him of the fire in her hair. He couldn't wait to see her face when he showed it to her.

Smiling, he watched the way the sun danced over the brilliant white diamond, then, at Reggie's soft knock, quickly returned the lid to the box and stuffed it back into the pocket of his tailcoat.

Reggie's homely face poked through the door. "Sorry to bother ye, Major, but Miss Whitney is come to see ye. I've shown her into the Gold Drawing Room."

Adam smiled. She wasn't supposed to be there. Everything had changed since the day she'd been cleared of the murder charges. She was the woman he intended to marry and he meant to treat her with the respect she deserved. Still, he hadn't cared about propriety before. He cared even less about it now. He simply wanted to see her.

He got up from his desk and followed Reggie down the hall. Jillian stood up as he walked in. Gowned in pale blue muslin sprigged with embroidered rosebuds, a bonnet hiding her glorious hair, she looked beautiful and innocent, and he felt a surge of love so strong, for an instant he couldn't speak.

"Jillian . . ." he said, nervous for no good reason, then he noticed the uncertain look on her face. "Sweeting, is everything all right?"

She nodded, smiled, and he thought that she was glad to see him, too. "I just needed to talk to you."

Catching both her gloved hands, he bent and kissed her cheek, though what he wanted to do was drag her into his arms and kiss her till neither of them could breathe.

"It's good to see you." He felt awkward as he never had before, as if he were suddenly wearing knee breeches and his tutor was about to tell his father he had sneaked off without doing his lessons.

"It's good to see you, too." She let him guide her over to the gold-striped sofa in front of the hearth, and he took a place beside her, still holding onto her hand. It was slender and delicate, and though her fingers should have been warmed by the gloves, they felt cold against his palm. He wondered if she might be feeling a little awkward, too.

"I hope you've been well," she said.

"I've missed you. I wish I'd never let you leave." But he had and now he just wanted her to marry him and come home where she belonged. He flashed her a smile brighter than most of the ones she had seen. They came easier since he had met her. He knew once she belonged to him, he would smile at her all the time.

"Yes, well . . . that is what I've come to talk to you about." For the first time he noticed how tense she was, the way her shoulders looked tight and straight, her chin angled up a little too high. It made his own nerves crank up a notch.

"You look pale. You aren't sick, are you? The last time I spoke to Clay, he said that you had been spending a lot of time up in your room, but he thought you were probably just recovering after all that you'd been through."

"I'm fine. Really. My health is not a problem, but . . . there is another matter we need to discuss." Her fingers gently curled around his hand. "First, I want to tell you how much I appreciate everything you've done for me. If it weren't for you, I would undoubtedly be spending the rest of my life in prison. I might even be facing the gallows."

Adam said nothing, but his instincts were telling him that something was very wrong and his heart jolted into a faster rhythm.

"I care for you greatly, Adam. I've never met a man I respect more than I do you. You're intelligent and kind and loyal. You're the best friend I've ever had."

He straightened a little, let go of her hand. He noticed that it trembled. "Is that all we are, Jillian? Friends?"

She swallowed, shook her head. "You know it isn't. We were . . . lovers. Making love to you wasn't something I did lightly."

He could see she was struggling. What amazed him was how much it bothered him to see her that way. "Why don't you just tell me what's going on?"

She swallowed, glanced down at the hands she clenched in her lap. "There are things I never told you. Things that happened in my life before I came to London." She looked back at him, her eyes as blue as the sea and yet there was something turbulent in them, like clouds building on the horizon.

"There was a man in my life once, someone that I loved. He was a friend of my father's. Just before my father died, he left for Oxford to complete some additional schooling. Then Father passed away. I moved to London and we ... we lost touch with each other. I never thought I would ever see him again."

This last was said softly, as if the memory of losing the man still pained her.

"But you did see him," Adam prompted, coaxing her to continue, yet not really wanting to hear what he feared she might say. His heart was thudding. He didn't know exactly where this was leading, but Jillian's lips were trembling and her eyes were filled with a deep regret.

"Yes ... I saw him again. One day on the street outside your house. I told you about it; I mentioned running into a friend of my father's." He remembered, but he had been worried about the trial. "Two days ago I-I ran into him again ... in Bond Street. It wasn't planned. I went shopping and there ... there he was. He said he had been planning to call on me, now that the trial was over. His name is Michael Aimes."

A pressure was building in his chest. He could feel every sluggish beat of his heart. "Go on," was all he said.

"Michael had read about the trial in the newspapers. I didn't know he had come to London purposely to find me until he said so that day." She swallowed. "He loves me, Adam. He says he has loved me for years. H-he ... wants to marry me."

I want to marry you, he thought, but not if she didn't love him.

Jillian reached over and gently took his hand.

"The days and nights we shared . . . they were wonderful. I-I told Michael about you. I couldn't lie about our friendship . . . or hide the fact that we were intimately involved. He says it doesn't matter. He says nothing matters, not as long as we're together."

Adam cleared his throat. It seemed to be squeezing off his air and it was getting hard to breathe. "You're telling me that you're in love with this man . . . this Michael Aimes?"

"I love him." She was shaking, forcing out each of her words. "I've loved him . . . for as long as I can remember." It occurred to him how difficult this was for her, how worried she was about him, how hard she was trying not to hurt him. She knew that she was and it was killing her.

He dragged in a steadying breath, willed his voice to come out even. "Well, if that is the case, then you are not in love with me." Adam got up from the sofa, paced over to the window, and stared out into the street. Clouds had begun to gather, hiding the sun and turning the morning cold and gray. A little boy played on the stoop of the house across the way. A door opened and his mother protectively scooped him back inside, out of the first drops of rain.

He turned back to Jillian. "I had hoped we might share a future together."

She nodded, swallowed. "There was a time I . . . I had hoped for that, too, but I would never have been happy as your mistress and now . . . now that I've found Michael again, I think this will be better for both of us."

There was a time he had wanted nothing so much as to be rid of her. He'd been afraid of his growing attachment, afraid she would hurt him. Even if it wasn't her intention, she was certainly doing that now.

She got up from the sofa and joined him at the window. "Please, Adam . . . please don't be angry. I'd never do anything to hurt you." Her voice broke. "I would have told you about Michael if I'd had the slightest notion he would ever have come back into my life." She glanced away for a moment and he caught the sheen of tears. "If I had known the way he felt . . . if he had come for me after my father died . . . none of this would ever have happened."

Adam looked into her anguished face. Her skin was ashen, her pretty blue eyes utterly bleak. She was hurting, he saw, hurting for him. He might not have known about Michael Aimes, but he knew a great deal about Jillian Whitney. He knew that when she cared about someone she cared about them deeply. And even if she thought of him only as a friend, she wouldn't want to hurt him.

She looked at him and her eyes welled with tears. He couldn't stand knowing that he was the cause, couldn't bear to see her suffer. Christ, hadn't she suffered enough already?

An odd calm settled over him. For the first time in his life he understood the true meaning of *love*. He understood that when you really loved someone, you cared about their happiness more than you did your own. He understood that you would do anything—anything—to save the person you loved from pain.

Even sacrifice everything you had ever wanted out of life.

Adam reached out, gently cupped her face in his

hand. "If none of this had happened, I never would have met you. We would never have made love, and I wouldn't have missed being with you for anything in the world."

She fought to keep from crying, but tears slid down her cheeks. "I'm sorry things didn't work out."

"Will you be happy with him, Jillian?"

She swallowed, nodded, forced a tremulous smile. "He's everything I've ever wanted."

Adam bent and softly kissed her mouth. It was the last kiss they would ever share and his heart felt as if it were crumbling into little pieces. Jillian leaned against him, went up on her toes and for an instant kissed him back. She kissed him with all the feelings she had once held for him, kissed him as if he meant everything in the world to her, as if it were he that she loved and not Michael Aimes. Then she stepped away.

"Be happy for me, Adam."

"Take care of yourself, my love."

"Tell Kitt and Clay . . . tell them I'll never forget what they've done for me."

"I'll tell them."

She caught his hand, pressed it against her cheek, tipped her face into his palm. "Don't forget me."

"I won't forget," he said, his voice rough. His throat was aching. Moisture burned his eyes and he knew if she didn't leave soon, he was going to embarrass himself. "You'd better go."

She nodded, but made no move to leave.

"Have a good life, Jillian."

More tears slid down her cheeks. "You, too, Adam." And then she was gone.

Adam stared at the place she had been. He hadn't

felt this deep, bottomless despair since the day he got news that his brother had died. He reached into his pocket and his fingers curled around the box that held the ring. It seemed to burn a hole through his hand. He took the box out, but he didn't open it.

Adam set it on the table, turned, and walked out of the room.

26

Jillian left London the following day. The magistrates had said her testimony wouldn't be needed at Madeleine's trial, that the word of a duke and an earl would suffice. With that worry aside, Jillian would be staying with friends of Michael's in Woburn Abbey until he could help her secure a position.

A week later, she moved into the country home of Phyllis and William Marston, Earl and Countess of Richmond, friends of Michael's father, the Marquess of Devlin. The earl was a man in his forties, handsome, with slightly graying hair and a warm, charming demeanor. His wife was several years younger, slender even after three children, a little bit shy, and obviously in love with her husband.

The couple had offered her a position as governess, and Jillian had accepted with a great deal of relief. Michael Aimes had given her the chance to begin a new life, and she would always be grateful for his kindness, support, and generosity.

But she was definitely not in love with him.

She was in love with the Earl of Blackwood and no matter how many bleak, empty, achingly lonely nights she endured without him that simply wasn't going to change.

Nearly a month had passed. Still Jillian stood at the window of her third floor schoolroom thinking about him, remembering the first time she had seen him, astride his magnificent black horse. She remembered the night of the murder when he had given her refuge, remembered his solid belief in her innocence that had ultimately saved her life. She remembered his strength and his gentleness, remembered his kisses and the hardness of his body moving inside her.

A hundred times these past dreary days, she had awakened in the night reaching out for him, only to find that Adam wasn't there. She had tried to forget him, tried to forget the pain in his face when she had told him that she loved someone else.

She had expected him to be angry. She had never expected he would be more concerned for her than he was for himself. He had said that he wouldn't forget her. Though Jillian wanted nothing so much as to bury her own bittersweet memories so deeply they would never resurface, she found that she could not forget him. A man like the Earl of Blackwood wasn't easy to forget and without him, her heart felt ravaged, irreparably torn in two.

At the patter of small feet running into the room, Jillian forced her thoughts in a different direction and walked over to the blackboard to erase yesterday's lesson in preparation for another round of teaching. She turned toward the three shining faces of the children busily seating themselves in small

wooden chairs lined up in front of the blackboard:
Winnie, the youngest, with her curly bright red hair;
Rachael, dark-haired and solemn; and Jeremy, the
oldest, tall and rail-thin, with the same charming demeanor as his father.

Three darling children whose innocent needs, she
hoped, would in time help her to emerge from the
black pit of grief she felt in losing Adam.

Dressed in a fashionable high-waisted gown of
turquoise brocaded taffeta, pleated beneath the
bosom and banded with matching turquoise velvet,
Maggie Hawthorne walked next to her aunt out of
the Royal Opera House where Garth had taken
them tonight. He had been squiring the two of them
all over London for the past several weeks, publicly
courting her, making his intentions clear.

Aunt Sophie was nearly overcome with joy and
Maggie was happier than she'd ever been in her life.
She didn't know if Jillian's refusal to marry her
brother and subsequent departure from London had
been a factor in Garth's pursuit, but there was every
possibility that it had been.

Maggie had received news of Adam's failed proposal with surprise and sadness and a fierce shot of
hope. Jillian's rejection had hurt Adam badly and
that made Maggie sad. Still, if the woman were truly
in love with someone else, as Adam had said, then
Maggie certainly didn't want him to marry her.

Garth's first invitation had come the day after Jillian left the city, inviting Maggie and Aunt Sophie to
accompany him to a play at the Haymarket Theatre.
Since then, Maggie had been caught up in a romantic
whirlwind that left little thought for anything else.

"Did you enjoy the opera?" Garth's deep voice cut into her thoughts. In the yellow glow of a street-lamp, she admired the faintly sensuous curve of his mouth and the sheen of his golden hair. Her heart stuttered, then started beating again. Dear Lord, the man was handsome.

"I liked it very much."

"Then we shall have to do this again."

God's teeth, she hoped so. She wanted to be with him every night, every minute. "I'm sure Aunt Sophie enjoyed it as well."

Garth said something to her aunt as he helped her climb into the carriage and the older woman laughed.

Aunt Sophie liked Garth Dutton.

Maggie loved him.

And she worried, still, that something might go wrong and his family would force him to end his courtship of her. She pondered that fear all the way back to her town house, though Garth was particularly charming and had her laughing by the time they arrived.

Once they reached the drawing room, he obtained permission from Aunt Sophie to speak to Maggie in private, and the conspiratorial glance that passed between the pair set her heart to pounding again. Had he already spoken to Adam? Dear Lord, if he had, this might be the moment she had been praying for.

Garth slid the doors closed behind them. He surprised her by reaching out and hauling her into his arms. For the past several weeks, he'd been excessively polite, doing little more than holding onto her hand. Maggie had begun to wonder if she had imagined the hot flare of passion they had shared out in the garden.

Then he bent his head and took possession of her mouth and conscious thought faded away. Sweet God, she wouldn't have believed a kiss could be so scorchingly hot and at the same time achingly tender. Maggie kissed him back and clung to him, her heart hammering with love and hope.

By the time Garth ended the kiss, her face was flushed, her pulse racing. Garth was breathing a little too hard, his green eyes blazing with the barely leashed desire he no longer tried to hide.

"Garth . . ." she whispered.

"Marry me," he said bluntly. "I may be a barrister, but right now the only thing I can think to say is how beautiful you are and how much I want to make love to you. I love you, Maggie Hawthorne. Say you will marry me."

Maggie threw her arms around his neck. "Oh, Garth, I love you, too." Tears welled, blurred the image of his handsome face. "Yes, yes, yes—I'll marry you! I love you so much." Maggie went up on her toes and kissed him with all the love she felt for him. She heard Garth's deep groan, then heat and desire swept over her, so strong it made her tremble.

"I don't want a long betrothal," Garth said between soft, sensuous kisses. "God knows, I couldn't survive it."

"We can post the banns tomorrow."

"We'll wait just long enough to satisfy the gossips."

She nodded, smiled back at him. "The sooner the better."

Garth grinned. "Then again, what's a little gossip? Perhaps we should marry by special license. Then the scandalmongers can sit round counting the months, trying to figure out why we wed in such a hurry. They'd never guess I simply couldn't bear another day without you."

He hugged her hard and Maggie wept with joy and relief. Garth loved her. She wasn't going to lose him.

Her brother's dark image crept into mind, the bleak set of his features the day he had told her that Jillian intended to marry someone else. The happier she was, the more she hurt for Adam.

If only her brother could have found happiness, too.

Adam strode into the stables of Blackwood Manor. He had arrived at the house late last evening, returning with Maude and Reggie, and little Christopher Derry. He should have come sooner, he thought, as he inhaled the sweet scent of hay, heard the soft creak of a harness being polished and the welcoming whicker of horses.

Instead, he'd stayed in the city, listless and numb, unable to do little more than grieve. It was insane to feel so abandoned, so lost, when he had known from the start his involvement with Jillian was doomed to fail.

Hadn't it always been so?

And yet, as he had told her, he was grateful that he had known her, that he had, even for a very short time, been part of Jillian's life. Though his nights seemed endless without her, dreams of the war no longer plagued him. His bitterness had faded and Jillian was the reason. She had helped him to deal with his painful past, and perhaps because of her, he and young Christopher were fast becoming friends.

Adam almost smiled. The boy's intelligence amazed him. He was curious about everything, fascinated by life and amazingly perceptive about it.

"Is Miss Whitney coming with us?" Chris had asked the morning they had left the city.

Adam felt a sharp pain in his heart. "No, Chris, I'm afraid she isn't."

The boy looked up at him. "Why not? I thought she liked us."

"I think she did. I think she especially liked you. But Miss Whitney is getting married. Someday she'll have a little boy of her own." Just saying it made his chest hurt.

Chris stared down at the small gold buckle on the toe of his shoe. "I miss her."

Adam's voice came out rough. "I miss her, too."

Perhaps it was the common loss of someone they both loved that drew the two of them together. And just being there in the country, in the rolling green hills of Blackwood Manor—surely it would help him to forget her.

As early morning sunlight filtered into the barn, Adam walked toward Jamie O'Connell, his head groom.

"Top o' the mornin' to ya, milord."

"Good morning, Jamie. Did my delivery arrive from London?"

"Aye. Ye've made a fine purchase, milord. 'E's fit as a fiddle and rarin' ta go. I'll fetch 'im outta his stall."

A few minutes later, Jamie led a little white Welsh pony out of one of the stalls, and together the men walked the animal out of the barn, his fine white coat gleaming in the sun.

"Ye've chosen well, milord. 'E's got a fine, sweet disposition, this one. He'll be followin' the boy round like a pet."

Adam nodded. "When I saw him at Tattersall's, that was one of the things that convinced me to buy him. A little girl was riding him and he seemed not to care in the least. Normally, I'm not much for ponies. Sometimes they're more difficult to handle than a full grown horse."

"Aye, but not this one. Gentle as a lamb, he is. Your boy will be ridin' like 'e was born ta the saddle in no time a'tall."

Your boy. Adam felt an odd tug at the words. Now that Jillian was gone, he would never have a child of his own. In a way, Christopher was an unexpected blessing. He'd left word with Maude that the child should come to the stable as soon as he had finished his breakfast. Adam smiled at the sight of the boy racing eagerly down the hill.

Chris slowed a little when he saw the pony, then started running again. He was a little out of breath when he slid to a halt in front of Adam and Jamie O'Connell.

"Mrs. Flynn said you wanted me to come to the stable." Though he spoke to Adam, Chris's eyes remained locked on the pint-sized horse.

"Yes, I did." Adam stroked the smooth, muscular neck, combed his fingers through the snowy mane. "His name is Ra. Ra was the Egyptian god of the sun. Do you like him?"

Chris reached over and tentatively stroked the horse. "He's a beauty, milord."

"You're eight years old. That's old enough for a boy to have a horse. I never got you a birthday present. Ra is yours. Happy birthday, Chris."

The boy stared up at him, green eyes tilted up in shock. He swallowed. "You aren't . . . you wouldn't be teasin' me, would you?"

Adam solemnly shook his head. "No, Chris. I wouldn't tease about something so important. Ra belongs to you."

White teeth flashed like small squares of fine bone china. "I never had anythin' so splendid. Will you teach me to ride 'im?"

Adam had thought 'im to have Jamie take care of it. Now, looking at the hope in Chris's face, the idea of teaching the boy himself held an odd appeal. "All right. We can start today, if you wish."

"Oh, yes! That would be ever so good."

After setting the boy in the pony saddle, Adam watched him walk Ra around the practice ring, his small hands gently guiding, his posture relaxed, quickly developing an ease in the saddle. Chris had a way with the animal that seemed to come naturally. It was the way Adam had been with horses since he was a boy.

The same uneasy feeling that had bothered him before crept over him. *What if Chris is my son?*

If he were, Adam would be proud to claim him.

Adam thought of Jillian and how fond she had been of the boy, how delighted she would be if she could see him now. God, he missed her. Wherever she was, he hoped that she was happy.

She was probably married by now.

His stomach muscles tightened. If Michael Aimes treated her badly. . . .

But there wasn't a thing he could do.

It was nearly two weeks later that Michael Aimes's name came up again. Adam was seated in his study, going over the account ledgers—a job he hated—wishing instead he were out in the sunshine with Chris.

"Beg pardon, Major." Reggie stood in the open doorway. "Ye've a visitor, sir."

Adam shoved his pen back into the inkwell. "Who is it?"

"Fellow says his name is Michael Aimes."

Muscles tightened at the back of his neck. Adam closed the heavy ledger and came to his feet. "I'll speak to him in here."

"Yes, milord." Reggie hurried away and a few minutes later, a tall, slim, brown-haired man walked through the door of the study.

Adam remained standing behind his desk, his stomach twisted into a knot the size of St. Paul's Cathedral. He steeled himself. "Would you care to sit down?"

"No, thank you. I'm fine right here."

"All right. What can I do for you, Mr. Aimes?"

"Technically, it's Lord Michael. My father is the Marquess of Devlin, but I'm not much concerned with that sort of thing."

God, one of Devlin's sons. The marquess was wealthy in the extreme. At least the man would be able to take care of her. "Exactly what *are* you concerned with, Lord Michael?"

"Professor Whitney was a friend of mine. He fostered my interest in Egyptian antiquities. I've heard you share a similar passion."

Adam's eyebrow arched. He was beginning to realize exactly who this younger man was, not just one of Devlin's sons, but the one who had built a solid reputation in the field of Egyptian historical studies. Though he had wanted Jillian to be happy, he had also been determined to dislike Michael Aimes. It was difficult when the man was someone who had already garnered a measure of Adam's respect.

"I was in Egypt with the army," Adam said. "I developed an interest in the country's history and antiquities while I was there." He walked to the front of his desk. He was perhaps an inch taller, but Aimes was at least five years younger, closer to Jillian's age and undeniably handsome. "I'm afraid, Lord Michael, I still don't know why you're here."

Eyes, a warm shade of brown, remained steady on Adam's face. "I'm here because of Miss Whitney. When she came to me for help, I promised that I would keep her secret, and I tried to, truly I did. But I went to see her recently—"

"I don't understand. I thought by now the two of you would have wed."

"Jillian and I never intended to marry. As I started to say, when I went to see her and saw how utterly miserable she was, I simply couldn't keep my silence any longer."

Adam's heart was thudding. He didn't know what was going on, but somehow he knew it was crucial. "What are you talking about?"

"I know what she told you. I agreed to the lie because I had offered her my aid and that is what she asked me to do. I knew she had suffered a great deal since her father died. I wanted to help in any way I could."

"Are you saying you're not in love with her?"

A corner of Michael's mouth curved up. "I don't think any man in his right mind could help falling a little in love with Jillian. More to the point—Jillian is not in love with me."

Adam exhaled a slow breath. He didn't know where this was going, but his instincts were screaming again. Unfortunately, he couldn't figure out what they were saying. "I think I need a drink."

Walking over to the sideboard, he lifted the crystal stopper off a decanter of brandy, poured himself a glass, and took a swallow. "Would you care for something?"

"No, thank you."

Adam turned to face him. "All right, let's try this again. If Jillian doesn't love you, who is she in love with?"

"*You.*"

He nearly choked on the sip of brandy he had taken. He swallowed a little more carefully and set the glass on the sideboard. "As much as I might wish that were true, I don't believe it is. The day she came to see me, Jillian made her feelings perfectly clear. And if she hasn't gone off to marry you, she must have gone off with someone else."

Michael Aimes shook his head. "You still don't understand. You're the man Jillian loves. She left London in order to protect you and your family. She knew you planned to ask her to marry. She gave you up because she loves you so much."

"That's impossible."

"I'm afraid it isn't. You see, your aunt came to see her at Rathmore Hall."

One of his eyebrows went up. "Aunt Sophie?"

Michael nodded. "She told Jillian that your sister, Maggie, was in love, and that the man Maggie loved wouldn't marry her if her brother wed a woman of Jillian's reputation."

His mind spun as pieces of the puzzle began to fall together. "My sister was recently betrothed to an attorney named Garth Dutton. He's the heir to the Schofield barony." And Garth's family was wildly concerned with reputation and social standing. In a way, Adam had been surprised when Garth had come to him for permission to marry Maggie.

He turned a hard assessing gaze on Michael Aimes. "You're certain about all this?"

"Jillian loves you. Of that much I'm sure."

The emotions Adam had been fighting threatened to boil to the surface. He didn't dare reach for his glass of brandy. His hand was shaking too badly. "Where is she?"

"Just outside Woburn Abbey, a little village called Bartonstoke. With my father's aid, I helped her secure a position there as governess to the Marquess of Richmond."

For the first time since Michael Aimes arrived, the tension in Adam's shoulders began to ease. Jillian loved him. She loved him. God, could it really be true?

"I'm grateful to you for coming, Lord Michael. You will never know how much."

"Michael is enough." He smiled with a hint of relief. "I assume you're going after her."

Adam's mouth curved. His heart was still beating

too fast, but this time it was thumping with joy and hope. Jillian had left to protect him and his family. She had loved him that much. He wanted to believe it was true. God, he wanted it so much.

And yet, as Jillian had known, there was Maggie to consider.

"There's something I have to do first. Then I'm off for Woburn Abbey."

As they walked to the door, Adam settled a hand on the younger man's shoulder. "I'll never forget what you've done. You'll always be welcome at Blackwood Manor."

Michael seemed pleased. "Take care of her."

"No matter what happens, you may count on that."

Michael left the study and the moment he was gone, Adam rang for Harley Smythe to pack his things. Half an hour later, he was aboard his carriage and rolling toward London, on his way to see Garth Dutton, the man who held his family's future happiness in his hands.

27

At the sound of a light rap on his office door, Garth set aside the document he had been studying, charges against the son of a nobleman for debts he refused to pay. Garth's secretary, a young man named Kent Wilson, stepped into the room.

"I'm sorry to interrupt, sir, but Lord Blackwood is here to see you. He says the matter is urgent."

Garth ignored a trickle of alarm that something might have happened to Maggie. "Send him in." He rounded his desk and strode to the door to greet the man who would soon be his brother-in-law.

"I hope nothing untoward has occurred," Garth said, trying unsuccessfully to read the expression on Adam's face.

Blackwood waited till Kent closed the door, making them private. "I suppose that depends on one's point of view."

Garth's alarm took a leap. "Is it Maggie? Is she all right?"

"As I said, that depends." Blackwood's eyes looked

hard. Garth sensed an underlying turbulence hidden beneath his outer control.

"Depends on what?"

"What you will say if I tell you I intend to marry Jillian Whitney."

Garth frowned, not quite sure he had heard correctly. "I thought Miss Whitney was marrying someone else."

"So did I. Apparently that was a ruse Jillian created in order to protect my sister."

"Your sister? What the devil are you talking about?"

"Before I explain, I need to know if your betrothal to Maggie will stand if I marry Jillian."

"For God's sake, man—what you and Miss Whitney do has nothing to do with your sister and me. I love Maggie. I would have married her already if I weren't concerned about the damnable gossip."

"That, I'm afraid, is exactly my point. The Dutton family has always been overly concerned with propriety. Maggie's name is bound to suffer from my marriage to a woman of Jillian's reputation—as undeserved as we both know it is. What will you do if your grandfather threatens to disinherit you?"

Garth was beginning to feel his own temper rising. "Let me get this straight. You're telling me that Jillian refused your suit because she was afraid that if she accepted, I wouldn't marry Maggie?"

"That's exactly what I'm saying. Jillian knew Maggie was in love with you. My aunt made certain of that. She also made sure Jillian was convinced you would never offer marriage if the two of us were to wed."

Garth shook his head. "Gad, what a coil." He

raked a hand through his hair. "It seemed obvious the two of you were in love. I was surprised to hear things didn't work out." He straightened. "I feel terrible about this, Adam. But make no mistake—Margaret Hawthorne has agreed to become my wife. Not my grandfather nor anyone else is going to keep that from happening."

The relief on Adam's face made Garth's chest feel tight. He knew how he would feel if he lost Maggie. Thank God, the truth had come out before it was too late for Adam.

"Thank you," Blackwood said, his voice a little gruff. "My sister is lucky to be marrying a man like you."

Garth smiled. "I'm the lucky one, I assure you. Tell Jillian I wish both of you the very best."

Adam nodded and started for the door.

"When you get back, don't be surprised to find out the wedding's been moved up. After listening to you, I don't want to take any chances."

Adam laughed, a carefree sound unlike anything Garth had ever heard from him before.

"Kiss the bride for me," Garth called out as the earl pulled open the door.

"Count on it," Adam called back over his shoulder.

Garth merely smiled.

Jillian sat curled on the sofa in the library of the Marquess of Richmond's country estate. It was getting late, nearly eleven o'clock, and she had to get up early. But a storm was building outside. She could hear the rumble of distant thunder, catch the occasional flash of lightning, and she wasn't the least bit sleepy.

Instead, she felt restless and edgy, as jittery as the branch trembling in the wind outside the mullioned windows. She sighed as she left the sofa and walked over to the hearth, knelt to add coal to the low-burning flames. It was warm in the room and yet her hands felt icy cold. She couldn't seem to warm them.

Little by little, her nerves slowly calmed and a deep, numbing lethargy replaced them, a feeling that gripped her every evening about this same time.

It was this time of night she thought of Adam, late in the evenings when she remembered how safe and solid he had felt lying next to her in bed. It was this time of night she ached for him, suffered the despair of knowing she had lost him. Her only consolation came from the notice she had read in the *Chronicle* of Maggie's betrothal to Garth. At least some good had come of all the grief.

With a leaden heart, Jillian walked back to the sofa to continue the book she had been reading, a text of Walter Scott poems. She had just reached to pick it up when the library door swung opened. Soft yellow light from the wall sconces down the hall illuminated the figure of a man, tall and spare, wide-shouldered, with wavy dark hair.

Her heart clutched. The book remained where it lay, draped over the arm of the sofa. She wanted to say the man's name but she was afraid to, afraid that if she did, the figure would step out of the shadows and it would be someone else. He started walking toward her, his long strides graceful and determined. For an instant, lamplight touched the side of his face, revealing the thin white scar along his jaw. There was no mistaking who it was and her leaden heart took wing.

"Adam . . ." she whispered, a thick lump swelling in her throat. She started shaking, tried to walk toward him, but couldn't get her legs to move. Adam just kept coming. He didn't stop until he stood directly in front of her and for an instant, she thought he meant to sweep her into his arms.

Her breath caught in anticipation and her eyes slid closed, but the moment never came. When she looked up at him again, she saw that he stood just inches away and it was all she could do not to reach out and touch him.

"Adam . . ." she repeated, the merest whisper of his name.

His eyes were dark, the lines of his face barely visible in the flickering firelight. "Michael Aimes came to see me."

Her lips trembled. "Oh, God."

"He told me the two of you never intended to marry."

Jillian said nothing. Her throat felt strangled and no words would come.

"Lord Michael says you don't love him. He says you never did. He says . . . he believes that you're in love with me. Is it true?"

She knew she should lie. Garth and Maggie weren't yet wed. But she loved him so much, and as she looked into his beautiful face, the beloved planes and valleys, dear God, she couldn't lie to him again.

Adam stood so close she could feel the heat of his body, breathe in his scent.

"I asked if you're in love with me."

Her eyes welled with tears. They spilled over onto her cheeks. "Desperately."

A shudder ran the length of his body. "Ah, God." And then she was in his arms. He was trembling nearly as badly as she. "I love you," he whispered against her hair. "I love you so much. I've never said that to any other woman."

Her hands slid into the thick black hair at the nape of his neck and she clung to him as if he might disappear, like the man who haunted her dreams.

"I thought I loved Caroline," he said softly, "but I never told her. Now I'm glad I didn't—because it wouldn't have been the truth."

Her throat ached so badly she couldn't speak. A soft little sob escaped and his arms tightened almost painfully around her.

"Adam . . ." She couldn't stop saying his name. It sounded a little funny with tears clogging her throat.

He eased away, looked into her face. "Will you marry me?"

She wanted to say yes. She had never wanted anything so badly. "What . . . what about Maggie?"

The corner of his mouth edged up. "Garth loves her. He means to marry her. Whatever we do, that isn't going to change."

Jillian leaned toward him, her arms still snug around his neck.

Adam caught her chin, tipped her head back, and kissed her. It was a fierce, thoroughly passionate kiss, yet it was amazingly tender.

"You haven't given me an answer," he said, kissing the side of her neck.

Jillian pressed her cheek to his. "There's nothing in this world I want, my lord, more than to marry you."

Adam drew away and actually grinned down at

her. "I was hoping that's what you'd say. I also hope you don't want a big wedding."

"I just want you," she said, meaning every word.

"Good. The vicar is waiting in the drawing room. I've obtained a special license. The Marstons have graciously offered the use of their home. If you say yes, we'll be married tonight."

Jillian blinked back tears and grinned. "Yes, then! Tonight. Now. This very minute!"

Adam lifted her up and spun her around. She was laughing when he set her back down on her feet and very soundly kissed her again.

Entwining her fingers with his, he started tugging her toward the door. "Come, my love. Let's get this over with. I've plans for you that don't include a vicar or anyone else." The hunger in his eyes was unmistakable. They were a deep, indigo blue that shimmered with love and the promise of what he meant to do to her, once they were wed. Just thinking of it made the little curls of heat spread out in her stomach.

Jillian married Adam in a brief ceremony in the Rose Drawing Room of the Earl of Richmond's country estate, Jillian dressed in the same gray batiste gown she had been wearing in the schoolroom, Adam still dressed in the slightly wrinkled blue tailcoat and snug gray breeches that he had been traveling in.

Lord and Lady Richmond stood beside them. Teary-eyed and smiling, Lady Richmond handed Jillian a long-stemmed red rose still moist with rain, hand-picked from her garden. The three Marston children were awakened for the special occasion of their governess's wedding to the Earl of Blackwood and attended the affair in their long white cotton night rails.

Afterward, they shared a late celebration supper that included champagne and a special custard with gooseberries served in the shape of a heart.

As the clock struck the hour, she felt Adam's hand at her waist. "Come, love. It's time we said good night." His eyes told her exactly what he intended to do to her once they got to their room, and love and desire shimmered through her.

She thanked Lord and Lady Marston and hugged each of the three Marston children, then took Adam's hand and they headed for the stairs.

She had wanted a new life. Adam had given her one.

He stopped when they reached the door to their second-story bedchamber and lifted her into his arms.

"You're mine now, Countess." He stepped through the door and shoved it closed with the side of his foot. "I'll never let you run from me again."

Jillian twined her arms around his neck and kissed him. "If I run, I'll be sure to go slow enough for you to catch me."

Adam laughed and the sound was deep and joyous. He kissed her as he carried her over to the bed. Jillian's new life had finally begun.

Epilogue

❧❧❧

Adam's life at Blackwood Manor had changed since his marriage. Each day seemed fuller, richer, filled with anticipation. He and Jillian had been married just three months and already he couldn't imagine life without her.

His wife had blossomed in the country. The serenity that had drawn him to her the first time he had seen her had returned. She smiled and laughed often, her cheeks glowed with life and health, and her too-slim body had regained its softly feminine curves. She brought peace and joy into his world and he loved her for it—more every day.

He smiled at her now as they left the ivy-covered church they attended every Sunday in the village, and Adam reached for her hand. He helped her climb into the carriage for the short ride home, settled Chris beside her, and sat down in the seat across from them.

Along with the wife he adored, Chris was now part of his family, along with his new brother-in-law

Garth Dutton, now that he and Maggie were also happily wed.

On meeting the bride, the future Baroness of Schofield, the cranky old baron, Garth's grandfather, had relented. Maggie had apparently charmed him as easily as she had done his grandson. There would be no disinheritance. Lady Margaret Dutton was welcomed with open arms into the Dutton clan.

The ride from the village was brief. Adam could hear the crash of the sea against the cliffs below the manor as the coach rolled along the circular driveway and pulled to a halt in front of the house. A liveried footman opened the door.

Adam glanced at the two people sitting very properly across from him. "We're home." He grinned. "Last one out is a hedgehog."

Christopher shrieked in delight and scrambled for the door. Jillian laughed and fell in behind him.

Chris was jumping up and down when Adam reached the bottom of the narrow iron stairs. "You're the hedgehog!" Chris said.

Adam ruffled the boy's thick brown hair. "Next time it's going to be you." Dressed in their Sunday finery, they crossed the gravel drive toward the wide porch steps below the portico in front of the double doors.

"Watch out for that mud puddle, son," Adam warned as the child spun around and started skipping backward toward the house. Chris stopped, waited till Jillian and Adam caught up with him.

"Sometimes you call me son." Big green eyes tilted up at him and something softened in the middle of Adam's chest. "I wish it was true. I wish I truly was your son."

Adam had been considering exactly that, a formal adoption officially making the boy a Hawthorne, but he wanted to talk to Jillian about it first.

Chris kicked a pebble with his shoe. "Do you think we could go riding?" The lightning-fast change of subject caught Adam a little off guard.

"Riding?"

He nodded. "Ra needs some exercise."

The stable boys regularly exercised the pony, but it was as good an excuse as any for an eight-year-old boy.

"I've got some paperwork to finish first. And you'll have to change your clothes, but I think we can manage an hour or two." He gazed at Jillian with tenderness. "Maybe Lady Blackwood will join us."

Chris's gaze swung to her. "Would you?" he asked hopefully, clearly as in love with Jillian as Adam was.

She smiled. "I'd love to go, Chris."

"Then it's settled," Adam said. "We'll have Cook pack us a lunch and make a day of it." He was more relaxed these days, more able to enjoy himself. And now that his nightmares were gone, he was sleeping like a child.

Adam reached out and caught Jillian's hand. He liked just holding on to her and any excuse would do. They had almost reached the porch when he saw his mother wandering down the path at the side of the house. The dowager countess had declined to accompany them this Sunday as she usually did. She was feeling a little poorly, she'd said. Apparently from the broad smile she wore beneath her straw hat she was perfectly all right now.

"Adam!" She waved and started toward them. "Yoohoo, Adam!" All three of them smiled and started walking toward her.

"Good morning, Mother," Adam called out to her, but her attention seemed focused on Chris instead of him. Adam frowned as he realized his mother had mistaken the boy for her son in his early years.

Lady Blackwood knelt on the path in front of Chris. "Adam—where on earth have you been? I've been looking all over."

Fortunately, in the last three months, Chris had become well-acquainted with the countess's odd lapses. He endured them good-naturedly and actually seemed to enjoy his brief excursions into the fantasy world in which the older woman lived.

Adam reached down and gently drew his mother to her feet. "That's Christopher, Mother. You remember young Chris."

The countess blinked up at him. She gazed around as if she were waking from a dream. Then she smiled. "Of course I remember him. Christopher is your son."

Adam felt a ripple of tension. He cast a glance at Chris, but the child's attention had wandered to a bee on a nearby blossom.

"Mother?"

She looked up and smiled. "Yes, Adam?"

At least she knew who he was. "Chris is Robert's son, Mother. You know that." Peter Fraser had confirmed a portion of the vicar's story. Caroline was indeed the boy's mother, but he'd found nothing to confirm that Robert was his sire.

The countess frowned. "Don't be silly. Christopher is my grandson. The boy is yours. He looks exactly like you."

That was the truth. Chris looked more like him every day. But that was hardly the point. "He looks like Robert as well."

She shook her head. "Christopher looks exactly the way you did at his same age. Besides, Robert can't have children."

Something cold slithered into the bottom of his stomach. "What are you talking about?"

"Surely you remember the summer Robert fell ill with that terrible swelling in his throat? He couldn't swallow and there were those awful big lumps on his neck. I was terrified you would come down with it, too."

Something was squeezing inside him. Now that she had reminded him, he did indeed remember. For years he had worked to block any thought of Robert from his head.

"It was the year after Father died," he said. "Robert had just turned sixteen. He'd come to see us the week before and I remember how terrified you were that I would come down with the illness, too."

The countess, completely lucid now, spoke to him as if he were still that boy. "And do you also remember the dreadful fever your cousin suffered? There was some sort of problem with his . . . with his masculine anatomy. The physician said that happened sometimes. He said there was simply no way he would ever be able to sire children."

Adam couldn't speak. He remembered that summer clearly now, remembered Robert's terrible sickness, remembered what the physician had said, and for a moment he hated Caroline Harding.

"Adam . . . ?" He felt Jillian's hand on his sleeve. "Are you all right?"

He swallowed. Apparently satisfied, his mother readjusted her hat and ambled back toward the dower house as if she hadn't just brought Adam's whole world tumbling down.

"That's why Caroline was so certain the child was mine," he said. "Robert must have told her he was sterile. Why didn't I remember?"

Jillian reached down and caught his hand. "Perhaps you didn't want to remember. You couldn't stand to think that your own son could have been treated so badly."

He watched his mother walking back up the hill and turned to find Christopher's solemn green eyes staring up at him.

"Is it true? Are you . . . are you really my father?"

As he looked down at the child any fool could see was his son, an ache rose in his throat. He went down on one knee beside the boy. "Yes, Chris, I am."

"Why didn't you want me?"

The ache swelled. "I didn't know about you until Vicar Donnellson brought you to the house that day. After that, I didn't know what to believe, but I started to love you anyway. Now I know for sure that you're my son. Your real name is Christopher Hawthorne."

Chris's eyes welled with tears and Adam pulled the child into his arms. "I'm your father, Chris. And when I call you son, now you'll know that it's true." Adam looked over his shoulder, saw the moisture in Jillian's eyes. She dabbed at them with a handkerchief she pulled from her reticule.

Adam came to his feet, lifting little Chris up onto

his shoulder, and the little boy's arms went around his neck. Adam reached for Jillian's hand, thinking no man had ever been more blessed.

"I love you," he said to her, then looked up at his son. "I love you both so very much." Entwining Jillian's fingers with his, Adam sent up a prayer of gratitude for all that he had been given and guided his family up the path toward the house.

Visit the
Simon & Schuster Web site:
www.SimonSays.com

and sign up for our
mystery e-mail updates!

Keep up on the latest
new releases, author appearances,
news, chats, special offers, and more!
We'll deliver the information
right to your inbox — if it's new,
you'll know about it.

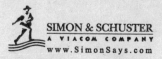

SIMON & SCHUSTER
A VIACOM COMPANY
www.SimonSays.com

POCKET BOOKS

SONNET
BOOKS